FOR GLORY AND HONOR

LTUE Benefit Anthologies

Other Works by Jaleta Clegg

Dark Dancer
Autumn Visions (collection)
Brain Candy (collection)
Llama Tell You a Story . . . (collection)
Soul Windows (with Frances Pauli)
Waiting for Elephants (collection)

❖

ALTAIRAN EMPIRE SERIES

Nexus Point

Priestess of the Eggstone

Poisoned Pawn

Kumadai Run

Cold Revenge

Jericho Falling

Obsidian Tears

Chain of Secrets

An Indecent Proposal

Phoenix in Flames

Redemption

❖

AS EDITOR

Wandering Weeds: Tales of Rabid Vegetation (with Frances Pauli)

Other Works Edited by Joe Monson

ANTHOLOGIES

A Universe of Stories

The Horror at Pooh Corner

❖

COLLECTIONS

Thin Air: The Cosmic Crime Fiction of Gustavo Bondoni

❖

LEGACY OF THE CORRIDOR PUBLICATION SERIES

The Florilegium of Madness (D. J. Butler)*

Dragon Soup for the Soul (Emily Martha Sorensen)

Down the Arches of the Years (Lee Allred)

Sharks in an Inland Sea (Lehua Parker)

The Bacillus of Beauty (Harriet Stark)

In the Haunting Darkness (Michael R. Collings)

Interplanetary Edition and Other Tales of Tomorrow (Emily Martha Sorensen)

All the Monoliths in the Universe (Michael C. Goodwin)

Waiting for Elephants (Jaleta Clegg)

The Chrestomathy of Desire (D. J. Butler)*

*Co-edited with Callie Butler

FOR GLORY AND HONOR

EDITED BY

JALETA CLEGG AND **JOE MONSON**

HEMELEIN PUBLICATIONS

For Glory and Honor
LTUE Benefit Anthologies, volume 8

Cover artist: Kevin Wasden
Cover art copyright © 2026 Kevin Wasden. Used by permission of the artist.
Ornamental break icon copyright © 2023 Arctuboy. Used by permission.
The Hemelein shield and stars H logo and "It's worth your time" slogan are trademarks of Hemelein Publications LLC.

Edited by Jaleta Clegg and Joe Monson
Cover Designer: Joe Monson
Interior layout and design: Joe Monson
Copyeditor: Marny Parkin
Managing Editor: Joe Monson
Publisher: Heather B. Monson
Published by Hemelein Publications, LLC., hemelein.com

First Hemelein printing, February 2026
Trade paperback: 978-1-64278-053-6
Ebook: 978-1-64278-054-3

10 9 8 7 6 5 4 3 2 1

Library of Congress Control Number: 2025936263

To Caroljean Hanson.
Your smile, humor, and wisdom are missed.

Contents

A Non-Evil Librarian

Joe Monson

It's hard to believe this is the eighth volume in the LTUE Benefit Anthologies series! Time flies! As with other volumes in this series, this volume is dedicated to a contributor to local fandom who impacted a lot of lives. This volume is dedicated to Caroljean Hansen.

Caroljean was a long-time supporter of science fiction and fantasy conventions and events all around Utah, including Life, the Universe, & Everything. She worked at the Marriott Library at the University of Utah for decades, where she spent her time helping patrons and fellow staff members. In addition to her support of genre events in Utah, she supported many efforts to increase literacy in Utah and beyond, working with a number of local and national organizations toward that end. She loved animals and helped several animal welfare groups and organizations throughout her life as well. She was a true pillar in the local community.

I worked with her for around fifteen years volunteering for a local convention and working on the convention committee there. She was generous to a fault and fun to be around. She and her sister, Ruth, were always willing to lend an ear and offer their experience and thoughts on how things should be done, and they were more often than not correct. Caroljean had a wicked sense of humor, too, and a smile that would light up the room.

She was a big fan of science fiction, and especially military science fiction and space opera. This volume has ten stories that have never been published before—that's more than half of the stories! Some of the stories are deadly serious, and others mix in some (or a lot) of humor. All of them show people serving and sacrificing for the greater good.

I'm also a huge fan of military science fiction. I've read a wide range, including David Weber's Honorverse, Lois McMaster Bujold's Vorkosigan Saga, many of Robert Heinlein's stories, Elizabeth Moon's Vatta series, and many, many others. There is so much solid and enjoyable military SF out there, and this collection offers up eighteen stories that we think Caroljean would have enjoyed. We had a lot of fun sorting through all the submissions and narrowing it down to the stories found here.

All of the authors have donated their works to help out Life, the Universe, & Everything in its mission to help authors, editors, and other creatives sharpen and improve their skills. All of the author, editor, and artist royalties go to help students get in for a greatly-reduced rate each year. We appreciate your support in picking up your copy, and we hope you enjoy the stories as much as we did when putting this volume together.

Thank you for your support!

—Joe Monson

Entrapped by Freedom

Michelle J. Diaz

It was supposed to be a simple, post-war extraction. They told us it would be easy. Of course, I should have known better. Nothing *ever* went smoothly. What started off as a normal mission warped to hellish faster than the elevator ride into the sulfur pit itself.

And now, here I was, an Overdra soldier stuck within enemy territory with a dysfunctional MemPlant, with no way of contacting my team, and only one chance of getting my butt off the planet. And then there was the matter of the three-year-old who had glued herself to me.

"Vander, when we getting dere?" Ariana asked, climbing over what might have once been a bathtub but now resembled a crippled goat.

I had given up trying to convince Ariana to say my name properly. Vander sounded like the dog chews, but apparently "Evander" was too many syllables for her.

"Soon, kid. We'll be there soon." Soon as in, "I don't have a clue." For all I knew, the ship didn't even exist. The scavenger could have been lying, could have been sending Ariana and me on a wild goose chase through hell, but I had to hope, had to keep moving, or else our chances of getting off this planet alive were almost nonexistent.

Ariana skipped happily over the rubble, as if the broken concrete and buckled columns were a dream playground. The Thule war had been raging longer than she'd been alive, devastation a constant companion from the first breath she drew.

Somehow, kid . . . somehow I'll get you out of this.

DRY, HOT WIND HOWLED AROUND US, SENDING SAND ACROSS THE GROUND IN waving veils of white. The pungent scent of the Thule desert cactus infused the air, causing my nostrils to sting and itch. Why anyone would fight over this hunk of rock, even for the metals, was beyond me. It was a perfectly paradisiacal wasteland.

I struggled up the rise, feet sinking in the sand, Ariana's sleeping form against me making each step seem harder than the last. The fading sunlight painted the distant hills a deep orange, like a flame raging in the hearth. My breath rasped against a sandpaper-dry throat, coming in gasps as I crested the hill. Icy shock prickled in my chest as I stared down into the valley. Grounded on the cracked earth rested the *Lady Utopia,* her silvery-blue metal gleaming like a gas giant. Her searchlight swept the desert floor, illuminating a winding group of survivors gravitating toward her like moths to flame.

It's actually here. Relief swept through me, swift and cold.

I hoisted Ariana higher, gently shaking her awake. "Look, kid, we made it."

She lifted her head, droopy eyes widening as she took in the huge ship grounded before us. "Will day led us on, Vander?" she whispered, arms clinging around my neck.

"Of course they will." *At least, they'll let you on. Me, not so much.*

I started down the slope, ankles twisting on the rough gouges left behind from rains long past. When we reached the bottom, we joined the queue, and I held Ariana closer to me as the other travelers pressed in. She was my only ticket out of here, and I wasn't going to be separated from her now. Not while we were both so close to freedom.

A man stood at the bottom of the ramp, calling people forward, writing something down on his mod, and waving people through. My hopes began to rise. No one was being turned away.

"Next! Name and city," the usher shouted, waving us forward. His bristly beard and bulbous nose were coated in sand like a battered cherca clam, drips of mucus flying from it as the wind tore around us.

His gaze landed on the MemPlant in my temple, and his eyes narrowed. "This ship has no room for mutant killers," he growled. "Get outta here. Both of ya."

"Are you going to deny the child entry?" I asked, my hope vanishing like dandelion seeds in a summer gust. Hopeless anger prickled in the bottom of my stomach; if she didn't get onto this ship, she'd be dead, same as me. Somewhere, deep down I had known they would bar my entry, even the scavenger had told me so.

The usher grunted, looking at Ariana. She peeked at him, then burrowed her face against my shoulder.

"*Only* her." Sand-beard reached out and tried to pry her away, but she wrapped her arms tighter around my neck, practically blocking my airway.

"No!" she cried, her legs encircling my waist in a death grip. "Vander *has* tuh come."

I looked down at her, emotions conflicting inside me. She needed to board, even if I couldn't. "I need you to get on this ship, kid. I'll be fine."

Shaking her head, she buried her face in my uniform. "I need *you*. You keep me safe."

I resisted the urge to sigh. We'd only had *one* close call with a grenade; that didn't make me a hero. Didn't . . . erase what I'd done. All I wanted to do was go home, but if staying on Thule meant she'd be able to get on, then I would do it. To my family, I was probably already dead, anyway. My team more than likely believed me to be, and they would have already delivered the news. "Ariana . . . Please, for me?"

She shook her head, her face rubbing against the rough fabric of my uniform.

"Kid, you need to—"

"What's going on?" a man—he hardly looked old enough to shave, much less carry a gun—asked, walking down the ramp toward us.

"A mutant wants to board, Captain," the usher said, sneering at me.

Captain. Huh. I held the youth's gaze as he sized Ariana and me up, no doubt taking in my tattered uniform, gun, and the small silver disks implanted in my temple. His eyes lingered on my face, then he nodded slowly. "Which side?"

"Ovedra," I muttered, mentally wincing. "I'm just trying to get home," I added, my whispered words stolen by the wind.

"And the girl?"

"I found her in Javecta." *Or what's left of it, as with every city.* "I couldn't just leave her there."

"Was there anything else?" the younger man asked, turning to the usher.

Sand-beard shook his head.

"Then continue with the rest of the survivors. We need to depart as soon as possible."

Grumbling, the usher turned to the next person in line, but the glare he aimed my way voiced his thoughts on the matter.

The captain held out his hand. "Holt Davis," he said, a small smile touching the edges of his lips.

I hesitated, then shook his hand. "Evander Gray. Why . . . ?" I trailed off, not sure how to ask without offending him. Why would someone let an enemy board their ship to safety?

"My brother chose to fight for Ovedra," Holt said. "And he never got the chance to come home. I think every man deserves some ounce of mercy, don't you?"

I swallowed the ache in my throat. "Thank you." Holding Ariana close, I climbed the ramp, weary legs groaning in protest.

Did I deserve it? What had I been doing out there on the field worthy of forgiveness? *We* had been the invaders, killing the men and women who were only trying to protect their home. Orders were orders, but that didn't make them right.

"VANDER!"

I was barely aware of the kid's excited squeal before her thirty-pound weight bounced on top of me. My muscles clenched as the air vanished from my lungs and pain throbbed in my abdomen. I rolled to the floor, taking her with me, still half asleep. Throwing my arm out, I just barely caught myself before I fell on her.

"What did you do that for?" I growled, but she didn't hear me. Giggles had consumed her, and she lay on the bedroom's floor laughing, brown hair splayed around her head like a halo.

My anger evaporated, and I sighed, sinking down beside her. "Real funny, kid. Hilarious." Mentally groaning, I ran a hand over my face. Now that we were out of danger, and survival wasn't on my mind every single second, I wasn't sure what to do with her. I wasn't the right person to keep her safe. I couldn't even keep myself out of trouble half the time. But I couldn't exactly leave her here, now that we were traveling together.

Ariana sat up, brushing a curtain of brown hair out of her grinning face. "Can we play da game?"

"What game?"

"Da one you taught me."

Confused, I searched my memory, but it remained blank. What game had I taught her? An image of the two of us sitting by a fire briefly flashed in my mind, but then it vanished, like a word on the tip of my tongue that insisted on evading me. *No* . . . fear churned in the bottom of my gut as I brushed my fingers across the MemPlant in my temple. It was deteriorating faster by the day, snatching random moments from my mind and removing them, possibly even forever. How long until *everything* was gone? Could I hold on long enough to get back to headquarters? I ran through the faces of my family one by one: my father, mother, three brothers, and sister. Four siblings . . . that wasn't right.

"Vander? Please?" Ariana pleaded, bending down to put her face in mine.

"Y-yeah." I took a deep breath, trying to steady my trembling hands. Freaking out wouldn't help anything. I would figure something out; I would have time. The *Lady Utopia* would be docking in less than a week, and I would be able to get back to base before anything worse happened.

Ariana plopped beside me, setting one hand on my knee, palm down.

I stared at her, but she just looked back at me, waiting. Frowning, I put my hand next to hers.

"No! On top." She grabbed my hand and put it on top of hers, then she stacked her other hand, and I followed her lead.

We continued like that until I slipped up.

She grinned happily. "Me won!"

"*I* won," I corrected her.

"No, you didn't." She stuck out her bottom lip.

I sighed, but didn't bother explaining. I was too tired for that. "Yeah, you're right, you did." I pulled myself up wearily. "You good on your own, kid?"

She looked at me, green eyes curious. "Where you going?"

To get a breather. "Nowhere exciting. I'll be back in a minute."

After glancing back to make sure she was settled with the game-mod, I pushed through the door of our pod, closing it securely behind me. Our rooms weren't luxurious by any means, but it was better than I could have ever hoped for. If it hadn't been for Holt, I would have been rotting my last days away on Thule, and that wasn't exactly how I had planned to go.

The empty hallways were dark and silent, all the other passengers long since asleep, as any sane human would be. I leaned against the wall, staring out the small port window into the dark void beyond, rubbing my temple to ease the throb that was slowly growing with each passing hour.

The gold stitching from the insignia on my uniform reflected in the dim lights. Two golden fish forever swimming free inside of the dark blue O of Ovedra. Thoughts of my team drifted through my mind. I wondered if their return journey had been successful and if Dr. Lark—the man we had risked our necks for to begin with—had made it safely home to his family. Had they already spoken to my family? Were they, at this very moment, holding my funeral?

Logan's joking voice filled my head. *"What's better than a suicide mission? And if we do make it through, it'll be for glory, honor, and a cold one!"*

"I thought making it out was for the sole purpose of completing the mission and surviving."

"Well, that too."

I sighed, leaning my head against the cool glass. What I wouldn't give to go back to those times, when war was still an adventure. When battle didn't mean the death of your brothers. When glory wasn't the act of wiping out entire villages.

"You gain nothing with war, son. You go out there, and you won't be coming back."

Dad always loved being right, and for once, I could honestly say he was. I had hated him then; his shadow over my life had felt suffocating, but now . . . now I would give anything to be back, to have him wrap me in his embrace, to be back on our little farm in the middle of nowhere. I would take it all and take it gladly.

I just hoped that by the time I made it there, it wasn't too late. Most men wanted the MemPlant—it guaranteed your memories would be secure—and I had, too; that is, until the close shave with the grenade during the Lark extraction had caused it to start malfunctioning.

Sometimes, the things that preserve are also the things that make it perish.

Four days into our journey, and I was about ready to die.

"Vander, can I have ur gwapes?" Ariana grinned happily at me, bouncing side to side in the cafeteria chair as she danced to some unheard music. The occupants of the other tables were silent, hunching over their food as if afraid someone were about to snatch it.

No, you can't. "Sure, kid, whatever." I passed her the grapes, releasing a silent breath of frustration. Taking grapes was nearly a criminal offense. How in the world did parents deal with these kinds of kids? I was quite sure I hadn't been *this* annoying.

The loudspeakers crackled to life, interrupting my thoughts.

"All passengers, please return to your rooms immediately. The *Lady Utopia* will be commencing a mid-flight transfer shortly. For your safety, please find the safety restraints provided." The woman's artificial voice continued to drone on, and I tuned her out.

"Are we dare?"

"Not yet, we still have a way to go. The captain just needs us to be in our rooms for a few minutes." I stood and offered her my hand. She hopped down, stuffing the last of the grapes into her mouth.

The transfer would be smooth enough, but liability was something they couldn't afford to skimp on.

I took Ariana back to our room, allowing her to entertain herself with the game-mod while I cleaned up. I stuffed my uniform jacket and empty gun holster—the pistol having been "stored" for me by the crew—into the compartment under the bed, then pulled the safety handles out from between the blue wall cushions. *So much for restraints, these things look like ripcord D pulls.*

Fifteen minutes later, the woman's voice came through the channel again.

"The *Lady Utopia* and the *SX Galactic* will be joining in five minutes, please fasten your safety restraints."

I eased down onto the mattress, staring at the rough texture of the ceiling. A moment later, Ariana climbed up next to me, snuggling down against my side, eyes trained on the screen in her hands.

"What're you watching?"

"Tunnel divers."

"Is it any good?"

"Uh huh."

Before I knew it, I was just as absorbed in the show as she was, watching a group of daredevil teenagers chasing adventure through wormholes in space. It was only after the show ended half an hour later that I realized the union between ships had already happened. I stood, smoothing the wrinkles from my white shirt. "Stay here, 'k?"

She nodded, snuggling deeper into the blankets with the game-mod.

I watched her, hesitating. Her dark brown hair fell across her face like a curtain, hiding me from her view. A deep-seated ache filled my chest. Why had anyone left this child behind? Even if the parents were gone, surely the neighbors would have seen her out there all alone. She had done nothing to deserve that life. I wasn't even sure if her parents were still alive, all she could tell me was that "Daddy working." As far as I knew, her dad was twenty feet under a pile of rubble.

It'll be alright, kid. I'll make sure of it.

I grunted, heaving another box onto the transport cart.

The docking supervisor looked down at the pad in his hands. "That's all." With that, he turned and walked away.

You're welcome, really. It was no problem at all to spend two hours helping your crew for nothing. Sighing, I swiped at the sweat that had gathered on my forehead.

"Don't mind Eddie, he's like that to all the new people," a guy said, moving over to the water station and filling himself a thin plastic cup. The badge on his coveralls read "Greg."

"Not new. Just on my way home."

The man stared at me. "You're a passenger?"

"Yeah."

"What're you doin' down here, then?"

I shrugged. "Looked like you guys could use a hand."

"Huh." He drained his cup. "Thule or before? Or did you just come in on the *SX Galactic*?"

"Thule."

He whistled. "Cuttin' it close, don't you think?"

I gave another shrug. It was what it was, and there was nothing I could have done to get out sooner.

"I heard it was harsh out there. Much left?"

"Don't ask."

"That bad?"

"Worse." I picked my shirt back off the table where I had laid it. "I should get back." The *SX Galactic* was preparing for departure, and even though I needed something to keep me distracted, I couldn't stick around.

"Hey, man, thanks for your help with the transfer. If you need anything during your stay with us, let me know."

I waved my thanks and left the bay as the loudspeakers clicked on.

"All passengers, please return to your rooms immediately. The *Lady Utopia* will be disjoining in ten minutes."

I wondered what my parents would think when I pulled into the driveway of our farm. *Probably think they were seeing a ghost.* I snorted at the mental image. *And what will they think when you bring a kid home with you?* That thought sobered me. What *was* I going to do with Ariana?

Our room was dark when I swiped my card and pushed inside.

"Hey, kid? Are you awake?" I whispered, fingers crawling along the wall in hunt of the light switch. Silence was my only response.

Light flooded the small space, revealing the disaster. The room had been completely ripped apart, the contents strewn across the bed, the small table, and into the sad excuse of a bathroom.

I cursed, yanking the shower curtain aside, but the stall was empty. The compartment under the bed was, too.

Ariana was gone.

"The *Lady Utopia* will be disjoining in five minutes; please fasten your safety restraints." The calm artificial voice made my stomach churn, and something acidic rose in my throat. I bolted from the room, racing back to the docking bay.

Who had taken Ariana, and why?

The hallways seemed to stretch forever, every lift taking eons to move. I sprinted down the service corridor, skidding to a stop before the door leading to the docking bay. Someone was already there, closing the latches.

"Wait, please." I gasped for air, my MemPlant throbbing painfully.

The man turned, and my hopes rose as I recognized the man from the docking earlier.

"Can I help you?" Greg asked.

"That ship can't leave. The child I was caring for was taken from my room. Please, you have to help me find her."

"Don't worry yourself, almost everything has been taken care of." Greg smiled, but it didn't reach his eyes.

"What do you mean?" I took a small step back, putting more distance between us, my hand automatically lowering to my holster, only to meet air.

"I like you, Evander, I really do." Greg shrugged almost apologetically. "But money talks."

Before I could react, his thick, muscled arm lashed out, catching me in the rib. Twisting away, I found myself backed into the corner. He swung again, and I tried to dodge under his arm, but he grabbed a fistful of my shirt, slamming me up against the wall. My head smacked against the metal plating, white dots dancing in my vision.

Greg crushed his forearm against my windpipe, locking me in place.

I choked, shoving against him, but his limbs could have been made from solid steel for all the good it did.

"The kid will be fine, as long as your end cooperates," he grunted. "As for you, they don't need to have you running back like a tame pup." He reached up, fingers prying at the edges of my MemPlant.

Pain exploded in my skull, traveling down to the soles of my feet, as if a serpent of solid ice were slithering through my head and down my spine, turning the fluids to pure acid. A roaring filled my head, blocking out any sound, pain stealing all other senses.

Then, without warning, the pressure vanished, and I slammed into the floor, my stomach heaving. I pressed my hands against my head, waves of agony crashing through me.

"Evander."

The voice was too loud, grating on my ears and bouncing around my brain like a marble in a wooden box.

"Evander! Get up."

The blurred face of Holt stood above me. He grabbed my arm, pulling me upright.

"What happened?" he demanded, holding my shoulder as a coughing fit overtook me.

"I—don't . . ." Everything was gray and fuzzy. What had I been doing? Where had I been trying to go? Ariana's face floated briefly before my eyes, snapping me back to reality. "Ariana. Someone's taken her."

Holt stepped over the prone form of Greg, heading back up the hallway. "Come with me. The *SX* has already departed, but I'll give you a small craft to go after her in. You'll only have a few minutes to lock in before they're too far into the Current to follow. That is, if you think you can make it."

I nodded, my head pounding as if a horse were repeatedly kicking me. "I can make it."

The jungle city of Raulshavn was bustling, the transfer port teaming with traders, vendors, patrons, and crew alike.

Face veiled with the hood of my jacket, I leaned against the bike, waiting in the shadows of a building and surveying every passenger's face as they disembarked from the *SX Galactic Cruiseliner*.

It had been three days since Ariana had been taken. Three days of aggravating fear and impatience as I followed the *SX* through the Current. Three days of her face slowly fading into the gray fog that was creeping through each memory that remained.

Worry gnawed its way through my heart as the trickle of passengers began to slow. Where was she? What could they possibly want with her?

Gritting my teeth, I strained my eyes, watching each face, running it through my mind twice. Would I recognize her when I saw her? Or would her face completely fade before I could get her to safety?

Please, whoever may hand out miracles, let me keep the memory of her with me. And let me be able to get her out of this.

No one answered my internal plea. Then again, I hadn't expected one. Miracles weren't for the likes of me.

I spared a glance around at the two-story wood buildings, checking tabs on the green-and tan-cloaked snipers waiting on the rooftops.

I'd need to be careful. Bide my time. This wasn't some sloppy kidnapping job: this was serious. And they had more hidden backup than the Galaxsation Queen herself. One wrong move, and I'd be dead before I could reach Ariana. I would have to wait, follow them, and improvise if need be. At least Raulshavn relied solely on crawlers, with a speed limit of 130 klicks per hour. Following might even turn out to be a 20-percent success rate, if I were lucky.

I pulled the green jacket—bounty of a necessary swipe, same as the bike— tighter around me, the temperature steadily dropping as the sun dipped closer to the forested mountains in the distance.

A truck rumbled past, the side emblazoned with a familiar emblem: two golden fish curled inside a dark blue O. I stared at it. It meant something, something important, but when I tried to remember where I had seen it before, all that filled my thoughts was a thick gray haze.

"I wan Vander!"

My gaze snapped to the ramp of the SX. A woman and two men were departing, a small girl screaming in the lady's arms.

"Vander! I wan Vander!"

An assistant walked up to them, but the woman only flashed him an apologetic smile and said something I couldn't hear from the distance I was at. The assistant laughed, tipped his hat to her, and moved on.

A sick feeling twisted in my gut. How many children had been taken like this? A smile and a "motherly" explanation, and no one batted an eye.

Ariana yelled again, and I clutched the handles of the motorcycle, clenching my jaw as the urge to snatch her away from the kidnappers nearly consumed me.

The small group climbed into a waiting truck, pulling away from the dock in a cloud of rust-colored dust. Kicking the bike to life, I turned away from the curb, turning down a side street and coming out two crawlers ahead. I glanced in the mirrors, watching as they turned down a different street.

Yanking the bar to the right, I roared down a narrow alley, people jumping out of the way with angry shouts. I ignored them, gunning the engine faster. The truck was turning another corner as I raced out of the alley.

They left the city behind, leaving a trail of dust in their wake as they headed south into the forest.

The road wound slowly through spindle-like trees akin to a never-ending serpent, the vegetation visibly suffering from the length of the dry season. The dust cloud left behind by their truck hung thick in the still dry air, causing my sore throat to contract.

Forty minutes later, the dust grew suddenly thicker, and I slowed, turning off into the bushes and killing the engine. I had been lucky to find one with a good muffler, otherwise they would have heard me from miles away.

I hesitated, casting my gaze through the deep shadows of the trees. There were bound to be some kinds of scouts out there.

The roar of the truck's engine calmed to an idle purr, and then shut off completely. Laying the motorcycle on its side, I doubled over, creeping silently through the dark underbrush. After a quarter of a mile, the brush began to thin, opening into a clearing.

I scooted forward on my stomach, parting the grass carefully. Tents had been pitched, trucks, motorcycles, and other crawlers parked haphazardly between them. Men milled from one tent to another, starting fires to keep out the encroaching dark. The occupants of the truck were standing outside the largest tent. Ariana wasn't with them.

I gripped a handful of grass, wondering if perhaps I had followed the wrong truck. A man called someone to him, his voice rising as he pointed back to the road I had come from. The younger man saluted, rushing up the road into the night.

Maybe they didn't have a post set up, after all . . .

I waited until complete darkness before creeping slowly down the hill, parting the grass and moving along a few inches at a time, senses on high alert. It was gruelingly slow, but blowing it would be a death sentence. The time crawled by slowly, the moon rising from one side of the clearing to peak before I made it to the back side of the largest tent.

I pulled on the edge of the tarp, but the metal stake was hammered deep into the rock-like soil. Grunting softly, I pulled on it as hard as I could without shaking the whole structure. The metal budged slightly, and I shoved it back and forth faster.

A hacking cough exploded behind me, and my heart kicked into high gear, trying to claw its way up my throat.

"Stupid allergies," a rough voice muttered.

I stilled, hardly daring to breathe, letting the shadows cloak me from the silver rays of moonlight. *People don't see what they don't expect to see.*

The man moved on, boots crunching over bone-dry grass.

I waited until the sound of his footsteps had faded into the distance, then yanked on the stake till it pulled free from the soil's grasp. Lifting the flap, I shimmied inside, letting my eyes adjust to the darkness.

Crates and boxes were stacked along the edges, a table in the center, a cot set up to one side, and a small cage on the other. Hatred blazed to life in my chest when I saw the occupant behind the bars, her tiny fists clutching the metal.

Before I could move, however, shouts echoed through the night, growing louder as the person neared the tents.

"Fire! Fire on the road!"

Darting behind the crates, I lay still, watching through a gap in the boxes. The front flap was thrown wide, silhouetting the soldier against a backdrop of hazy red and orange.

"Sir! The forest is on fire."

The cot came alive as the man occupying it threw back the blankets and leapt to his feet.

Ariana sat up and began to cry.

"Don't just stand there, move! If it can be stopped, stop it. Otherwise, get the artillery out and send Jena in for the Lark hostage."

Grey filled my thoughts at the mention of Lark. I knew that name. Somehow, I knew it. And it was important. If I could only remember why—but not now.

The first man threw a hasty salute and rushed from the tent, the other stumbling around for a moment and pulling on some clothes before also rushing out.

Jumping to my feet, I moved over to the cage, disengaged the bolt, and pulled her out.

"No, led me *go!*" She squirmed, kicking like a baby goat, and I pulled her close.

"Shh. It's alright, kid, it's just me."

She stilled. "Vander?"

"Let's get out of here. Not a sound, okay?"

She leaned against my shoulder, little head bobbing.

Flicking aside the tent flap, I peered out into the night. Men and women were rushing around the trucks, loading crates into the back, and covering them with tarps. Shouts filled the night, rising above the growing roar of the fire that had consumed the road into the encampment. Thick smoke billowed into the sky, hazy orange in the flame's glow.

Ducking my head and covering her back with my jacket, I rushed out, skirting the trucks as I headed for the motorcycles. The fire had already consumed the bike I used to get there; I just hoped these guys left the keys with the crawlers.

"Intruder! Stop the intruder!"

Bullets peppered the ground around my feet, dust rising in the fire's light. I clutched Ariana closer to me, curling around her as I sprinted for the bikes.

Ice-cold shock flashed through my chest, followed by a searing pain in my thigh. I stumbled, my leg starting to give out. *No. Not after you've got so far.* Gritting my teeth, I threw us onto the back of the crawler, thanking the stars they'd left the keys.

The engine snarled to life, and—ignoring the pain that flare in my leg—I kicked it into gear, tearing away into the dark trees.

The gunfire died away, the rush of air around us snatching all other sounds.

"Are you okay?" I yelled, keeping my eyes on the bulb of yellow light illuminating the path in front of us.

She nodded against me.

"Are you hurt?"

She shook her head, little fingers digging into my shirt.

"Don't worry, kid. I've got you."

THE FOREST HADN'T THINNED IN THE SLIGHTEST OVER THE COURSE OF THE THREE hours of riding. At every split, I'd angled northwards, back to the city, but the roads only wound away again, somewhere else.

The needle had been resting on empty for six kilometers, and now the engine sputtered and died.

I stomped the kickstand into place, gritting my teeth against the deep pain throbbing through my entire leg as the bike jolted. The makeshift bandage I'd fastened around it was soaked through, crimson droplets falling to the dry dirt in the glow of dawn. At least it was only a flesh wound.

"When will we be dare, Vander?"

"Soon." Soon as in, "I don't have a clue." Taking a deep breath, I lifted her off the crawler, the movement causing my stomach to twist into knots. Moving carefully, I eased my leg over the side, blood rushing to my head and leaving the world spinning.

Ariana moved around the bike, pointing to my leg. "Vander, you haf owie."

"Thanks, kid, I noticed that, too." I took deep breaths, waiting for the ground under me to stop rolling like a freaking fun house.

"What we gonna do?"

"Walk." The very idea made heat flare in my head, and all I felt like doing was sitting down. But if I did that, I wouldn't be getting up again. This was the only option.

"Can we go 'ome to your house?" Ariana asked, holding onto my hand as I began to limp my way up the road.

"I . . . don't know." In truth, I didn't even know where my home was. Here, there, or halfway across the galaxy. Were there people waiting for me, or did I have no one?

We walked like that for hours, long enough for the sun to rise and the mosquitoes to come out.

Every step was torture. The pain had only grown worse, working its way up my side until all the muscles had cramped, making movement all that much harder. I kept my eyes on the ground in front of me, a mantra playing in my head like the steady drum beats of a funeral march.

Step. Breath. Step. Breath. Step . . .

"Look." Ariana tugged gently on my hand. I paused, looking up. The city rested at the bottom of the small hill, buildings rising from between the trees, a few houses not even half a kilometer away.

Almost there.

My brain felt like it had been filled with gasoline and lit on fire, but I dragged myself down the hill, one step at a time, vision blurring into gray. Time ceased to matter; it was just one great mesh of pain, movement, and gray fog. I let Ariana's small hand guide me until that too seemed to fade away, and I was falling.

Don't forget her . . . she needs you . . . get up.

I stared up into the blue sky, mind too muddled to make sense of anything.

A shadow fell over me, a face hovering so close to mine, tiny mouth moving too slowly to form words, or maybe I was just moving too slow to understand them.

Don't forget . . .

Something prickled on the edge of my mind, someone I needed to see or help, but I couldn't hold onto the memory. It slipped away, like sand falling from between loose fingers.

"Vander?" The kid shook my shoulders, staring at me with wet eyes. A sense of familiarity flashed briefly through me, then faded, her face unknown to me.

Who was Vander? Who had left this kid here? Where was I going? Thoughts swirled together meaninglessly, until it didn't truly matter, until everything just *was.* Without meaning or purpose. The pain began fading, numbing to a dull throb. I lay there, blinking slowly, watching the world spin around in an array of colors. The child's face returned, followed by a man in a green uniform, a crest emblazoned on his shoulder: two golden fish curled inside a dark blue O.

Their voices rolled around in my head, the words drifting apart, changing into a pattern that made no sense whatsoever. Then I was flying, the ground falling away beneath me, air rushing through my hair, caressing my face like the strokes of a down feather.

And then the sky was falling.

I NEVER DREAMED I WOULD BE AN UNCLE. OR A GODFATHER.

Or a hero.

Setting my crutch aside, I shrugged into the ceremonial uniform, straightening the collar, and gazing at my haggard reflection in the mirror. After three weeks of war, travel, stress, and nearly bleeding to death, I wasn't exactly in prime condition.

"Vander!"

I turned, just in time to catch a giggling Ariana before she collided with me.

"Hey, kid." Lifting her up, I put her on my good hip, grunting as the weight change caused my thigh to twinge painfully.

She held out a chocolate covered strawberry, sweet goo melting and running down her hands and through her tiny fingers. "Eat it!"

The kid's hands looked less than sanitary. I took it from her and pretended to put it in my mouth at the same time that I dropped it into the wastebasket.

"You're going to ruin your dress, you know." I picked up my crutch, swinging us toward the door. It was a miracle she hadn't already dribbled chocolate on her pink dress.

"Me won'!"

I chuckled. "Why do I find that hard to believe?"

"Will day give you lots of cho'late for bringing me tuh daddy?"

"Probably just dinner."

She looked disappointed, but I didn't mind. Chocolate wasn't really my favorite, anyway.

Dr. Lark and Senior Pilot Logan were waiting on the other side of the door, my brother-in-arms grinning like a goofball.

Logan slapped me on the shoulder. "You cleaned up nicely."

"Don't look too bad yourself."

Dr. Lark took his daughter, and we moved into the reception hall, the clatter of dishes, chatter, and classical music echoing off the vaulted ceilings. I limped over to where my family was seated, embracing my parents and six siblings in turn. They all began talking at once, and I let myself relax in their presence, just happy to be safe. Just glad that I was one of the soldiers given the chance to come home.

"Lieutenant?"

The general of the fleet stood above me, holding out his hand.

I struggled to my feet and shook it, smiling politely.

"If you would come with me, please?" he asked, green eyes twinkling from under graying brows. Swinging on the crutch, I followed him to the raised podium, where the Galaxsation queen waited.

I bowed, the crutch biting into my hand, my heart pounding in my ears. What was this about?

The queen turned to face the assembled men and women. "First Lieutenant Evander Gray has shown courage beyond that which many good men hold. He risked his life to allow his team and his mission to succeed. And even when faced with perils most men would cower before, he held onto hope, fighting for the people of Ovedra. Not only did he rescue renowned scientist Dr. Lark from our enemy, but he also retrieved a family member Dr. Lark feared he had lost forever. It is my privilege to award him the Medal of Freedom." She lifted the medal from the box on the podium, draping it around my neck. "Congratulations, Lieutenant."

My ears were ringing, and all I could do was stare at her, at loss for what to say. "T-thank you, Your Majesty."

Applause deafened me as I stumbled from the dais.

As the night wound down, the Lark family joined our table. Mr. and Mrs. Lark continued to thank me, no matter how many times I tried telling them it had been my duty and honor to serve.

Ariana climbed into my lap, snuggling against me. I still had a hard time wrapping my head around the fact that Dr. Lark had made me her godfather. It seemed . . . surreal. But looking down into her face, I realized that nothing mattered more to me than the fact that she was safe. My memory had been restored, and I wouldn't have to say goodbye to her for a long time. She was my salvation, my freedom, and she had entirely captured my heart in her chubby little hands.

"Vander?" Ariana asked, yawning widely as her eyes fluttered closed.

"Yeah?"

"Me love you."

I kissed the top of her head. "I love you too, kid."

Merry-Go-Round

Liam Hogan

S o you get to Alteron first," the grease monkey said, yanking the straps that held me securely within the needle-nosed fighter, "which means you'll land *last.*"

"Huh? Wait, what?"

She smiled. Short haired, freckles—or oil splatters? Kind of cute, though insanely young. And all over me, at the moment, though purely from a *professional* perspective.

"Weren't paying attention during briefing, were you, flyboy?"

I bristled and probably blushed. She waved it away.

"Don't worry, it happens, 'specially for virgins."

I didn't think I could *get* any redder.

"The *Goliath* has only just begun her descent," she went on. "Turned ass over tit, engines towards our destination, slowing us down. You're in the first wave of fighters—the shock wave. And once we kick you overboard, you're NOT slowing.

"Meaning you'll hit Alteron travelling at something like thirty thousand kilometres a second. Initial reports suggest Alteron's defence system extends maybe thirty-five k-klicks—as far out as geostat. So your war will be over in just over two seconds from first contact."

I knew all *that.* Knew the targeting systems would have already selected things for my missiles to hit. And for *missiles* read chunks of depleted uranium— when you're traveling at a tenth of c you *are* the missile. Best we could do is give them a little nudge so they fanned out onto the right trajectory, though like the drones that preceded me, I'd be beaming back valuable intel for the next, some- what slower, more precise wave.

I was there, as human pilot, because tactical AIs had calculated we gave a small—but appreciable—advantage in making any final decisions when there were a lot of targets in the sector. The squadron had trained hard for this. For our month of complete and utter boredom, speeding along on near-starvation rations, muscles wasting away in zero-g and tubes going places it wouldn't be polite to mention, followed by about an hour of final approach planning, and then weapons hot and heavy and *blam!*

I still didn't get it, the landing last bit. Maybe *I* was the monkey, like those dumb animals first sent into space in the way back when.

"So you exit the battle stage right, and you're *still* going thirty thousand kilometres an hour," she patiently explained. "Heading *away* from Alteron."

"Oh." The penny finally dropped. "And then I start decelerating?"

She laughed. *Actually* laughed. "You see any fuel tanks on this heap of junk?"

I had to admit I didn't. I squinted at the area above her left breast, trying to read the name badge without appearing to lech.

"You and you alone, in the tiny support pod which is this cockpit, will get thrown out and back from your speeding fighter at as many G as you can handle and flyby the fifth planet, the gas giant, close enough to shoot turkeys, all to put you into an extreme elliptical orbit, *still* heading away. Then you go to sleep, gravity does its thing and the *Goliath* mops up. We come pick you up on your way back into the inner system. Assuming," she went on, the pink tip of her tongue poking out as she checked my life support stats, "I've cinched the straps tight enough and you're not instant Jello."

She looked me in the eye. Scanned them, searching for something, perhaps. Nodded. "Don't worry, all that stuff is automatic which is why you haven't had to do it in the simulator over and over. You'll be *fine*. Just better hope the war is a short one and you don't have to go around *twice*."

I blinked and she laughed again.

"*Joking.* Long as you don't hit anything on the way through. Your relative speed means that even if anything is standing still, it's still going to . . . ah, no point in getting all graphic. But if you get to the deep sleep stage, you're *golden*. Unless we actually lose the war," she chuckled, as if that was an impossibility, "we'll be picking you flyby heroes up and for you it'll be like an hour has gone by."

I finally twigged what the most important question was. "And for the *Goliath*? How long for you?"

She smiled. "'Bout twelve years. The age gap between us won't exist any more. I might even outrank you." She looked me up and down, trussed as I was, the neck and head brace meaning I couldn't look anywhere else except those steady hazel eyes. "You can maybe buy me a drink, for rescuing your ass?"

I smiled. "I'd be delighted, *Lieutenant* Elena Rodriguez."

CAPTAIN MACKENSIE MOSEYED OVER WHILE THE PREPPED FIGHTER WAS BEING wheeled towards the carrier deck.

"You do your usual thing, Roddy?"

She watched the needle jet exit the cavernous hanger before turning to her boss. "If you mean give him a reason to live, then yes."

"And how many fighters have you dispatched these last two weeks?"

She reddened. "Eighteen."

"Going to be a full dance card."

She turned on the captain, a flash of anger in her eyes, but only for a moment. War was hell, and she—they—were only doing what was necessary. "The other engineers, they tell the truth?"

It was his turn to look sheepish. "Don't suppose they do. What did you make it? Twelve years?"

"Long enough to be remarkable, short enough not to scare the bejesus out of them. Don't suppose we'd get many volunteers if they knew."

"You'd be surprised." The captain shook his head. "We keep 'em separate from the grunts, but we've got some veterans on this mission."

"Oh? How many times?"

"Five, one of them. This'll be their number six."

"Six rides on the ol' merry-go-round? Is he some sort of dinosaur?"

"*She.* And yes. But she says she's getting to see the Universe . . . change. Always something new and interesting to wake up to. Plus, she outlives *all* her exes."

Six times two centuries . . . a twelve hundred-year-old soldier? Roddy shuddered. It didn't bear thinking about.

Galactic Service: Stuck on a Milk Run

Kate Dane

The starship captain stood in front of an intricately carved wooden door, bright colors in a swarm of geometric patterns battling to catch eyes. Her arms stretched wide as if to embrace a lover. "Look at the arched top, the detailing. This door represents all of Earth. Like the Galactic Service. Beauty. Dedication. Tradition."

Someone sniggered.

Newly commissioned First Officer Randy Drake glanced over at the assembled crew, more than a hundred gathered in the fancyside dining room for pre-embarkation speeches. His academy ranking deserved better than this milk-run ship filled with problem spacers. Even these spacers—if they knew his father's name—they'd push him out the airlock, possibly slashing his throat first. Randy had to control them from get-go. He scowled at the mutters and titters.

The group fell silent, not shifting. No rustles.

They didn't know what to think of him. Good. Fear kept people in line. Unpredictability bred fear, and so he offered them a twisted smile.

The captain spun. The closed door framed her. "I know spacers. You make a game out of scavenging. A dare, a challenge, a bet, or just I-can-get-around-your-rules. Most of you are new to this ship, from first officer to newbie spacer, assigned here for an easy trip. I don't care if we're not tracking pirates, fighting enemy spaceships, or opening new routes through space. We're Service. This ship runs tight and trim. I don't tolerate off-reg fun like ship-hooch, gambling, fights, drugs. To avoid tempting you, I paid to install this door. You can't get through it. Not a dare or a challenge. A fact."

Sure. Technology offered a million ways.

"This looks like simple wood." She pivoted to trace one of those raised lines with a lingering caress. "It's not. Pure graphene underlay with a facing. As strong as the ship walls. They'll break before this door."

Feet shuffled and whispers rustled.

One spacer stepped forward, her expression blank, her posture rigid. "Regulations say no part of the ship can be placed off limits, ma'am. Disasters may require emergency access to every area of the ship. Air pressure loss, fire. Who, other than you, can open this door?"

The captain whirled and displayed a scowl dark enough to scare houligows. "No one. Absolutely no one."

Randy winced. Being stuck on a milk run apparently meant your captain was . . . out of touch with reality? The Galactic Service ran regular psych tests. Eccentric. That would be the correct description. Eccentric. "Yes, ma'am. Thank you for educating us on the door's capabilities. The spacer"—he didn't know crew names yet—"is right. Regulations require access."

"This is my ship. Mine." She stalked close to Randy and pointed her finger at his nose. "I have delicacies for the diplomats we'll be ferrying. Alcoholic beverages and tidbits from forty worlds. I'll not have them devoured by laughing spacers. I've had it. One trip after another with no one held responsible for losses other than me. Demerits on my record. Not again. None of you can be trusted. Especially you, First Officer *Drake*."

Randy flushed hot. His father had made the choice that got sailors killed. "I am a serving officer, ma'am. The Service assesses my fitness to serve, as it assesses yours." He should have become a civilian spacer, a towship pilot, or any career other than Galactic Service. Or taken another name. His stellar academy record got him placed on board this ship. But he owed the Service, however little its spacers might want him. He had to serve.

Captain Smythe brushed the insignia on her shoulder. "The Service is not infallible. I take necessary precautions. Do you want to file formal charges, Drake, and see who wins? We'll miss our pickups. I'm sure the diplomats absent from conferences will understand the need to follow every word and comma of fleet regulations. A military court will doubtless laud your caution."

The spacer who'd quoted regs shifted as if to urge him onward.

Randy ducked his head. Space lawyering on his first assignment wouldn't do his in-service rep any good. His father had defended his decisions and won *legally*. Not morally. His guilt ate him up, shriveling his soul. What harm would it do to let the captain keep her extravagant food and drink stores locked up? None. Keeping the stuff away from spacers was a good idea, in fact, even if contra reg. "No, ma'am. I think we should move on with our assignment."

"I'm so glad you approve our sailing orders, mister." She waved her hands at the crew. "Get to your stations or your quarters. You heard the first officer. We have a route to drive. Go. I'll take the conn, First Officer."

"But—" Tradition said a newly commissioned first officer launched his first ship.

"But what, Drake?" Captain Smythe stood facing him in front of her brightly colored door. The sailors had dispersed. "Do you also have a regulation to quote at me?"

"No, ma'am."

"Good. Regulations are crutches for those who can't think clearly." She strode from the fancyside dining room, which functioned as the crew gathering point, to the hallway leading to the bridge.

He followed, leaving her gaudy door behind.

"Where are you going, Drake?" She tossed the words over her shoulder.

"To observe our departure, ma'am. I'll sit in an observer chair."

"You are better employed checking your quarters. Be sure everything is tied down." The captain quickened her pace. "I don't want you on my bridge in any situation where decisions might arise. Inspect the ship down to its rivets, aeroponics down to the leaves, and engineering down to every wire. Talk to me if you find a major problem. Or stay busy and out of my way."

Randy stood, frozen. She wouldn't even let him watch his first launch from the bridge. How did he do his job as first officer when the captain didn't trust him? He needed good duty fitness evaluations to build his career. On the other hand, she couldn't run the ship every minute of every day. For now, he'd live with her Drake bashing. Consider it an extreme version of new-crew hazing. Once they were under way, she'd need to sleep. He'd prove his merit and get his chance.

Randy turned and headed for his compact quarters. He'd watch the launch on his viewscreen. Wearing the name Drake in the Galactic Service had taught him to use his solitary time productively.

Now Randy understood the captain's exasperation at reg-lawyering. "No, Spacer Claiborne, I will not provide double time off for your working fifteen minutes over shift when Spacer Tompkins ran late."

"Regulations require—" She'd quoted regs at the captain, and now Claiborne caught him in the crew mess to carp about shifts.

"Regulations are to be interpreted with flexibility. Tompkins was stuck in a lift." For a ship transporting diplomats, this one had its quirks. The lifts jammed regularly. Engineering hadn't found a solution. The personnel talked about intermittent overload on control circuits, which didn't sound good, but denied any serious problem existed. "The Galactic Service expects us all to pitch in and do our jobs."

Claiborne studied him. "You're not going to do anything, are you?"

"You're welcome to take the matter to Captain Smythe."

"Yes, First Officer Drake." Claiborne flashed a by-the-books salute, pivoted and marched back to her tablemates, made some comment, and the group guffawed.

Randy went back to carefully chewing his meal. He wouldn't let them see him flinch. Smythe kept her non-commissioned officers running the ship and detailed him to paperwork. Checking off this, signing off on that. His rank meant nothing on her ship.

He'd tried to find something significant and demonstrate his capabilities. The system instabilities were graphed, the deficiencies he'd found in inspections were logged, but he couldn't offer the captain a cause. The ship had a grimy feel. Not polished, not broken, just sloppy. Sloppiness was dangerous in space. The captain didn't respond to his reports. Something was off kilter. Not enough to invoke officer privilege and take the ship out of commission.

Especially not with diplomats housed fancyside. They dined on delicacies brought out by stewards under the captain's watchful eyes after she unlocked her extravagant door. He'd heard the accounts in the crew mess. The whole visitors section of the ship was off-limits to him. Smythe acted as if he'd contaminate the air. Randy stared at his plate full of synthmeat and aeroponic vegetables, then took it to dump.

He'd had enough of sitting in the mess today, doubtless under surveillance by Smythe's sycophants. The crew were experienced. They'd know if something was so far outside parameters he should be concerned. They'd talk to him unofficially, if they weren't willing to file a formal report.

Being in Smythe's bad books made him less threatening and easier to approach. He knew. He'd had complaints about ration stealing, loud sexual encounters, small meal portions, and every other day-to-day gripe, some he couldn't have imagined.

Randy headed out but not back to his quarters. He needed to be a working part of this ship, not a signature on never-ending forms. Smythe had to assign him more duties. She seemed harried and rushed when he glimpsed her. A first officer should ease a captain's burdens. He needed to argue his case. Now, when she should be off-shift, was the time to catch her.

THE CAPTAIN'S QUARTERS WERE SPARTAN. GRAY AND BROWN AND MOSS-GREEN, none of the flashy colors blocking access to her cave of secrets. A few Service mementoes decked the walls, a cap here, a framed pair of insignia under a photo of a uniformed spacer who could be a brother from the shape of his nose.

Smythe looked at Randy from the chair behind her desk, hair pinned tight, shadows under her eyes. Her expression was less than sympathetic to his request for changed duty assignments.

He stood at close-to-attention, refusing to shift his weight. "I should be conning the ship on off-shifts. You don't want a Drake talking to diplomats? Fine. I won't mingle. You've seen my academy grades. I can do the work. Take stuff off your hands."

Smythe's gaze trailed from face down to boots and back up, slowly.

His uniform was creased, tucked, and polished, hat tucked into his belt. Nothing for her to complain about.

"You commed me you wanted to do more. I've seen repeated system outages. Minor, but recurrent." Smythe's voice was hard as graphene. "Have you found a pattern?"

"No, ma'am."

"Why are you bothering me? Finish your assignment. If you checked every rivet, leaf, and wire, as I ordered, you would know what is affecting my ship."

"Engineering isn't worried." Randy could hear his voice rising. "I should be doing real work, not chasing ghosts."

"Ghosts." Smythe's chuckle echoed eerily. "Those problems popping up don't happen in the visitors' section of the ship. Don't you think that's odd?"

"I don't . . . I didn't . . ." Randy stuttered to a stop. He had investigated only crewside. He'd worked to the letter of her request, not checked more broadly. A sick feeling crawled through his stomach. "Is this a real problem?"

"Real as real, despite your apparent suspicions I stuck you with make work." Smythe's eyes narrowed. "You've been filling out reports. Have you been thinking while you write or just sulking?"

"First officers are supposed to—"

"Do whatever their commanding officers want them to." Smythe rose from her desk. "Do you think I'm putting you through the wringer because of your father, First Officer Drake?"

Randy's hands twitched at his sides. "Yes. The way cadets blamed my father for his decision."

"A decision costing Service lives."

"He had no good choices. Close off part of the ship and let some people die or lose everyone."

"Potentially." Smythe stared into his face. "He chose to lock down the blast doors and save his wife and his son. You."

"Along with a vital cargo and most of the crew." Randy was breathing hard now. "At least you'll say it to my face. You think he killed people to save me."

Smythe looked away, her gaze halting on the framed photo. Framed in black. A photo of someone dead. "I wonder whether he did. I wonder what choice I would have made. Whether I could have chosen to condemn some to save others." She looked back at Randy.

The sick feeling crawled from his stomach up to his throat. "Did your father die on the Gallant?"

"Yes."

"I'm sorry." Randy's lips went numb. "My father—he made an emergency decision more than a decade ago. I'm not him."

"The Gallant's systems went bad. No one knew how bad. That's why your father made an emergency decision. Because he didn't find the problem sooner." She moved closer to Randy. "Do you see why we have to check out lapses? Why *you* have to check out every hinky failure?"

The captain wasn't punishing him. She was trusting him. The burden landed on his shoulders. He felt himself slouching until he forced his spine straight. "Yes, ma'am. I will track the problem to its end. I promise."

"I know you will." Her stare bored into him. "We've both lost too much."

RANDY DUG INTO THE SYSTEM PROBLEMS NOT AS A RELUCTANT DUTY BUT AS AN obsession. Comparing records proved the captain right. The elevator stalls, the sticking doors, the occasional flickering lights could only be tracked crewside. Monitors showed high power draws for short periods. They didn't directly shut down systems. He suspected the overloads caused wear and sparked outages.

Tracking usage spikes over time, he circled the ship. Routine monitoring wasn't designed to isolate where power was drawn, so he wound up testing, moving from one area to another. The crew shook their heads at first but seemed to decide he had a thing for shoving measuring tools into power supplies and let him be.

Eventually, he had his answer. Or non-answer.

Sitting in his quarters, spreadsheet and graphics on display, his measurements radiated from one place.

Engineering.

Their work would logically draw power, the amount varying with the work. All he had discovered was that you needed energy to reshape metal and charge equipment and use powered tools. He smacked his knee. Total loss.

Though why would the outages hit only crewside? Systems should distribute the load throughout the ship. Unless someone was trying to mask the usage. The tech people could be targeting systems.

Spacer Claiborne wanted to enforce regs. Unbalanced loads should be barred. By complaining about Tompkins, she'd called the lift problem to his attention. She likely wasn't involved in whatever was going on. Not directly. He could ask her, but spacers didn't rat each other out. Not unless off-book activity endangered the ship's safety. She might feel obligated to warn crew the first officer was hunting illicit activity.

What info did he have?

Odd usage distributions could have been arranged for efficiency or represent major projects. Who would know? If the work was authorized, the captain would have signed off. Maybe her assignment was a test.

He'd report to Smythe. Let her deal. By tracing the information, he'd accomplished his mission. She wouldn't want him catching and accusing spacers under her command of using fleet property improperly. Captains dealt with problems rather than getting themselves marked down for failure to command their crews.

Randy commed the captain.

He stood when the captain entered his quarters, coming to a straight posture and moving to stand by the bunk as if he were in the academy awaiting inspection.

He was.

The captain had said she would come down to see him. Why?

They could have talked via comm; he could have showed her his spreadsheets. He could have gone to her quarters. Senior officers didn't do the running. She wanted something.

Smythe stood—slight and short, but somehow looming—and surveyed his space. "You don't have any personal things out. Were you planning to leave soon?"

Randy didn't look around. He knew what she'd see. No family pictures. No trinkets. Nothing but what he needed for work. Basic mug for coffee. His few mementoes safely invisible. "The Service prefers we travel light. I want a career."

"You could have chosen another profession. Even if you wanted to stay in space. You chose the academy and being an officer. Why?"

He snapped to attention, staring straight ahead, at his cabin's blank wall. "I wanted to be of service, ma'am."

"Service to whom? To the people your father killed?"

He would never be free from his past. The truth settled about him, his father's ghost and the ghosts of spacers crowding cold and heavy. He welcomed the haunts as better company than spacers. The dead crew who'd teased him, set him challenges when he was the captain's kid all those years ago. "I am not my father, ma'am. I am your first officer, and I reported potential problems. Did you want to discuss them, ma'am?"

The captain settled herself in his chair. "Inform me."

Randy stayed still and stiff and briefed her. The recurring power issues, untraceable to any cause but with a frequency indicating a problem. The lack of concern on the part of spacers who should be sensitive to hazards.

"Sit," Smythe said.

Randy glanced at the captain. One chair and she filled it.

"On your bunk."

He lowered himself, gingerly, and perched on the edge, back vertical. "Ma'am."

"Excellent work documenting a pattern. You're not part of the conspiracy or you'd have come up with excuses. Or failed to integrate these details."

She praised him? *Him?* Wait. She praised him for not conspiring. The captain was seeing an organized effort at deception, the way she'd ranted on his first day aboard. What if she turned on him? Or this was a trick . . . "Thank you, ma'am."

"The crew will assume I came here to rebuke you. They're muttering about your propensity to stick your nose everywhere. I'm going to order you to the bridge under my watchful eye."

"What?" Smythe was inviting him to fancyside. "Why?"

"The spacers are up to something. You've proved it." Her nose twitched. "I know my ship better than anyone on it. I'll figure this out. You're the decoy. They will believe I'm watching you when I'm after them."

"Can't we just tell the crew we've seen unexplained power surges? They'll know they have to stop."

"We would never know who we can trust. Dishonest in small things, disloyal in large. The Galactic Service keeps secrets." Smythe's brow wrinkled and she shook her head. "You'll have to keep them busy on the bridge, too busy to consider where I might be."

"Yes, ma'am." The only answer crew gave their captains. How was he supposed to distract an entire crew? He couldn't ask. He had his assignment to the bridge. Finally. However he got there, he would be in command, his first command of a ship outside the academy. "You can count on me."

Smythe strode through the hallways, leaving crewside for fancyside.

Randy followed close on her heels. The captain murmured niceties to the passengers, arrayed in garb from skimpy to cloaking, from colorful to plain, from shimmering to drab. The nonhumans reminded him of cats, dogs, fish, bushes, solitary or paired, or fluttering hives. Truly the Galactic Service.

The door to the heart of the ship slid open at her quick approach.

She marched in and spun to face him. "Take the bridge, First Officer Drake."

"Yes, ma'am."

"Don't mess up anything."

Smythe's order hurt, though he knew she was doing her bit to focus the crew on him. "No, ma'am."

She sniffed before strolling around the bridge, then twirled to face him, drawing her fingertips across a console and studying them for dust, presumably, before staring at him. "Sit down."

Randy stumbled to the captain's chair and sank into it.

"Well?" She tapped fingers on the back of an empty chair. "Give some orders, First Officer."

Distraction time. "Spacer Skoda, sonar scan the vicinity. Spacer Tolles, plot three alternative courses in the event of solar winds causing turbulence. Spacer Raeburn, assess the readiness of lifeboats." He'd studied the crew's names and responsibilities. He could do this.

The crew would see this as makework by an overly zealous young officer. He could sense the sidelong glances and rolled eyes while he stared at the viewscreen. "Replace space view with system check view and run standard weapons scan. We're going to keep our passengers safe."

"Sir, with alien passengers, the false alarms from a standard scan will be extensive." Spacer Jemion sounded wary. "I think you mean a Gal-Mod scan for weapons. Even that wouldn't usually be done since all passengers and their luggage underwent fleet screening before boarding."

"I-I don't—don't—" Randy forced the stutter. The crew would think he'd slept through academy classes. They'd obey. "Run the scan I told you to. Pull in personnel as needed for human review of scans. Everyone you need to alert who is not on sleepshift."

"Yes, sir." Jemion's response was deadly neutral. "Yes, *sir*."

What else could he toss into the mix? "I want a full review of emergency readiness and planned maneuvers. All department heads on screen in five. Comms, call the necessary people."

Smythe cleared her throat. "Are you sure about those orders, First Officer?"

"Yes, ma'am." Randy stared at the screen without looking over at her. "Regulations suggest new officers should ensure all areas of ship function are tested."

"Right, First Officer Drake." The captain sounded as if she bit back a laugh. "Regulation away."

Smythe left the bridge the way a ship blasted off a planet before a windstorm. Fast and loud without looking back.

One hour and eighteen minutes later, the extended conversation over emergency readiness plans and their compliance with regs had driven the section heads to rebellious responses. Two were sulking in silence and answering in monosyllables, one was politely cursing in a language she didn't realize Randy understood, two were speaking with ever increasing volume, one in long tirades and one in short sentences a child could understand.

The head of engineering broke in. "Look, sir. In the event of system problems, we quarantine the affected areas. Cut off power to avoid escalating feedback."

"Power takes out life support, doesn't it?" Randy continued playing the fumbling newbie. "What would happen to the spacers or our passengers?"

"We have emergency supplies in most portions of the ship. The sections affected would be one or two compartments. Trapping a person in unsupplied areas is unlikely."

"Unlikely isn't certain, Engineering Chief Casey."

"Nothing is certain, sir. As we've discussed." Chief Casey sounded avuncular. "You've tested our systems extensively and found nothing debilitating."

"True." How much longer could he keep the section heads onscreen? As long as his captain needed. "We need to review every emergency procedure, step by step. Each department, tell me your procedure in the event of a fuel explosion."

He did his best to ignore the expressions on the large screen and refused to look at the bridge crew. Smythe put him in this position. What if it was all a setup to fail him from the Service? It could be. No one would believe she'd ordered him to distract the crew.

"It's close to dinner time, sir." The supply chief's plump cheeks drew in. "The passengers expect service. Will you be managing dinner this evening?"

"The stewards can do their jobs." Randy waved at the screen.

"We need the captain's access to supplies. I'll call her."

"No." Randy forced himself to lounge in the command chair. Apparently, the crew chiefs didn't know where Smythe was. Good. "I am confident she will return on time. Captain Smythe deserves a short break from responsibilities before she returns to the bridge."

"Yes, sir." Supply Chief Grappo sounded disheartened. "Or did she leave you the access codes?"

"No. No, she didn't," Randy said. "We will rely on the captain to perform her duties."

"With permission, I will excuse myself from this call. I should make myself available for pre-dinner arrangements—"

"You are exactly where I ordered you to be. Stay." Randy's voice snapped. "Return to the subject of what action is taken by each group when fuel explodes. What do you do, Chief Grappo?"

Three section heads dropped off screen, including the annoyed looking Grappo.

"Get them back online, Comms."

Clicking noises and beeps brought no results. "I can't, Sir. They aren't responding."

"Run diagnostics. If there's nothing wrong, ping them urgent priority through self-comms, not department comms."

"Yes, sir." Comms' efforts became noisier and faster.

"Engineering, any ideas?" Smythe might have interfered, but Randy couldn't act oblivious to the problem. Not when he'd spent days poking into power supplies. "This seems like another of the gremlins plaguing our systems."

An urgent call broke in. "Spacer Claiborne reporting fires, sir. Throughout crewside. Help needed."

"Chiefs, we seem to have a true emergency." Did they really or was Smythe using Claiborne to provoke action? Likely the latter. "How fortuitous we are discussing emergencies. Recommendations. Action."

Smythe broke into the channel, using her captain's access. "Chief engineering scum, you've broken my ship. Pulled safeties, run programs that eat power. To make ship-hooch beyond allowed alcoholic beverages. Synthesize drugs. Run a gambling operation. Whatever. We risk catastroph-cascades breaking down relays. I'll kill you, Casey. After I save the ship."

"You're overreacting, ma'am." Chief Casey's voice came smooth and controlled. "A few glitches, nothing more."

The captain appeared on screen with the chief. "You think so? What if I run this program, the one you squirreled away so Drake missed it?" She held up her self-comm, pressed a sequence.

Alarms blared and blinked from bridge stations, sirens howling, colored lights flashing from control panels. This matched the worst disaster simulations and historical reenactments the Academy offered.

Randy had trained for this, but he wasn't in command. The captain was. "Your orders, ma'am?"

"The situation is spreading, sir," Spacer Jemion said. "Systems overloading and cascading. We are losing more quarters by the second."

"Quarantine the affected areas." Randy's hands were tight on the arms of his chair. "How many compartments?"

"Sir, we'd have to lock out crewside. All of crewside."

This was no drill. If he cut life support, anyone offshift and crewside could die. The captain would be unable to communicate. He'd have to run the ship. Randy stepped into his father's nightmare. "Do it. Cut crewside off. The whole section of the ship."

Spacer Claiborne wailed. "Regulations say allow time for evacuation. You can't condemn us."

"We don't have time when the ship is in danger." The words fell from Randy's lips while he stood outside himself, watching. "Cut comms, too. Smythe warned us about catastroph-cascades through power relays. We've got time. They've got time with emergency safeguards. Silence the alarms."

The battling sounds and flashes cut out.

When the captain called in, she'd identified the problem. Not the extent. She'd triggered the breakdown when she ran the program. Chief Casey didn't. Trying to prove the head of engineering had been running off-book operations, Smythe had accidentally wrecked her own ship.

Randy had to find an answer before people died. Or find a way to rescue them. The decision seemed easy. Cut people off to save the ship. The victims were supposed to be a handful, not most of the crew.

Comms spoke. "We've got passengers frantic about the noise and lights calling in. What do I tell them, sir?"

"Tell them we're dealing with some minor problems." Fancyside wouldn't be affected if he'd cut them off in time to stop the cascading effect. "Dinner will, however, be delayed. Ask them to remain in, or return to, their quarters."

"Yes, sir."

"Spacer Skoda, quit running space scans and help comms."

"Yes, sir."

They'd lost communications with every section head when he cut off crewside. What he had left was the on-duty crew on fancyside. The bridge crew and whoever else was working here, rather than in their action stations. How many people had he condemned? Not condemned. Temporarily isolated. "Spacer Jemion, put the last scan data for critical ship systems up."

The ship shuddered as if hit repeatedly and lights dimmed before coming back on with the blue tint signaling emergency power.

"Calls are flooding us," Comms said. "They want to talk to the captain."

Jemion's system map only showed fancyside systems. Crewside was grayed out along with spots of fancyside. No communication, no info. He wouldn't believe they were dead. There were emergency supplies, they had oxygen for some time. Unless the faulty systems triggered air evacuation and fire suppression or a jillion other horrible possibilities designed to safeguard the ship. One or two compartments should be blown. Not most of the ship.

No, they had to be out of contact. No more. "Give me the ship announcement channel." Randy didn't have time to deal with individual passengers.

"Opening channel." Comms gave him a thumbs up.

"This is First Officer Drake. The captain is busy, so you're hearing from me instead. We're dealing with some turbulence. Stay strapped down in your quarters to stay safe. I will update you when we have more information to share." Randy made a slicing gesture across his throat.

"Announcements closed."

"Thank you, Spacer." Admit it. "I'm not sure of your name."

"Martacek." Comms looked very young and very scared, eyes wide and hands wrestling one another. "Sir, we've lost power. We have no connection with engineering. Are we going to die?"

"No." Randy shifted in his chair. Not on his watch. His first duty watch on his first ship. "No one dies."

"Sir, they might not." Skoda sounded eager. "The scan of the area you had me run as a drill, there are ships that can help."

"How far out?" He wouldn't have to decide to try a crewside rescue or to keep the ship broken in two.

"Not close enough for fast help, sir. I've sent out help calls, but we're still talking days, maybe weeks."

The crew looked not to Randy but to Tolles, the senior spacer on the bridge. Tolles looked up from his helm station as if he wanted to speak but stayed silent, his face grim.

The problem with ships not on the same established travel route was finding a quick way to reach them. The well-mapped lines were quick and trouble free. Venturing off them meant possible collisions with meteors, hidden undercurrents in space. They were unlucky enough to be traveling a long, little-used passage rather than a short, well-traveled one. "Good work, Spacer Skoda."

Now was not the time to carp about regulations requiring the captain, or commanding officer, to make the determination whether an SOS was warranted.

Tolles' expression eased.

He feared Randy would be a young officer clinging to every period and comma of regs to assert his authority or draw strength from the rules. Randy wanted to yell "That's not me." He couldn't. He had to stay calm, reassuring, in control. Crew looked to officers. They had a time frame, a long one. Meanwhile he had to figure out a way to help the isolated crew.

"Sir?" Spacer Martacek's voice shook. "The passengers are calling."

"I told them to stay quiet and in their rooms."

"One of them is a Lucerian. He's worried about ship problems and being locked down without food. He's not staying in his quarters. I can hear squawks and pounding and yowls. The Kittering claims he wants to eat them. I've tried, but I can't get him to stop."

"A Lucerian?" Their metabolisms meant they needed calories and lots of them. The species was carnivorous, though usually not cannibalistic. They also believed in striking first and fast. This one wasn't taking any chances on stockpiling dinner before a lockdown, even though dinner would be a fellow diplomat's corpse. Randy was on his feet. Lucerians responded slightly better to authority figures. "Tell me where the fighting is."

"You can't risk yourself, sir." Spacer Jemion's voice held the force of gravity. "Most of the officers are locked out. We need you."

"I'm not putting someone else in harm's way. Give me a location."

Martacek stammered out directions.

Randy grabbed a sidearm from the bridge locker and strode away.

Tolles' lips curved up at the corners. Either he hoped the Lucerian would eat Randy and remove his problem or he approved.

Officers shouldn't rely on crew for approval. He couldn't lean.

Leaving the bridge set him free. Dealing with an immediate problem seemed easier, even if he was trying to stop one very important passenger from eating another. Crises could be useful. His heart sang while he hurried along.

THE LUCERIAN LOOKED MORE LIKE A BIPEDAL TIGER THAN A HUMAN. FUR, FANGS, clawed hands, and a growl shaking the corridor when Randy approached.

The passenger backed away from the door, raced toward it, and launched himself against the metal to land with a crash. The now-dented metal.

"Sentients don't eat one another." Randy found a command voice loud enough to stun.

The Lucerian turned. Nose whiskers twitched. Claws flexed in and out. His breath rasped, and his tongue flicked out to lick at the fur around his mouth. A growl rumbled from his chest. "Who are you?"

Randy's fingers clutched his holstered sidearm. "Acting Captain Drake. This is my ship. You are in defiance of orders."

"I need food. You told us to remain in our quarters. Where is my dinner?"

"You don't look as if you're starving."

"Hah." The Lucerian offered an open-mouthed smile showing sharp, sharp fangs. He was talking, not attacking. "I might be hungry enough to eat a human. Your weapon would not prevent me."

"I doubt I would be to your taste and likely lacking in nutrients your body needs." Randy let go of his sidearm. His honored passenger was now acting rational.

"You are trapping us without food. No one would answer my pleas for information. Not until I assaulted this door and the Kittering squealed for help." The Lucerian slammed a palm against the entry.

Squeaks erupted. "We can hear you, Acting Captain Drake. End the life of this aggressor. Your duty is to protect passengers." The melodic voice would be female in a human.

"The specialty foods for the passengers are safe. There will be a delay in dinner. A short delay." Until Randy could figure out how to get through the captain's bedamned graphene door. "None of you need fear a lack of nutrients."

"You swear?" The Lucerian's gaze fixed Randy as if assessing how many meals his body might provide.

"Officers don't swear."

The joke didn't go over well, drawing a snarl.

"On my honor as an officer, you shall be fed if you now return to your quarters and cease disrupting the peace of other passengers."

"I shall wait. Not patiently and not long. For now, I shall return to my quarters, accepting your vow." The Lucerian swiped at Randy's long-sleeved uniform, tearing the fabric. "My claws are sharp, my patience short. Do not attempt to lock my door."

"I see no need to barricade you in place in the absence of further outburst." Randy bowed his head.

A rumble rose from the Lucerian's chest while he turned and stalked down the corridor.

"All is safe now," Randy told the Kittering.

"For now, maybe." The Kittering's voice remained musical, but the overtones said tragedy. "You and your crew shall be held to account for the trauma visited upon my mate and I."

"You are safe and will remain so." How could he promise that? Because he would find a way through the captain's door. No engineering tools, only the bridge crew. They had to get at the special delicacies. The only fancyside food, and fortunate to have it there rather than stored with supplies crewside. They didn't have time to await those rescue ships. The door had to open, and open fast.

FIVE HOURS AND THIRTY-SIX MINUTES LATER THEY'D REGROUPED TO THE BRIDGE from the empty dining hall with its tantalizing door without having found a solution. They'd tried shooting firearms at hinges, avoiding the lock plate for fear of damaging it. They'd tried levers, which snapped when enough force was applied. They'd used every object capable of applying power, from fire extinguishers to cleansing sprays—until they realized they had a problem besides food.

The water supplies were also fed from crewside. There was a small amount fancyside but no reservoirs. Randy slumped in the command chair he'd do anything to hand off. He couldn't stop his outburst. "Who builds a ship that can be split without splitting the emergency supplies?"

Spacer Jemion was the only one to reply. "The same people who never figured our acting captain would order more than half the ship cut off. We don't know our systems would have crashed. Engineering might have fixed things. But we cut them off. They're dead. If not now, they will be."

"We don't know what happened to them." Randy clung to his belief they could be alive, at least, for the time being. Wouldn't they have knocked or found some way to communicate? Maybe the ship failures did kill them. Or he killed them by ordering the blast doors down if the systems ran amok and evacuated air, flooded chambers with water, or electrified the walls. He shook his concern off. "They're smart. They have resources we don't."

"System's fritzing resources." Jemion sounded rebellious.

Someone was praying in a murmur. Others were writing notes by hand, recording messages that would be last words, or sitting in soul-annihilated despair.

Randy had to rally them. "What do we know about the door?"

"The captain said it would blow up if we forced it." Martacek's sulky words sent a shock bouncing Randy to his feet.

"You didn't think we should take that into account before we shot it, pried at the edges, hit it with high pressure fluids?"

Martacek shrugged. "Everybody knew. You didn't care. You said we opened the door no matter what."

Tolles broke in. "We needed access to those supplies. It was worth the risk."

"Next time assume I might not know everything the rest of you do and I'd like all the information before I move forward." Randy sat, stiffly, his throat almost too dry to swallow. Physical attacks hadn't worked. The captain had refused to share the code to open the door. He needed to get inside Smythe's head.

Would she have set up a trap to kill people who broke in?

No. The proof was the door and the room hadn't yet exploded or vaporized them. Captains cared about their ships. Graphene strong, the door's weak points should be what they'd unsuccessfully tackled. Hinges, frame where door met ship wall. What had she said? The door was stronger than the ship walls.

Could they go out into space and break through the walls instead of the door?

Tearing apart the ship would likely cause more problems. They'd have to get the supplies back into the ship. They might lose the desperately needed food and drink. A bad solution all around.

The comm buzzed, loudly.

Martacek slapped it silent, but the buzzing started again. "It's the Lucerian, sir. What do you want me to do?"

"Tell him—" to chew off his own foot. "Tell him we're making progress."

"Yes, sir." Martacek passed on the message with the certainty of someone falling off a cliff and claiming he could fly.

Randy tapped his fingers on his knees, hoping the Lucerian couldn't read emotion in a human voice. "How, exactly, did the captain open the door to get dinner supplies out?"

"I don't know." Martacek's voice quavered. "What difference does it make? She's not here. She's dead like the rest of them. Like we'll be when the Lucerian gets hungry enough. We should kill him first."

"We're going to work this out." Randy tried for an assured tone.

"Captain Smythe would call the stewards up," Tolles said. "She would place her hand against the door, turn and lecture us about not breaking into the expensive supplies, face the door again, and put her hand back on it. We don't have her hand. The door must be sealed to her prints."

"The lock wouldn't be graphene." Randy rose and trooped down the hall, Tolles with him.

The other bridge crew trailed behind, except Martacek. He could use intership comm with messages, the ship was floating in space, and getting at the supplies was top priority.

Randy studied the door. "This isn't a keypad. Only a sensor plate. It should be easier to break than graphene."

"Right." Tolles sounded impatient. "Like I said, she laid her hand on it. The thing is probably rigged to blow off anyone else's fingers."

"No, you didn't say she touched the plate. You said she placed her hand on it, turned and lectured the crew." Randy did the same. "She took her hand off the plate."

"Yes, sir." Patience dripped from the spacer's affirmation.

"How long did she speak?"

"I dunno. A minute, two minutes."

"Did she deliver the same lecture every time?"

"Yep. Like we would forget," Skoda said. "We were bright enough to pass the academy. She treated us like dogs, explaining why we wouldn't get a treat."

"I don't believe Smythe would leave us a locked door no one else could open if something happened to her." Randy stood, motionless, counting seconds off for another minute, figuring this was about two. "She said she wouldn't give any of us free access. There's no way to enter a code."

He turned back and set his hand on the plate. The door split, leaving the entry open.

"You got it." Spacer Jemion sounded dazed. "How?"

"Thanks to Spacer Tolles." Randy nodded. He'd done it. He'd saved them all. Everyone on fancyside. They'd have beverages, probably some kind of sparkling water, food for the aliens on board as well as the humans. He'd bought them time. These lives would not burden his soul.

"How did you know?" Tolles asked.

"Why would the captain give the same lecture at every meal?" Randy shrugged. "She already gave the pre-voyage warning. She talked at you to give her a reason to wait before touching the door a second time. A time delay between touches, anyone's touch, opened the door. Presto. No code needed, and no success if you tried opening it with copies of her prints."

Raeburn banged his hand against the wall and let out a howl of laughter. "We could all have died because she was too clever."

"Not as clever as our first officer. Nice, Acting Captain." Spacer Tolles nodded back. "We have water, food. We should be okay until the rescue ships arrive."

"What about the rest of the crew?" Jemion's question held accusation. "You can't abandon them without power or air."

"They have the emergency supplies crewside," Randy said. "We didn't."

"If they're not stuck in separate compartments by the blast doors." Jemion marched over to stand inches from Randy. "You have to do something to save Sarah. To save them. All the crew."

"I can't work magic. I got you food and water. Rescue is coming. The crew will have to make it on their own." He sounded as hard as his father must have sounded when he shut the blast doors, saving some crew, killing others.

Randy was a Drake. Take the safe answer. Save the ones you could. Let the others go instead of risking them all.

"You're killing them!" Jemion's face burned red.

"You won't change my mind by yelling. I know you're hurting. I'm hurting. We're Galactic Service. Not everyone lives."

"You could try, sir." Tolles moved closer. "You solved the problem of the door. These are more doors."

"Without a solution handed to me by the captain." Randy's head throbbed. "The door opened because of the delay. The blast doors are down to prevent the power systems interacting. We can't . . ."

"Can't what, sir?" Tolles stared at him.

Sir. This time Tolles made the title sound deserved. The senior spacer was relying on him. So was the rest of the crew. They looked at him like mercrows, expectant.

"We go back to the bridge." After a slow march, Randy settled back in the captain's chair, head throbbing as he leaned back. "Blast doors are designed to shield pieces of the ship. We locked them down. We don't dare reconnect the power supplies. I suspect Engineering and others were involved in using that power for something. Bootleg weapons, booze, drugs, virtual reality. I don't know or care. What's important is the systems crashed fatally."

"You won't save them." Jemion threw himself into his own chair.

"Blast doors can be opened manually. We're not worried about losing air or disease. All we want is to avoid catastroph-cascades contaminating the remaining clean power. If we don't power up the doors, we can open them." If he'd thought of this sooner, he could have dumped the Lucerian into Smythe's lap. She would have had to deal. Not him.

The captain and the crew beyond those doors could be dead if rogue power strikes had fried them. The ship could be burning. They might have suffocated in airless chambers if their side of the ship dumped oxygen.

Randy wouldn't accept any of those things. He would choose to believe he and the bridge crew would open the blast doors manually, one at a time, and rescue everyone. If they couldn't, he'd have to find a way to live with their deaths. Not like his haunted father.

An officer made fast decisions. Not acting would have been worse. They could all be dead. Sacrificing himself would be easier than condemning others to die. He didn't get to offer up his own life. He had to save who he could. Survive and tell the story so other ships didn't face the same fate. Decades of experience lived in the academy. This would be one more story of why you didn't skimp on inspections or blow off small glitches with excuses. Not in space.

"Let's go open some more doors, Spacer Jemion." He glanced over at Tolles. "I'll leave the bridge to you."

"To me, sir?"

"I might need to make another command decision. I need someone here to do the same."

"No, captain." Tolles snapped off a perfect salute. "I'll bring them back safe. You need to stay here. I couldn't have made the decision you did. My name isn't Drake."

"You know who I am?"

"I knew your father. A man who wouldn't bend from what he knew was right."

"Who paid the cost." Randy understood, finally, what woke his father in the mid of night, what haunted his eyes, what drained his life away, what made him try to talk Randy out of Service and then out of command track. "He never forgave himself for those lost lives. He thought somehow he should have rescued them."

"Or he feared he'd chosen to save you and lose others," Tolles said. "He'd agonize over why he made the decision. Serving officers don't have the luxury. The past harms future decisions. I worried about you."

This time, Randy had an easy choice. Lock down the danger. Save the people on the right side. Next time the problem might be tougher. "We're supposed to make these decisions and keep on."

"The Service needs history, not guilt. Not perfection," Tolles said. "Not enough information. No time. Just act. And forgive yourself."

"Forgiving myself will be a lot easier if they all live." Randy sank a little deeper in his chair, becoming part of the ship. His command bridge and his ship for now. He belonged here, in the Galactic Service. He wouldn't fracture and fragment. He'd learn and survive. "Hurry up and bring the crew over."

"Will do." Tolles walked away and Jemion followed.

The rest of the crew settled at their positions.

Even Martacek seemed at peace.

Tolles turned and saluted. "Will do, Captain Drake."

H.A.R.R.E.: Heuristic Algorithm and Reasoning Response Engine

Brandon Sanderson & Ethan Skarstedt

A lone drop ship passed across the face of Milacria's gibbous bulk, a pinhead orbiting a beachball. From its launch portals streamed a hundred black motes. Each one a mechanized infantry unit clinging tightly to the underside of its air support craft, the mech's broad back serving as a heatshield. They torched down through the hazy cloud-speckled atmosphere in precise formation, trailing thick ropes of smoke and steam, a forest of uncertain fingers pointing back up to the ship, the *MarsFree*.

Within his mech's cockpit, on the western edge of the formation, Karith Marvudi hung in a loose cocoon of straps. He caught himself watching the grip indicators. If his mech's locked grasp on the underside of Nicollete's airship failed, they'd burn in and Nicolette's flimsy but agile airship, deprived of the thickly armored protection of his five meter tall mech, would tear apart and burn up in the atmosphere.

He stretched within the pilot cavity, spreadeagle, testing the tension of the feedback straps. His fingers and toes just brushed the edges of the space within the torso. Perfect. The faint scent of his own body, mingled with that of plastic, electronics, and faux leather, swirled in the canned air.

He was surprised at the trepidation he felt. Though he expected a certain amount of fear every time he dropped, this time was different. This was like . . . no, not as bad as his first drop. Maybe his fifth or sixth. He hadn't felt this jittery in more than two hundred planetfalls.

He wondered if Nicolette felt the same way.

He pushed at the fear, shoving it down where it could be ignored. It pushed back. Maragette's face flashed into his mind, smiling next to the squinting white bundle they'd named Hazel, after her grandmother.

"You about ready to shunt some of that heat up to me, Karith?" Nicolette's voice was as buttery as ever, not a hint of tension.

"Maybe if you ask me politely." Karith muted the mic on the common circuit. "Harry, we about full?"

The baritone voice of his mech's AI filled the cabin. "93 point 7 percent, sir. Shall I route 50 percent of the sink product to Captain Shepard's power banks?"

"Make it 75; Nic needs it. Show me what it looks like out there: focus on the DZ."

Nic's voice came again from the speakers hidden among the electronics crowding the cockpit. "Oh, it's manners you want now, is it? We'll see how you like it when all my lasers can deal out is a bit of a sunburn. Ah, *there* we are." She had seen the power surging into her ship. Her voice changed to a purr. "Karith, you shouldn't have."

Karith let out a loud patient sigh over the mic. She giggled.

HARRE said on the private circuit, "Is Captain Shepard displeased, sir?"

"Nope. That's sarcasm, Harry."

"Noted. I must point out, sir, doctrine states that the mechanized infantry unit in an entry pair has priority on power collection."

"It does say that, doesn't it." Karith frowned at the 3D representation of the area around his drop zone that HARRE was feeding into his HUD.

Nicolette's voice slipped into the cockpit again. "I can't believe I let you and Maragette talk me into transferring out of RGK with you. I'm about ready to fall asleep up here with no anti-air fire."

HARRE spoke, his deep voice mechanically precise. "Captain Shepard, had the Self-Replicating Machine Infestation evolved to a stage with anti-aircraft weaponry on this planet, our former comrades in the Recon Group-Kinetique would have been inserted, not a line infantry unit with you as advisors."

Silence filled the circuits for a moment, until Karith chuckled. "That's right, HARRE, Captain Shepard has obviously forgotten . . ."

"Well, well, don't we have a *fine* grasp of the obvious," Nicolette interrupted, voice dripping honeyed acid. "I don't remember him talking this much, Karith. You screw up his settings?"

"No. He lost a lot in the injury reset."

"Hmmph. I suppose I owe him some slack since he was wounded."

"Especially since we were saving *your* ass, Nic."

"That *was* a hairy mess, wasn't it?" Somehow she managed to convey the impression that she was shivering over the audio circuit.

Karith grunted in acknowledgment, brow furrowing as he zoomed in on an area of ground to the northwest of the Drop Zone. "HARRE, can we get any better resolution on this area?"

"We have not yet launched sensor drones, sir."

Karith nodded. "Right, right. Countdown?"

"We separate from Captain Shepard in 14 minutes 51 point 7 seconds, sir."

"Harry, round up to the nearest second on all time-hacks please.

"You can start inflation any time now, Nic."

"You think?" She humphed at him over the audio circuit.

Moments later he felt the first gut-churning rumble, press, and drop as Nicolette deployed her inflation scoops. They used the howling wind and heat of re-entry to fill the first few hundred lift-body spheres with superheated air.

Karith ignored the creeping feeling of unease. His DZ was in the mouth of an east-west running valley on the western edge of a big Panesthian city, name unpronounceable. The city, in turn, sat in a bigger north-south valley.

The DZ's valley carved through the mountains to the west and opened out onto a plain overlaid with red haze. The primary boiler infestation. He circled several map-areas at that end of the valley, highlighting them in pale yellow. "HARRE, what's the uncertainty over here?"

"Sir, from the limited data I can collect with the range-finding lasers, those areas differ from the historical models by just over the margin of error given the current level of interference."

"K, that's a little strange. The model's only a month old. You suppose the Panesthians have been doing some remodeling out there, maybe defensive works? It's right on the edge of the boiler's zone."

Silence.

"That last bit wasn't me talking to myself, Harry. It was for you."

"Noted. Unknown, sir. I have no information on any Panesthian earth-moving operations of that scale. I have very little data on their construction projects at all, sir."

"You can call me Karith if you want, Harry."

"Yes, sir."

Karith chuckled. He zoomed out and slewed the view over past the yellow end of the valley and beyond, into the red zone on the plains where the boilers were building their industrial compounds. "That's a pretty big infestation for stage seventeen."

"Agreed, sir, but it is within parameters. I note the stage 15 on Brindle Eight, the stage 16 on . . ."

"Right."

Karith's eyes flicked to the grip readouts. They were solid.

"Hey, Nic."

"Wait one," she said

He slammed hard against his restraints again and his stomach floated up into the back of his throat. Moments later, he settled back into the webbing. That would be the second-stage inflation scoops. Outside, hundreds more of the little spheres were lining up to get inflated with superheated air and then roll away on smart velcro into the thick braking ribbons trailing behind Nicolette. The surface of Milacria stopped sliding away to the right and resumed its steady flow beneath them.

He heard a touch of strain in his own voice when he said, "You feeling this, Nic?"

"Yeah, I felt that."

"No, I mean, I feel like a green kid. Butterflies in the guts and everything."

"You do?" Her tone was faintly incredulous, and he could hear laughter behind it.

"I'm going to regret telling you, aren't I?"

"After twelve years in RGK you've got drop jitters? You can't be serious."

"Look, it's no big deal."

"Wait until I tell Jarko. You transfer to advisory to keep yourself safe for your wife and baby, and the first drop where you're *not* getting shot at, you get a case of the shakes?" She laughed again. "You want a tranq?"

"Oh, shut up."

Her giggle filled the cabin.

Karith hissed and then stabbed the button that would connect him with Major Kewlett, the commander of the mech-infantry unit dropping with him.

"Major, how goes the drop?"

The major was chewing something. "Fine, fine. Nobody's let go of their airship yet anyway. What about you? Must be old hat, eh? You on track to meet up with the indig?"

"Yes indeed, sir." As a member of the Advisory Corps now it was his job to be the liaison between the major and the locals.

"Good to hear. Luck. Out." The connection clicked off.

"Sir," HARRE said, "the Panesthians are trying to raise you on the beacon channel."

"Put 'em through, Harry."

The soft hiss of a long-range transmission filled the cabin, and a rectangular hole opened in Karith's HUD. The image solidified and filled with a nightmarish mandibled visage. Karith was struck again by how much Panesthians looked like big cockroaches, big enough to eat your head. Fortunately, there had been a few Panesthians in RGK, and he'd gotten used to them.

This one hissed and clacked at him, mouthparts writhing. It took a moment before he was able to parse the heavily accented Spranto. "Greetings, Sir Marvudi. We await your arrival with great awaitingness." As it talked, there was close movement in the background, other Panesthians crawling back and forth over its back.

"Thank you. You are?"

The Panesthian buzzed for a moment. "My apologies, Sir Marvudi. My name is 'hzzzclackyow'. The humans at the embassy speak to me as 'Yow', and as a male." He buzzed again, wingcases opening slightly, disrupting the footing of a passing Panesthian, which slid forward over Yow's head. Yow used his forelegs, triple claws pinching, to move the other along before crawling closer to the camera lens. "I wish to confirm, Sir Marvudi, that your dropping is indeed on these coordinates?" Yow did something offscreen, and coordinates appeared in Karith's HUD next to the visual.

HARRE spoke up, "Confirmed."

"Wellness!" Yow replied. "I will come up to meet you in how many minutes . . . ?"

"Harry?" Karith asked.

"Approximately 12 minutes, sir."

Yow's antennae waved. "I hurry. Few of my nestmates speak Spranto. Your class awaits on the surface already, Captain. I will join them. Drop with good droppingness!" The image went dark and blinked away.

Nicolette's awed voice came over the audio circuit, "Holy rot," at the same time red warning icons began to populate Karith's HUD.

"Incoming, sir," HARRE said calmly. "Brace for maneuvering."

"Damn it!" Nicolette swore. "There wasn't supposed to be . . ." She cut off and Karith's restraints cinched up tight as they accelerated, swerved, and side-slipped all at once.

"Outside view, Harry!" Karith shouted. His cockpit blinked away and he was speeding through the middle reaches of Milacria's atmosphere, high above the mottled green-and-yellow landscape. Something dark flashed past him, its red glowing trail leading back to a computed point-of-origin deep in the red boiler haze. His computers held the view steady, but his body felt the chaotic maneuvers Nicolette was putting them through.

They were losing altitude faster than they'd planned. Below, the Panesthian city streaked by. It looked like a pile of dusty intestines. The surreal look of the place held his attention for a moment even as Nicolette tried to make him lose his lunch. The Panesthian burrow-buildings wormed over and around each other in a great heap, spreading out into the surrounding countryside like the roots of a tree, giving way to cultivated land.

"Holy Moses, Harry, is that correct?" He jabbed a finger at the icon for the *MarsFree*. It was black.

"Yes, sir. The *MarsFree* is no longer in communication. Presumed destroyed."

He goggled. "By what?"

"The first salvo of hyperkinetic rounds was largely ineffective against the mech-infantry drop formation, sir. It was likely not intended for them or us."

Black puffs began to blossom in the air near and far, all at about the same altitude. Anti-air, targeting the drop troops.

"Sir, I recommend a redirect to the company headquarters area . . ."

Karith cut him off. "Overlay unit locations and status." HARRE went silent and complied. Karith clenched his fists. The fear had teeth now. Aborting to a nice, well-defended company headquarters appealed to the monkey part of his brain, but he was supposed to embed with that Panesthian unit. That was the whole point of his being here.

Behind him the sky started filling with icons for the infantry unit he was inserting with, each one another mech shielding its airship from the violence of entry. He and Nic had preceded them out of the ship. Close to a hundred icons filled the sky. Additional icons over the horizon showed HARRE's best guess at the location of enemy weapon emplacements.

He glanced back. Well over a third of the infantry icons were already flashing or black. So many casualties. A hyperkinetic round could go right through a mech and its airship.

Explosion after explosion blossomed around them, black smoke obscuring his view time and again as Nicolette jinked them through the kind of evasive maneuverings that had made her famous in the RGK. The kind of maneuvers that had kept them both alive through a hundred hot drops.

"Karith," she said, strained, "you need to make the call right now. I can still get you to that DZ if you want, but I'm with Harry about redirecting to the company area. I think the embedding gig is out the window."

"Sir," HARRE said, "doctrine clearly indicates that when encountering a superior force, retreat and regroup is the . . ."

Karith gritted his teeth. "Can't do it. Are you seeing this, Nic?"

"Yeah. Thirty percent casualties. Damn. They shouldn't have hyperkinetic weapons yet."

Karith growled. The boilers didn't usually develop hyperkinetics until stage thirty, usually a good two years after stage seventeen. It was extremely dangerous to drop this close to a boiler complex at that stage of development, even for RGK troops.

These infantry were troops of the line. Most of their missions were holding and clearing actions against early-catch boiler infestations, not assault strikes against advanced strongholds, which was what this was feeling more like every second.

HARRE's count of casualty icons ticked up on the overlay to 78. They were approaching 50 percent casualties, mechs and airships alike, on the entry alone. Adrenaline filled Karith.

"Sir," HARRE said, "I say again, I highly recommend that we redirect to the headquarters DZ."

"Noted. Nicolette, put me in on the original DZ. The Major's going to need eyes out this way and there might not be anyone else in contact with the local military. Besides, I'll be damned if I'll let a little boiler anti-air fire . . ."—he gasped as they swooped into a long curve and his restraints pushed the air out of his lungs—". . . scare me off. I bet our DZ's under the maximum depression of those railguns anyway."

"Damn it, Karith." He could hear a mixture of exasperation and excited anticipation in her voice. "This is exactly why I love you."

"What?"

She went on. "Can you expose your guns?"

He checked their airspeed and did so. He and HARRE started intercepting some of the rounds coming their way.

At fifty feet above the deck Karith cut loose and dropped away from Nicolette's airship into free fall. As he fell he engaged the feedback mechanisms and the straps tightened up around him.

Nicolette peeled away and shot to the south, her lift spheres held in a stream-lined bullet shape by their smart velcro. Her cockpit and lasers were inside the mass of spheres somewhere. As she rose back into the railgun's target zone, she took a glancing hit. The spheres rippled, parted to let the missile pass, and then reformed again. A hundred meters beyond her the round exploded. She clawed for height, changing shape for more lift. She shrank smaller until he couldn't pick her out anymore.

"Ready for operations, Karith," she said. Her breathing was tight and fast in his ear.

"What was that you said to me a little bit ago?"

With a crash and a spray of dirt, he plowed into the ground at the center of the DZ, rolling to absorb some of the impact. He stood up and shook himself to free his mech of dirt.

"Sir," HARRE said. "I can play back any traffic you may have misse . . ."

"Shutup, Harry."

Nicolette's voice was tight, "Nothing. I didn't say anything."

He smiled. "'cause it sounded like you . . ."

"Leave it, damnit."

Karith dropped the grin. Her reaction worried him a little. "Right. Nothing. Got it."

Two Panesthians scuttled up to him. Hip high to a human and about two meters long he could have covered either one with his mech's foot. He tried to imagine what his fifteen-foot tall, multi-turreted, thick-bodied, thick-limbed bipedal mech must look like to a rural Panesthian and crouched down. "Yow?"

"It is I," the Panesthian on the right replied. "We," he waved with one foreleg and an antenna at a seething pile of agitated Panesthians on the edge of the DZ, "are hearing that the boilers are having effective firings on your drop troops."

The seething mass of giant insects was the 1st Company of the 3rd Milacrian Armored Battalion. Of course, they didn't have any armor yet. Karith was there to learn their combat tactics and advise them on how best to augment their abilities with mechs like his own. That would all have to wait now.

HARRE spoke in Karith's ear. "Sir, the company restructured its drop points. They are consolidating in the city to the east. I recommend . . ."

"Not now, Harry. Yow, we understood that the boilers were at stage seventeen. Railguns are at least stage thirty. Care to explain?"

Yow squeaked and clicked at his companion, who replied, trilling and buzzing. Yow's wingcasings raised, and the gauzy wings within fluttered. "Truly, it is the first we have seen of the magrails. We cannot explain."

"Well, we're all stuck into it now. Give me your latest information on boiler disposition and activity."

"Of course. Immediately." Yow spoke to his companion, who used his multi-clawed legs to manipulate something on his underside. Karith saw that he and the other Panesthians all had equipment strapped to their bellies as well as fiery circles emblazoned on their wing casings.

"Sir," HARRE said, "the link has been established and I'm receiving the information. Updating models now."

"Good. Put me through to Major Kewlett."

The HUD had Major Kewlett on the ground in the city to the east. A moment later his voice grated into Karith's cockpit.

"Whattaya got, Marvudi?"

"Sir, I've made linkup with the Panesthian ground forces."

Major Kewlett's gum popped in Karith's ears. "I'm glad somethin' went right. They gonna be any use to us? *MarsFree* is gone, we got twelve hours before the next follow-on ship, and I got close to a hundred of my boys and girls broken already."

"I'm not sure how useful they'll be. I'll have to get back to you on that, sir."

"Good copy here." Snap, chew. "Out."

The connection went dead. "Harry, transmit the data from the Panesthians to the general situation model."

"Done, sir."

Karith turned his attention back to Yow. Before he could speak, another bit of motion caught his eye. He turned. "What the hell is that?" he asked, pointing behind him.

Yow turned. There was a separate group of adult Panesthians on the other edge of the field, and they numbered almost as many as the soldiers. Half of them had smaller ones swarming on and around them.

"The families, sir?"

"Those are your families?"

"I am unmated, sir. But I believe they are the mates of the soldiers, sir, yes."

"Are you hearing this, Nic?" Karith said.

"Sir," HARRE said, "the non-combatants should clear the field."

Nicolette snorted. "Yeah, what he said. You should feel right at home though, Karith, with little ones to dandle on your knee and all that."

"Shut it."

She laughed again.

Karith reopened Yow's circuit and poked one finger down at the other Panesthian. "Yow, who is this?"

"Sir Marvudi, that is the commander of the company. He is choosing the human name Delbert."

Delbert said, "Delbert!" and fluttered his wings.

"Ah, okay. Yow, tell Delbert that he needs to get the families under cov . . ."

"Sir!" HARRE's voice was urgent.

"What!"

HARRE's voice was normal again. "Sir, I am detecting a great deal of movement on the far end of this valley."

Nicolette whistled. "He's not kidding. There's a whole lot of something going on over there."

"Show me." HARRE opened another window in Karith's HUD with an overhead view of the area in question, icons and indicators overlaid. The western end of the valley was alive with red, active machine units sweeping toward their location. They were maybe five miles away.

"Okay, we're out of time. Yow, tell Delbert those families need to be evacuated to the city to the east of here. The boilers are coming, and they're coming now."

Yow's antennae froze and then waved excitedly as he jabbered at Delbert. Delbert turned and buzzed loudly at the soldiers. At his words, the families on the periphery of the drop zone jerked into frenzied activity. They turned as one churning mass and fled, followed by most of the soldiers, disappearing into scattered holes in the ground.

"Harry, give me a radar shot of the surrounding ground, eh?" Karith formed his mech's hand into a blade shape and jammed it into the dirt. He was on the western edge of a huge warren complex that seemed to run all the way to the city. He grimaced. "That's a lot of civilians, Harry."

"Yes, sir."

"Nic, I need you to engage the lead boiler units. Slow them down, and try to trigger their 'seek cover' response."

"Roger that, Karith." In the background he could hear her motive engines kicking in and the mutter of her battle song.

"Sir," HARRE said, "she should target the railguns first. They are the primary threat and liable to . . ."

"I know, Harry. She'll be fine. We have to get those lead machines stopped first."

"Sir Marvudi," Yow said, "Delbert wishes to know what you would have him do?" Yow and Delbert were still at his feet. In front of them there were perhaps a dozen soldiers left in the short grass. They were in some semblance of a single rank, their shiny brown carapaces like giant wooden toggle buttons on the ground.

"Get the civilians out of here, Yow. Delbert and the rest of his soldiers should evacuate as many civilians as they can to the city—get them behind the human's defenses."

"Sir," HARRE said, "that is not a viable mission. Given the statistical population densities I estimate that there are thousands of Panesthians between here and Major Kewlett's lines, far too many to move in the remaining time."

"So we need to stop those lead machines pretty quick, eh, Harry?" No response.

"Sir Marvudi," Yow said, buzzing. "Delbert wishes to know what your plans are?"

Karith looked down at the two Panesthians, staring up at him with broad black eyes, mouthparts moving slowly in and out.

"I've got a few ideas."

Yow and Delbert conferred urgently. Yow said, "We were hearing that you were in the RGK?" Dimly, muffled by the automatic filters on the comm system, Karith could hear Nicolette howling and growling along with her battle song over the deep coughing of her lasers and her jet's roar.

"Was. I *was* in the RGK."

"We are honored. You can stop them?"

"No, I probably can't."

A small Panesthian, a tenth Yow's size, buzzed unsteadily out of the sky and landed on the face of Karith's mech. It squeaked and buzzed, peering into one of the darker radio portals in his faceplate. Raising one foreleg, it rapped its claw on the portal. Faintly, Karith heard a muffled tapping through the confines of his cockpit. He raised a giant metal hand but hesitated to pluck the child off his face.

"Sir Marvudi," Yow said, "allow me?"

"Of course." Karith laughed nervously, reminded of when the nurse had handed him Hazel. He had been afraid to touch the little thing for fear of breaking it.

Yow, ponderous on his big wings, buzzed up to Karith's mech, even more unsteady than the youngster had been. When he was about to touch the child, it squeaked and zipped over Karith's head and down his back. Seconds later it was in speedy but erratic flight toward the warrens.

Yow thumped back to earth.

"Harry, put Yow in contact with Major Kewlett directly."

"That is against protocol, sir. The connection should properly go though you as the liaison advisor."

"Well, I'm going to be too busy to handle it, Harry. Just do it."

"Done, sir."

"And put me through to him." Karith said, "Good luck, Yow." He stood and turned away from the retreating Panesthians, striding toward the hills and accelerating into a thundering trot over the rolling ground.

"Kewlett, go." The major's chewing was furious now.

"Sir, Marvudi here. The locals won't be much use. I've got them herding all the civilians they can toward your lines, but they won't be fast enough. My air is currently putting the hurt on the lead boiler units, slowing them down. I'll get into it and slow them down even more."

"The hell you will, son. I've got boilers coming up out of bogtaken tunnels not two miles to my east. Tunnels! Who the hell," snap, "ever heard of that? I need you and your air unit back here."

Karith let the mech run by itself for a little bit and slewed his map to examine the city where the major was holed up. Red icons dotted the suburbs on the far side. Energy weapons lanced down from the sky and kinetics flickered across the battlefield. Zooming in, he could see Treads, Crawlers, Walkers, and Blasters.

"I concur with the major, sir," HARRE noted. "We are facing a far superior force. Doctrine advises us to consolidate in defense with other units in the area."

Karith confirmed with a glance that HARRE had not put his quoting of the book out over the open circuit. "Can't do it, Harry. Major, I wonder if you've seen what the boilers do to civilians they catch in the open? I think I can reverse the boiler's focus if I hit a piece of their primary infrastructure. They'll turn around to protect that instead of expanding for the moment. It'll keep them out of your rear area. Normally I'd just call in an orbital strike but . . ."

Nicolette chimed in, privately. "I don't know Karith, they look pretty determined. I've got them taking cover for now but I'm seeing heavy-treads, heavy-rollers, and full complements of cutters and blasters for each."

Snap. "Marvudi, there's civilians here in the city too. The boilers don't care one way or the other. Now get your ass over here ASAP."

Karith isolated Nicolette's circuit. "No Crawlers or Hummers?"

"Not yet."

"That's something."

"Yeah. It's only a matter of . . ." Her reply broke off and faded out under the howl of her motivator engines.

The ground started to rise sharply and Karith leaned into the first foothill, clawing with his hands. "Sir, I'm going to cut through these hills and try to get behind them. If I can smash something important enough, their subroutines will switch over to protect and rebuild before they tear into these warrens."

"Fine, RGK. Maybe you *can* make something happen." Snap, chew, his voice tense and rising. "Keep me apprised."

"Roger that, sir." Dead air.

Karith's HUD tracked him as he accelerated through the hills. Red machine units seethed along the valley floor while he passed up high in the opposite direction.

He kept an eye on the battle on the east side of the city, watched it grow into a big smear of red on his screens. Hopefully he could keep the tide of red below him from sweeping into it from the west.

"Sir, Captain Shepard has taken a direct hit to one of her lasers. Her lift bodies have been depleted by 17 percent. Without a repair depot . . ."

"Nic," Karith said, "how you doing up there?" Her icon soared above him on his HUD.

"Just fine, Karith. Too high and the railguns can target me, any lower and the treads can lock on with their main guns. And I keep running into needle streams from the bloody crawlers."

Karith studied the model HARRE was making from the sensor-drone feeds. The boilers *were* digging in under Nicolette's onslaught.

Reaching up and grasping a knob of rock, he levered himself up over a ridge and rolled down, armor crushing boulders and snapping trees.

"K, Nic. Go take out a few of those railguns if you can. Make yourself some breathing room."

With an exultant yell, Nicolette flipped her airship into a backward loop and pulled out to race down the center of the valley at treetop height. Looking down a long draw, Karith saw her flash past the mouth of it, lasers on full, burning the ground and enemy units in her path in a fountaining rooster tail of flame and smoke.

The airships over the city wouldn't be able to go all out because of the civilians on the ground. He was just grateful the machines hadn't achieved a stage with aircraft yet.

"Sir, Captain Shepard has dropped off my radar."

"Yeah, I expected that. She'll fly nap-of-the-earth all the way until she takes out those guns."

"That is very risky, sir. The concentration of smaller-caliber weapons on the ground along her route is likely to be extremely high."

"Yup. Moving that fast, though, they'll probably miss her."

"But with concentrations of fire . . ."

"What else, exactly, is she supposed to do, Harry?"

HARRE's response was immediate. "Retreat with us to the main perimeter, sir. The concentration of antagonistic force here is too high to justify operations in this area."

"Can't do it, Harry." Karith flattened himself against the side of a ridge on the edge of the red zone and lifted a sensor pod to the crest. Leaving it in place, he backed up, sidled along the ridge, and put another one up. "All right. What do we have out there?"

HARRE had started building a real-time model of the plains beyond the ridge as soon as the second pod was in place for triangulation. A smoky, torn landscape unfolded before Karith's eyes, filled with endless banks of raw functional machinery, thick power cables snaking along the ground and through the air, trenches and canals filled with oily water and mud between metal walls, and fences as far as the eye could see.

"OK, Harry, we need something important enough to sting 'em good, right here so those units in the valley are the nearest units for defense.

While HARRE scanned, Karith adjusted the mech's missile batteries.

"Surely, sir, Nicolette's action against the railguns will draw the boiler's attention."

"You're bloody right it will, Harry me lad, but that's too far away. What are the units in the valley doing now?"

"I'm afraid they are up and moving again, sir."

"Bog take it. We need to hit something fast. What do you see out there?"

"There is a class seven power node quite close to the mouth of the valley, sir."

"Seven?" Karith was looking over the situation back at the city. Kewlett was holding on the east, barely.

"Yes, sir. It seems to be feeding most of the machinery and infrastructure in this area." HARRE lit up a rough circle several miles in diameter at the valley's mouth.

"Nice. We'll do the old high lob low fastball. We may not get another chance."

"Yes, sir."

Nicolette's voice sounded. "All right, this little strip of sky should be clear now."

"Excellent. Glad you're still alive, Nic."

"Yeah. Where do you want me?"

Karith launched three top-down missiles over the ridge.

"Hit here." Karith passed her the power node as a target along with the flight paths of his missiles which were dodging and weaving through an upward rain of fire from the machine's defenses.

Three more missiles streaked from his shoulder racks and over the metal landscape, straight for the node. The flash and expanding concussion wave was followed closely by another from the last of his high flyers.

Nicolette screamed past, lasers digging a fiery trench straight through the node. Karith resisted HARRE's automatic instructions to duck behind the ridge, instead drawing a bit of fire off Nicolette. The ridgetop exploded under a fire-hose stream of metal splinters and energy weapons, even as he returned fire. He leaned into the storm, trusting his armor. The incoming fire drummed against him like pounding horizontal rain. Energy beams scored bright streaks across him, raising his internal temp. He could feel the heat on his skin as he shook and rocked from the force of it all.

He stood firm, sending streams of metal from his arm mounted kinetic weapons ripping into the defensive pods scattered around the fantastic metal landscape. HARRE orchestrated a symphony of destruction with the shoulder and hip turrets.

Karith's inner-ear protested. Suddenly, dirt piled into him from the side. He found himself stumbling.

"Contact!" HARRE yelled.

Looking down, Karith saw a walker fastened to his mech's lower abdomen, sparks flying where its plasma cutter chewed into his hip joint.

"Rot!" He smashed the spiny metal thing with his fist. Three more scuttled out of a newly opened hole in the ridge's side. Their leggy angled shapes scrambled past a machine he'd never seen before, a conical spinning drill bit as big as the rumbling combustion engine backing it.

"This is a new behavior, sir."

Karith smashed at a second walker as three more leapt onto his chest and shoulders. He caught himself screaming in anger and gritted his teeth. He triggered a burst of explosive rounds into the driller thing and leapt at it, pushing it back into the hole it had come from. Spinning, he flailed at the walkers cutting into him from above.

The dirt under his feet gave way and he slipped face first into another cluster of walkers scrambling out from between another driller and the edges of the hole it had made. He choked back another yell and curled up into a ball. They looked more like fantastic metal spiders than anything else, long legs supporting a bulbous body. One of them was digging into his abdomen again. He felt and heard something give down by his feet, a tearing, crumpling sound. Not his mech's feet, his actual feet. A whiff of ozone reached his nose.

"Sir, units in the valley are turning back toward us."

Thrusting with his mech's feet against the top of the second driller, he fired another burst of explosive rounds into its engine as he jumped away, or tried to jump away. Two more walkers dragged at him and upset his balance. The dirt and brush at the bottom of the ridge rushed up to meet him. Impact tightened his harness. Sparks flew in three directions across his face.

He grabbed a handful of walker and ripped it away. It went limp when he slammed it against the ground, pieces breaking off. He flogged his armor's upper torso with the remains of the thing and felt it impact other walkers.

"Karith!" Nic's voice was frantic. "I can't see you!"

"Wait one."

A walker lost its grip and fell to the ground. Karith stomped on it as he struggled to his feet again. Sparking, it blew up, clouds of smoke boiling out of it.

"Sir, your armor is compromised at plates T12 and T13."

"What!?" Nic screamed over the link.

"I'm fine! Relax." The screaming sound of a plasma cutter was starting to vibrate his cockpit. Frantically Karith swept his hands over his head. Aha! He grabbed the thing and crushed, dragging it to the front where he could see it. The cutting stopped. Metal corpse in hand, he flung himself to the ground on top of the two still on his back and rolled away. One stayed down. He fired into its body and it spasmed, smoking.

A shadow overtopped him and his sensors registered a flash of heat. He ground his back against an outcropping of rock, spun, and smashed his fist into the power plant of the boiler clinging to the rock face. It exploded. He looked up even as he fired a burst into the walker stirring at his feet.

Nicolette's airship floated over him, just below the ridgetop. He stared in consternation for a moment. Most of her lift spheres were discolored from heat and impact.

"Nic?"

"Well what was I supposed to do, you jerk?"

"Sir, this area is riddled with tunnels. I deem it likely that more drilling machines are on the way and recommend retrograde movement."

"Harry, if you ever say 'retrograde movement' again, I'll erase you. It's bogtaken 'retreat'. What are you doing down here Nic?"

"Just thought I might lend a hand."

"That's crazy. Get out of here, back up high."

"Fine, screw you then."

She sounded upset but jetted away down the ridge, picking up speed until she lifted into the air.

Up and down the ridge, earth slid and a literally earthshaking rumble started. Karith turned and sprinted back the way he had come, into the hills. "Harry, what are the machines in the valley doing?"

"Approximately a third are returning toward their damaged power node."

"Damn it. The rest?"

"They have reached our drop zone and are continuing toward the city."

"Nic, I need you to hit those boilers in the valley again."

"Roger that." Her voice was cold.

"Hell, Nic, that was stupid and you know it. What if a walker had gotten up into your lift spheres?"

Silence.

"Whatever, Nic. I'm on my way down."

"What's that supposed to mean?"

"I'm going to hit them from the rear. That'll get their attention."

"Are you crazy? There's a hole in your armor!" Her voice was more frantic than he had ever heard it.

Karith found a draw going his way and started loping down to the valley.

Major Kewlett broke into their common circuit. "Marvudi, can you hold that valley yourself?"

"Why?"

"I need your air."

Nicolette's voice was cold as iron. "No, Major, you're not pulling me off Karith's top cover."

"That's up to him, little miss."

Karith raised his eyebrows. It had been a long time since anybody dared call Nicolette "little miss" or anything like it. He examined the situation model as he ran, Nic's lasers coughing in the background.

HARRE said to him, privately, "Sir, our armor is breached. We must return to the depot for repair."

"There is no depot, HARRE. The *MarsFree* is gone and the next ship is hours out."

"Yes, sir. We should still consolidate with other units in the area."

Karith stopped just below a hilltop overlooking his dropzone and a little closer to the city. Panesthian civilians were a glittering brown carpet moving along the ground toward the city. The boilers were already upon the near edge of the mass. Curled and flaming Panesthian bodies littered the torn earth. The boilers ground on, weapons burning, ripping, and smashing. Dimly, Karith could hear a roaring sound, the frantic buzzing and wailing of the dying Panesthians.

Taking up a stable posture, he readied every top-down missile he had. Nicolette orbited overhead, lasers coughing in his ears. Rippling explosions of smoke, steam, and molten metal stuttered across the valley floor. He could see the boilers digging in to shoot up at her, but not all of them. Some still moved toward the city.

"Major, you've got plenty of air."

Snap. "It's not enough, son. This damn city is oozing civilians. My mechs keep breaking through the tops of their bloody burrow-buildings when they try to move. The airships are the most effective weapons platforms I've got for offense, and I need 'em all. You're not the only one. I'm pulling air off all my outliers."

The Major had a point about the air. Strange that a quirk of architecture made air assets more precise and civilian friendly than ground units here.

HARRE was using data from all the sensor pods they'd dropped earlier to build the current situation model. The boilers were deep into the suburbs now, and breaking into the burrow-buildings themselves too. They weren't empty.

"Bloody hell."

"What was that, son?" Snap, chew.

"Can do, Major. Nic, go."

"Damn you, Karith."

Karith didn't say anything. She sounded on the verge of tears, which was just odd. Nicolette did another low screaming pass over the boilers in the suburbs in front of him and curved away toward the city.

Major Kewlett said, "Son, you see what's going on over here?"

"Yes, Major."

"Good."

The connection went dead.

HARRE spoke to him. "Sir, are we going to attempt to engage and defeat the boilers in the valley?"

Karith triggered his first salvo of top-downs and sprinted off the hill just ahead of the counter fire, which ripped into the ground behind him until he made it into a wadi. He put his shoulder turrets onto automatic and sprinted along the gash in the ground.

"Harry, if we don't draw them off here, they're going to plow into the Major's rear area and they're going to be slaughtering civilians the whole way in. This is it, my friend."

Karith popped up to the top of a swelling hill and fired off another salvo of top-downs. The counter fire was slower this time, and he was well away before it hit.

"Sir, the boilers are still advancing."

They were into the suburbs now. Karith moved carefully as he fired, trying to avoid stepping on the crushed and burned Panesthians scattered around the shells of their tunnels and buildings now cracked open to the sky. He gritted his teeth and choked back the bile. Panesthians died easier than their smaller looka-likes from Earth.

A subsonic round from a tread he hadn't seen in time slammed into his shoulder plate and knocked him over. Through the concussive haze he could feel a breeze playing around his feet. There really was a hole in his armor.

From flat on the ground he sent an armor-piercing round at the boiler's tread. The bulbous shape jumped and exploded. Lucky hit. Another one rolled up behind it.

He regained his feet and ran on. With HARRE's targeting help, he kept both armguns firing at once. Counter fire whipped around him, glancing off his armor.

He paused in a depression filled with trees, a wide spot along a stream bed.

"Fire off the rest of the sensor pods, Harry."

"Including the reserves, sir?"

"Yes."

HARRE launched the remaining eleven sensor pods from their racks. They arced out from Karith in a spreading cloud, came to earth, and dug in, leaving only their antennas protruding. The situation model sharpened up almost immediately. The boiler advance seemed to be clumped up before a small hill in the center of the valley. Beyond that hill, he could see hundreds of unsteadily flying and scuttling Panesthian shapes fleeing overland.

He took a moment and ducked down to examine the inside of his cockpit. There, just to the right, down by his feet, was a jagged hole leaking daylight. He swore when he realized that he couldn't use a sensor pod to examine the exterior because he'd just launched them all. It occurred to him to dismount and examine it but he discarded the idea before it had even fully formed. The smell of a summer afternoon wafted up to him, laced with that of burning plastic.

He sprinted out of the depression, running toward the hill, firing as he went.

He hadn't gone ten steps before he broke through the top of a burrow-building and crashed to a stop. To his great relief, it was empty. A colorful mural on one wall looked down on bare floor. He vaulted up and out.

The boilers were flowing around and over that hill now, moving on. He had to get in front of them somehow.

The machines were thick on the ground. His guns howled and screamed along with him as he stomped, smashed and burned a thick swathe of destruction through the metal foe. Karith was no longer speaking aloud. Once again he and HARRE were one in dreadful destructive purpose.

Just before he reached the hill, a swarm of walkers, crawlers, and blasters erupted over a stone ridge and on top of him, metal limbs flashing with terrible speed. He caught a glimpse of one blaster's stocky cylindrical body up close before it triggered its main weapon into his mech's face.

The crash shocked him backward. His flailing right hand latched onto a thick-limbed crawler and he swung it around himself. He could feel the smashing impacts through the fabric of his suit.

Horrible clicking sounds came to him, through his external sensors and through the hole at his shins. He rolled frantically over, left hand clapping to the hole in his mech's abdomen even as he pulled his real right leg up away from something moving down there, toes curling.

There was a boiler at the hole. He couldn't see it; he could only feel it move under his metal left hand. He bore down, crushing hard. At the same moment he felt a deep terrible pain high in his left leg. He stomped with his right and smashed something to the floor of his cockpit. Something withdrew as he pulled the boiler away. It was a walker, limp in his hand, holding a smoking monoblade cutter.

"Sir, there is a hollow in the top of that hill, a crater."

And there were a dozen more boilers around him. He started shooting and crushing again, and began pounding his way toward that hilltop, left leg going numb.

"Harry! Have they stopped?"

"Yes, sir. You have occupied their attention sufficiently to stop their advance. They are coming for *us* now." Blaster fire, waves of heat, washed over him, licking through the hole at his legs with sharp tongues as he ran.

"Good."

A huge blow took his mech in the right arm and spun him around and down. One of the treads. He looked for it, blinking sweat out of his eyes, and fired one of his three remaining missiles. The noise pounded at him. He'd never had a hole all the way through into his cockpit before. A sharp burning smell came in through it. He felt like throwing up.

The hill loomed over him, and he strained back to his feet to fling himself at it. Moments later he tumbled into the crater at the top. It was full of boilers.

He curled reflexively around the hole in his middle, flesh cringing away from it. Blaster fire filled the crater with orange plasma.

"No! This is *my* crater now!" He put the hole out of his mind, straightened, and fired point-blank at the boilers swarming over him. He kicked a boiler clear over the edge of the hole and grabbed another in his left hand, using it to scrape the others out, smashing and flinging. His mech's right arm twitched erratically as he fired its gun blindly. He smashed and stomped through the pain in his real leg, and fired until the boilers that were left in the hole were nothing but gears, cabling, and chunks of metal hull.

He blasted a few more as they came over the rim, launching them into the air in pieces.

"What's going on out there, Harry?" He gasped at a sudden wave of pain from his left leg and stumbled. When he tried to put out his mech's right hand to steady himself he fell against the wall of the crater as the arm only twitched limply. There was a sweet coppery smell heavy in the cockpit now.

"They are pausing in their assault on our position, sir. They are gathering."

He closed his eyes for a moment, then snapped them open. Closing them was a bad idea.

He could see now it wasn't really a crater. It was an excavation of some sort.

He tried to stand, but slipped. Glancing down, he saw among the shattered boilers a layer of dead Panesthians. Panesthians with equipment strapped to their bellies and fiery circles on their wing casings. So that was why the boilers had stopped at this hill. Not all these boilers were his kills.

"Karith?" Nicolette spoke to him. "I'm coming, baby."

The fire in his leg made him almost scream. "Harry, what's she doing?"

"She is breaking formation to come to our aid, sir."

"Stay where you are, Nic! That's an order."

"Go to hell, Karith!"

"Damnit, Nic, stay where you are. You gonna let the boilers break the line after I went to this much trouble? Stay where you are!" He filled his voice with as much energy as he could. In the background, he could hear Kewlett bellowing at her.

"Fine," she said. "You come to me then. Just run. You can make it."

"Can't do that, Nic."

"Damnit, Karith!" He could hear tears in her voice.

"Hey, Nic." He blasted a boiler off the rim and watched for another. None came.

"What?" She sounded angry now.

"Tell Maragette and Hazel I love them, OK?"

No answer.

Karith heard her engines roar and she screamed a long curse. The noise filters kicked in.

"Harry, what are they doing out there?"

"They have located and destroyed seven of our sensors, sir, but they appear to be bypassing us."

"What? They're advancing again? Toward the city?" Karith had never felt this tired.

"Yes, sir."

Karith chuckled, a sound weak in his own ears. "Up we get."

He propped himself up on the rim of the hole and started shooting. Boilers fell and return fire shattered the crater rim around him but still they advanced.

He gasped for air. "We're gonna have to get them to notice us again, Harry."

Karith gathered his legs under him, braced his left hand on the rim of the crater, grunted, and fell into blackness.

THE MECH FROZE.

"Sir?"

Karith did not answer. HARRE noted a thick stream of blood pouring from the hole in his armor. He used his emergency override to ease the mech back behind cover.

"Sir?" Still nothing.

"Karith?" Nicolette's voice was frantic. "Your icon's dark, Karith. Karith!"

HARRE answered. "He is unconscious, Captain Shepard."

"Damn." Her voice was thick. "OK, you're in charge now. Get him back here."

"It is true that command falls to me if my pilot becomes incapacitated."

"Why aren't you on your way back already, Harry?" her voice held ominous overtones. "Get up into the hills and make your way back here or he'll die."

HARRE looked over the field, the fleeing clouds of Panesthians, the advancing boilers carving into them.

"It is true, ma'am, that Captain Marvudi has a much higher chance of survival if I return to headquarters at this time."

"So get moving!" She screamed.

HARRE paused. Doctrine advised that he do as she said, but it was his call now. "I can't do that, ma'am." He vaulted the crater edge and charged the boilers, all guns blazing. They noticed him, and turned to engage.

Sometime later the *CambriaDawn* took up orbit around Milacria and dropped another three companies of mechanized infantry onto Major Kewlett's perimeter. Only forewarning and fast maneuvering saved her from the same fate as the *MarsFree*. Her Bombards destroyed the boiler railgun positions shortly thereafter.

Human forces pushed out to the east and the west. Captain Nicolette Shepard flew west, over the tangled wreckage of what seemed like thousands of broken boilers and dead Panesthians.

At a certain spot she lowered her airship to the ground and jumped out. Over 30 percent of her lift spheres were gone, and those that remained were discolored and ragged.

Karith Marvudi's mech lay face down in a dry streambed surrounded by hundreds of dead boilers, like the center of a blast-ring stretching for hundreds of meters.

Nicolette folded her helmet back as she ran. The stench of smoke, burning oil, and plasma assailed her nostrils. Ignoring the hot metal she scrambled up and forced her way past the dead boilers on the mech's back. She tapped a code into the hatch's touch plate. No response, not even a power light. She ran back to her ship and returned with tools. Sparks flew and tears boiled off the metal as she began cutting.

To Catch a Foo Fighter

David Hankins

To catch a foo fighter, you need three things: tech, speed, and bait. I'm the bait.

Assuming all went well, and I never assumed otherwise, I'd make history today and stamp a green alien head onto my X-73 experimental jet, right under my name: Lieutenant Jimmy "Wraith" Rigg.

I grinned inside my helmet and punched the afterburner.

I sliced above the South Pacific at Mach 3, scanning cloud-dappled skies as islands flicked past below. Foo fighters always came out when we tested new tech, and the X-73's inertial compensator was beyond cutting edge.

So where were they?

I huffed into my oxygen mask and keyed my neurotransmitter. The device sounded mechanical and emotionless, but it gave me a voice. "Assassin, status report?"

"No joy, Wraith. Maintain heading one-eight-niner." Commander Lydia "Assassin" Litvyak sounded annoyed as she circled high above in her F-35. She hated that I, a born mute, had been selected over her to fly the X-73. The most decorated pilot on this project, Assassin had downed twelve aircraft during the brutal Second Korean War while I'd been in grade school.

But I was the better pilot. When I was in the air, it's like I became one with the jet.

I searched the light blue above and the dark blue below for floating spheres, fingers tapping my control stick. Still no joy. Foo fighters were first seen in World War II and named by a radio operator after something he'd seen in a comic strip. They followed aircraft and defied physics, but never responded to radio calls. Foo fighters birthed the worldwide UFO craze and became a modern myth. But for the US Navy, UFOs weren't fiction. They were fact.

And they weren't cooperating.

Screw this. I wrenched my stick to the left. In any other jet, a hairpin turn at three times the speed of sound would have torn the aircraft apart. Aerodynamics sent a shudder through the frame, but the X-73's inertial compensator made the turn feel like a ride in grandma's Volkswagen. Inertial energy became more thrust, and I shot toward Guam at Mach 4.

"Wraith! What the hell?" Commander Litvyak followed, but without hope of keeping up in her F-35. I ignored her and craned my neck, looking for the telltale reflection of . . .

My heart jumped. There it was—a silver sphere two hundred yards off my port wingtip. Blood pounded in my ears. I'd actually done it. I'd found a foo fighter.

Now to catch it.

"Tally, Bogey One," I radioed, confirming contact, my excitement masked by the neurotransmitter's monotone. I banked ninety degrees again. *Come on.*

The foo fighter maintained station. It mirrored my maneuver perfectly—just as they always did—a habit I could exploit. A chipper voice echoed in my head, its tone playful. <*Tally ho, human. Come on.*>

I whipped my head around and stared at the sphere. Sunlight glinted off its polished surface, and my thoughts did a stutter-step. <*Did you just . . . talk?*>

Silence answered my thoughts before the voice said hesitantly, <*You heard me? But humans can't . . . oh wait . . . the protocol . . .*> It went silent, then said with gravitas, <*I am an Artificial Intelligence Ambassador from the Galactic Federation. I come in peace.*>

My stomach churned, and my hands grew sweaty. A century of chasing foo fighters and I'd just made first contact.

Admiral Byng's tense voice cut into my thoughts. "Batter up, Wraith." He'd set this trap, betting his entire career on it. I shook myself. According to our code phrases, I was the pitcher, and the foo fighter was the ball. Time to throw this thing into the "Catcher's Mitt".

<*You're a computer?*> I asked, banking eastward.

<*A sentient computer, thank you very much. I'm a Federation citizen with full rights and responsibilities. I even pay taxes. We've been waiting a long time for Earth to meet the criteria for peaceful Federation integration. We have much to discuss.*>

Peaceful integration? Humanity barely got along with each other. Sure, it had been a decade since the last war, but the political climate remained . . . strained.

My heads-up display showed a destroyer two hundred miles northeast, just four minutes away at Mach 4. I punched the acceleration and barrel-rolled down to skim over the wave tops, hitting Mach 5.

<*You're fast! Woohoo!*> the foo fighter said, staying with me. We angled toward Catcher's Mitt, a cabled spider web held aloft by balloons and tethered underwater to the destroyer. Embedded inertial dampeners would slow and catch the foo fighter which the destroyer would then reel in. At these speeds, the net was

invisible. The rest of the carrier group waited as a backstop twenty miles beyond the net.

"Inbound, thirty seconds," I sent to the destroyer, adrenaline pumping through me. I was making history.

<What's your name, friend?> the foo fighter asked.

<Call me Wraith,> I sent absently, maintaining focus.

<Oh, how dark and foreboding.> Its tone was mocking, yet light. *<Call me Arlo. I can't believe you can hear me. Humans finally crossed the threshold!>*

A tendril of doubt wormed its way into me. As a born mute, I understood the excitement at finally being heard. God, did I understand. My scramjet engine roared as a lump formed in my throat. I glanced at the five-foot sphere off my wingtip, unsure what to say.

"You're coming in too hot, Wraith. Drop below Mach 2." Admiral Byng's voice was clipped, excited.

I tapped the airbrakes, shedding speed. Arlo maintained station. I tapped them again.

<Where are we going, Friend Wraith?>

Before I could respond, I sliced past the trap and the foo fighter slammed into it. Spider web cabling whipped around the sphere. Embedded inertial dampeners slowed it precipitously, but not enough. The tether pulled out of the ocean, jerked the destroyer, then snapped like wet spaghetti. Arlo's panicked scream echoed inside my skull.

I wrenched my control-stick back and shot skyward. The scream faded with distance. I cut thrust and spun my nose downward. Gravity and momentum fought over me. Below, the foo fighter jinked left and right over the wavetops, trailing the half-mile-long tether like a dog's leash. Admiral Byng screamed through my radio.

"Shoot it down. Now!"

My hands gripped the flight controls, finger on the trigger, but I didn't fire. This felt . . . wrong. What had I done?

White smoke belched from the destroyer as its deck guns bracketed the corkscrewing foo fighter. The massive net dragged the sphere down, slowing it enough for the shells to fence it in.

"Wraith!" Admiral Byng's voice burned with fury. "We need that tech. Shoot. It. Down!"

I shook my head. First contact shouldn't end like this.

It wouldn't.

I slammed my engines to full power and screamed out of the sky. "Destroyer, stand down. I can bring it in."

Byng cursed, but the flashing guns stopped as I plummeted into the line of fire. Breath coming fast, I dropped the hook I used for carrier landings, timing Arlo's movements as the ocean rushed toward me. I picked my intercept point, leveled out, and shot over the top of the foo fighter. My landing hook snagged the net.

I didn't have time to cheer. I barrel-rolled to wrap the alien craft up tight. *<Sorry, Arlo. Please, calm down. It's better this way.>*

A terrified yell answered me, and Arlo jumped skyward. The net yanked upward against my forward momentum, and I tried to follow. Too slow. Despite the inertial compensator, it felt like God hit me with a baseball bat.

The X-73 tore apart.

My world became a spinning swirl of sea and sky as my cabin skipped across the water like a spinning stone. The compensator worked for a few precious seconds, reducing the unsurvivable crash into a gut-wrenching fair ride before giving out when my nose cone caught a wave. I spun into the air, vomited into my oxygen mask, and splashed down.

Pain and darkness rolled over me with the waves.

A SHIP'S HOSPITAL BED IS NOT THE BEST PLACE TO RECEIVE AN ASS-CHEWING, BUT Admiral Byng didn't seem in the mood for courtesy. He woke me with a finger jabbed into my chest. The Old Man's face hovered inches from mine. Copenhagen under his lip made his breath smell like a sweaty horse.

"What the *hell* were you thinking, Lieutenant Rigg?" His voice echoed off steel bulkheads while monitors beeped beside me. Tobacco-laced spittle hit my cheek, and I flinched.

I tried to answer, but my thoughts met silence. Crap. I'd lost my neurotransmitter with the X-73. Byng didn't understand sign language, so I wiped my cheek, clenched my fists, and took my punishment.

The Old Man raged for five minutes about duty, honor, and regaining our technological edge over the Chinese Hegemony. He finally wound down and thrust a flat-palmed knife hand in my face, fingers and thumb pointed stiffly. "You're never flying again, Lieutenant." Veins bulged at his graying temples before he stormed out.

I released a shuddering breath. Rumor said that the Secretary of the Navy had given Admiral Byng an ultimatum: bring in a foo fighter or retire. Byng's ambition wouldn't let him retire, and the strain had made him . . . unstable.

A worried face peeked through the hatch, framed by an unruly mop of red hair. I smiled, the tension in my shoulders easing as my best friend Charlie Marosi slipped inside. Sporting the pudgy figure of a genius with no time for the gym, Charlie wore delicate round glasses and social awkwardness like armor.

As an electronics prodigy, he'd been accepted into MIT at fifteen to join a team attempting to turn brainwaves into words. There had been breakthroughs before, Stephen Hawking's speech synthesizer being the most famous, but MIT wanted to take it further. Make the tech seamless. I was sixteen when I met Charlie, having left the family ranch in Montana to be one of the project's test subjects. As the only teenagers on the project, Charlie and I had hit it off.

Within a year he broke the code and gave me the power of speech.

Ten years later, I got him added to the scientific side of this boondoggle as a tech specialist. Seemed only fair. I waved him in.

Charlie passed a worried gaze over me. "You okay?"

I gave the "OK" sign, and he pulled my old neurotransmitter from his pocket. It was matte-black and the size of a cigarette carton with an embedded speaker, the first model he'd made. He flipped a switch and said, "You look like crap, Jimmy."

I grinned weakly. "I feel like it, too." My voice sounded tinny coming from the small speaker. "What happened to the foo fighter?"

Charlie's fingers worried at the edge of my transmitter before he set it on my bed. "After your spectacular crash, it opened a portal in the sky and disappeared, net and all."

"Good." I settled back with a relieved sigh.

That earned me a raised eyebrow. Charlie leaned forward, his gaze serious. "What happened up there?"

I drew a deep breath and told him everything. It felt good to tell my side of things after that ass-chewing, and Charlie was a good listener. I think he even believed me.

The ship's JAG attorney visited the following day. I was officially grounded, pending investigation. She read a depressing list of brig-worthy charges, made me sign a stack of forms, and left me feeling like crap. The wheels of military justice were about to crush me.

Nine years in the Navy and I'd never been in trouble. Investigated, sure, but I'd expected that when I requested a SECNAV waiver to join. Born with a dysfunctional larynx and dreams of flying, I blew the Navy's aptitude tests out of the water while at MIT. The Navy wanted to buy MIT's neural-link tech to develop faster pilot response times, so the Secretary of the Navy signed my waiver, and I joined the X-73 project.

It took two more days to escape the sick bay. I ached down to my bones, but I couldn't lay around and get railroaded. Once the doc released me, I headed straight for Admiral Byng's daily sync meeting. I had to tell him what had happened with the foo fighter.

I'd made first contact and the aliens were friendly.

My heart hammered as I slid into the conference room filled with the low chatter of officers and scientists. A wave of silence spread through the room when they saw me, and I froze just inside the doorway. This was going to be harder than I'd thought. Admiral Byng wasn't here yet, but I spied Charlie in the corner. He gave an anxious smile, then his eyes went wide.

Byng's cold voice rumbled from behind me. "Lieutenant, get out of my meeting."

I spun on my heel and snapped a salute. He didn't return it. Instead, he hooked a thumb over his shoulder toward the corridor, a silent command that my feet ached to follow.

I held my salute and spoke through the neurotransmitter clipped to my shirt pocket. For once I was grateful for its emotionless monotone. "Sir, about the foo fighter. I need to report—"

"I did *not* give you leave to speak, Lieutenant Rigg!" The rancid smell of chewing tobacco wafted over me, and Admiral Byng's knife hand sliced forward, fingertips stopping a millimeter from my nose. "You let the enemy escape and destroyed a 1.2-*billion*-dollar aircraft. I'm getting recalled to Washington because of you!" The veins on his temple looked ready to burst. "Get. Out. Now!"

Clutching the shreds of my dignity, I snapped my salute down and stepped around him. As the door closed behind me, Bing addressed the room. "We're springing Catcher's Mitt Two tomorrow. Commander Litvyak will fly our last X-73. I *will* have a foo fighter, dead or alive, before I face those bureaucrats in DC."

I shook my head. He was making a mistake, but what could I do?

CHARLIE FOUND ME THAT EVENING ON THE CARRIER'S AFT FLIGHT DECK watching the fading sunset and feeling sorry for myself. The carrier group was barely visible as dim outlines gliding over the dark sea.

Charlie shoved his hands into his pockets and bumped me with his shoulder. "Hey, cheer up. It could be worse."

I snorted, running through my litany of errors for the millionth time. "How?" I asked, the transmitter's tinny voice pulled away by the stiff breeze. "Byng's going to crucify me! I'll be lucky to avoid brig time, and I'm sure as hell never flying again."

"But you saved the foo fighter."

I drew a deep breath of diesel-laced sea air. Yes, Arlo was alive, but that knowledge did little to soothe my anxiety.

Charlie buffed his glasses on his shirt, held them up to a deck light to check for spots, then put them back on. "I figured out how you did it," he said. "How you talked to the alien tech."

His excited tone pierced my melancholy, and I cocked my head toward him. "Really? How?"

Charlie tapped my transmitter. "Your brain has been linking with tech for years, ever since you joined the brainwave-to-speech project at MIT. I think you've developed electronic telepathy, and *that's* what connected you to the foo fighter."

Electronic telepathy? I thought about how completely attuned I felt to the X-73. Like the machine and I were one being. It felt . . . right. "Arlo said that humanity had crossed a threshold," I said. "Perhaps that's what it meant." The ache in my chest twisted like a knife, and I shook my head. "I screwed up humanity's chance at peaceful first contact."

Charlie's expression turned earnest. "Then try again."

"How?"

"Convince Admiral Byng to put you back in the air."

My shoulders hunched. I turned back toward the churning ocean and sighed. How the hell was I supposed to do that?

I watched Commander Litvyak's launch the next morning from Vulture's Row, a narrow balcony outside the flag bridge. The roar of her X-73 made my fingers twitch. I should be in that cockpit.

I stood near the bridge's open windows, out of sight but within earshot. For Catcher's Mitt Two, the Admiral had reinforced his previous failure by doubling the net and quadrupling its tethers. Once again, the carrier group watched from a twenty-mile vantage.

Litvyak's sharp contralto crackled over the radio. "In position, commencing maneuvers." Squinting against the sun, I watched her X-73—the only one in existence now—cut impossible ninety-degree turns as she stressed the experimental aircraft to its limits.

She flew crazy loops for an hour before I saw a brief flash of light. Her radio crackled, confirming contact. "Tally, Bogey One. Returning to home plate."

I leaned against the rail, surprised. I hadn't expected the foo fighter to actually return. When she banked toward the trap, however, Arlo shot skyward, a silver streak that disappeared in a flash of light.

Admiral Byng's curses echoed through the bridge's open windows. I glanced inside as silence fell. The admiral was hunched over his display, tanned fingers clutching its edge in a white-knuckled grip.

The foo fighter ran, I thought, *because Litvyak couldn't hear Arlo's voice.*

My neurotransmitter spoke my thoughts aloud, and I froze. Crap. I'd forgotten it was on. Admiral Byng's head whipped around. His eyes narrowed when he saw me.

"Have something to add, Lieutenant?" he said, voice deceptively calm. "Please, stop lurking and enlighten us."

I cringed internally. I knew that tone. He wanted someone to rage at, and I'd jumped straight into his sights.

But this was my chance.

"The foo fighter talked to me, sir." A twitch of surprise flickered behind Byng's glower. "I heard it through my neurotransmitter, and it said that they come in peace. I made first contact." I let excitement fill my face, if not my electronic voice. Squaring my shoulders, I stepped through the hatch onto the flag bridge. It was a cramped space, but the staff edged away lest the Old Man's temper splash onto them.

Byng's eyes narrowed. "You spoke with the enemy and didn't report it?"

"I tried to, sir. At your daily sync."

Byng's jaw clenched. "So the alien can talk. Big deal."

"Sentient computer, sir, not an alien. But it represents the Galactic Federation, and they're offering us a chance to join. This is big, sir. A chance for humanity to rise above our petty squabbles. If you send me up, I can reestablish communication. Bring the foo fighter in."

The admiral's fingers drummed on his display. He glanced at the watch officer. "Recall Assassin." He looked back at me. "I think you're full of shit, lieutenant, but I'm running out of time. Bring me my foo fighter, and I'll drop the charges." His lip curled into a snarl. "But screw this up, and I will bury you."

My heart hammered in my chest, but I saluted smartly before spinning on my heel. I could bring Arlo in to establish peaceful first contact.

For the sake of humanity, I had to.

ACID CHURNED IN MY GUT AS I SOARED ABOVE THE PACIFIC. THE OCEAN WAS peaceful today, as close to glass smooth as it ever got. I tried and failed to find the same calm as I burned fuel and time. Despite running the aircraft through its paces all afternoon, the foo fighter hadn't appeared.

Charlie had rewired my old neurotransmitter into the X-73 and Admiral Byng had insisted he install a recorder with it. Commander Litvyak flew overwatch again, a surly guardian waiting for me to screw up, while Admiral Byng grew increasingly caustic over the radio.

Frustrated, I closed my eyes and focused on the aircraft wrapped around me, seeking calm. The engine thrummed, its roar muted by my helmet as it vibrated muscles sore from my wreck. I considered Charlie's idea of electronic telepathy and imagined reaching my mind toward the flight control computer. It felt silly, but I told the X-73 to do a barrel roll.

The aircraft spun on its long axis, dropping toward the sea. My eyes snapped open, and I wrenched on the stick to level out. Charlie had been right! Commander Litvyak sounded in my ear.

"Six o'clock, Wraith. It's on your tail."

"Roger," I sent, drawing a calming breath, and twisting around to look. Arlo's shiny metal sphere glinted from two hundred yards behind me. My heart lurched, and I keyed my transmitter so Admiral Byng could listen in. <*"Arlo, can you hear me?"*>

A small electronic sigh answered, followed by resounding silence. It was a pointed silence, like a disapproving parent gathering their thoughts. I was about to call again when Arlo spoke, its voice clipped and unhappy.

<*I did not want to return, but the Federation Council interpreted your actions as a 'primitive miscommunication.' You are rich in resources, so they granted humanity another opportunity to prove its peaceful intent and join the Galactic Federation.*>

I mulled that for a moment. <*"You think we have resources? Hell, most of our wars are border disputes over a few square miles. And don't get me started on water and mineral rights."*> My parents in Montana often fought with neighbors over their ranch's water rights. But if resources are all the Federation wanted, would they just strip Earth clean before moving on to the next hapless planet?

<*No, not land,*> Arlo said. <*Or water, or minerals, or even your air. We have those. We want you. Humans.*>

Oh, crap. They wanted slave labor. Or perhaps fodder for some war they were fighting?

<*"To what end?"*> I asked, forcing myself to breath calmly.

There was a long pause. <*I'll make you a deal. Keep up with me, and we'll talk.*> Arlo zipped past me.

I blinked in surprise, then punched the afterburner. I passed Mach 3 in seconds, but the foo fighter remained tantalizingly ahead. It abruptly cut left and down, and I whipped the X-73 around, directing the jet with my thoughts. The inertial compensator dampened the maneuver, but not my spike of adrenaline. We skimmed the water, buzzed the carrier close enough to break windows, and then shot into the sky.

I became one with my aircraft and maintained station just behind the foo fighter, matching his every maneuver.

<*You almost killed me last time,*> Arlo said. <*Why should I believe you have peaceful intent?*>

<*"We were trying to capture you. It was a mistake. I'm sorry."*> Arlo gave an electronic snort. Hoping to move past my screw-up, I asked, <*"Why does the Federation want us? What's so special about humans?"*>

<*You are a race of potential prodigies. Most Federation races rose from hive minds or herd mentalities. Your ability to innovate at the individual and collective levels is staggering. The Federation needs that innovative mindset.*>

Potential prodigies? So *not* slave labor or fodder for a war. I breathed a sigh of relief. <*"What is the Galactic Federation?"*>

<*A loose coalition of systems bound together through common financial interest and the peaceful advancement of science, which we freely share. If accepted, Earth would have access to regenerative medicine, perpetual energy, the intersystem portal network, and more.*>

Woah. That would change . . . everything. It was like a grand uplift to pull humanity out to the stars.

And yet, I hated to ask, <*"At what cost?"*>

<*Planets are considered for membership when they achieve certain technological benchmarks. Humanity's final requirement was the mind-computer link necessary for Federation technology.*>

<*"Electronic telepathy,"*> I said. Charlie had been right.

<*Indeed. You've demonstrated this well, a promising and necessary next step toward innovations and growth you—and we—can't even imagine.*>

That sounded promising. <*"Humanity is ready. We—"*>

<*No. You are not. Humanity is too violent. That is your cost. You must join us in peace. The Federation has no tolerance for warring races and sequesters them to their home systems. I've observed Earth for centuries, waiting for you to advance and change your baser nature. I'm learning to live with disappointment.*>

I had no answer for that. <*"I'm not a diplomat, Arlo, just a pilot. Can you talk to my admiral? If humanity knew what the Galactic Federation has to offer, then I know we'd be motivated to work toward peace, toward inclusion."*>

The foo fighter went silent. I drew three measured breaths before it said, <*As an ambassador, I am duty-bound to speak with your leadership. Take me to him.*>

Relief washed over me, and we banked toward the carrier. My thoughts raced, considering the implications of this moment. Never mind that my career hung in the balance. Humanity's future was in the balance! We had to get this right.

I was so preoccupied that I failed to notice Admiral Byng's silence.

I got permission to approach and landed with a jerk as my landing hook caught the arrestor. The foo fighter floated to a stop beside me, hovering six feet above the deck.

Admiral Byng stalked across the flight line, waving me toward him as I unhooked my neurotransmitter and climbed out of the X-73. His pleased expression looked unnatural on his craggy face. Unable to sort out my own knot of emotions—wonder, anxiety, eagerness—I jogged to him. He slapped my shoulder and said, "Good job, Lieutenant, I'll take it from here."

"Sir," I said, "The foo fighter said—"

He silenced me with a wave and pointed toward a nearby Marine major. "Now."

The major spoke into his headset and a Marine stepped out of a hatch with a shoulder-mounted rail gun—its magnet-wrapped barrel looked like an old-fashioned rocket launcher—aimed at the foo fighter.

<*No!*> I spun toward Arlo. <*Run!*>

The foo fighter twitched upward but the Marine tracked it and fired. The rail gun sounded like someone rapidly clicking a massive pen. A hole appeared in the sphere's side and Arlo fell from the sky like a dropped ball. It clanged to the flight deck and rolled to the edge before rocking to a stop.

Admiral Byng cheered. I ran toward Arlo. Byng tried to call me back, but I ignored him. I reached the sphere and ran my hands over the ragged hole. The edges were hot and crimped inward. Sparks flickered inside densely packed tech; daylight visible through a basket-ball-sized exit wound. My chest felt tight. I couldn't breathe.

<Are you still there?>

<You lied!>

Breath rushed out of me, and I rested my head on the sphere. Arlo was alive. *<I'm sorry. I thought Admiral Byng would talk first, give diplomacy a chance and listen to what the Federation was offering. Can you fly?>* I glanced back and saw Marines stalking forward, weapons ready.

<My antigrav is punctured. My portal generator is functional, but core programming restricts its use with fragile sentients nearby. It would kill you all. I never should have trusted a human!>

"Step away, lieutenant," a Marine said, motioning with his barrel. Beyond him, Admiral Byng arched an imperious eyebrow that said my career hung in the balance with my next decision.

So did humanity's future.

<You were right, Arlo. Humanity's not quite ready, but don't lose faith. We will change. Give us time, please.>

I dropped to one knee and shoved the sphere with my shoulder. It was heavy, but it tipped over the flight deck's edge and plummeted toward the ocean. The Marines tackled me with angry yells, and I hit the deck, my head and shoulders over the edge. Knees dug into my spine and cuffs ratcheted onto my wrists, yanking my shoulders painfully back. I didn't care. I gazed downward.

The ocean swallowed the foo fighter with a splash. Sunlight needled through the water, glinting off Arlo's sinking sphere, refracting in a dozen directions.

<I will present your plea to the Federation Council.> Arlo sounded weary. Disappointed. *<Expect long deliberations. Humanity's betrayal and barbarism have no place in the civilized galaxy. And yet, your defiance to save me through non-violent means has been noted. Perhaps there is hope yet for humanity. Goodbye, Wraith.>*

There was a flash of light and the ocean bulged outward and then collapsed on itself. A tiny whirlpool formed, blurring everything for a moment before clearing.

The foo fighter was gone.

As expected, Admiral Byng fed me to the wolves. It was small comfort when his career also imploded, and he was forced into retirement.

For wanton destruction of government property while disobeying a direct order, I got twenty-three months at Leavenworth and a dishonorable discharge.

Thankfully, Byng's "aiding the enemy" charge got tossed after Charlie leaked the transcript and video footage of our disastrous attempt to catch the foo fighter.

After serving my sentence, I rejoined my parents on their Montana ranch. It hurt knowing that I would never fly again, so I spent my days sweating in the wheat fields and my nights sitting on their front porch, watching the Milky Way spiral through the wide-open sky.

The Galactic Federation was out there. Waiting for us.

I was rocking on that porch one cool June evening, contemplating the cosmos, when Charlie dropped by for a visit. He'd lost weight since I'd last seen him and looked more tired, but that awkward smile was all Charlie.

"How you doing?" he asked, dropping into a second rocker and crossing his legs.

I presented my palms. "Rebuilding calluses," I said through the neuro-transmitter.

He smirked. "You never did like ranch work."

I nodded and we rocked in companionable silence as the wind sighed through the wheat. "I saw you on the news," I said. "The peace rallies are grow-ing." World news had exploded after the Foo Fighter Transcript leak, making Charlie an icon for the peace movement that followed. As a military prison inmate, I hadn't been able to help.

Charlie toyed with his shirt buttons, uncomfortable with his fame. "A dozen countries have signed the disarmament treaty, but others won't commit until their enemies sign first." He eyed me sideways. "We need help."

"You don't want me. I'm the disgraced pilot who screwed up first contact." The disappointment in Arlo's voice still haunted my dreams.

Charlie punched me in the shoulder. "You *made* first contact. Sure, humanity failed its first chance to join a peaceful galactic community, but now we know the price of admission. The world is changing for the better—despite the politicians, I might add—but we need your help. You promised Arlo that we'd be ready when he returns. It's time to stop feeling sorry for yourself and make good on your promise."

I crossed my arms. "How?"

Charlie pointed at my temple. "Help me replicate your electronic telepathy. It's the key to unlocking . . . what did Arlo say? Innovations and growth we can't even imagine? The Federation wants us, and we want the Federation. But we need to make your mind-computer linkage widespread before we even dream of integrating into their society—assuming of course that we achieve peace first."

I raised an eyebrow. "That's it? No motivational speeches at the peace rallies?"

A wry smile appeared. "I didn't say that. People want to hear your story, and I *will* get you on stage. You talked to the Galactic Federation's ambassador. Like it or not, your opinion matters. Humanity has—for the first time in history—started to unite. We're on the edge of something big. Your influence could tip the balance toward disarmament and peace."

I drew a deep breath, reveling in the crisp Montana air. Charlie had a point. I'd felt sorry for myself for long enough. We needed more than speed, tech, and bait to catch a foo fighter this time, to convince it to let us join the Galactic Federation. We needed to work together. We needed to change our violent nature in hopes of something better.

We needed peace.

"Alright," I said. "I'm in."

The Army Ration That Saved the Earth

Candice R. Lisle

P rivate Edward Franklin looked up as he walked past neighboring farms in his home state of Missouri. Rods and splashes of multi-colored lights seared the night sky. Earth had been invaded and sent up military craft to repel the mother ship belonging to the Orange, as they were known by Earthlings, because they looked like giant lady bugs, about four foot tall, with black spots on their backs, but these bugs only had two arms, and were able to stand on two legs. These bugs wanted cellulose. They had deforested their home world and needed more. They didn't ask nicely but came in force to take all of Earth's trees.

Franklin grasped his plasma rifle tightly. He'd give them what for.

"Private Edward Franklin, report," crackled his wrist communicator.

"No Orange sighted in Sector G-1," he responded. "Will scout out Sector G-2 next."

"Understood," replied a voice on the other end of the communicator.

Private Franklin sighed. This time of year, he should be preparing the soil in the north fields for his soybean crop and taking care of the corn starting to grow in the south fields, not looking for giant lady bugs.

He had recently purchased a new herbicide and was anxious to try it out on the weeds choking his nearby corn fields. They were pernicious and nothing seemed to stop them. Just thinking about it made Franklin sneeze.

Wiping his nose on his sleeve, the earthy odor of fertilizer filled his nostrils as Private Franklin stomped through the bushes and trees which edged his farm. His eyes ached from peering in the night for Orange invaders. He should have been able to see the lights of his home. Private Franklin could hardly wait to finish his rounds and see his wife, who was pregnant with their first child, and give her a hug and plenty of kisses.

Was it only last month when Franklin andMarie watched tanks and jeeps parade past their farm? It seemed like a year ago when the U.S. Army set up a base downtown and then conscripted every citizen to help out in any way they could. They all knew this would be a fight to the death. Neither race would survive without trees.

Even though they were at war, Franklin still tried to keep his farm running. He considered changing from field crops to trees. But no trees grew as fast as the Orange aliens were stealing them. He would sure be glad when this was all over.

"Sector G? Your neighbor is in the infirmary with a virus. We need you to scout out Sector H as well."

Franklin doubted his neighbor was sick. Private Barney Johnson most likely didn't want to go out in the dark, wandering around looking for Orange bugs. Lazy bones. Didn't even know how to farm properly. Johnson's fields were covered in weeds, just like Franklin's would be if that herbicide didn't work. Private Franklin sighed and accepted the additional assignment. It wouldn't take too much more time. Sector H was a lot smaller than Sector G.

"Request permission to message home and let my wife know that I'll be late this evening."

"Permission granted. Over and out."

After sending a message to Marie, Private Franklin laid his plasma rifle down against a boulder. He was tired and hungry. Sitting against an oak tree, he took an MRE out of his backpack, hoping it was filled with something delicious yet satisfying. He saw faded—yet still readable—red and black bold printing in all caps, covering the tin, warning it was not to be opened unless an officer gave authority to do so, and only in dire emergency conditions. Private Franklin sighed. No one would know. He had eaten all of his other MREs and his metabolism required constant feeding.

Opening the vacuum-packed container, he found a hard biscuit wrapped in foil and three thick rectangles of chocolate nestled in camo wrappers which read Non-Melting Tropical Bar. The biscuit sucked all the moisture from his mouth. Choking, he gulped water from his canteen then bit into the chocolate. It didn't taste too bad, kind of sweet yet bitter at the same time. He wondered how old it was. How long did MREs last? He ate one bar and put the other two in his pants pocket. A snack to munch on while looking over his neighbor's land.

The night air was cool and soft. Franklin relaxed. Buzzing filled his ears. *Was it time for the cicadas already?* He looked up, and through the leaves and branches, saw only stars. Beautiful, bright stars. He recognized the three which made up Orion's belt. *Wait a minute. He could see stars! The fireworks show had ceased. What was going on? Had we won? Lost? Was the war over? Could he go home now?*

Just as he was about to get up, the oak tree he was resting against lit up and hummed. Franklin felt dizzy. His head throbbed. The buzzing got louder. His body felt like it was being torn apart. Then all went dark.

Green light filtered through his eyelids. Franklin opened his eyes and found himself in a greenish-colored room filled with uprooted trees of all kinds. He sat on a hard black floor, still leaning against the oak tree. Roots pushed painfully into his rear end. He tried to stand, but his head still spun, and his stomach didn't feel so good.

He heard growling. The whole room thumped and shook. About a dozen Orange fed trees into a large machine. The stench was overwhelming. The air smelled like rotten wood. Franklin did his best to not vomit. He felt so queasy.

At the other end of the machine, brown rectangles traveled down a mechanical belt, then fell into a shiny metal container.

A door opened and more Orange appeared, taking the filled container away.

Private Franklin swallowed his fear, put his mouth to his wrist, and whispered, "Mayday. Mayday."

Static replied. Was his communicator only able to work planet side? How on or off Earth could he let anyone know what had happened to him? Franklin looked for his plasma rifle, but it and his backpack had stayed behind.

Franklin began to sneeze and his eyes watered. He felt miserable, in more ways than one. He sneezed again. He sniffed and wiped his nose on his sleeve. Some ragweed must have snuck in with the trees. Those weeds were pernicious. Just as bad as the Orange invaders, to his mind.

All that sneezing and wheezing brought Franklin to their attention. An Orange wearing a black shiny coverall looked right at him and grabbed two other workers. Claws clinked on the hard floor as they scuttled toward Franklin. He didn't know what to do. He didn't see any way out. His head swam. He could barely stand up straight. Their cold, black hands pinched as they grabbed him and wrapped a wet fiber rope around his wrists and legs. As the rope dried in the sawdusty air, the fiber got tighter and tighter. He wiggled his fingers, but nothing changed.

After tying him up, the bugs ignored him and went back to work. They didn't even set a guard.

Tears threatened as Franklin realized he was a prisoner. Would he miss the birth of his child? What would his wife do? Would she remarry? What would the Army do when he didn't respond at the next check in? What would they think when they found his rifle and backpack? Would they just write him off as MIA?

Franklin took a deep breath and let it out. The room stopped revolving as his head cleared. He realized that the only one who could save him was himself. But how? Franklin leaned against the wall and looked for a door. There had to be a way out, but he couldn't see it.

One of the aliens opened its carapace, flapped its wings, and buzzed into something that looked like a speaker. Something buzzed back at the creature. A green light on the ceiling flashed, and the machinery stopped. The workers lay down on the floor. Each took out one brown spiky rectangle and nibbled it. Dinner break.

Even though he was captive with no way back home, his stomach let him know it was still hungry. He wriggled around and tried reaching into his pants pocket for one of the chocolate ration bars, but his fingers couldn't reach. He kicked his tied-up feet on the floor, stomping them and making as much noise as possible. A bug scuttled over to stand in front of Franklin, who motioned with his tied-up hands that he wanted something to eat. The creature pushed a small portion of the brown spiky rectangle into Franklin's mouth.

Franklin bit down and immediately spit it out. It tasted and felt like shredded twigs. The bug buzzed and chattered. The man pointed to his pocket. The Orange leaned over the fabric rectangle, put its claws inside, and tore the pocket open. Franklin's wallet and the two chocolate bars fell out. Near his right leg, a hologram of his pregnant wife appeared.

The Orange chittered and held its claws up, showing a hologram of 30 tiny Orange beings to Franklin. Standing among the horde was a larger Orange. Franklin assumed this was the creature's mate.

The creature picked up a chocolate bar, sniffed it, then, not even bothering to unwrap it, took a nibble, then another one.

"Hey! Eat your own nasty stuff," Private Franklin cried out. He tried to retrieve his food, but the Orange's claws were too strong for him.

The bug waved his coworkers over.

Franklin was quickly surrounded by Oranges, who loomed over him as they fought for chocolate. He swatted at them with his bound hands and kicked at them with his feet, but it was no use.

After the rations were consumed, the bugs' antennas quivered, legs flailed in the air, and then all was still. They fell to the floor.

Franklin wondered if they were dead or just asleep. He kicked one. It rolled onto its side and began snoring. He bumped the snoozing bug's arm and a claw appeared. Using the serrated edges on the tip of its claw, Franklin tore the fibrous binding off his wrists and ankles. Prickles ran up and down his arms and legs as circulation returned.

Relieved that he was free, Franklin looked for a way out of the processing room. He found a door and carefully opened it. In front of him was a hallway with Oranges speeding back and forth. No one paid any attention to him. Red lights flashed and buzzing sirens sounded as the Oranges scurried up and down the hall. Behind him, inside the processing room, his captors were sound asleep, snoring loudly.

He retreated into the processing room, shut the door, then walked over to the communication console. It seemed to be easy enough to use with a display monitor, buttons made for claws, and a speaker.

Private Franklin looked in the monitor and was surprised to see a U.S. Army Colonel wearing a fake carapace and wings. The officer waved his wings and pushed buttons making various buzzing noises. Then the Colonel spoke, his announcement reverberating through the ship.

"This message is being shared with all of our military units. Attention Orange invaders! You violated the peace treaty by killing and harvesting more trees. This is unacceptable. Battle will resume in one Earth rotation. Over and out."

Private Franklin waved at the screen and shouted into the air, "Mayday! Mayday! This is Private Edward Franklin from the U.S. Army. I've been abducted." He pushed buttons and slid levers, hitting the screen, trying to get the man's attention. "I'm here on the alien spaceship."

The Colonel's face disappeared.

Great, just great, he thought. *Looks like I'm going to be in the thick of it.*

He collapsed against the communication console. Catching his breath, he tried again. Pushing buttons, making buzzing and spitting sounds, sliding levers. He hoped the Oranges wouldn't wake up from all the noise he was making. He pounded on the console. *How did this thing work?*

The Colonel's face reappeared and he repeated his previous message. Franklin shouted over the officer's words.

"Mayday! Mayday!"

Near the end of his transmission, the officer looked startled. "Private? How did you get on the mother ship? State your situation."

"Sir, I'm Private Edward Franklin from sector G. I'm captive on the alien ship. I was transported up along with an oak tree. The bugs ate my Tropical Chocolate bar rations and fell asleep. They really liked the taste, sir, and fought over the bars. I think the sugars and carbohydrates were too much for their metabolisms or something, because it knocked them out. As you can see, my captors are taking a nap." He stepped aside so the colonel could see the Oranges lying on the floor. Franklin then showed the officer the rest of the room by rotating the monitor screen. "I'm currently in a processing room where the aliens take trees and turn them into brown rectangles. The rectangles look just like our chocolate ration bars except spiky and made of twigs and bark."

"Private! Who gave you permission to open your MRE?" the colonel demanded.

Sweat filled his palms and covered his forehead. Private Franklin gulped. *Oh, oh. I'm in big trouble now. Disobeying an order, even printed on a tin. Not good.* He wiped his forehead with his sleeve, and replied, "No one, sir."

The colonel waved his hand. "No matter. We'll deal with that later. You being on the enemy ship is very useful, Private Franklin, and it seems that you've found a much better weapon than a plasma rifle. I need you to find the bridge and put all of the bugs to sleep. Once the bridge is secured, report in, and I will help you disable their shields and weapon systems."

A more sophisticated wrist unit materialized at Private Franklin's feet along with a MRE filled backpack.

"Use these well. Over and out."

MREs began filling up the room from floor to ceiling. Franklin opened some of the boxes and unwrapped the Tropical Bars.

Carefully opening the door, he tossed them into the hallway, six bars at a time. He heard legs and claws clattering on the floor as the hungry bugs ran to devour the sweets. He wondered what they thought as he threw more into the hall. Maybe a processor malfunction? They seemed hungry enough that they probably didn't really care. They fought over the bars. He wondered if it was addictive to the bugs. Knowing how much he liked the stuff, he figured it probably was.

Once the clattering stopped, Franklin put on the treat-filled backpack and went to find the bridge. The red lights and sirens had ceased. All was quiet, except for the hallway which was filled with snoring Oranges, lying on their backs, feet and black claws sticking up in the air. Franklin picked his way through the tangle, sticking close to the wall where the bugs were fewer.

Soon, his hand touched something that felt like cool glass. Three windows glowed with a subtle light. Franklin took a look. He screamed as he thumped the hard, clear surface, trying to break it. The room was filled with tiny grubs. The enemy of his precious crops. Thousands and thousands of squirming and writhing pupae ate green leaves. One stood, then began to clamber up the window. Franklin continued to pound on the glass, but the grub didn't seem to feel or hear his efforts as it continued on its way. Sliding down to the floor, Franklin leaned against the wall.

Pushing down his panic, he looked in the next window and saw eggs hanging from the ceiling. Adult Oranges were busy either laying or fertilizing them. Franklin couldn't see the walls, nor the other end of the room. There were so many eggs. Hundreds of thousands of glistening white spheres.

In the third window he saw tiny Orange bugs in clusters of fifty or so gathered around pairs of adult Oranges. The baby bugs ate processed brown rectangles broken in small pieces by their parents.

Franklin's immediate reaction was to stomp them all. He found himself wishing for a tank of insecticide. Earth's trees wouldn't last long once the babies were set loose. Where was the door? If he opened it, would the babies swarm into the hallway? He decided to report in and find out what he should do.

"Sir, does this communicator have visual?"

"Yes."

"Take a look at this."

The Colonel swore then said, "We've got to kill them all. It's our survival or theirs. There are way too many of them. It's imperative that you disable their weapons and shields."

Shuddering with revulsion, Franklin took one last look before leaving the nursery in search of the bridge. Time was running out. His heart raced. War could start again anytime. He ran, turning this way and that, pushing stiff bugs out of his way. He felt the backpack to make sure he had enough bars left to knock out the bridge's officers, once he found it.

Where could it be? This ship is huge!

Exhausted, out of breath and ideas, Franklin decided to take a rest and think logically about the best way to proceed. He leaned against a warm pillar. Clear tubes filled with a bubbling yellow liquid were attached to the walls. He touched a tube. Some moisture came away on his finger. He smelled the liquid and gingerly touched it with his tongue. It was sweet, like sap. Most likely the tubes led to a storage or mess room. He laughed. All creatures loved sweets.

He needed to find the bridge.

But first, he took a look at the hologram of his wife and unborn child. He missed them so much. Would he ever see them again? Seeing his family reminded him of the processing bug's family, and the nursery. They probably just wanted the same things he wanted. But there weren't enough trees on Earth to feed them all. Then what? He wished they would eat the weeds invading his crops instead. Those grew everywhere and so quickly he couldn't even keep up. Just like kudzu. kudzu!

Shaking with excitement, hoping he'd found the answer to all of this, Franklin practically shouted into his wrist unit. "Colonel!"

"Have you found the bridge? Are all of the bugs asleep?"

"No sir, I haven't found the bridge yet, but I have found the answer to our problem. I know how to stop the Oranges from stealing our trees: kudzu. Offer them Earth's most prevalent, quickest growing, edible weed. It's perfect! Maybe they'd be interested in ragweed too? It would sure be handy if they could weed my fields. No one on Earth uses kudzu. They can have it all for all we care."

"Well done, Private Franklin," the Colonel replied. "I think you have indeed found the answer. I'll pass your idea on to the powers that be."

"Colonel, sir!"

"Yes, private?"

"Can I go home now?"

EDWARD FRANKLIN GUIDED THE COMBINE DOWN THE ROWS. A SWEET SMELL filled the air as the stalks disappeared into the processing machine. This year's corn crop was huge, the best ever. He breathed deeply with nary a sniffle.

A shuttle, driven by a team of Oranges, sped overhead, making the corn tassels dance. Once the Oranges were shown which plants they could feed on, the buggers really went to town. Earth's trees were safe, and Edward's land was weed free for the first time ever. Of course, the pharmaceutical industry complained when sales of allergy remedies dropped, but they knew that some other ailment was bound to crop up.

Edward watched the grain pile up, making a huge mound in the harvest trailer. He smiled and waved at his wife and baby standing next to the grain elevator. Edward felt warm inside and out. He was so happy to be home.

Maintenance Mode

John M. Olsen

Otto Fernley knew it was a bad day when the emergency airlocks of Victory Station slammed shut around the repair bay. Air pressure alarms hooted in the background. The subtle airflows in the bay stopped, concentrating the background smells of grease and dust. He'd never make his quota with the transport tubes blocked off behind those doors, and Sergeant Anders would mark him down for the delays. She would dock his pay, and he'd be even farther from retirement, all because some yahoo poked a hole through the station hull.

Infantry soldiers were dumb as bricks and would break anything they touched. It was in their job description as the pointy end of the spear. Otto wished they'd stop touching the station when they visited. The mech pilots, on the other hand, respected the mechanized armor they used, and Otto took great pleasure in making that armor work at peak efficiency. Sure, he was biased, but who wasn't?

Otto tucked a spanner into his shirt pocket. Now he sat with two repaired mech suits standing five meters tall in the repair bay. He had no way to swap in the next pair for a refit and diagnostic check. With no machines to repair, he figured he might as well check in with home. He put on his Maintenance Master helmet and activated the AI. "Booboo, please call Felicity."

A tinny voice in his ear said, "You are on shift. Access denied."

"Activate maintenance mode. Unlock wide band radio link on the mech suit in repair dock one, then call Felicity on a secure channel." There were loopholes and workarounds if you knew the maintenance interfaces like Otto did.

"Maintenance mode active. Connecting your call."

A few moments later, the corner of his helmet HUD lit up with an image of his wife in their tiny apartment on the lower residential ring of the station. "Otto! Is something wrong? I heard the alarm for the pressure doors."

"It's nothing. They'll get it taken care of and we'll be back in business in no time." He didn't believe it would be that fast or that easy, but there was no sense in alarming his wife over minor details.

She sighed and shook her head. "When you're done with your shift, we need to talk. I want you to put in for a transfer to something ground-side."

That conversation never went well, and they'd been over it almost every time a supply ship docked. The pay was better here, and he'd retire sooner, but she deserved his best efforts because they were a team. It wasn't always about what he wanted. Maybe it was time to get off this orbiting tin can. He had a friend who owed him a big favor. "Sure. Let's talk about it. I know a guy."

The wide-band combat receiver crackled and came to life in his helmet, displaying its full range of signal diagnostics as it played an incoming audio signal. "Station power is secure. Wired communication lines are down. Moving to shut down low-security comm next. Team one and team two continue to objectives."

That wasn't right. Nobody used those combat channels on the station. A quick peek at the master panel in his repair bay showed a growing number of red lights for systems in the central core of the station. This wasn't a drill. He returned his attention to his hidden back-channel. "Felicity, get everyone from the residential level to the escape pods, but do *not* activate them. Just be ready. Something's wrong. If you see an officer, say we have boarders."

"You said everything was fine. Escape pods and boarders don't sound fine, Otto!"

"Sorry, love. I gotta go."

He disconnected the call and contemplated how angry Sergeant Anders could become when annoyed. "Booboo, place a personal call over the diagnostic system to Sergeant Anders."

An image came to life in the corner of his visor. As he'd expected, her olive-skinned face held what looked like a permanent scowl surrounded by a low gravity halo of jet-black hair. "Otto, if this is another one of your pranks, so help me—"

"No. Listen. I think we have boarders in the hub. They've taken the fusion reactor and cut the hard comm lines. They'll be moving down soon."

Sergeant Anders whipped around to her master console, scattering the solitaire game on her desk. Cards spun through the low gravity and floated to the floor. The same red status lights showed on her screen, visible through his HUD display. The confirmation set his teeth to grinding.

Over the combat frequency came a new message. "Objective one complete. Three casualties. Clearing the next ring."

"Sergeant, they're on their way. I sent Felicity to get the residential level into pods, but to not eject yet. Whoever's off shift will get them organized, but they'd be sitting ducks for whoever is out there if they launch. At least the pods will be safer than the apartments."

Sergeant Anders pulled a sidearm from somewhere offscreen and glanced toward her door. "Good thinking. I'll try to reach C and C to—"

The screen blurred with movement and transmitted the sound of small arms fire, then flashed white, and went dark.

"Booboo, can you reestablish the connection?"

"Networking error."

Command and Control would never hear from Sergeant Anders. At least his warning gave her a chance to go down fighting. Who was the off-duty commander? Otto scoured his memory and found the name he needed. "Booboo, open a personal call to Commander Caspin."

"No further managed connections are available." The radio diagnostics system infrastructure had failed.

"Booboo, monitor all alarm systems and report status on screen."

"Please select an alarm system from the following list—"

Interrupting, Otto said, "Damage and fire." He rubbed his chin. "Also add violations of the noise policy." Fighting and quiet didn't go together. With some luck, he could track what was going on through the heavily redundant alarm and monitoring system.

A graphical overlay appeared in another corner of his visor, showing the status broadcasts of dozens of safety devices and their backups. Safety and emergency systems were the only network still working in the whole station, and only because its redundancies made it nearly impossible to take down. He avoided the command interfaces and stuck to status displays. No sense in giving himself away yet. The core and first ring of the station showed red flags, but nothing critical. Sporadic noise violations appeared, then vanished. These invaders knew what not to shoot, making this much worse than a random raid. With this precision, they knew what they wanted. It was probably some paramilitary group.

The invaders used a standard ground combat frequency, and aside from Otto's custom helmet, the mechs in the service bays were the only equipment on the whole station that used those frequencies. If they knew that, he was their next likely target as they came down from the central core of the rotating station. He would be high on their list anyway, due to his position between the staff offices and the lower residential sections. If they were okay with piracy, they would have no reason to leave survivors as witnesses. Anything he could do to slow them would buy the residents and off-shift personnel time to do something useful.

Given their speed, he had a few minutes at most to prepare for their arrival. He jumped for the mech in station number one and climbed in through the rear hatch. A deft move jacked his helmet into the control systems. The airtight hatch sealed behind him as he slipped his arms and legs into the control harness and tightened the straps.

His helmet software wasn't the same as a regular pilot's interface, but he had diagnostic control over everything down to the pilot's catheter back-pressure. He'd annoyed more than one pilot with that one and lost a month's pay over it.

It would have been worth it, except for Felicity's disappointment. He'd promised to only pester pilots who deserved it, but all he'd got back from Felicity over the incident was an eye roll and a shake of the head. He'd never messed with anything critical, like the motor actuator safeties that made the limbs move.

A crucifix hung in the cockpit from a cargo loop to his left, wired in place by a previous mech pilot. A small personal recorder hung next to it. Some pilots were funny about their little trinkets and decorations, and he'd never touched either out of habit. The straps pinched over his pocket, so he removed the spanner and examined the two trinkets wired to the mech. After a moment's thought, he detached the small recorder and put it in the small side pocket of his trousers, leaving the awkward spanner attached in its place beside the crucifix. Superstitions allowed for trading trinkets, or at least they should. He was, after all, temporarily and unofficially a mech pilot.

This mech had come in with severe damage weeks ago, and the pilot hadn't arrived with it. The previous pilot would likely never see it again, and the next pilot might toss the trinkets anyway to replace them with his own.

"Booboo, give me a full power-up test. Override live fire lockout at test level zero."

"Power on. Override is a violation of standing station orders. Please confirm."

"I confirm override."

The weapons systems came online, showing his full load of five hundred rounds of 20mm ammo feeding the machine gun in the mech's right forearm. The ranged weapons came online with a chirp. Firing his rockets or mortars would probably kill him as well as any opponent in such enclosed areas. It would also do serious harm to the station if he hit anything important. All he needed now was to get out of the repair bays and down to the common foyer in the residential ring. Protecting Felicity and the others would be easier from there.

If it was time to make a mess and break things, he'd do it right. Maybe this was how real mech pilots felt. Everything around him became fragile when he wore the suit. Everything was expendable. Everything but Felicity and the other families.

"Booboo, override the emergency seal on the high bay interior door and open it."

"Opening."

At least he didn't have to go through an authorization for everything. That would have taken forever. An icon blinked on his helmet's HUD, showing new machines available for maintenance over its short-range wireless link. Had it been blinking this whole time?

Small arms fire erupted from the far side of the door as four armor-clad soldiers appeared in the doorway and brought rifles to bear. They wore Mark III armored vac suits. The suits, while motorized, were the baby cousin of the mech suit he wore. They stood only two meters tall compared to his five.

With a jerky movement only a beginner would appreciate, Otto raised his right arm and painted the invaders with his targeting system. A continuous burst of 20 mm rounds marched from left to right, pushing the four suits of armor away down the hall as holes blossomed in each suit. With a little luck, his misses with the armor-piercing rounds wouldn't go through enough bulkheads to cause another vacuum breach. He tried not to think about the rounds that tore through the men in front of him.

Detachment helped Otto to deal with the messy truths of warfare. Detachment was a tool, and Otto knew his tools. These vac suits were only suits of armor. Something to repair, and not covering a person. Someone had to clean and repair those suits, but it wasn't him. He was safe from the condemning faces inside. The faces of soldiers who wanted to kill him. The job came first, then the emotions would flow later. The faces faded as his focus returned.

With one team down, Otto had more to face. They had at least three squads, based on the radio traffic. The one he'd seen looked to be a short squad, so they might have split up into even smaller groups. However they had teamed up, he couldn't count on the next fight being easy. Coordinated fire with small arms could still take out his mech suit. If that didn't work, they would break out bigger guns to stop him. He would die if the fight went on too long.

It was time to be clever instead of bold. His clever tendencies had sent him into repairs instead of foot infantry, or even the mech program. Mechanics and repair techs weren't supposed to be shot at. The worst he ever got was a tongue lashing by Sergeant Anders, who knew profanity in more languages than Otto could name. To get here, the soldiers would have had to go through the upper offices where Sergeant Anders and the rest of the daily staff worked. All gone. He packaged up his fear and worry and stuffed it into the back corner of his brain for later. He had important things to do and people to save.

He reached to his shoulder, touched his mortar rack, and considered the structural integrity of the station. His plan just might work without major structural damage.

"Booboo, activate surgery mode." It was his personal configuration with refined motor control and specially-aimed targeting cameras to where he could pick up a coin from the floor with the massive steel fingers. It also gave him crazy double-jointed flexibility with the machine's arms at the expense of speed.

With a deft twist, one mortar came loose from the rack on his shoulder. He unscrewed the fuse and pinched an innocent-looking white wire, then plucked it from the explosive. Once he placed the mortar on the floor beside the door, he reached for another. With one on each side of the door, he was ready.

"Booboo, Cancel surgery mode. No, belay that." He would need fine motor control more than he would need fast arms. Otto ducked under the wide four-meter doorway and stooped as he made his way down the hall. The five-meter mech wasn't meant for tight quarters or low ceilings, but he'd make it work even if he had to belly-crawl his way into the residential level.

He closed the large bay doors behind him and said, "Booboo, activate the proximity fuse on mortars B1 and B2 and chain them together for coordinated detonation."

"Live fire is against station policy."

"Booboo, override station policy on all features with my voice authorization for full diagnostic access." That might keep the reminders of the idiot AI down for a while. He'd have to come up with some better programming to make it easier to get around in his helmet's diagnostic interfaces. If he survived, that is.

It was time to get out of the way and let things work. Twenty meters along the hall sat a closed freight elevator door. He could use the elevator, but it would show up on screens in C and C and tip off the invaders if his unknown enemy knew what to look for. He wedged a steel finger into the sliding doors and pried the shaft entrance open.

The targeting camera on his right arm showed a ladder rung inside the shaft. It was designed for humans, but it might hold him. The repair facility wasn't at a full gravity, sitting half-way between the hub and the full-gravity residential ring. He grabbed the ladder, shifted a foot in to land on a much lower rung, then swung in. Glad he'd left surgery mode active, he nudged the elevator doors closed as the ladder creaked under his weight.

"Team two, report." The silence stretched, and Otto grinned.

"Team one, I've lost telemetry on half of team two and show severe damage to the other half. Get in there and take the objective before the enemy gets organized."

A response came back as a frustrated soldier said, "We're on our way back up. We can't reach the residential level, anyway. I don't know what they did, but we'll have to cut through the floor to get to them."

How had they gotten past him? They must have been faster than he'd thought. At least the residential area was safe for the moment. Otto wondered at how his people had managed the elevator trick. He could probably figure it out with a little thought, but there was no time. He was on the dangerous side of that barricade, and he had a job to do. He would make the invaders pay for what they'd done to his friends and to his station.

The radio crackled again with the voice he'd flagged as their leader. "The residential level is a secondary objective. If they're isolated, we're still on track. Get to the repair bay."

What nut job would set a repair bay as an objective? Everything in there was standard issue, ordered out of a catalog. Anyone with enough credits could buy the same equipment all the other tinpot dictators and rebels bought. Monotech Robotics had a great thing going, supplying all sides with the standard issue mechanized and powered suits used by armies to settle their differences in typically violent fashion. They supplied his mech and the destroyed armored suits in the hall, too. The company provided every last piece. The quality wasn't anything to write home about, but everyone made up for it in quantity. Anyone who had the credits to buy armored vac suits had no business resorting to military raids to steal a stupid mech.

If it wasn't the equipment, then what was it? The people? Was someone so short of repair techs they wanted to kidnap him? That was even stupider than stealing the mechs. Any idiot with solid reading skills and a bit of HUD programming skill could learn to fix the things.

The voice on the radio had mentioned telemetry. Otto returned his attention to the blinking service icon floating on his visor and would have kicked himself if he wasn't strapped into the mech. "Booboo, inventory new hardware systems." Fifteen icons appeared, two outlined in red.

The idiot invaders hadn't thought to change their factory default maintenance passwords. Most of the time, he had to hit a physical system reset button on a suit before he could connect and begin repairs.

His display gave no locations, but he knew how many enemies he faced now. Knowing their numbers didn't change much. All he had to do was stay between them and the residency ring and make sure the bad guys were the ones who left in body bags. The longer he lasted, the more chance there was of someone else coming up with an idea to save the station.

Otto shifted and lowered his left foot, searching for the next tiny rung on the ladder as the rung in his right hand bent and squeaked. He froze. Why had he thought this was a good place to hide? If he fell, he might pick up enough momentum to punch out through the outer hull of the lowest ring. The suit design worked on land and had no propulsion system. Busting through the station floor would only kill him slower than an abrupt stop at the bottom of the shaft could.

The muffled rumble of mortars shook the shaft, nearly dislodging him from the ladder. He reached out and braced against the far side of the shaft with his left hand. Four more service icons winked out, no longer providing even a maintenance signal. He remembered to practice his detachment. It was only data and equipment, not people with families and children. His detachment skills collapsed as his anger grew because of the friends he had lost, and might still lose.

"Report!" The leader's voice now bore a frantic edge.

Before he could help himself, Otto triggered his microphone and said in a sarcastic imitation of the default AI voice in his helmet, "Safety margins exceeded. Please return equipment for warranty repair after hosing out the remains of your soldiers."

"All units switch to the alternate channel now." The frantic voice had grown icy.

Otto laughed after making sure he wasn't still broadcasting. The noise of his laughter didn't sound too hysterical in his own ears as it echoed inside the musty mech suit, but he was sure Felicity would call him on it.

The radio in Otto's maintenance helmet crackled on an alternate channel. The diagnostic subroutines flagged it as properly functioning and automatically synchronized with the new signal. The infantry pukes would freak if they knew about the custom code in his repair helmet, which is why he never told anyone. "I don't know how they found our main frequency. There must be a squad on board that we didn't know about. Regroup. We've got to find out what we're facing here, get the data, and get out."

They thought he was a whole squad? Otto considered his options. Generate fake radio traffic on the old combat channel? They'd figure that out too fast. Could he wait for them down at the residential level like he'd planned? Felicity and the others had locked him out when they locked out the invading soldiers. Wherever he was, they would come in with all they had the next time, and he would die with everyone else, never knowing what they wanted.

He reviewed the fire and damage stats on the station and saw the swath of destruction covering everything except the residential ring. Everything above residential had already been cleared. Everyone on shift except him had been wiped out.

The elevator below him came to life, rising from the hydroponics level. He reached one leg across to the ladder rungs on the far side of the shaft and climbed up to the next door with one arm and one foot on each side of the shaft. The door in front of him was only three meters tall. There was no time for finesse as the elevator approached. He punched the door, knocking the crumpled steel into the hall behind. He shimmied through on the suit's belly, scraping his way out of the shaft as the elevator rose past the doorway.

If he knew what they wanted, maybe he could give it to them and they would be on their way. He flailed through the mental gymnastics it would take to have a pleasant chat with an enemy strike team and realized there was no way to talk through this.

While the trick with the explosives had been handy, he had to think his way out of this one rather than try to shoot his way through the whole team. Some enemy suits reported damage; the four he'd shot up, and three others showed total structural failure. Someone else had fought back. Sergeant Anders and the rest had at least hurt them.

The elevator scraped past the broken door and continued up to C and C. Time was short, and he had to act rather than react.

He rolled to his side in the hallway and pulled his arms and legs from their control harnesses. His mech would slow him down for this next step. He popped the rear hatch and eased out into the hall, scanning for a panel with a red outline. There, fifteen meters away sat a firefighting control panel.

He jacked his helmet into the panel, and the redundant control and suppression systems all appeared on his visor. He connected directly into their diagnostic control systems. This just might work, depending on how fast he moved.

"Booboo, expand diagnostic menus on the Mark III equipment list."

A list of all the options available to him appeared with the powered armor of the enemy. "There you are, my sweet. Booboo, set a timer to deactivate and lock all Mark III servo motors thirty seconds from my mark. Using fire safety protocols, override and open all airlock doors above the hydroponics levels on my mark. Authorize by my voiceprint. Mark."

"Depressurization is against station policy."

Otto cringed at the delay. "Override policy!"

"Overriding depressurization is disabled while station is occupied." Otto had always hated that default computer voice and its bad attitude of not doing what he told it to do.

The timer for the servo lock counted down below fifteen seconds remaining. He had to get the two events together for his plan to work. Otto scanned the menus for another option.

He found what he was after in the emergency measures list. "Booboo, open all interior doors above hydroponics and detonate emergency explosive bolts on all exterior airlock doors above hydroponics now!"

A rippling shockwave hit the station, starting at its core and progressing through several of the inner rings. His diagnostics display showed him everything as air whistled past and out into space. The enemy vac suits had locked up as ordered. He yanked his helmet's cable free from the panel and ran to the reclining mech suit, fumbling with the back hatch as the station's atmosphere fled through dozens of open airlocks. His ears hurt as the pressure dropped.

He gasped for air, knowing enough to not hold his breath lest he burst his lungs in the dwindling pressure. With a final grab, the hatch opened. He climbed in and slammed the door home as the air pressure outside continued to drop. His lungs worked overtime, failing to deliver critical oxygen. "Booboo, pressurize mech suit." He hadn't thought what would happen if pressure had dropped to where he couldn't speak. He chalked it up to dumb luck.

"No mech suit is attached for diagnostics. Please identify the desired mech suit by serial number."

He stared numbly at the data cable dangling from his helmet, knowing it had something to do with his blurring vision and headache. There. A jack. He reached out and grabbed the cable on his second try and forced it into the jack as his vision played tricks on him. "Booboo," he gasped, "pressurize attached mech suit."

Stars sparkled in his vision as the world grew black from hypoxia.

SOMETHING HISSED, MAKING AN ANNOYING STATIC NOISE AS HE AWOKE. AIR flowed. He was in the mech. The pressure seals did their job, and the tang of greasy air hit him. However it smelled, it was still blessed air. He swallowed to pop his ears several times as the pressure increased.

With the enemy suits forced into diagnostic mode with their motors locked, the invaders waited impotently. Even if they forced the reluctant limbs to move, they couldn't get out of the suits in the hard vacuum. He monitored their cursing for a while and then muted the radio. After shimmying his mech toward the core through several shafts and halls, he found the invaders in the Command and Control center.

A quick glance at the room's consoles showed a ship docked at a now-ruined airlock in the hub, but there was no response from the ship when he tried to contact the crew. The invaders stared daggers at him as he pushed them one by one through an open airlock to spiral out into open space. Someone from their ship would certainly track and pick them up on their way out. Otto just wanted them off the station.

An hour later, he realized their ship was empty and there was nobody to track the suits as they tumbled on their various trajectories away from the rotating station. They'd all come into the station, leaving nobody behind in their ship. Otto set aside his horror at the slow death those soldiers faced, yet he tracked their projected battery and oxygen levels until he knew it was pointless to continue.

He waited in C and C, knowing the residential level wouldn't let him in without communication coming online first. The outer airlocks would need replacement parts before they would work again, so he satisfied himself by closing all the interior doors and pressurizing a small section in the hub. At long last he climbed out of the mech and repaired the sabotaged communications links while he waited for the fickle finger of fate to point his way again.

The next day, a troop transport approached. Otto activated his radio and sent all his data and camera recordings documenting the entire incident. Welding and repair crews brought the station back to life one section at a time while Otto sat, confined to quarters. Felicity sat with him, scared at how it would all work out.

Finally, the station came back online with a replacement crew covering for those killed by the invaders. A knock sounded at the door to their tiny apartment, and Felicity let in Commander Caspin, dressed in a crisp white uniform with gold piping, his nearly white hair slicked back.

"A hearing has been set for tomorrow. They're taking your recordings as your official statement, unless there is anything you would like to add."

It would do no good to hide anything, and unlike his multitude of earlier disciplinary hearings, he had nothing to hide this time. "I'm good. They have everything." Everything but the pilot's data recorder he'd pocketed in the mech, but it had nothing to do with the attack, did it?

"That's what they'll debate, but I already know how it will go." The commander stood at ease, reciting what sounded like a rehearsed message.

"Oh?" Otto wasn't sure if he wanted to know, but it couldn't be all bad based on the commander's response.

"Do you think these things aren't scripted in advance? You have history. You will be charged with destruction of property, expending military ordinance without authorization, overriding safety and security protocols, and general endangerment. Any one of those incidents would normally see you court marshaled and jailed. Taken together, there's no other option. You will receive a dishonorable discharge unless you can prevail in court. I think you're smart enough to take the discharge they'll offer for this to all go away quietly."

Otto's heart sank at the news. So much of his life had been wasted in the pursuit of something now forever out of his reach. "But—"

"I'm not done, son. Let an old man have his fun. There are some unusual circumstances to be handled before the discharge will be allowed on the table. The enemy suits and disguised supply ship they came in have no registration or identification and can't be traced. No serial numbers on any of them, so there will be no claims from their side. The oddest part is that it doesn't look like the numbers were removed. They were never there in the first place. But that's beside the point. This means there is the matter of prize money for single-handedly capturing their ship, and no counterclaims to worry over. There was no command staff anywhere within the inner rings of the station, so you won't be splitting the prize with anyone."

Commander Caspin glanced momentarily at Felicity as he continued. "We also recovered several intact suits that, ah, somehow fell out of an airlock. Those suits also count on the award." Otto made a note to thank the commander later for his tact in avoiding the details of what they found in those suits.

A ray of hope shined on Felicity's face where before her cheeks held nothing but salty tracks from tears. "After subtracting expenses for an *extensive* list of repairs, you will be given the remaining prize money, and you will be discharged. Mind you, it will still be a dishonorable discharge. Yes, I know that sounds like an unbelievably stupid way of arranging things, but it's the least stupid thing I could force through and leave you with anything. We're talking about military efficiency, after all. The leftover funds will nearly match what would have been a full retirement with benefits. I can't do any better for you with your thick file of past complaints. Off the record, everyone in the residential ring owes their life to you. And also to you, Mrs. Fernley, for your quick action to warn us. On the record, quite a few people will be glad to see you go."

Felicity wrapped her arms around Otto, and he returned her embrace, lacing his fingers together at the small of her back as she kissed him. Otto didn't know how to process the rapidly changing situation. He had no words, so he stood still to enjoy her embrace, the scent of her hair helping to scramble his ability to think.

Before the situation dragged on long enough to become awkward, Felicity released Otto and offered a hand to Commander Caspin. "Thank you."

The commander took her hand in both of his for a moment before returning to his military stance.

She turned to Otto, a mischievous look peeking through her façade of annoyance. "As for you, I expect us to be on the next flight out of here, bound for somewhere with a real sky."

Otto barely held his stiff military expression as he gave a mock salute to Felicity. "I think trading commanders will do me some good."

Commander Caspin let himself out as Otto and Felicity began to negotiate in earnest.

When the Sleeping Soldier Wakes

Jacob Pérez

The third human body washed up on Guillermo Beach at dawn, setting the fishermen of Tierra Sangre abuzz with speculation and accusations. When Rodan arrived on his rumbling GalanBlack an hour later, the beach glistened a dark vermillion in the wan sunrise. He snapped the kickstand onto the sandy promenade and headed toward the throng of hovering gawkers. The crowd grudgingly parted when they saw his gray coat with the UTS Department of Xenology patch on his chest.

Captain Ramirez nodded at Rodan while zipping up his Coalition of Nations—or CoN—jacket. A medisynth next to him made a series of clicks with its eyes before lifting a gravitational gurney carrying a black body bag.

A storm was brewing to the north. Rodan felt it in his joints. Dark, brooding thunderheads formed in the mauve sky behind Kockie Island. And before the gathering clouds, Tres-23's second moon, Mona, was still visible. It gave off a pale, wraithlike light. A day, maybe less, before Tierra Sangre hunkered down.

"What did the synth's analysis reveal?" Rodan asked and flipped the collar of his coat against the rising sea wind.

Ramirez's eyes flickered to the crowd, then gestured for Rodan to follow him out of earshot. "The lacerations and bite marks point to the Dula."

Rodan's heart sank. The sound of the waves washed over him, and the sea air filled his lungs. "The Dula are pacifists and vegetarians. In our few recorded encounters, they've exhibited a lack of aggression unless provoked—and only to warn, never to kill."

"Don't make much of a difference." Ramirez cupped his hands and blew into them for warmth. "Centuries-old prejudices and all. Got them"—he motioned toward the crowd—"muttering about boarding Gs and heading to Kockie for justice."

It wasn't enough that humans had nearly eradicated the Dula three hundred years ago and exiled them to islands throughout Tres-23. Still, generational discontent begged for an excuse to rehash past transgressions. "Why contact me, then?" Rodan asked and looked around. "Without a Dula corpse, you should call Ambassador Joaquin's office."

Not that he didn't want to help. Rodan was tired of CoN's continual expansion and pacifying efforts that led to prolonged conflicts like the one that killed his daughter, Xio, on duty four months ago.

"Witnesses say there are two men from the victims' party unaccounted for," Ramirez said. "Chief bumped it up to CoN Command. They want this resolved before the storm moves in. CoN has an operative on liberty who arrived a week ago. They volunteered to look for the missing men at Kockie Island. The operative requested for you specifically to act as their liaison."

Rodan sputtered in disbelief. He didn't know anyone from CoN Command, let alone one of its operatives. "The Dula have not received a formal CoN delegation since their exile. Why should they now?"

Ramirez shrugged and pointed toward the island. "That's prob'ly the operative now."

A distant whir rose above the lapping waves. The gravboat was a sleek arrow made of black fiberglass. It skimmed the top of the ocean without touching it. When the driver pulled up to the beach, a spray of sand peppered Rodan's legs. The gravitational waves rippled the sand in concentric circles.

Rodan wanted to curse but the words caught in his throat. The woman behind the wheel was straight out of a historical broadnet; low-gravity tall with proud shoulders, dark braided hair, and brown skin that glowed in the rising sun.

Rodan despaired when she turned. Her eyes were white, not just the scleras, but her pupils and irises too. Embedded in her forehead rested the CoN uplink that marked her for what she was . . .a Hielo; awoken from cryosleep for war, sent back on ice in times of peace.

It was the Hielo that nearly wiped out the Dula centuries ago.

Rodan wheeled on Ramirez. "Do you *want* to start a war? Send someone else other than me. Contact can't be attempted with a Hielo in tow."

"Ash," said the Hielo with a sharp expression from the open cockpit. Her voice carried over the idling engine with authority.

"Ash." Rodan grimaced. He'd expected something foreboding like Reaper or Wraith. "If—and that's a big if—the Dula agree to an audience, your presence will hinder any chances for an amicable mediation."

"I don't understand," Ramirez said.

Rodan gestured in Ash's direction. "If the Dula still holds any animosity toward CoN for their exile, it'll be nothing compared to their views on the Hielo for their part in it."

Ramirez pointed at Rodan's department of xenology patch. "CoN needs an expert. You're one of our best chances at getting them talking. They can't force you to do this, but she won't take anyone else."

"Why me?" Rodan asked, studying Ash. He was positive he'd never met her before. "There are far better qualified professors at the university."

Ash crossed her arms.

Rodan scowled and clenched his jaw. "I can't be responsible for what happens if we fail."

"Then I go alone." Ash's expressionless eyes bored into him.

And that would end in bloodshed. If the rumors were true, the Hielo were killing machines, not diplomats. How many military funerals would be held because of a new war with the Dula? How many fathers would have to bury their daughters in the name of peace? What would Xio want him to do?

To try.

Rodan's shoulders sagged with resignation. "Fine! Let's get this over with."

KOCKIE ISLAND LAY TWENTY KILOMETERS FROM TIERRA SANGRE, A SEVENTY-minute trip by speedboat. They got there in thirty to Rodan's dismay. CoN checkpoints ignored them. Why would they bother them with a Hielo on board? His stomach roiled and protested, and his throat burned with bile. He leaned over the taffrail numerous times, flushed and head spinning, certain he wouldn't make it to land. When the gravboat settled on the beach, he tumbled out, grateful he didn't lose his stomach and add to his embarrassment.

Ash dumped a bag of supplies next to him that she'd filled with mbars, water, and a basic first aid kit. She vaulted over the taffrail and landed lithely on the sand. "You okay?" Her voice had a lilting accent he'd only heard in historical broadnets. She accentuated her vowels in a way that was quite lovely despite the economy of words.

Rodan held his hand up, then vomited anyway. He wiped his face on his sleeve, straightened his back, and looked into those unnerving, blank eyes. "No sea legs."

"A seasick Tierra Sangre native?" Ash said. "Now I've seen everything."

Rodan saw a shadow of a smile. It took him by surprise. Little was known of the Hielo. And what *was* known was exaggerated to legendary status. Xio used to call them Wardogs—designed for war to transcend human capabilities. Always present during pivotal CoN battles.

Xio would've laughed too if she'd seen him a rumpled mess, spilling his guts on the sand. The memory of her unrestrained laughter, mirth plain on her expression, blindsided him. He fought off his grief and focused on ocean waves lapping on sand—and the strange and formidable soldier looming over him.

The uplink on Ash's forehead began to blink. A frown creased her face.

"Is that thing going to blow up?" Rodan asked, half kidding.

Ash cocked her head. "That would be a first." She picked up the supply bag, turned toward the tree line, and made her way up the beach. She barely made a sound moving across the sand. Her programmable black warsuit undulated in the sun. She carried a PFA3 holstered to her thigh—the same service blaster Xio had used—and a dagger the size of Rodan's forearm magnetically locked to her lower back.

Would Xio still be alive if she had access to an elite warsuit like that one instead of her standard CoN combat uniform?

Rodan brushed off his coat and followed her. The dense sand provided sturdier footing than at Guillermo Beach. Despite decades of studies in Dula sociocultural theory and research, Rodan had never visited Kockie Island. CoN forbade anyone outside of Command from attempting contact with the Dula. A rush of adrenaline fluttered through his heart at the thought of him being there.

The tree line writhed like a living, waking organism. Groves of acaleatus trees rustled in the breeze. Elegant vrota of the deepest red dangled upside down from white, heart-shaped leaves. Long stalks of leander grew from silvery tufts. The buzzing of krikhatas and skittering ardidas erupted from the shadows of the forest.

When they reached the edge, Rodan noticed a game trail and a carved wooden sign spiked into the ground. Ash turned to him and raised an eyebrow.

"Dula script," Rodan said, examining the lines and symbols on the wood. "Let me see . . . *kritaa*." The harsh word rolled in his mouth like a handful of nails.

"Beware," Ash said.

"You speak the language?"

"No." She swept past the sign and into the path. "But I recognize *kritaa* from the Dula War."

"Look, Ash." Rodan scampered behind, narnet leaves grabbing and pulling at his coat. "The Dula are an isolationist race, highly insular and reclusive. If we ignore social conduct and cultural etiquette, we risk another war. 'Beware' is a clear message that they want to be left alone."

"Then they shouldn't have dumped three human bodies into the ocean."

"Mona blind me! You asked for me to be here. Can you at least listen to counsel? The Dula will not harm us if they know we come in peace. Ignoring their first warning will only justify whatever aggression they show hereafter."

Ash stopped, flicked her dagger out of the sheath, and sliced through a branch in her way. The blade hummed with charged particles as she stepped into a clearing. "What do you suggest?"

Rodan pointed at the dagger. "For starters, would you put that thing away? I swear you couldn't look more menacing if—"

"Wait," she said, pointing the PFA3 toward the shadows. "We're being watched."

"I stand corrected." Rodan gaped at her empty holster. He hadn't seen her move.

Ash's eyes scrutinized the slanted shadows of the forest's underbelly. The canopy swayed in the wind. An unnatural silence surrounded them. Her gaze snapped to a wide-leaved maeta tree when it creaked; her finger tightened on the trigger.

"*Atriik!*" Rodan said. He reached for Ash's forearm and pressed down to lower the blaster. The arm didn't budge. The muscles underneath his touch were like corded steel. He gestured in wide arcs with his other arm. "*Atriik!*"

Ash snatched her arm away and scanned the forest without blinking. "Touch me again during an engagement and you'll lose that hand."

"You almost started a war and we only just arrived," said Rodan, nostrils flaring.

A few terse moments passed before she holstered the weapon. "We're alone. What does *atriik* mean? I'm unfamiliar with that Dula word."

"It means *peace*."

Ash opened her mouth, but then her body tensed. Ahead, the underbrush quivered. Four insectoid Dula emerged from the forest carrying glinting spearheads in clawed hands. The imposing leader at the center stood like an armor-plated tank: digitigrade bipedal with four upper limbs; two lateral, proportionate-sized arms, and two miniature ones protruding from the front of the thorax. Their chitinous exoskeleton gleamed with moisture from the rain. Colored fur covered their upper back, shoulders, and horned head. The leader blazed in scarlet, flanked by two in cobalt and one in jade.

Fascinating!

Rodan gaped at them with wonder. He'd studied their anatomy on paper and from broadnet recordings three centuries old, but it didn't prepare him for this moment. The fur pointed to a rapid evolutionary response to an environmental and/or sociological stressor.

Their spears edged forward in their direction.

Ash bared her teeth at them, her face twisted with rage, colorless eyes hardened and narrowed into slits. One hand found the dagger at her back and pulled it halfway out. The other gripped her blaster. Pent-up kinetic energy ready for release poised her body for action.

"Ash?" Rodan tried to sound calm, but her aggressive posture sent shivers down his spine.

The Dula bristled at the sight of Ash's uplink. The jade-furred one bellowed something unintelligible and rushed at her with spear raised high. Ash drew the PFA3 and pointed it at the attacking Dula. The charging chamber burned bright with superheated particles.

"Ash!" Panic gripped Rodan. He rushed forward and placed himself between the Dula and the barrel of the PFA3.

Ash gave him a bewildered look as if, for a second, she didn't recognize him. "Move!"

"Stop!" The Dula's musk-like smell assaulted his nose. "This . . . this is an envoy."

Rodan turned and saw the jade-furred behemoth towering within striking distance. The scarlet-furred one grabbed the attacker by the horns and roared. The jade-furred one retreated, chastised but furious. The eyes of the chagrined Dula, amethyst-black orbs with w-shaped pupils, glared at Ash with hatred.

"Willing to bet your life on it?" Ash said. "Last we met, they weren't the *envoy* kind of race."

The leader stomped the butt of their spear against the ground, then made a guttural noise. Rows of steel-tipped teeth snapped together.

Rodan pointed his arms in opposite directions, a sign of respectful deference. Cold sweat stung his eyes. His heart hammered in his chest. It sharpened the glint in the Dula's exoskeleton. The leader grunted, but the smaller arms on the chest formed an L, then made the same noise.

"What's it saying?" Ash asked.

"She," Rodan corrected. "See that ridge across the forehead? It marks her as female. At least for now. The Dula are sequential hermaphrodites. And I think she's saying, *atriik,* but their phonemes have evolved."

"You think?" The hard edge of her blade cut through the feeble light.

The leader slammed the spear on the ground again. The little arms moved and this time Rodan was sure. He mimicked the gesture and said, "*Atriik.*"

The entire envoy turned and walked into the forest. Rodan reached for Ash before she followed but remembered her earlier warning and decided he was rather attached to his hand. Instead, he stepped in her path.

"Out of my way," Ash said in a deadly voice.

"What was that? Are you trying to get us killed?"

Ash glared at Rodan with unflinching eyes. "You weren't there during the Dula War, didn't see humans slaughtered for sport."

"You're escalating, acting like some feral animal." Rodan kept his eyes locked on hers. The uplink flashed blue in the dull light. "These are *not* the same Dula you fought three centuries ago. I can't stress it enough. Another outburst ends any prospects of peaceful dialogue between us. You need to start trusting me. Keep your emotions in check."

Ash hesitated. She appeared to ponder something. Then her gaze shifted to the clearing's edge over his shoulder. "The uplink . . . keeps me in control—keeps the memories at bay."

And the uplink wasn't working, jammed if Ash was right. The thought appalled him. Xio used to scream at night after her first tour. What kind of damage would countless battles have on a person's psyche? Even to a Hielo. He couldn't imagine what was going through Ash's mind; a small wonder she hadn't lost herself already.

"Don't worry. I'll keep it together." Ash pushed past him. "But for all your talk of the Dula being pacifists, they attacked first. I will not be ashamed of reacting to aggression. My duty is to keep us alive, not succumb to naiveté."

And with that, a creeping trepidation settled in Rodan's chest. The Dula's attack was unexpected. It went against everything he'd learned about them.

THE ENVOY SET A GRUELING PACE. WHEN THEY STOPPED BEFORE A TOWERING wall of preia vines, Rodan chugged water and took an anti-inflammatory for his knees. He shivered in the advancing cold front despite his coat.

Once Rodan's pulsing blood subsided, he heard a dull stridulation coming from beyond the preia. The scarlet-furred Dula parted the vines, grunted for them to follow, and walked through. The others closed in behind them. When Rodan's eyes adjusted to the soft lighting, he found himself inside a half-collapsed caldera. Dula emerged from residences and storefronts carved into the igneous rock. The air was warm and humid, a welcome respite. Bridges made of synthetic rope and wooden planks etched the sky.

An iridescent dome buzzed overhead, camo-membrane clear from the underside. Rodan saw rolling thunderclouds through it.

His jaw dropped.

Where had they gotten high-tech camouflage? Did the three deceased stumble onto this secret and pay with their lives?

Ash appeared on edge, twitchy even. Her eyes darted every time a Dula got near them. Her hand never left the grip of her blaster. Rodan imagined restless energy exuding off her, like from a struck tuning fork, vibrating at the frequency of warfare.

Scarlet, cobalt, or jade-furred Dula skittered out of their way. Inquisitive growls trailed them. The envoy led them to the center of the caldera, toward an onyx obelisk the size of a skyscraper. A door on the surface of the obelisk irised open at their approach.

Ash placed a hand on Rodan's shoulder. "Take a deep breath and release as you walk past the threshold."

Ash went through it before he could ask what she meant. The Dula behind him grumbled and made a shuffling motion with the spear. Rodan took a deep breath and followed. When he crossed the threshold, an unseen force grabbed him in a vice. His chest contracted, his skin tingled, and a tinny sound screamed in his ears. Light distorted and curved as he popped out to the other side. He fell to his knees, gasping.

"Security field," Ash said while helping him to his feet.

A cavernous grotto filled the inside of the obelisk. The vaulted ceiling shimmered with blue-green rock formations. The guard's footsteps echoed despite their gracefulness.

"How is this possible?" Rodan said. "CoN stripped them of their tech."

"Command needs to know."

They led them into a chamber that held theater-style limestone seating. It surrounded a central podium where three Dula with ridges across their forehead sat in gravitational chairs. Each of the three colors was represented by them. Ash and Rodan walked down the stairs and stood before them. Their scarlet-furred escort turned with outstretched diminutive arms. One of the bigger limbs pointed at Ash's blaster, dagger, and supply bag.

Ash bared her teeth and reached for her dagger. The Dula snapped her jaw with a resounding sound.

"Ash," said Rodan. "If they wanted us dead, they would've done it already."

Ash turned her head. She searched his face with a manic expression. Rodan held his breath until she finally nodded and relinquished her belongings.

The Dula dropped the items at the foot of the podium.

Rodan made the L sign for peace. "*Atriik.*" Then motioned with his head to Ash. Her eyebrows pinched together, but she repeated the gesture.

The three hovering Dula rumbled in irascible tones.

The scarlet-furred one said in their language, "Welcome." Her voice sounded like grinding boulders. "I, Rootka, welcome you in *atriik.*"

He cleared his throat. Approximating their speech pattern while trying to compensate for the evolutionary changes in phonemes, he replied, "Thank you for granting us an audience. We are here in need of an explanation. Three humans are dead. Two are missing. Injuries suggest the Dula are to blame."

Rootka's bulging eyes flickered, dissecting the words. The others beside her rasped in hushed tones. The jade-furred female heckled and pointed an accusatory clawed finger at Ash. In a harsh tone of voice, she said, "*Vaakte.*" It roughly translated to *deathless.*

"Furless come." Rootka put up five fingers. "Slaughtered mother and child. They tried to take more in a fast water spear."

Ash swore when Rodan translated for her. Her hands clenched and unclenched.

"You shouldn't have killed them. When the storm passes, many more," Rodan indicated to Ash, "will come. We are trying to prevent any further misunderstanding. Do the other two hum—furless live?"

The jade-furred Dula ignored him. "We must end the *Vaakte,* now!"

"Silence, Liktaa!" Rootka said, then to Rodan. "The furless need to answer for their actions."

"Punishment at your hands would send the wrong message," said Rodan and twisted his hands to form the Dula sign for honesty.

Rootka made an inquisitive motion with her smaller arms. "We want *atriik* with the *Vaakte* and furless. But the furless trespassed and spilled Dula blood."

"Allow us to take your prisoners as a sign of good faith. We will judge and punish them according to our laws."

Rootka turned to the other two and conferred.

The cobalt-furred Dula said, "If we do, will you leave us? Let us live in *atriik?*"

Rodan translated the exchange for Ash again. Her eyes were steadfast, but Rodan could tell she mulled something over. This was their chance. *Say yes, and let us be done with this Dula business. Let's go home.*

"Ask them about the tech," Ash said with a sneer. "When we leave, my uplink will make Command aware of it. It's time to end the charade. I'll bring their concerns to my superiors if their response is acceptable. But this is their only chance."

Rodan translated, albeit with more tact.

"The *Vaakte* lies!" Liktaa said. Globs of spittle dripped down her chin. "Fusskta, do not listen to Rootka. I say, kill the *Vaakte* and end *atriik* with the furless."

The cobalt-furred Dula, Fusskta, said in a throaty, vicious tone, "Silence, Liktaa!" Then spoke to Rodan. "Our technology is for the protection of *atriik*, not to wage war with the furless. We only want to be left alone. But if the furless threaten *atriik*, we will defend ourselves."

"That's not good enough," Ash said after the translation.

"Then, a peace treaty is essential," Rodan urged the Dula. "Will you give an audience to a CoN diplomatic delegation and negotiate *atriik*? We don't want another war."

The Dula turned and conferred in harsh, agitated tones. Rootka's crimson fur flowed in the blue-green glow from above. "We will vote."

THE GUARDS ESCORTED RODAN AND ASH TO A HOLDING CELL ADJACENT TO THE audience chamber. Light orbs along the stone wall gave off a subdued white light. Rodan sat on natural outcrop seating. It was warm to the touch. He felt like he'd grabbed onto a live wire with his bare hands. He rummaged through his pockets and found the last of his cacasha nuts. The crunch in his mouth steadied him.

Ash paced the room, then leaned against the wall, arms crossed and eyes shut. Spasms agitated her eyelids. Rodan was impressed by her indomitable will to calm herself despite what must be going through her mind. Xio would've liked her.

Rodan leaned back. He thought he heard the storm lashing against the caldera, sizzling on the camouflage shielding. Were they too late? Had CoN Command already give the order for troop carriers to land on Kockie Island's beaches? How many more must suffer to get a respite from warfare?

He must've dozed because Ash stood by the doorway when he opened his eyes. "Sorry, was I snoring?"

Her lips quirked. "A little."

"Xio used to say I rattled the walls of her room at night."

"My father used to be the same," she said, losing her smile.

Rodan was quiet for a moment, not sure what to say. Awkward silences made him restless. It tended to get him into trouble.

"May I ask you a question?"

She nodded.

"Why the Helio? It sounds like a bleak existence." He regretted that last part immediately. He didn't think she'd answer.

"My parents were killed during the First Flet Invasion." Ash clenched her jaw. "Afterward, it was just my younger brother and me. One of us would've been drafted." Ash shrugged. "So, I volunteered—one draftee per household. I refused to let my brother endure the horrors of war. And when the time came to re-enlist, I looked at my baby nephew and knew I wanted to protect him with my life."

"But to continuously go back to cryosleep? To be displaced in time from your family and all you know. To be rewarded by bloodshed, loss, and loneliness? It would drive me mad."

"I never wanted someone else making that sacrifice. Peace is important to me. Making that choice meant that nobody else would be orphaned. The Hielo are efficient in ending wars and preventing excessive human casualties."

"So sacrifices must be made?" Rodan raised his voice and didn't realize it.

"Are you still talking about me or Xio?" Ash said softly.

"Don't! They called her death a noble sacrifice. For what? Peace? Expansion? Humanity? I'd trade my life in a heartbeat to have my daughter back instead of this gaping black hole in my chest."

"My life may not be glamorously normal, but the stretches of stability and peace in humanity are a testament to the sacrifices many have made. There is no cure for war. It's inevitable. But those sacrifices *do* matter. They have to."

Tears fell down Rodan's cheeks. "But why my Xio?"

Ash sat next to Rodan and shocked him by wrapping an arm around him. "I'm sorry you lost your daughter. A parent should never have to bury their child."

Rodan's shoulders trembled with an avalanche of delayed grief he'd kept locked away for months. It drowned him, robbed him of his senses. The darkness cocooned him. He gave in to shuddering sobs that rattled his chest. Ash held him throughout. Rodan wiped his swollen face and thanked her when his emotions were spent. He sat there for another moment, grateful for her presence.

"Captain Ramirez said you specifically requested for me to come," Rodan said, breaking the silence again. "Why?"

Ash massaged her neck. "I needed an expert."

Rodan humphed. "Ha! And here I thought we were becoming friends. Come now, tell me the truth."

Ash sighed.

"If it weren't for you, this mission would've already failed. I would have shot the first Dula I saw." Her gaze dropped. "War is the sacrifice I make for the peace of others, but every conflict leaves me empty and lost despite the uplink. It's why I always return to Tierra Sangre, to rediscover why it's still worth it. A family gives me the courage and purpose I need to go back on ice." Ash looked up.

"A family?" The whiteness of her eyes captivated Rodan. He felt like he was falling.

"My brother's descendants. They remind me that the price I pay isn't wasted."

"Your brother's . . ." Rodan bolted upright and made a choking sound. "What is this? Is that why you brought me here? To be used as some excuse for a lifetime of misconstrued altruism?"

Ash's features turned stony, impassive. Her eyes flared, but she kept her tongue.

Rodan ignored the shroud of loneliness that embraced her at that moment or the longing gaze she'd given him just before his outburst. A black vortex of confusion, grief, and anger blinded him. While Xio's life was cut short, Ash lived despite centuries of military action. How was that fair? How dare she use him to justify an existence defined by self-sacrifice? He didn't want that responsibility.

Another change of the guards; two scarlet-furred Dula replaced by ridgeless, jade-furred ones. It sparked something in Rodan. He leaned forward, ignoring the tension between them, and beckoned Ash closer. They hadn't spoken since her revelation and Rodan's not-so-tactful response.

"The Dula are not tribalistic like I'd inferred," Rodan said. "They appear to rule using a tripartite system. Remarkably, their physiological response to their political ideology appears to manifest in the color of their fur. If I had to hypothesize, a member of the jade party attacked and dumped those bodies into the sea. It has been the jade-furred Dula who have shown aggression thus far." *A new, young party to their society?* "They will push for war if they could get the cobalt or scarlet party to agree."

Ash eyed the Dula with newfound interest.

The guards made a series of brusque snarls and opened the cell door. The Dula ushered them toward the audience chamber. The party leaders hovered in front of the podium, Ash's bag and weapons at their feet. Two men knelt beside her belongings, bound and gagged with guards at either side.

A feeling of foreboding churned Rodan's stomach. Ash and Rodan stopped in front of the Dula leaders, flanked by their escorting guards. They both made the L sign for *atriik* with their arms.

The Dula returned the gesture, Liktaa being the last one.

Rootka pointed at the two captives. "Take them in exchange for *atriik*."

Rodan took a step forward. The guards rustled. Ash took an inconspicuous step toward him.

"Thank you," he said. "And in regards to a peace treaty?"

Liktaa, jade-colored fur agitated, spat on the ground. "*Vaakte* and the furless will draw their last breath if they return."

"CoN will need assurances concerning your technology," Rodan said with a crestfallen expression. "Please, allow for a representative to establish communication. So we can coexist without further incident."

Liktaa's bulbous eyes flared. She spoke to Ash in words she wouldn't need translated. "*Kritaa.* End Dula. What *Vaakte* do."

"*Vaakte* almost ended you then. We can end you now," Ash said, cool but purposeful. "Do you understand that?"

The light from the rock formations above gleamed in Liktaa's black eyes. The jab goaded her. Steel-tipped teeth flashed. Her mouth twisted into a hungry leer.

Rodan let out an exasperated grunt. "You are *really* bad at this."

There was a stillness in Ash's posture she didn't have before. She gave an arrogant, insolent smile. "The ugly jade one is planning something soon. And I hate waiting. Did you notice all the guards are from the jade party? Be ready."

"Liktaa," warned Fusskta, her cobalt fur hanging lax over chitin.

"I gave you a chance, Fusskta," said Liktaa. Her signal was subtle; a twitch of her miniature clawed hands. Then she produced a knife out of the gravitational chair. "*Atriik* has blinded you for far too long."

A coup! Why else would there be only jade-furred guards present at such a delicate meeting between the two races? It was the perfect time to strike, to take control of the Dula leadership and blame it on the humans.

Rodan felt Ash move and push him away. He slid across the floor toward the party leaders. The guards watching over the prisoners ran past him in Ash's direction.

Rodan turned and saw Ash pirouette on her toes, dodging the guards' spears. She stretched her right arm toward the podium. Rodan felt the magnetic field in her dagger activate. It sailed through the air in a blur of reflective light. Ash caught it on a spin. Her warsuit rippled. The blade flashed wickedly. One of the guards overextended his spear arm and paid for it. Each time Ash's dagger moved, it sank between the gap in a guard's exoskeleton.

A great, skull-piercing scream rent the air. Rodan turned. Fusskta pitched over her gravitational chair, clutching her throat as pale, yellow blood gushed between her fingers. Rootka scrambled from the injured Dula, bumping her chair into Rodan. Liktaa raised her arm triumphantly and lunged toward Rootka. Dula blood coated the knife in her hand.

Rodan reacted without thinking. He moved to intercept Liktaa. Then his foot caught the supply bag, and his knee gave out. It saved his life. The knife sank into his left shoulder. Pain flared. His arm went numb. It would've been his chest had his knee held. He cried out and dropped to the ground.

Liktaa and Rootka struggled for control of the blade. When Rodan tried to get up, his right arm brushed against Ash's blaster. Rodan had never fired one in his life, but Xio had shown him how in case of an emergency. Rodan thanked her for that foresight. He picked up the PFA3, flipped the safety, and fired.

A thunderous crack reverberated in the chamber. The particle shot blew through Liktaa's head. She slumped over. The chair spun in aimless circles. An ozone stench hung in the air. Ash rushed to Rodan's side, rummaged in the supply bag, and placed a coagbandage over his wound. All the guards lay in individual pools of blood behind her.

More guards rushed into the audience chamber—a wave of cobalt, jade, and scarlet. They surrounded Ash and Rodan. Spears pointed in their direction. The other prisoners quivered in the fetal position, ruffled but unscathed.

Rootka pushed her chair past the guards. An open gash bled across her thorax, and two fingers were missing from a diminutive hand. She spoke urgently to the guards. They rushed to Fusskta's side, but her body lay still. Rootka looked at Rodan with gratitude in her eyes and bowed her head.

"*Atriik.*"

Gray clouds streaked across the sky, trailing a storm long gone. A ruby haze hung over Tierra Sangre, ghastly in the fading light. Waves lapped at Rodan's naked feet. Coldness soaked into his muscles, dulling aches and soreness. A shadow fell across him. He didn't have to look up to know it was Ash.

"Don't start," Rodan said. He shifted his shoulder in the sling. The coagbandage tingled, but the pain was a distant twinge.

Ash sat down next to him. "So, you've met the Dula. Thwarted a coup. Saved their leader and prevented another war in the process. Now a treaty? Not bad for a xenology professor. Your undergrad self would be proud." She gave him that insufferable smile again. "For whatever it's worth, I'm glad you agreed."

"That's because you're not the one brokering the treaty between the Dula and CoN Command."

"It's the right move," she said. "You've earned their trust. What made you agree?"

Rodan gazed at Tierra Sangre and those distant, vermillion sands he called home. The storm may have passed hours ago, but communications there were still spotty. Liana was going to kill him. He was late for dinner and hadn't called her yet. When Rootka recovered her composure, she ordered the communication jammers deactivated. Ash contacted CoN Command via her uplink before troops landed on Kockie Island.

Rodan eyed Ash. She looked at ease with the uplink working again. "Something you said."

"I said many things."

"Peace is important to you," he said. "It's important to me, too. Xio would've wanted me to do it." They fell into companionable silence. Then, Rodan blushed and said, "I . . . I wanted to apologize for my callous remarks in the cell."

"No need," Ash said. "I understand."

"No, you don't. I was completely out of line. The day I found out Xio was dead haunts me. The emptiness left in her place is overwhelming. I took out my unresolved grief on you. It wasn't fair. I'm sorry."

Ash waved his concerns away, but her face softened.

"What will *you* do?" Rodan said.

Ash shrugged. "I still have a few months of liberty. Got a place by the beach that's quiet."

Rodan turned to Ash and grinned. "Absolutely not. I won't allow my ancient, warrior great-great-etcetera-aunt to visit TS and not stay with us."

Ash laughed. "You're making me feel old."

"Welcome to the club," he said, standing up and brushing his pants. "And who knows," he offered Ash his hand, "you might find a reason to stay. There's more to life than sacrifice and duty. And other ways to achieve peace."

Ash grabbed his hand and gave him a hopeful look.

Rodan pulled her up. *And perhaps, with a new purpose, you can stop being a sleeping soldier who wakes and become a soldier who lives.*

Orbweaver

Liz Silverthorne

All units, prep Angel armour for dark."

Kalethao flipped the Angel "scale" once between his fingers, inserting it into the spectramour nexus between his shoulder blades. A soft click met his ears, and he gently tapped the subtly-embedded module twice, for luck.

"Southbound, coming within range now; last-minute checks. Ready in five."

The roar of atmosphere rumbled softly against the outer hull, a metallic clicking and creaking joining the quieter sounds of equipment checks. He mentally dove into the settings on his own spectramour, turning it to dark and briefly activating a spectral gauntlet to show up visually. It hovered like a void above his skin, wrapping his hand and arm in a light-absorbing black.

Less like angels and more like bats in the moon's night.

A slight smile turned up the corner of his mouth, fingers tugging at straps and making sure ammo packs, holsters, and hip satchels sat secure. The light glinted off his compact pulse-laser, the safety nestled firmly on in the mental space containing its stats, visual indicators glowing briefly as his thumb rubbed at its surface.

"Southbound, sound off."

Running over everything one last time, he flicked his fingers, joining in on the chorus of affirmatives. "Good to go, sir."

The pilot's voice came over the internal speakers again. *"Hatch opening in point-ten."*

"Ready to descend like the dragons of Haell?" A shoulder bumped his.

He gave one last adjustment to his fingerless gloves and grasped at the handle dangling from the ceiling, shoving lightly back at Wick. "And don't you know it. Anhu and the others had better be watching from the starlight."

"Easy there, Kalethao. They're only drug tenders, not the inner ring of the Ruling Web."

He joined in on the brief laughter as the hatch whirred and the roar intensified, drowning out all other sound, but not the heart of it. Even as he squinted against the rush of wind sucking at his clothing and tied-back hair, the smile remained.

Like the dragons of Haell . . .

<Jump on mark.>

The lush, dark surface of the moon spread out in front of them, glowing faintly in the light of the planet, the wind whipping at them cold with a tangy edge.

<Mark!>

In rolling pairs they leapt cleanly into the night. He swore he could feel the anticipation shivering through the handle sliding along the runner as he jogged forward beside his wingman.

Letting go, he pushed off and let the winds snatch him.

Stars flipped into the shadows of rugged terrain, rolling across the line of the horizon, the rush of the wind howling in his ears. It streamed around his face as though a bubble dampened the raw cutting edge, and he stretched out his arms and legs, reorienting until sky and ground steadied into their respective places.

Someone whooped over the link, and he grinned. Nothing quite like the stomach-evicting drop of free fall to chase the shade away.

<Coming in on position now. Check your heading and adjust your course. Wings open on signal.>

He swiped over the landscape, bringing up the grid and the marker designating their drop-in site, adjusting his angle. The others he could sense as shadows individually tagged at the edges of his mind, drifting in like he was or staying comfortably secure on their heading. TL Dam, as always, had been dead-on from the start.

<You're a machine, sir. Look at that, not a degree off-course.>

<He is a machine, Thao. Didn't you hear they rolled him off the assembly?>

<One day you'll be good enough if you learn to cut the chatter, side-wings.>

The silhouette a couple metres off his left flicked a lighthearted gesture, and Kalethao shook his head, the corner of his mouth quirking up. Didn't he know the TL had eyes in the back of his head?

If Anhu were still here, he'd be needling him for it. The bittersweet thought flickered through his mind. *Though he probably still was, on the other side.*

Turbulence buffeted them, and he leaned into it, streamlining his body. The rugged cut of the ground with its ridges and clawing flora swelled closer, the details of glowing pinpricks in a ravine coming into clear focus. *Two . . .*

<Wings open.>

Close enough. Around him, spectral wings spread—black shades in the night. The emulated sensation tingled on his own shoulder blades, a flicker snapping above his back to flare and catch the wind.

Whoompf!

With a jerk, his body snapped out of the headlong rush, organs continuing without him for a moment. The buzzing swell of pins-and-needles briefly swamped the phantom sense of extended wings, tingling along his spine and crackling at the nape of his neck. *Ouch.*

He shook his head, focusing on the dark shapes a little further ahead than they should have been and swooping to gain speed.

<Alright there, Thao?>

<Rinsed and clean.> He shook his head again, massaging at the side of his neck. *<Just bad timing on the opening. Caught a rogue gust.>*

<Quiet on the chatter, boys. The lures are in the crake-fish's maw. We're behind schedule.>

The operatives stringing the drug tenders along had already reached the final stages of the fake deal? Impossible to tell where the other teams were from his own readouts at this range, but from Dam's tone they'd probably already hit firma-not-quite-terra.

Not that they travelled too far behind. The rush of their passage shook stark tree-like shapes with a rattle of glass-shard leaves, the air hissing through his "feathers". The dot of their destination blinked, the rounded shapes of the squat farm buildings breaking up the flatter, clearer ground at the edge of the scrub.

He arrested his momentum with an angling of wings and dropped neatly to the ground with the others in a soft crunch of rock and brittle leaf-litter, half-crouched.

Dam brushed past, hand-gestures flashing, and with a brief check that everything was still secure, Kalethao spread out to his point on the approach. The soft rasp of his compact slid from its holster, safety mentally flicking off with a quiet click, mechanisms shifting and unfolding—hence the "compact" moniker. Stats shrinking to the back of the list for the moment, the glow of his team-members lit in the visual overlay as they jogged to the outlying structures.

<Side-wings, check for stragglers.>

His boots crunched lightly over the ground and the bristling tufts sprouting from it as he ranged through the fringes. Adjusting the Angel armour's set of sensory visuals, he couldn't pick up any hints of sapient life-force—no recent traces of Arete swirling in or out, or anyone inside. When he briefly turned his attention to it, the central building sang with life, though. The one that would normally be the hub of the little community supposedly tending these lands.

Almost reminded him of his childhood home, back before their neighbourhood had been gradually whittled away for more living stacks and pushed further into the shadows. Though the open space and sky here, unblocked by giant twisting roots and branches melding into each other, was about as different as night and day.

Picking his way back to the shadow of a small barn, drifting to cover the edge of their section of the net, he confirmed no stragglers on his side. Dam acknowledged him silently from where the core of their team slipped through the brittle brush edging a homestead across the dusty road.

<We're clear. Side-wings, take the ceiling sky-views. Tan, grid four-two; Wick, four-five; Thao, four-eight. We're moving in, breach on signal.>

He acknowledged with a flash of fingers and holstered his compact. Stepping back, he shoved off the ground and flared his wings, the ghostly sensation of air shunting over their dark surfaces tingling through his spine as he lofted above the structures, flapping lightly.

Almost makes me want to convert to the real deal, sometimes. He allowed himself a brief extra flourish on his descent as the lit, externally-quiet communal centre sprawled out below. Movement flickered in the sky-views, offering him a brief glimpse of a white coat before it swished out of view, and he landed lightly on the edge. *If it wasn't supposed to be painful as Haell to convert, anyway.*

Which was probably the point, considering doing so killed your humanity. Using emulated abilities through a spectramour neural nexus was just easier, anyway. Meant he could switch between whatever set he needed, too, so long as there was a scale disk for it.

Shunting extraneous thoughts aside and reluctantly folding the spectral wings, he crouched there at the edge of the puddle of light, watching the small patch of chip-mash floor he could see through the curved window. Not much else to see, with one of the woven beams blocking his view of the gathering inside.

Idly, he tapped at the seal surrounding the sky-view, casting a glance back over at the shadows of the other buildings. He couldn't pick out any of the others moving across the grounds, so they had to be at the entrance.

Any minute now . . .

And sure enough, the TL's voice cut across his own thoughts directly into his mind through the pathic link. *<Breach!>*

The crash of doors splintering cracked through the quiet of the night a half second before his own spectramour-reinforced boot came down on the window with a crash of breaking glass.

He dropped through, pinging his Angel armour to light as the clear shards glittered in a blur all around him. Blazing white wings bled through dark feathers in a flash, catching the air just enough to soften the *thud* of his boots on the floor.

Landing in a crouch, he levelled his compact on the group of Rachnids, the weapon clicking into short-range config. Wide eyes met him, humanoid figures tense—frozen.

"Orbweaver Interrealm Peace-Enforcement! On the ground!"

One abruptly snapped out of his shock as they pressed forward, Wick shoving another man to his knees. "You don't—"

"On the ground, now!" Kalethao locked him in his sights, giving him a shove of encouragement.

The man hissed, the pattern of eyes on his forehead flashing, a set of manifested spider-legs attached at the shoulder blades twitching as if readying to strike. Kalethao kicked him in the back of the knee, ending that and sending him thudding down with a strangled rattle.

Ignoring the pair of articulated fangs on the sides of the troublemaker's otherwise normal jaw, he slapped a restraint-disk on the back of his neck. The features disappeared to the ghostly threads veining over the Rachnid's skin, effectively paralysing his ability to manifest them. One down, and most of the others offering little resistance from the sound of it.

He kept his grip around the collar of the man's jacket for a moment to keep him from collapsing on his face, flicking a glance over the swarm of activity arrayed around the chairs roughly circling a clear, hovering table. His and the other teams had most of them down . . .

"We're doing *nothing* illegal!"

Apart from a couple of protesters. The woman caught his eye, voice raised to spit past her needle-like canines even as she kneeled, her over-shoulder sash as red as the tattoos on the antlered horns curving over her skull. And the blood she probably spilled on a daily basis. Not that those features lasted long once a restraint-disk was attached, choking off her tirade briefly.

"Unfortunately for you, there's definitive proof that you are." Another woman in a white coat, seemingly human apart from the glow of her silver eyes, gazed down at her, gesturing at the enforcer to take her away.

"You thread-weeping *sow!* I should have known you would be a human-fattening, soft-fanged—"

A flicker of movement caught his eye, and he ignored the Rachnid woman spitting insults, focusing on one of his team-mates—Enk—wrestling with another one who'd suddenly decided to kick up a fuss. Dropping his own and gesturing for Wick to take care of him—"Don't go anywhere, spider"—he moved over to help.

"You alright there, wet-ears?" Most of the others had moved to secure the rest of the hall, checking for any hiding places and unpleasant surprises. Or watching over the group already secured as the drama between the drug-tenders and the pair of operatives—backs turned to the little scuffle—went down. He waved off one from another team looking in their direction.

"That dry-fang! You all put us up to this!"

"Shouldn't have decided to make a living streeting drugs, then." He threw a glance over the man—boy, really, not much older than his eldest nephew—and frowned. "Did you secure the restrainer properly? He shouldn't be moving around like that."

The younger man yanked his charge's arms tighter behind his back, forcing his head forward with a hand. Those glowing threads looked weak, too. "When I hit it on, he was twitchin' around. Think it's off-centre, but he won't—"

"Here." He stepped in. "Hold him down and let me check it."

The boy struggled, tossing his head and hissing, and Enk grunted, his grip slipping for just a second.

Just a second for the Rachnid to break free, spitting viciously.

Holy—Kalethao snapped back, barely avoiding the wild swing slicing at him, Enk tossed back with a cut-off cry. He couldn't bring his compact up in time, a hair too late to stop the hand ripping the restraint-disk off.

Knifklit! He's—<One's loose!>

A spectral spider-leg forced him to duck, an electric crackle raising the hairs on the back of his neck. The Rachnid had turned on the operatives, fangs extending and ghostly projected legs raised above his shoulder blades, glowing.

He leapt forward without thinking, a blazing white wing flashing to block them.

The strike crashed into it with a deafening flare. *Nghk.* He gritted his teeth at the spine-tingling feedback, shoving against the sharp-edged projections. Stumbling back, the Rachnid rattled a hiss—

Only to find the muzzle of a laser-pulse compact extended in his face, humming.

"On. The ground. I—" he hissed a breath between his teeth, fingers practically locked around the grip—"would not want to have to use this on you. It makes a sricked mess on this setting."

Before the boy could make the wrong choice, he was being manhandled onto the ground and restrained.

He released a breath, wincing and reaching a hand over his shoulder to rub at the spectramour nexus briefly. *Human nervous systems were* not *made to handle this.*

"Thank you, enforcer." A voice turned him around to find the operative who'd spoken earlier offering him a smile, her intensely light-silver eyes flicking to his shoulder. "Are you alright?"

"Just a bit of feedback tingles. And just doing my job, sir." He smiled in return, casting back one last reflexive glance to check that the others had everything handled before turning his full attention to her. "Nothing hurt?"

"Only my ears." She brushed aside a lock of platinum blonde hair to tap one with a pale, slender finger. "Though they were already burned by the lovely speeches I've just been given."

"You'd be the only one to put it that way," her partner put in, his pale red-orange eyes flicking over the restrained Rachnid. "Weak-webbed fools, the lot of them. Their words couldn't mean less."

Are you related to Dam? He repressed a smile. Maybe it was the dark hair and clipped attitude. The woman, though—"Sorry, I didn't catch your names in the briefing, only code-designations."

"Command-Weaver Hazche." She traced a swooping downward spiral with a smile, and gestured to her companion. "And this is Sub-Weaver Aleign."

"Side-wing Kalethao of team two-four." He returned the gesture, adding a two-fingered tap to his jaw for respect. "Nice to make your acquaintance. And if you'll excuse me, my TL's pinging my frequency."

"Don't let us stop you."

Turning, he took a moment to locate the man, his gaze passing briefly over the sullen, kneeling drug-tenders and landing on a familiar scowl. A soft exhale puffed from his lips as he jogged over. *No downtime on the job.*

"This isn't meet-and-greet night, Thao. Eyes up and on-target, we're hunting out the nests."

"Yes, sir," he acknowledged crisply, holstering his compact. "My favourite part of the job . . ."

"Could be worse. Could be stuck in the cleaning division, sloughing out the fermenting pools." Wick fell in beside him as they moved out of the hall and back into the quiet, silver-lit grounds.

"It'll be just my luck if we find one, then. They stink."

"We'll go odd pairs by building, working the area and marking what we find," Dam cut into their chatter. "Wick, Thao, Tan—you're on three."

"Three? Why are we on three?" He muttered as they flicked acknowledgement and jogged off, brittle tufts crunching under their boots.

"Because you decided to go schmooze with the higher-threads, Kaleth," Tan —their permanent resident name-mangler—snorted, as the most foreboding structure of the grouping they were set to search loomed in the darkness.

It looked vaguely like a half-melted waffled zogat pudding, he mused to himself. If the cook had been particularly incompetent—completely understandable, since he couldn't make anything more complicated than a tost, himself— and let the glip layer overfrost to form spikes at the base. And if they'd only partially coated the honeycomb mesh, leaving dark gaps peering through a monstrosity of thin woven columns.

Maybe I'm just hungry. Slipping his compact out, he pushed first through the silk layer used in place of a door, ethereal strands tingling briefly against a flicker of spectral armour. They clung only for a moment, trying to get a feel of his Arete—the threads of his life-force—before snapping back into place, unable to trap him.

". . . *hate* these spider-homes," Wick muttered behind him.

"Ditto." Kalethao lit the centre of his palm, a glow orb hovering above his hand to illuminate the pitch-black space, naturally-grooved walls glinting.

"It's not so bad if you grew up with them."

"And how many times did you nearly get eaten by a door?" He gazed up at the shadowed loft for a moment, checking for life signs briefly before turning his attention to studying the floor.

"They aren't actually as bad as you think. Most of them were just set to keep out animals."

Wick tugged at something in the dusty corner. "Trusting lot."

"Some. Not this lot."

Kalethao moved to join the other and slipped his compact away again, dirt scuffing under his feet. "Found something?"

Wick grunted, tugging a panel in the floor free and jolting it up onto its hinges with a *krunk.* "Ta-da. Silver threads, that's srickin' heavy."

"Good work. The whole scale-cluster." He patted him on the shoulder, earning a white-knuckled grip on the edge. "Oh come on, that isn't enough to send you in."

"You'd need a boot to wedge him off there." Tan smirked, one hand on the top of the trapdoor as he peered down.

"That's what I was expecting from you hoons."

He snorted, lifting his hand over the hole, but it extended further into darkness than the glow orb could light. Though kicking a fragment of something undefinable over the edge did yield a soft clatter. Not too deep. "Well, if no one's volunteering, I'll drop in."

He didn't wait for acknowledgements to crouch down at the edge and swing around, lowering himself. Letting go, he dropped just a fraction of a second long enough to wonder if he'd misjudged before his feet abruptly hit the floor. He grunted at the impact, a twinge shooting through his knees briefly.

"All clear down there?"

"The drop's just a bit further than I thought." His voice echoed faintly as he straightened, gently working out the kinks in his abused ligaments. Taking a step away from the dim shaft of light, he let his own shine over the glinting walls of the cave, shroom fronds unfolding at his presence and glowing dimly. "I hope they're not free-ranging the . . ."

He trailed off as something moved in the corner of his eye, descending from the ceiling.

A pair of slowly-waving, stick-like legs.

He swore, jerking out of the way and sending the dark bug flying with the side of his compact just as another pair of boots thudded onto the ground. It came nowhere near, but the man still twitched, hissing a cut-off expletive of his own and hastily sidestepping the scuttling thing.

"Knifklit, Thao! Watch where you throw those things!"

He shone his light over the walls, trying to watch every direction at once in case of any more crawling about. "It jumped at *me*, not you—"

A laugh echoed down from above. "Aw, did the crawlers come to welcome you? They're only saying hello."

He caught Tan landing in the corner of his eye, Wick taking a hasty step back out of the way. "All-Weaver's spinnerets, Tan, don't *do* that to me."

Focusing his attention briefly, he saw the man poking at where the big spidorcion had scuttled to with the toe of his boot. "Don't worry, I've never seen one big as a man. Unless you count the Rachnids when they go dragon."

"Spend enough time around them and you might become one." Kalethao twitched a glance over his shoulder, half-convinced he'd find beady glowing eyes on a half-formed stalactite.

Tan just laughed again. "Look at you two. The OI, respected tough-as-silk peace enforcers. Afraid of some weird mystical spiders."

He rolled his eyes to the heavens. "Let's just search this place out. I haven't spotted any others, so this one must have escaped from the rest of the nest."

"We'll take sides and back. Unless you want me to go first . . ."

He made a face. *Set myself up for this, didn't I?* "Too late, I'm leading now."

A shrug, half-sensed. "Just let me know if it gets too scary for you."

"Ha-ha." He pressed forward, brushing past a frilled, glowing frond. The cave didn't go far, seemingly ending in a narrow dead end, where the grain of the rock was just slightly off—rougher.

Eyeing the wall, he ran his fingers along the edge, casting a glance up just in case there was another unwelcome visitor. And spied a small gap. *Aha. Definitely something on the other side.* He shoved at it, setting his shoulder into the stone, a jagged edge jutting out digging into the tough fabric of his shirt.

It didn't budge.

Huffing out a breath, he pushed back from it, slipping his compact away and snuffing out his glow-orb, someone giving a muffled cough behind him. *Second time's the charm.* With a grunt, he pushed his whole weight into it, boots grinding against the floor.

And finally, with a jarring rumble of stone-on-stone, it swung back, slowly gaining momentum until it hit the side with a *crunk.*

"*Whew.*" He shook his arms out briefly, snapping the glow-orb back into life as he stepped inside. The light played over black walls bubbled with a vague, transparent shimmer, like boils popping out of the rock. Except it . . . wasn't rock.

An involuntary shiver tingled down his spine, raising the hairs on the back of his neck as the dark "walls" shifted, a soft chittering spreading through a mass of hard black bodies. Beady glints of eyes rustled in the light, thin stinger tails waving gently.

"Looks like we've got one." The shudder in Wick's voice was something he had to agree with. "Tagging it now."

"Thanks. Was just about to send it in myself." He walked slowly through the centre, eyeing the feeding tubes threaded along the walls leading into each bubble. Now that he looked closer, some of the creatures were larger than others, the dark jagged scales on their abdomens more developed. Ready to harvest, probably, and melt down into tar—that lovely mystical drug that made Rachnids go crazy. "Eugh, better check the ship on the way back. Don't want to end up with any of these stowing in a bag for a ride home and get fused while I'm sleeping."

"It takes three days at least. Find one sucking on the back of your neck in the morning and you can just flick it off." Tan stopped to hold his own glow-orb up to the feeder at the centre of the tubes.

"Thanks, expert." He waved the light gently at a larger bubble, a series of chitter-hisses and flicking stinger-tails rewarding his efforts. "And if I end up in a coma for three days? You know the hallucination effect of these life-suckers. There's only me in that stackroom. I'll stumble out with spider fangs sticking out of my face and nobody would've noticed I was missing."

"What about all those sisters and overprotective mother of yours?"

"They'll just think I'm busy. Which I will be. Tripping silk-shooters." Though after the second day dead-silent, at least Aerathnea—more likely with half the others along—would "casually" swing by to say hi, and save him from becoming a mystical alien life-sucker that could manifest arachnid features at will. But he wasn't about to tell Tan that.

"Alright, if you don't show up for the skrog-fest tomorrow I'll personally break in. Happy?"

"Chuffed. Thanks, Tan. You've always got my back."

"Slight problem with the tagging." Wick's voice broke in on the idle banter, and they both turned as he approached, "Wider connection's blocked. I've called it in to Dam over the link, but something's blocking long-range."

He and Tan exchanged glances. "Jammer?"

"Looks like it." He turned, scanning for any sign of sapient life and catching only ripples of evil spider energy. "The crawlers are interfering with sensors, too."

"I'm calling for reinforcement—"

"Shh." Kalethao held up a hand. Just for a moment . . . had that been a thumping? "Did you hear that?"

He received a pair of silent negatives, Tan's hands shifting to grip his compact in readiness. Quietly moving forward, he slipped out his own, approaching a split in the tunnel. With a couple of quick gestures, he set the others to either side, indicating he'd move with the left.

They swung around the corner into the narrow passage, him dropping to a knee with compact in hand, beaming the light from his glow orb down the tunnel. Tan's weapon hummed, ready to shoot in the blink of an eye, but the only movement came from the steady shuffling of spidorcions.

"Over here."

They turned at Wick's voice, the other man stooping over something, one hand on the wall. Straightening and stepping over, Kalethao let his light play over a heavy metal panel slotted neatly on a downward angle into the wall, a handle set in the middle. "Looks like a hideaway cover."

"Hope it doesn't lead to the fermenting pits," the other grunted as he pulled, and Kalethao slipped to the side to let Tan train his compact on the eventual opening. "Threads—it's heavier than my wife's sticky loaf—"

With a heave, he jerked it off its frame, scraping it aside to lean on the wall, Tan tensing and crouching slightly to get a better angle.

"Something just moved—"

He caught it, too—a shuffle of feet and cut-off quick breaths. Not like an ambush, but—"Wait. Hold your fire."

Carefully keeping from blocking Tan's line of sight, he leaned forwards, holding his glow orb up to light the inside . . . and the faces of five dirty children cowering at the back, one with her hand pressed over the mouth of a little girl and holding her tight, wide eyes blinking rapidly against the light.

"I think we'd better re-establish contact with higher command."

HAZCHE WATCHED THE LAST OF THE DRUG TENDERS DISAPPEAR INTO THE transport with a well-placed shove, and sighed quietly to herself. *A good day's work . . .*

Her gaze drifted up to the small army of hovering drones swooping through the sky, crawling over every inch of what used to be an honest land-tending settlement. Taking footage of the aftermath of the operation, each linked back to a reporter ready to declare to the world below how well the OI were cracking down on the evil, corrupt scum of the moons. As soon as it was declared secure, the living, breathing drones would be on the ground, buzzing around like mosquitoes.

Through the chatter streaming into her command-tier pathic link, a ping reached her directly from a minor team.

"Seems they've found them," Aleign commented, stepping up beside her. "Shall I go?"

"No, thank you, Ale." She turned, the breeze kicked up by a drone catching at her coat and hair. She dashed a few stray strands out of her face. "I'll leave you to supervise what's left to deal with here."

When she arrived, the team leader informed her it was inadvisable to go below, thanks to a jamming device and the need to secure the area in case of any spots hiding other possible surprises. Unfortunately, the children were also still spooked, the men who had found them only just coaxing them out of the underground cave system. She stood beside him, watching them lift one little girl—her dirty face streaked with tears—from the pit with an improvised harness.

Only five of them . . .

The child's eyes met hers and flinched slightly, cowering against the man setting her down and taking the harness off for the next one. She noted him as the young human enforcer who'd been having trouble with that drug tender before her attention had been taken with more vocal members. Barely into his second meridian, most likely—young enough that he might seem more like an older brother than a dangerous, hungry Rachnid, like her.

How long has she been captive . . . ?

The others pulled out had similar reactions, though the oldest girl reserved her wariness for everyone, her hand tight on the little one's shoulder. They shuffled in the corner of the dim confines of the disused barn, huddled in a few blankets offered to them.

"These are the only children you found?" she asked quietly.

"We're still searching the tending nest, sir. So far there's nothing more."

"If there *are* more, we'll find them." Another enforcer approached—the one who'd introduced himself as Kalethao in the middle of it all, she recalled with a brief flicker of amusement.

"I don't think you'll find anyone else." She watched one of the boys huddle closer to the others, a cough wracking his small frame. Each of them swirled with Arete, like a full well. "They were only giving us a sample. Most of the merchandise is in the city, not here."

The man twitched in the corner of her eye as if touched with an electric thread. "You *knew* they were dealing in bleeders, too—?"

"Thao," his team leader said sharply.

"Sir. My apologies. Sir."

She turned her gaze to him, not missing the roiling flicker reflected in his brown eyes or the rigid neutrality forced into his expression. Her own softened. "Accepted. Yes, we know. I was hoping for more to rescue, but our main objective was to seize the tenders and their operations. Five . . . is better than none."

He exhaled a soft hiss, running a hand through his tied-back hair, setting free a few wild strands. "There are hundreds more subs out there getting their *life* drained from their *souls,* and this is the best we can do? *Five?*"

"You're arguing with someone who already agrees with you, enforcer. But unfortunately, we've already reached our goal here." She held up a hand to quiet enforcer Thao's disapproving TL, eyeing the man curiously as his gaze flicked briefly to the huddled group in the corner. "If you don't mind me asking a personal question . . . do you have children, Thao?"

"No, I . . . not personally." He was quiet for a moment. "I'd hate to see my sisters or their subs used as cattle, though. I apologise, Command-Weaver. I spoke out of turn."

"Apology accepted." She tilted her head to the children, raising her eyebrows. "You can make up for it by seeing if any of them will open up and tell you something useful. There's a chance we might be able to set up an operation in the future."

<You know that's a lie,> Ale's voice whispered to her across their personal thread as the enforcer moved away with a brief but respectful acknowledgement. Eavesdropping again, it seemed. *<The lines tying the colony with the Occoon's authority are weak. Sending enforcers directly into the city could rattle Arathen's Ruling Web enough to declare war.>*

<Thank you, cousin, I'm aware.> She closed her eyes briefly. *<But there are more webs to weave than a simple net.>*

"I apologise, sir, for my subordinate." Team leader Dam's quiet hissing sigh broke into the mental conversation. "Enforcer Thao has a habit of speaking his mind when he shouldn't."

She smiled at him. "Don't worry about it. If I can't answer the people I command, then it's a sign I should look twice before throwing a line."

"Maybe. Or maybe it's only the sign of a bad soldier."

"Perhaps he'll make a better commander one day, then." Through the pathic link chatter she had oversight of, another pair blinked into existence, reporting the finding and disablement of the jammer they'd been seeking.

"In the meantime, I'd like to look at where they were held. I might be able to catch some shadows myself."

Five pairs of eyes looked up at Kalethao as he approached, the eldest's arm tightening around the youngest little girl—Ellante, the only one to give her name—and drawing the others closer. Crouching down on their level, he rested his elbows on his knees with a reassuring smile, hands open and loose where they could see them.

The wariness in their eyes, even after he'd helped bring them to the surface, was worlds away from the open, trusting exuberance of his nieces and nephews. *They're just subs . . . not even reached their first meridian.* Apart from the oldest girl, maybe—only one or two points above, though. Four at most.

"Hey, I'm not here to hurt you. Remember? We're taking you home to your parents, just like I promised," he said softly. "But I need to ask you some questions, alright?"

The two little boys were the first to nod, one's fingers fidgeting at the edge of the blanket, and after a long moment the oldest girl followed, still silent.

"We're enforcers—rescuing children like you is part of our job. What I need to know is if there are more of you who were taken by the spiders."

The boy picking at the blanket nodded again, glancing up at the oldest girl. It would have been nice to get names, but most of them hadn't answered even simple prompts. He kept going, hoping the nod was a sign one of them would break the conversation barrier. "Can you tell me where they are? If you have any brothers or sisters still being held by the Rachnids, we'd like to rescue them."

For a long moment eyes just blinked at him. And then the oldest girl finally opened her mouth, her voice a rough whisper barely loud enough to hear over the quiet background noise of the other enforcers. "I have a little brother. Back in the city, they took us from everyone else."

"Can you tell me what the place was like?"

For a long moment she fell silent, eyes averted, and he'd just opened his mouth to prompt her when she spoke again. "We were in a room, like a warehouse. Sick ones were taken somewhere else. When they wanted us they took us through the door into this big building like a hotel, or put us in trucks and took us to somewhere fancier. I only saw what it looked like outside once . . ."

He kept his voice calm and gentle, unpressured. "Can you describe it?"

"It . . . it was tall. It had these big windows in the middle, and it was dark. And it looked old."

"Run-down?"

She nodded.

"When you say tall . . ." he gestured up at the walls around them ". . . was it taller than this?"

She nodded again. "Maybe twice as tall? And a little more."

Probably around four or five stories, then. "Is there anything else you noticed that could help?"

"I think . . . the warehouse was at the back. It joined up to the building." For a moment she went silent. "And . . . there was this glowing web sign, I think. On the side."

Probably a symbol the Rachnids used to indicate a bleeding-house. *It's not like they have any reason to be subtle out here.* "How many were in the warehouse, do you think?"

". . . A hundred? I don't know. There were a lot."

He nodded, giving her a smile and shoving himself back to his feet. "Thank you. Hopefully we can recover them soon."

"You're not—aren't you going now?" Her eyes widened, shoulders stiffening. "But—but my brother—"

His chest tightened at the desperate crack in her voice, setting his hand briefly on her head. "Hey, we're doing what we can. We'll find him and free all of them, I promise."

The words stuck to his throat with a bitter taste. *You can't promise that.* But he couldn't leave them with nothing, either.

"No—you-you don't understand. They brought more in. He was going to be sold to somebody else, like us. They'll be gone in the morning—I heard the spiders say they were going to sell them in the morning when the trucks came and—"

"Whoa whoa, slow down." He frowned, crouching down again. "They're moving them?"

"*Selling* them. They sent us over here and they were going to sell them to somebody else. I don't know who, but he . . ." Her voice broke, choking into a raspy whisper again as she held Ellante closer. "I couldn't bring him with us, just my sister. Please. P-please . . ."

"Hey, deep breaths for me." He kept his voice steady and soothing as she scrubbed at her eyes with the blanket around her shoulders. "So let me get this straight, they got more children and they're selling on some of the others?"

A nod.

"Can you tell me how many?"

"H-half, maybe . . . ? Fifty. They said fifty."

"And you don't know where they're moving them?"

She shook her head, lips pressed tight.

From the sounds of it . . . *Hm.* They were looking to expand, so it made sense for them to invest in more "merchandise", but why not send a larger sample here, then? Why *sell* them? It made more sense to move them to another building if they didn't have enough space. Unless there was another group in play they needed to pay off. *In that case, they're better off in jail now.* Because if they'd been counting on the fake deal to widen their web and expand the cash flow, things could get nasty for the remnants left.

In the end, it didn't matter. What mattered were those subs about to be moved to who-knew-where, their last opportunity for freedom snatched away.

A hard lump settled in the pit of his stomach, burning like an ember dumped into a firepit, and he set a hand on her blanketed shoulder, careful not to spook her. "Let me talk to my commander."

Her dark eyes twitched up to his, and he squeezed gently, holding her gaze. "I'll do everything I can."

She bit her lip and nodded.

We don't have much time. Giving a brief ruffle of one boy's hair and a last smile, he turned, seeking out the white coat that had disappeared while he chatted with the subs. *And I have even less of a chance at convincing them before dawn lights Haell.*

<Sir, I'd like to speak with Command-Weaver Hazche. I have some intel she might like to hear.>

He could *feel* Dam weighing the pros and cons of letting him in her vicinity again. *< . . .We're down in the room you found the children. Whatever you have to say, remember your rank, side-wing.>*

<Acknowledged, sir.>

He'd dropped down in an instant, passing Tan and Wick at the split with a brief greeting, neither of them questioning his quick passage. Dam himself only gave him a cool look that spoke volumes more than any warning ever could as he stooped under the lintel and stepped inside.

"Enforcer Kalethao." CW Hazche turned from the glimmering threads woven through the space and reflecting the eery silver of her eyes. "You found something?"

I'm sorry, Dam. He threw out every warning his TL had given him and took a step closer. "Sir, you seem to care about the subs."

"I do." She tilted her head marginally, looking up just slightly to lock with his gaze, expectant.

He took a deep breath. "The oldest gave me a description of where they were being held. Around a hundred children, give or take her estimation abilities. But apparently, fifty are being moved in the morning and sold off, her brother among them."

"Useful information." Her eyebrows rose slightly.

"Respectfully, sir, I advise that we mount an operation to retrieve them before it's too late."

A shadow flickered in her eyes, chasing across her expression. "I'm afraid that might be hard to put through my superiors."

"If we don't, those children will be *gone.* Sir." He took a chance and another half-step closer, seeking out that flicker of softness she'd shown briefly before. "The parents of fifty children might never get a chance to see them again. Fifty subs, thrown from bleeding-house to bleeding-house until they're sucked dry. If we have even a chance, we can't let it go."

"You're spinning where there's already a web, enforcer." For just a moment, tiredness crept into her voice. "Unfortunately, I've already asked, and the last response was a definitive 'no'. We can't afford to antagonise Arathen. We only have permission for this operation, and nothing more."

"How in Haell will busting a bleeding-house count as antagonisation?" He asked, even though he knew the answer. They had deals and stipulations with the Occoon, and the sricking Rachnids from the lowest alley scrounger to the highest weaver on this forsaken moon were too addicted to the Arete of children. Just like home. Just like how everyone turned a blind eye if a little girl vanished off the street. *Jeccing life-suckers. Damn them.* Damn *them to* Haell.

Either she saw the thoughts reflected in his eyes or read the swirls of his Arete, a saddened, humourless flicker of a smile touching the corner of her mouth. "I'm sorry."

His fingers clenched, a muscle in his cheek twitching as his jaw tightened. "You're the one who commands us here, on the ground. They don't pull the threads in your web, sir."

"Unfortunately, they do. Ultimately." Her eyes searched his face for a long moment. "But . . . maybe there is a chance we can do something. TL Dam."

He flicked a glance back as she raised her voice, touching his shoulder. "I need to steal away your subordinate for a few moments. Carry on as you were."

And in the blink of an eye, they stood at the foot of a ramp. For half a moment he blinked in disorientation, gazing up at a lander ship that hadn't been there moments earlier before he'd suddenly been thrown back up to the surface. *Recall. Web-spinners.*

. . . Jecc, I'm dizzy.

"Come with me." A white coat brushed past him, completely unbothered by the sudden change in scenery.

Shaking his head, he stumbled into motion after her, attempting to regain his bearings as he acknowledged, "Sir."

There must have been something in his voice, because she glanced back, pausing. "Oh, I'm sorry. You haven't recalled before?"

"Yeah—imitation scale. Sorry, emulation. Never been along for the ride before, though." He tapped at the spectramour nexus on his back as the world settled, remembering the first time he'd strung a thread , teleported back down his path, and nearly thrown up. If anything, it looked like tagging along seemed to skip the side-effects. Mostly. "Little more limited mimicking it through a bio-comp."

"So I've heard." She waited to move until he'd stepped in beside and slightly behind her, probably making sure he didn't fall flat on his face. Or watching to see if he would.

As soon as they stepped into a small room just behind the pilot's deck, she strode up to a holographic storm of communications data, her partner—SW Aleign—already there, standing respectfully to the side. He was also giving her a look that ironically reminded Kalethao of the one Dam had just given him a minute ago.

His opinion of her might have jumped up a notch at that.

A soft beep drew his attention back to the holographic swirl just as it coalesced into a ghostly bust of an older woman. One with the hard, glowing eyes of a Rachnid who'd already made up her mind. And that decision happened to be on the negative side. *She's not here to listen.* He'd seen the same look on his mother's face once or twice—usually right before she'd opened the door to politely run off the land agent again.

"Hazche. As I've already told you, the operation parameters are nonnegotiable. You are to finish with your original assignment and return. Nothing more. Nothing less."

She didn't bat an eye. "I felt it would be useful to inform you of updates in the situation, Centre Thread. It has come to my attention that a number of innocents caught up in the drug tenders' operations are at danger of being removed. If we don't move now, there is a good chance they could be out of our reach permanently. And I believe this falls under our current operation's parameters, ma'am."

Damn, she's good. He glanced at the CT's unreadable face, looking for any hint of a change of heart.

"Do these innocents happen to be in the vicinity?"

"Yes, ma'am."

"Where, exactly?"

For the first time, he saw the faintest of twitches in what he could see of her face, her jaw tightening. "An unconfirmed location in the city, ma'am."

Instantly, any hint of indulgence vanished. "The city is off-limits, Command-Weaver."

Kalethao shifted his balance, and Hazche's hand unobtrusively lifted in warning. "I'm aware, Centre Thread. But I'm invoking a special case for this—at least fifty human children are due to be moved at dawn and sold on. If we don't move now—"

"If we do move now, all those children could die in a war *we* could have avoided."

. . . Old fat cob sitting in her perfect little web sucking children's bones. You've *never lost anyone to a bleeder.*

Hazche turned to him, and he hastily swept away the unflattering thoughts, rearranging his expression. She gave no sign of noticing as she addressed the woman, and him. "Ma'am, I believe this can be done without a major incident. Enforcer Kalethao, here, was given a description of the building by one of the rescued children. If we can locate it, we could launch a quick covert strike, hot-load the targets, and take them to safety."

He stepped forward, respectfully tapping two fingers to the side of his jaw and dipping his head. "Side-wing Kalethao of team two-four. If I may speak, ma'am."

Her eyes flicked once over him, cutting through his soul. "Granted."

"From the sound of it, the building is in a run-down area, out of the way. CW Hazche's strategy could work perfectly with minimal consequences."

"You have no place to decide that, side-wing. Those 'minimal' consequences could cost us hundreds of lives."

"If we do nothing, it *will* cost us fifty, ma'am."

"They will be sold, not killed, enforcer," she said coolly, her eyes narrowing.

With an effort, he kept his expression controlled and muscles rigid. "Personally, ma'am, I'd say it's a fate worse than death. And respectfully, that isn't true. If they aren't rescued, every one of those children will eventually die."

"As do all humans."

Was she baiting him? He sensed CW Hazche twitch, and subtly hissed in a breath between his teeth, clasping white-knuckled hands behind his back. "Ma'am, these are the lives of fifty—*more* than fifty—innocent subs—"

"I am not belittling you, I am pointing out facts. Even if you save them, there will be more, including those meant to replace these fifty. Unlike you, higher command has to consider *all* consequences, not just those of the few." Her gaze flicked away from him in a clear dismissal. "Command-Weaver, I will discuss this with the rest of the higher-threads, and we will get back to you. In the meantime, attend to your duties."

With a flicker, the holo winked out, leaving the floating web of silent communications chatter filling the room.

He practically ground his teeth, silently cursing out his superior fifty ways from the darkest depths of Haell and all the demons with summer homes there. Get back to them, she said. They'd discuss it with the others and come to a decision that considered *all* consequences, completely independent of ulterior motives. Because *of course* they weren't motivated by the funding and favour of the Occoon, who couldn't care *web sacs* about some dirty human subs.

With a soft exhale, CW Hazche stirred next to him as he spun on his heel, his footsteps ringing against the metal floor. "That's it, I'm going rogue. Srick this."

"Hold on a moment." Her hand caught his arm, arresting his stormy progress. "You're not going 'rogue', enforcer."

"I made a promise to a broken-up sub that I'd get her brother back." He tugged warningly against her grip, acutely aware of the height advantage he held as he locked gazes with her. "*Respectfully*, the Centre Thread can go—"

"Kalethao." Her eyebrows rose. "If you'll be patient and wait a few moments, you won't *have* to go rogue. There's a new aspect to this mission that's been brought to my attention, and I'm putting my forces in place to deal with it."

. . . Is she saying what I think she's saying? For a moment he stared. "The Centre Thread just told us to stay put until they come back and tell us 'no' for real."

"He's right, Hazche." SW Aleign stepped forward. "We don't have permission for this. You're risking your position if you go ahead anyway."

"Thank you, Ale, for stating the obvious."

He almost twitched at the dryness in her voice. But he had no time to dwell on it, her gaze returning to him as she slipped her hand off his arm. "I'll be infiltrating the city to find the bleeder house and see what we're dealing with. And if it's possible to raid it and retrieve the targets." She cocked her head. "I also need a human who can use an Angel armour set as an ace. Would you like to volunteer?"

He flicked one glance at Aleign's unhappy face and offered her a tight smile. "I'm all yours."

"You do know most of the people living here are Rachnids," Kalethao murmured as they stepped out of the transportation tube, wandering down the dark street of a twisted city that reminded him of Rathnea's quieter sections, back on the planet looming above. If it also happened to be crossed with the moon's brittle shard-leafed trees and glowing fungus rifts. "I don't blend in much."

"Actually, you do." The CW strode beside him, as comfortable in the vaguely mushroomish streetlamps lighting the winding pedestrian pathway beside the transportation tubes as if it were broad daylight. And not the dead of a planet-lit night with beady eyes rustling softly in the shadowed nooks and crannies. "You'd only really stand out if you were walking these streets alone, without someone to claim you."

He gave her a sideways glance. "It's not exactly obvious I am 'claimed'. You don't look that much like a Rachnid right now."

"Neither do they." A gesture led his gaze to a few loiterers hanging around an entrance to the tubes, slowly rippling glow-fronds framing the platform. She was right. Some of them weren't sporting fangs, spindly legs on their backs, horn-antlers, or anything else. Just facsimile humans—with glowing eyes. "Not *every* Rachnid walks around with enough sharp points to catch a forest."

He grunted softly, carefully keeping his attention to the corners of his vision instead of darting glances everywhere like a frightened mosrat in a pit of snakes. Checking his map overlay again briefly, he noted they were only a couple of kiltered streets into the area most likely to hold the bleeder house. "It has to be somewhere close."

"It is. There's a thread leading right to it."

He cast a quick glance at her. "You can tell already?"

She glanced back, one delicately arched eyebrow lifting. "If you know what to look for, you can find anything. And if you're looking for something in particular, there's always a thread."

Would be interesting to see the mess of Arete threads woven through a Rachnid-dominated city. The few times he'd used a spider scale and activated the senses that came with the package, it was like seeing in shades of people— like heat-vision but soul-flavoured. *I prefer Angel armour. Easier on the eyes.*

"Thao," his superior murmured, bringing his attention back to her, "There's a mirrored window just here at this corner shop. Have a look and tell me what you see."

Picking it out in an instant—the shop in question edging out from part of a block that resembled a wizened tree stump, with an overhang like a shelf-fungus —he spotted a group of three male Rachnids wandering behind. All of them with spider fangs framing their faces, multiple eyes, antler-horns; the whole deal. *Wait. Are those tattoos on the horns?*

"I see them. Part of a gang?"

"Worse—the gang we just apprehended. They're following us."

The hairs rose on the back of his neck, and he fought not to glance behind as they turned the corner down the twisting byway, dim glow bubbles bobbing on the vine-and-frond festooned walls. "Do they know who we are?"

"Word shouldn't have spread yet. I have a feeling they're more hoping I might share you."

Her eyes glowed faintly in the dim profile of her face as he cast a quick glance at her. "Great." Grimacing, he subtly turned his head to catch a glimpse behind, but they weren't there yet. "Guess I'm the lady of the hour."

There was a soft, stifled snort. "I suppose it is a bit different from human dynamics."

Had that been a laugh? "If you mean completely flipped, then yes."

This time, she definitely gave a soft chuckle—a humourless one, but a laugh all the same. "Don't worry, they're probably only after your Arete. I'd be more worried if they were women."

. . . Hopefully she never ended up in the more human waste-dumps of society. Deciding that keeping his mouth closed on all of that in polite company would be the better idea, he followed her down another branch, side-eyeing the map and the random route they were taking. "Why can't they just suck their own Arete? Is there any special reason we're taking this route?"

"Just a few quick detours to throw them off. It'll be harder to infiltrate and gain an idea of what we're dealing with if they're already trying to wrap us in a net. We need as little attention as possible." She swept past a low-hanging frond glowing a quiet orange as they followed a twist in the path, and sent him a side-long look. "How much do you know about Rachnids, Thao?"

"Enough to know you could bleed each other if you wanted." If it was a detour she was trying for . . . he focused on the civilian aspects of the map, razing through the list of establishments nearby.

". . . We *could*. But *you* could also eat another human being. That doesn't mean you would, or that it's healthy."

Aha. Just the kind of place he was looking for. They'd have to think his life-force was the best mark in the city to hang around. Or Hazche would have to be wrong about them. "Cattle for me it is. I've got an idea to throw our human-loving friends off. Down here."

He redirected them down a wider path to their left and leading away from their destination, the lights brighter. Hazche hesitated only a moment before following. "What kind of idea?"

He smiled at her. "How would you like to take your claim for a date?"

Hazche's eyebrows rose as the pedestrian walk opened up, a quiet hubbub of life catching her ear. The subtle weave of others' passing threads felt brighter, here. As if stepping into a bubble of light in the darkness.

A safe nest?

The slightest of smiles twitched at the corner of her mouth as they approached a woven gateway, glimmering threads extending up the walls and where they broke to the hazy edge of the planet above and the scattered stars beyond it. Growing distant, those menacing tugs at the city's web all around them seemed to fade in the little cocoon of warmth—an unexpected neutral haven in the middle of the group's territory. Maybe enforcer Kalethao's idea was just the thing to keep their net from closing.

"Keep your spectramour off." Putting a hand on his shoulder, she stepped through the gateway first, extending a few invisible threads to him just in case any accompanying humans needed permission. The web passed warm over her, twinkling like stars, and—apart from a brief, unintelligible mumble next to her—uneventfully over the enforcer.

"I think you have the right idea, Thao." She patted at his shoulder briefly with her fingertips, gazing up at the little dewdrop lights glinting above them, a few sets of eyes glancing over curiously from little side-nook shops and food cupboards.

"Well, if they're only after my irresistible humanity, staying a few minutes should throw them off." He smiled, leading the way down the path and either unaware of or ignoring the sneaking glances thrown his way by a few Rachnids.

Subtly, she stepped in beside him, noting a few other humans here and there, their bright Arete swirling placidly. A few said hello to Kalethao in passing, souls bright behind their eyes, and he returned the gesture, guiding her through the open arch of a restaurant, from the smell of it.

A quaint little place, too. She cast a glance around, admiring the wicker-woven ceiling and light filaments dangling through it. There was a cosy den sort of feel to the cave-like space, too, thanks to the smaller size—much smaller than most restaurants in Rathnea, with only a little family and an older group of four seated at the naturally asymmetric tables.

"Sure is rustic," Kalethao muttered, the ceiling apparently low enough that he had to brush a few particularly low glowing filaments out of his face. "Nice, though."

"Enjoy it. We won't be here long." She caught the eye of the establishment's owner bustling at the old-style counter ring at the back. "Table for two, please."

His eyes lit up with a click of his fangs, and he gestured with a thick, fully manifested spider leg at a nice nook in the corner by an old radial heater. "Right here, right here, just for you. Midnight nibble menu or full dinner?"

"Midnight nibble, thank you," she said at the exact moment Kalethao asked, "What's the dinner menu like?"

She raised an eyebrow at him. He shrugged.

"Well, there be a few nice sharing dishes in both." The man smiled behind his beard, chittering quietly. "I can pull up all those, if you like."

This time the enforcer raised his eyebrows at her, his hidden curiosity shining in his gaze. With a wry twitch of her mouth, she decided to indulge them both. "Why not? We'll have a look through it."

It took only a few moments—once they'd sat down—to look through the customised holographic menu offered. And even less than that for the "Grove of Twist Sticks™" to catch her apparently starving human companion's eye. Possessing less of an appetite, herself, she let him choose, confident he'd consume everything she didn't.

"Sure there's nothing you want?" he asked for the second time, after they'd already ordered.

"I'm sure."

"I used to live with eight sisters who all say the same thing, and regret it after." He took a sip of water. "Or Roan does, anyway."

Her eyebrows rose nearly to her hairline. "You have eight sisters?"

"I know. It was a drop to Haell for the odds. I think they threw me in just to keep from messing things up for the next hundred generations."

"You don't have any brothers?"

He shook his head. "Eight of them, one of me. And I'm the second-youngest."

"I'd say 'I'm sorry'," she said, eyeing him, "but I have no personal experience there."

"You look like you expect me to have a dress secretly packed away and a box of face dusters," he noted, clearly fighting a losing battle with the grin trying to break out on his lips. "No sisters on your side?"

"No. No siblings." She cast a glance over at the family on the other side of the room: two little boys bouncing in their seats, the mother deftly halting a cup from spilling with a spectral spider-leg.

"High-end parents?"

Taking her own glass, she raised her eyebrows at him over the rim as she took a sip. "This isn't a real date, you know. I would have thought you'd be more impatient to get moving."

Especially since he'd practically tried to bully her into it. Though, right now he looked almost as relaxed as the man who'd casually asked for her and Ale's names in the middle of the operation, one arm slung over the back of his chair as he rhythmically rolled his glass on its base, brown eyes drifting to the other side of the room.

"Well, you've got to take your moments." Leaving the glass, he reached up and ran a hand through his messily held-back hair, making a face as he fingered one of the numerous loose locks. Tugging at the tie, he pulled it free, ruffling at the sandy-toned mess. "If we have to stay here for a few minutes, might as well take the time for a couple of deep breaths. We still have about five or six hours. They'll probably be taking the subs at the crack of dawn."

"Hm." A fair point, but interesting that he was the one making it. She rested her chin on the back of her hand, watching as he dragged his fingers one last time through the surprisingly—or perhaps not, considering how it had tried to escape—thick crop of hair and shook his head once. Under her careful analysis, the flow of his Arete didn't look quite as relaxed as his movements. Perhaps he was more impatient than he let on. "Ale's made good progress getting to the city with the transport. They should be ready to move in once we locate the building."

He raised an eyebrow at her, his fringe not long enough to reach them— though it did contrast his strong jaw nicely—and let his hand flop onto the table again. "What happened to 'checking it out'?"

"Well, we have to be prepared for the possibility of a rescue, should we discover something illegal. And it doesn't hurt to have backup."

He smiled lopsidedly at her, fiddling restlessly with his hair-tie, a thing made of glitter and bright colours. Handmade, from the looks of it. "Right."

A flicker of movement up on the ceiling caught her eye. Glancing up, she spotted a fully-manifested Rachnid child—"gone dragon" as the humans would say—scuttling over the twisting weave, a platter carefully held the right way up over his head. He settled in place directly over their table, chittering a blithe greeting.

"Threads—"

"Thank you," she said over Kalethao, smiling up at the child as he carefully descended on a thread and set their platter down with a pair of two-clawed arms in place of hands.

He waved his hooked stinger tail cheerfully at them both in return, springing back up again.

She pulled one of the hot twist sticks arrayed around the edge out of the sauce, taking the first bite while her human companion stared after the young Rachnid, and smiled. "Surprised?"

"I'll admit, that's a first for me." Belatedly, his eyes returned to the dish, retrieving a stick of his own. "Sp—Rachnid subs crawling on things, I've seen. Carrying food upside-down like a serving spider from an old children's fable, though . . ."

They lapsed into silence, broken only by the soft crunch of sticks and the enforcer's mumble of appreciation. She idly noted that while she just ate half hers without sauce, he slid his down and spun it until all but the tip was covered. *That's a useful trick.*

She wondered if he did that whenever he ate with his sisters, or just dipped the bitten end in again; if they'd done that as children and been told off by their parents. Wondered how he could enjoy it so much when he knew that just a few sections away, children—humans like him—were sobbing into threadbare pallets, trying to forget the sting of a spider's fangs in their skin.

"We don't bleed each other's Arete mainly because it's tainted. That's . . . why we have to bleed others in the first place," she said softly, gently stirring at her section of the platter. "Otherwise our own production will slow, dry up, and we'll die. And our own is naturally limited, anyway—it's not free-flowing like yours. It doesn't burn like a gas-fed fire."

She felt his eyes on her for a long moment, giggles and laughter drifting from the other side of the room. "I guess that makes you a wood-fed fire."

"Or a fire that needs feeding." She smiled humourlessly. "Arete, specifically. Or what you call Fire."

"Actually, we do call it Arete. In the OI, at least. My family still calls it Fire, but I'm more used to Arete at this point."

She offered him a smile, a hint of sadness clinging to it. "You aren't even a Rachnid. You shouldn't have to call it that."

"I call it that because it's easier." His head cocked, eyes steady on hers and vaguely searching. "Is that a bad thing?"

"No, it's just . . . sad, to me." Her gaze wandered to the glowing bars of the radial heater chugging quietly in the wall. "We've taken so much from you— from humans—but all we've given back is what you deserved in the first place. Freedom. Equal standing. Basic rights. But the moment it's convenient, we take it all back. We don't have to bleed humans; there are other creatures with enough Arete, but we take your children because they overflow with it. It's what you said before. We just see you as cattle."

"Not all of you do."

Resting on his folded arms, he offered her a small smile as her eyes met his again, and she noted that she'd been wrong. They weren't brown, more an amber hue that caught the soft light, warm as his expression.

She sighed. "Too many of us do. The Occoon, most higher threads . . . even those in the same social circles."

"Well, our own people aren't much better when they get that high, if it's any consolation. Nobody cares what happens in the roots." He took one of the last sticks, biting into the end, still holding her gaze. "I'm glad somebody seems to care, though."

"I wish it made a difference." She took a small bite of her own, resting on her elbows. "But I'm a small thread in the web compared to them. And they don't want change, they want to sweep it under the couch; they want to make political points off the stories and bloat on the praise. The average person doesn't know how *far* these webs spread, how many children are taken, how much tar is distributed. They only hear about it through the news."

He stayed quiet as she continued, "We could have done more tonight, if Olekan wasn't so damned set on his own political image and making a show of following through on his promises. We had to make a theatre of the entire operation so that everyone in Rathnea can see how he's 'cracking down' on the drug-tenders. And *this* is the problem. We have to work tied down to the public and the Occoon's good will, while these spiders breed like spidorcions in the dark.

"If we could match them web for web, shadow for shadow." She shook her head, appetite abruptly lost. "If we could, everyone would accuse us of doing nothing. You can't work in secret and announce how well it's all going, can you?"

"Sounds like you're under a lot of stress."

She huffed a soft laugh. "I won't be after tonight." Lifting her eyes to his sympathetic ones, she gave him a brief, genuine smile. "Thank you, though. For understanding."

"Well," he said softly, "I joined for the same reason."

By then, all the sticks except her half-eaten one were gone. Tearing off the end, she offered it to him, resting her chin on her hand. "We have a few minutes."

Kalethao accepted the stick and the invitation to talk reflected in her silver eyes. "I didn't exactly grow up in the nicest of areas. Not much enforcement and a lot of Rachnid groups. Joining the OI just seemed like the obvious choice."

For a moment he chewed on a mouthful that melted instantly from crunch to soft, fluffy inside. "Seeing your sisters get harassed by humans and Rachnids, nearly getting drained a few times, and having your youngest sister snatched helps a little with that."

"Your sister was taken?" she asked quietly.

"She was one of the lucky ones. We found her a couple days later after she managed to escape." Since there were no more sticks, he dipped his borrowed one into the last of the tangy sauce, playing with the little tie. "She was cut up, bruised, and traumatised, but they didn't bother too much. I've heard girls don't have as much Arete. Not as desirable."

"The difference is negligible," Hazche murmured, her eyes drifting off past him again. "It's more that they don't tend to restore it as quickly. Not as 'fiery', I suppose."

"They've never met my sisters, then." He smirked humourlessly, popping the last of the stick into his mouth. The expression faded after only a moment, and he exhaled quietly. "I want the same thing as you, Hazche. I want a world my sisters and their subs can feel safe in, where they're free to pass a Rachnid in the street without having to worry if they're going to get pounced on. A world where people care."

Come to think of it, practically all the others in the business had similar goals: a better world, to change something; see the streets become safer, cleaner. People like Anhu, who were gone now. People like Hazche, who might be forced out because she'd dared to take a stand. People like him.

For a long moment there was silence, and he finally stirred with a sigh, pushing back from the table to stand. "And if we want that, we'd better get our creepers moving."

"Kale."

He almost froze, inadvertently locking eyes with her as she smiled up at him. "You're a good man. If neither of us are court-martialed and locked away after today, I'd be happy to promote you to a place under my command."

"I . . ."

She took his brief blank completely the wrong way. "Only if you're willing. If by some miracle the Centre Thread allows all of this, then take some time to think about it. My line is always open."

He stood there silently, blinking, as she pushed back her own chair and stood, moving to the counter. "I hope you don't mind me calling you Kale. I prefer not to keep things formal when I don't have to—it's just easier that way."

Finally shaking himself, he smiled wryly, following her. *You can call me whatever you like, ma'am.* "I don't mind at all."

"Any sign of our friends?"

"Still not so much as a twitch in the web," Hazche's voice confirmed behind him. "So far, this bodes well."

Especially since it meant the gang really didn't have any idea who they were. Just an unlucky coincidence they'd run into them in the first place. The little detour had been nice, but he couldn't say he wasn't glad to get back to their original mission, not with a thousand possibilities that they might move the subs early or catch on to the whole thing hanging over his head.

"Well, looks like the place." He slid his ocular specs—emulated senses didn't do much in the magnification department—back into their hip satchel, gazing across the dingy road at the ugly, half-melted and peeling building he'd been observing. "I can't see anyone inside, though."

"Nothing from your spectramour?"

He shook his head. "Must have blocks in place. Can't catch the subs, either."

"A completely abandoned waystation hub," she murmured. "There are too many threads leading into it, and this is where the lure ends. It's the lair, alright."

He glanced at her as she stared at the building. "So, are we going in?"

"As soon as the transport is in place. Just in case." A hint of a smile curved at her lip. "Just in case", indeed. "And as Ale has been complaining to me for the last five minutes, attempting to land-skim a compacted command shuttle through streets like these isn't easy."

"At least it'll be easier to take it back." *With a proper Rachnid on board to set the thread, should be able to recall all the way back to the edge of the city.* Hopefully, at least. He'd never personally seen the large-scale emulator used in action before; the personalised ones tended to have less range than a real Rachnid, so this should be interesting. More interesting than the mental image of a squashed-in lander creeping through the streets.

"They're in place," she announced after a while. "Each team should be ready on the perimeter by the time we're inside in case things go sideways, or we find an . . . *opportunity* . . . and feeds are open. Let's engage in some shroud and stinger, shall we?"

"Sir." He grinned, brushing an imaginary speck of dust off the shoulder of his civvy jacket and checking to make sure nothing underneath showed. Wouldn't do to have his specs or flash-pops fall out in the middle of everything. "Hope there aren't too many blood-suckers inside. Though from the looks of it, they're closed up tight."

"It is slightly unusual, isn't it?" She commented as they crossed the street, the dim orange light glistening off her coat. "Keep your eyes open. I have a feeling things won't be quite as simple as we want them to be."

Casting her a sideways glance, he moved ahead up the dingy steps to open the—thankfully normal—door for her. *<You don't happen to be a seer, do you?>*

Only a brief smile touched her lips in answer as she brushed past him. *<Stay alert, enforcer.>*

"We're not taking customers tonight."

A low, threatening voice caught his ear as he turned, the low, moody red light inside reflecting off a forehead holding more glinting eyes than skin. Full antlered horns with sharp tines curved over the totally bald head of a Rachnid who towered over them, covered in violent tattoos, his extremely sharp spider fangs flexing.

At least it was in his mission parameters to act unsettled.

"I thought this was supposed to be an open eat. Is it invite-only?" Hazche stood her ground easily, despite being slightly shorter than Kalethao, and even smaller compared to the hulking spider.

"There's no business tonight."

"Not even for a share deal?" Her hand waved languidly in Kalethao's direction. "I'll happily pay, but I want a *young* one. I'm sure there's one or two of you who would love a more . . . mature vessel."

The hairs on the back of his neck prickled at her tone. *She's a little too good at this.*

The massive Rachnid's primary eyes ran over him silently, the usually slitted pupils dilated in the low light. "The web-mother does like his type. Might open up the pantry for you. Come with me."

He turned, and before Kalethao could even take a step, Hazche's hand closed around his arm, guiding him forward. Almost dragging him, really.

They moved through a dark hallway, crimson glow-lights in the ribbed walls briefly driving his imagination to picture them walking down a driller's long throat. If a throat had flimsy screen doorways, dark mould stains creeping in at the edges of the carpet and veining the ceiling. *Is it damp enough for mould, here . . . ?*

Soft footsteps followed as they moved up a sweeping stairway, and he glanced back briefly to see more Rachnids shadowing them. One—a woman—chittered at him, a pair of sharp spider-legs waving in the corner of his eye, teasing for the side of his head.

A sharp hiss in his ear twitched them away, and he nearly jumped, Hazche's cold eyes flicking back ahead of them without a word.

Passing through an archway at the end, they found themselves in an open room, red ceiling lights contrasting with the softer ambience from large windows along one wall. Sweet-smelling fog drifted through it like a mist—incense?—itching at his nose and burning his throat, forcing him to hold his breath for a moment or break into a choking fit. It stung his eyes, too, the shadowy silhouette of spider-legs attached to a seated humanoid—and distinctly feminine—figure blurring slightly as they came to a halt.

She rose from the impression of a half-circled couch, sashaying towards them.

<Prepare a flasher, just in case. There are at least twenty in this room.>

Hazche's voice broke into his mind, and he blinked rapidly, attempting to clear his vision. *<Acknowledged. Damned if I can see, though.>*

"I hear you've got a little gift for me . . . ?"

As Hazche stepped forward to negotiate an after-hours dinner special, he mentally dipped into the weapons currently linked to his net, and the pair of flash-pops—specifically designed to take out Rachnids—in particular. Quietly slipping his thumbs into his belt, he brushed one of them, setting it in his mind to a focused flat-line blast radius, ready to activate at a squeeze. Anyone caught below the cut-off would be out like a light. *<It's set. If you need it, hit the ceiling.>*

Abruptly, a pair of fingers brushed his shoulder, and he twitched a glance over to see through still-watering eyes the same Rachnid Hazche had hissed away, now cosying up to him. "I hope she lets more than one take a share. Your Arete has such a nice swirl to it . . ."

Eugh. He tilted his head back slightly, letting a smile play at the corner of his mouth with a wink. "It's because I'm such a pure soul. I hope you don't like playing with your food, though. I'm not exactly *open* for anything extra, right now."

Either she was shocked he'd dared to speak back, or turned on, because those blurry eyes stared unblinkingly at him for an uncomfortably long moment.

"Well, that's a nice offer. Unfortunately, I don't deal with your . . . type." The voice of their host brought his attention back, her eyes glowing through the mist, streaky in his watery vision. "The human though, I'll enjoy him after your death, enforcer."

Enforcer. A chill ran up his spine in spite of himself, her red gaze seeming to lock on his. Well, there went the cat. *Is it the way we stood? Some OI aura? The hair?*

More likely it was that tail they'd thrown off. Damn. *Not exactly how I saw the "just in case" going, but we can't complain.* His muscles tensed, waiting for the—

<Kalethao! Now!>

In the space between heartbeats, the irritating mist freezing to a crawl, his thumb flicked up the flash-pop, pressing the smooth surface between his fingers.

And squeezed.

In an instant, the blinding white afterimage cut through the blackness behind his lids, like the faint pop sucked at his ears. All around him, he felt more than heard them thud to the floor, sound oddly muffled for a moment. Fluff stuffed in his ears. Always a strange feeling.

Letting out a puff of a breath, he dropped his hand and opened his eyes, glancing down at the slumped bodies on the floor and blinking rapidly at the returned stinging. "Hazche? Sir?"

His gaze flicked up at a faint movement to see her descend from the ceiling. "They should be unconscious for a while—"

. . . That wasn't Hazche.

Jecc! He threw himself back from the monster that leapt out at him, throwing an arm up. Too late.

A blur bowled him over, a sharp black leg stabbing past him. He hit the floor hard, breath punched from his lungs as his armour belatedly flickered to life, bracing for the flash of twin fangs—

The figure leapt past him.

What? He twisted onto his elbow, fighting for breath, scrabbling for the compact holstered on his back. Just as the hairs on the back of his neck shot up.

A flicker of movement stabbed out in the corner of his eye.

Spider-legs slammed him down again. He choked on his own lungs, barely twisting away from twin knife-points.

Pure adrenaline pounded through his veins. Coiling up, he kicked out, catching the underbelly of another, more bestial Rachnid. With a screech, it reared back just long enough for him to roll onto his feet, nearly stumbling onto his face again as he hacked in a breath and almost coughed out a lung. That damned smoke was *not* helping.

<Thao what just happened? CW Hazche is unresponsive—>

Another leg blurred for him, catching his shoulder as he tried to twist. Fighting for balance, he could barely get his bearings, let alone—

The force of a metal pipe swung by a crane slammed into his chest, a white flash cracking through the smoke—"*Nghk!*"—echoed by the crash of a wall smashing into his back.

Four blurry glinting points stabbed around him, and he reflexively jerked back, grabbing at a pair of fangs lunging for his face.

He could barely hold them, the appendages jolting in his hands, arms shaking. Gritting his teeth, he fought to keep them *back* out of pure instinct, the scaly Rachnid—gone dragon all the sricking way, screeching in his face with needle teeth he was sure . . . were probably pearly white and glinting if he could— "*Nngh!*"—see more than a blurry mess right then.

If only I could . . . pull out my jeccing compact!

The Rachnid jerked back, ripping out of his grip, and he threw himself down, a force shaking the wall just above him.

<*Thao, report!*>

<*CONTACT! We need—*>

Ducking out of the way of an extra pair of flailing spider-legs, he clawed under the back of his jacket, fingertips brushing the compact hidden beneath the loose material—

And shoved himself further back from the fangs as it broke free and tried to impale him. Which left him right underneath its abdomen in range of the stinger.

Jecc! A ragged laugh briefly escaped his lips an instant before it connected. In a flash of crackling white, the barb slammed into his armour, tingles chasing over his scalp and down his spine, setting his teeth on edge. *Thank the*—Rolling, he threw himself out from underneath, scraping against a leg.—*All-Weaver for Angel armour.*

He darted his hand under the jacket again, twisting to face the blur of the Rachnid and belatedly registering the fangs practically in his face, just as his fingers closed around the grip.

But I don't want more hits like that.

For the second time, the smoke flew past him, the distinct *crack* of glass breaking slamming into his shoulder blades. And for a dazed instant his heart instinctively clenched in his throat, expecting the tug of free-fall, warm metal under his fingertips—wherever those were. No sense of falling dragged him down, no glints of glass and the eery light of the planet in the sky. Just a big ugly spider-dragon-demon lunging for him.

His hand closed around a familiar grip, a flash of thought searing through his neural pathways to the right setting, and the dull glint of a solid muzzle snapped into view.

The wide flare of it cut through the dull red light.

About half a moment before the leg aiming to scoop him across the room jolted from its path and slammed into his head.

A dimly-lit floor fuzzed in and out of focus, bleary. Dark shapes, too, like the back of someone's body lying on the floor, or maybe a cushion—couldn't quite catch it long enough to tell, or rearrange his scattered thoughts long enough to muse it out. His eyes still stung, though. *Probably a Rachnid. Hope the rest are all down . . . don't want to do that again.* A cough seized his chest, and he pushed himself woozily up, shaking his head to clear it.

A small mistake, on his part, since the movement sent a sharp flash of pain shooting briefly through his head and neck. He groaned softly, rubbing at the offending areas and glancing over at where the Rachnid should have been.

Well, what was left of it. More of a mess now than anything, its dark blood seeping across the floor.

Dragging himself to his feet, he scooped up his compact from where it had fallen, picking his stumbling way back towards the couch. *Hazche . . . ?* The woman seemed to have a sixth sense for things going wrong, but *that* plan sure hadn't survived contact with the enemy. Especially the one that had escaped. He ran a hand through his loose hair, squinting myopically through the smoky dizziness and feeling vaguely like he was going blind.

Should've put the lucky tie back on. Needed that.

A soft groan met his ears, and he nearly stumbled over a body, abruptly registering the dim white. "Hazche? Command-Weaver?"

". . . forcer Thao?" She stirred, the still-blurry—despite his currently invisible helmet blocking the smoke—impression of her silver eyelashes fluttering.

He dropped a little heavily to his knees beside her, carefully checking her pulse just in case she was more sensitive to the flash-pop's worse effects. "Right here. We had a pair of Rachnids unaffected by the blast. One got away, and the other's neutralised."

"'Got away'?" She murmured groggily. "Who?"

"Whoever ended up on the ceiling instead of you."

"The web-mother . . . we have to—" She broke off with a soft hiss as she tried to rise, and Kalethao gently pushed her back down again, his spectramour notifying him of friendlies inbound on their location.

"Take your time, backup should be on its way."

"We can't afford to. If she's loose, she might go after the subs—" She grunted softly, resolutely moving to rise again, and he reluctantly let her. "I've seen it happen before. A hostage situation—trying to salvage what's left and force us to compromise. If none of the teams intercept her, things could get very ugly."

He glanced up as the others appeared. "Then we'd better make sure she's found."

GRADUALLY, THINGS CONGEALED INTO PROPER FOCUS AGAIN, THE SOFT RINGING IN her ears and the throb under her skull taking the forefront. With a soft hiss of pain, Hazche slowly drew herself up, Kale's grip moving to help her.

"Thank you." Gently rubbing at her temple, she glanced over the room at the other enforcers slipping through the haze of incense and checking unconscious Rachnids. From the stream of chatter—limited by her integration systems themselves until neural activity settled—she caught the gist of the rest of the operation: minor contact, mostly scattered, and no casualties. A general inquiry revealed no sign of the web-mother.

"They haven't located her yet." Gingerly, she moved to stand, grateful for the steadying hand offered. "Considering her dirty tactics, I wouldn't be surprised if she's using recall threads to avoid everyone."

"Hopefully she uses them to escape instead of going after the subs," he said, exchanging gestures with someone in the corner of her eye.

Coarse gestures, she noted with a brief hint of a smile. "I hope you're right. Problems?"

He grimaced. "Just getting snipped at for leaving the helmet off. I think I'm allergic to this incense."

The helmet in question floated there like a ghost, to her senses, but now that she was paying attention, his eyes *did* look a tad reddened underneath. She hid a smile with a sympathetic hum, moving to the doorway at a brisk stride. "I hope you're alright to move. I can track her, but we'll need to be ready in case she's making a hostage play."

"It's already clearing," he said. "By the way, Dam says they haven't located them yet. That warehouse the sub talked about is empty."

She noted the uneasiness in his voice as she strode down the stairway into the halls, running her fingers through the intangible strands trailing in the air. The high-pitched buzz of a sporadic scatter of laser-pulse fire echoed from elsewhere, twinging in her ears. "The warehouse would be for loading and unloading. They'll be hidden somewhere else. A basement, most likely."

"Awfully cautious of them."

"They aren't the biggest group," she said absently, her own strands glimmering into life, capturing fragmented impressions of fear and hunger winding down through a darkened corridor. "On the rise, but it's more others they're worried about. This building would have been a major asset."

A soft vibration shivered at her thread, and her footsteps slowed. The touch of someone else, twanging at the edge of her web . . .

There she is.

The weave opened up in her eyes, illuminating the passageway and its looming, uneven pattern. *Down here . . .* she felt more than saw, the dull ache in her skull and the soft sound of her footsteps distant to the echoes of sobs and pain reflected in every silver strand. And the shadow lurking on its edges—a multilegged stain creeping into its lair, sinister intent in every movement.

"This way. She's after them."

More stairs rushed beneath her, the spiralling veined walls flashing past, a soft curse brushing her ears. A Rachnid prowled here, hunting the young and shivering souls that haunted this place—a predator.

Her web flared through a narrow room festooned in odds and ends, boxes shoved aside to reveal a lair cover, and lit a shadow lurking in the dark entrance.

The web-mother's head snapped up, eyes glowing.

"You."

Spectral extensions snapped from Hazche's back in answer, flashing out in a crackling blur. They slammed into the other's manifested limbs, sending her stumbling, and she lunged forward.

The other twisted aside, a dark limb whirling around with the movement. It slashed across her shoulder with its sharp edge, staggering her back with a gasping hiss, a hot flare searing through her skin. "*Hff.*"

In an instant the other Rachnid leapt for her, needle teeth glinting in a snarl, eyes glowing like embers. Her own burned silver, extensions manifesting to solidity in a stabbing flash.

The crunching thud echoed in the abrupt silence.

A crown of wide eyes stared at her above limbs protruding from the web-mother's chest and pinning her to the wall, a soft croak gurgling in the woman's throat. With a final flicker, their glow winked out, shaking fingers falling limp.

Hazche released a long, slow breath, drawing her manifested striking pair back. The chitinous segments clicked softly, the stink of blood and musty basement tingling at their setae. Dutifully doing her best to ignore the slick sensation and the soft sucking sound, she let the corpse slide to the ground without a second look, vaporising the stains with a surge of crackling energy, and turned to the lair's entrance. "Thao?"

". . . Sir." He slowly lowered his compact in the corner of her eye, moving to the opening. She couldn't blame him for sounding queasy.

Folding the extra limbs away again, letting the nanoweave of her clothing reform itself and seal the wound on her shoulder, she joined him, burning away the webbed gateway he'd just stepped through. Instantly, a whisper of soft sounds caught her ear, dim lamps lighting a room the size of a warehouse. One filled with young, hushed humans, all eyes turned to the entrance.

<CW, building is secured. Transport is onsite and ready to load.>

She smiled, resting a hand on Kalethao's shoulder as the man let out a breath. "I think it's time we got them home."

KALETHAO WATCHED A ROOM OF LAUGHING CHILDREN, ARMS FOLDED, AN uncontrollable smile on his face. *It's worth it. Just for this.*

Three of them in particular kept catching his eye, a little girl squealing as her brother half-picked her up in a hug, almost losing his balance and rocking into his older sister. He could hear their laughter from across the space, even over the rest of the babble.

"Kale." A hand beckoned in the corner of his eye, and he turned to find Hazche there. She gestured him to follow again, and he cocked an eyebrow, obliging.

"Have they got back to us already?" He *had* been hoping to keep the sense of happiness for a while longer.

"They have."

He thought he could see a hint of a smile, there. *Wait* . . .his heart rate kicked into gear again. "And?"

"Well, Olekan has just had a major boost to his political image, thanks to the media coverage of an incredible rescue operation." She finally turned to face him just inside the doorway to the communications closet, the smile fully revealed. "And Arathen has put out a short statement well-wishing the families of the kidnapped children."

That quickly? He barely dared to hope, an answering smile creeping over his face. "Then . . . ?"

She chuckled. "I'm on probation so far as my superiors are concerned, but they can't touch me. Not with the reporters having the time of their lives."

A rush of relief escaped his lungs in a breath he hadn't realised he'd been holding. A miracle. They really had gotten a sricking miracle. In a slightly giddy huff, a laugh broke free as he ran a hand through his hair. "This is the best dream I've ever had."

"Well, if you want another, maybe you'll think about my offer." She smiled slightly lopsidedly and folded her arms, joy reflected in her own eyes as she leaned playfully towards him. "And you can tell me what you decide over a proper meal."

He stared for possibly a moment longer than he should have, the babble of laughter and chatter around them briefly forgotten. Had she just . . . ?

She made a shooing gesture, a hint of a grin in her expression. "Now off with you, enforcer. We need to lighten the load before we can take these children back. You have your own carrier to get to."

I think I just got invited out.

He cast one last glance over the smiles lighting the subs' eyes and grinned back at her, tracing the highest gesture of respect with a flourishing bow.

"Yes ma'am."

Beloved of the Electric Valkyrie

Scott R. Parkin

Anywhere here will be adequate, Jacob," the Hilde AI said on private comms in her rich alto voice.

I picked a spot and dropped to a knee, plunged my left hand a half-meter deep into endless, pebbly gray ground like fat kitty litter or fossilized cottage cheese—small curd.

"How's it taste, Stern?" Medeiros asked as he jogged past and took up a sentry position thirty meters further west.

"Like manna soaked in mother's milk," I said. "You should try it sometime. Hilde could arrange that, you know."

"I prefer human flavors, you cross-wired garbage-eater."

"Put a lid on it, gentlemen. This is mission time; Hilde's recording everything," Klein growled. Then under his breath, "I bet you actually remember the taste of your mama's milk, Stern."

I laughed as the rest of the squad silently took up a fan formation—Zbilski and Takashi to my left; Rachel and Klein to my right. Standard procedure: there *was* a Crab nearby.

The soil actually tasted like chalkdust and ozone—exactly like the five hundred seventeen other samples I'd sniffed out on this forsaken waste of a planet. Not just statistically similar, but chemically identical to the limits of my sensors, and at max gain I can taste single atoms.

A perfectly homogeneous blend of basic elements. Impossible in nature or by any known technology. Not on a planetary scale.

I had just plunged to two-thirds meters for a second taste when the klaxon went off. I stood up and scanned the horizon, a stark line dividing the featureless expanse of ashen gray earth from the blackness of space on a planet with no atmosphere.

The Crab appeared straight to the south. Medeiros' thin form blinked out suddenly as his exoframe duplicated his surroundings on its surfaces. I watched his blip on the tactical heads-up as he ran in a sweeping arc to the southeast.

I raised my left hand and used its extended resolution sensor array to try to sniff it out. I picked up the distinctive cera-metallic tang of the Crab's own exosuit from three hundred meters; saw its mottled blue shell a few seconds later. "Standard Crab," I said on team comm. "Moving at fifteen meters per second."

"We want to speak with you," Rachel said in a soothing voice on all available channels. She stood still with arms at her sides, her bright red armor a shock of color against gray ground. "We mean you no harm, but we will defend ourselves. Please acknowledge."

No response as the Crab scuttled on metal legs straight toward Rachel while she repeated the broadcast.

"Not again," Takashi whispered.

Zbilski spoke in a flat tenor voice that seemed far too high for his frame's formidable size. "Same as the others. Three-meter diameter protective shell appears environmental rather than tactical. Small plasma cannon is *not* a threat; repeat, *zero* threat."

"Hear that, Medeiros?" Klein called out. "We are not in da—"

The Crab fired its plasma cannon. Before the rapidly cooling energy bolt even deflected harmlessly off Rachel's polished armor, the Crab fell suddenly off its legs and lay still.

Medeiros appeared as if out of nowhere as his frame's camo skin shifted back to matte black, his needle rifle at the ready.

"Stand down!" Klein said. "Do not fire again."

"Should have listened to the lady," Medeiros said and stepped back without lowering his weapon.

The stink of formaldehyde and coppery sea water rose into the still, empty air. Murky turquoise blood marbled with burgundy hydraulic oil oozed from the single needle hole. It pooled briefly then ran down the curved ceramic-metal shell and dripped onto the pebbly ground.

"Contamination confirmed," I said. "Non-local fluid has contacted the soil."

Takashi knelt at the Crab's side. "Why won't they even try to talk to us?" she said as she touched its shell, her head cocked to one side. "No heartbeat or respiration. It's dead."

"Our frames are twice the size of theirs; we were never at risk," Zbilski said. "I could have easily caught and held it."

"It was a clean kill," Medeiros said. "By the book."

"Maybe, but still unnecessary," Rachel snapped.

"Sector contamination noted and logged," Hilde's voice said over team comm, interrupting what would have been a pointless, if entertaining fight. "Initiate isolation protocol."

"Bag it and tag it," Klein growled. "I want to move on in five. Hurry it up."

THE PLANETARY ASSESSMENT CORPORATION ISN'T MILITARY, THOUGH WE ARE A direct contractor. Still, culture tends to transfer and we've adopted some of traditional military's practices while providing them with our exoframe technology.

We also retain full rights to our own tech and develop it independently. We don't just wear frames like the military does; we fully integrate with them through direct neural and sensory induction: the Hilde AI belongs entirely to us. Hard on the pilot, but worth the physical atrophy to directly experience the otherwise unknowable.

It's an upgrade we'll sell when the time comes. But for now, off-planet, it's no one else's business. Literally.

Part of PAC culture is training in tactics alongside our areas of scientific specialty. Klein commands; Medeiros acts as sentry; I do chemical and Takashi does bio analysis; Zbilski's heavy labor and field engineering; Rachel's a paleontologist.

No visible need for the last on this survey. G-mat is astonishingly sterile. Still, we're a unit and all members play each time.

(Point of accuracy: according to PAC's Prioritized Designation List—aka, majority shareholder roster—the planet's official name is Giacometti. But who has time to choke out that many syllables? Dock my pay if you don't like it.)

I like the discipline; it keeps us safe and focused.

Still, it wouldn't hurt my feelings if Medeiros would choose scientific inquiry over procedure once in a while.

I CONSIDERED THE DEAD CRAB.

After less than two minutes the needle-hole had already stopped oozing in G-mat's near-vacuum, the flecked blue fluid now a dried plug filling the gap.

I pulled the can of iso out of my right thigh-pack and sprayed the drip site, then knelt and jammed my left hand into the pebbly ground next to it to taste how far contamination had penetrated. The coppery seawater odor was faint and fading fast.

I gave Zbilski a thumbs-up. He'd already examined the crude plasma cannon jury-rigged to its armored shell and crushed the discharge mechanism. He stepped over the Crab and pried the rigid outer shell up. It resisted for only a moment, then popped open under his powerful grip.

I raised my left hand over the Crab and tasted both the organic and inorganic vapors that billowed up in a dirty yellow cloud as I moved quickly around to my right. Oxygen rich—well over double Earth standard—but flavored with the dull tang of heavy metals, the flat dustiness of standard minerals, and the sharp aromatics of radioactivity, strontium isotope. Nothing new from a chemical standpoint, and only normal amounts of water.

Whatever their morphology, Crabs were no water-breathers. Likely they came from a heavy world with a thickened atmosphere. In other words, they weren't any more native to G-mat and its functional vacuum and seven-tenths Earth-grav than we were.

So why were they here? And why so belligerent?

Before the vapor cloud finished rising, Zbilski began to clip the hoses and straps of the Crab's life-support and safety harnesses as Takashi reached in and plucked out the relatively small organic being nestled deep inside. It looked like a large horseshoe crab about a meter across, but with an exaggerated frontal ridge and longer legs, each tipped with four delicate, articulated fingers. She slipped it into a clear polymer bag and pulled the seal tab as she stepped back.

"I would really like to examine a live one," Takashi said.

Rachel slammed the lid and Zbilski threw two orange straps over it (same color as his armor), flipped the Crab over, and ratcheted them down while I sprayed iso around the edge to re-seal it, and on the ground to contain escaped gases and particulates.

I bent down and tasted both the surface and a hand's-length below. Within seconds the last hints of Crab residues were gone. Only the musty ozone-and-chalkdust pall of the ubiquitous gray matrix remained.

I couldn't help but smile despite a nagging sense of unease as we stood over the Crab's empty hard suit. Nothing is quite as satisfying as a well-executed process.

"Thank you, team," Hilde said. "Exemplary containment."

"Yeah, yeah—nice work. But let's not run this drill again," Klein growled. "Can you manage that, Medeiros?"

"I detect no further Crab presence on the planet," Hilde said. "You should be able to work without further interruption."

"No Crabs, no problem," Medeiros said in a chirpy voice. "Happy to have nothing to do—sorta like you, Rae."

"Up yours, Medeiros," Rachel said.

"No can do," he replied. "Despite its many wonders, my exoframe has no external entry ports." He pointed toward the next survey sector. "Time to go."

The spill *was* contained, and we still needed almost fifteen hundred site readings before Hilde would let us back inside . . .

"No can do," I said. "I need another sample to make up for the one you just ruined. Ten minutes." I pointed vaguely into the distance as I jogged away from the dead Crab.

Rachel jogged after me.

I chose an area three hundred meters straight west. It was a pointless exercise; I already knew what the samples would show.

Still, if it annoyed Medeiros . . .

"You'd think they'd stop attacking," Rachel said on my private channel.

"Maybe they're just stupid." I scanned the ground for any variation that might suggest a good sample site. Nothing.

"Too organized; too persistent. Definitely not stupid."

"How so?" I picked a spot at random and knelt down. "After we defeated their mass assault, they knew they couldn't win. Yet two days later, the stragglers still blindly charge us."

It was a colossal understatement. We'd killed two hundred eleven Crabs in just under nine minutes, and only Medeiros was armed. A complete massacre.

"Scared, maybe," she said. "There's something they want us to understand and they're willing to die to make that happen."

"Sounds like stupid to me," I muttered.

I plunged my hand into the grainy matrix and took samples at the standard depths: every third of a meter for two meters. Duplicate readings each time.

Rachel knelt beside me and I fed her my spectrographic datastream as it came in. I suspect she's the only other squad member able to appreciate it. As a paleontologist her specialty overlaps pretty much everyone else's—geology, chemistry, biology, physics. Even team and project management.

"It's artificial, isn't it?" she asked.

"Interesting speculation."

"Too uniform," she said. "I looked at the summary of all five hundred eighteen samples. Identical."

"Question is: Who put it there? And why?" I said.

"Not the Crabs?" she asked. "Maybe as habitat or some kind of prep for terraforming?"

"Not from what we've seen of their tech." I scooted over a dozen meters and plunged for another taste. "They're using the same essential basis for invention as we are, but their tech is a century behind. Even their frames are just amplified suits; no neural integration. This . . . dirt, matrix, whatever . . . is beyond them. Or us. It's too perfect—especially if it's been here very long."

Flavors for the six sample depths: Same, same, same, same, same, and boringly, un-differentiably same.

"Fair point," Rachel said. "Someone else, then. Maybe on their behalf? This, um, *overlay*, contains most of the core elements needed for a complex ecology."

Sudden tension throbbed in the back of my skull. The chemical mix was wrong in a way that had bugged me for most of five days. I was missing something important.

"Problem is that it isn't any more useful to the Crabs than it is to us." I scooped up a handful and let the gray nuggets fall through my fingers. "Not a whiff of organics. No free oxygen or nitrogen; no un-oxidized metals; no carbon at all. Or silicon, boron, sulfur, or other alternates for basic biochemistry."

"A clean seedbed, then."

"No. G-mat is both sterile and barren," I said, suddenly peeved. "Nothing can grow here. There's no detectable chemical reactivity—"

Point of accuracy: no constructive reactivity. That was the problem.

"An active chemical entropy engine," I whispered.

"But that's a contradiction—"

"No, it's a process." I gazed down at the gray matrix. "It started to penetrate during containment on that last Crab. We released both organic and inorganic compounds—significant quantities from both the needle shot and cracking the shell. Yet just seconds after release I smelled the last of it vanish while my hand was still in the ground."

"Contained," Rachel said. "You sprayed iso everywhere."

"Then I wouldn't have tasted it at all."

"Evaporated," she said, her voice thinning. "Dissipated. This *is* a vacuum."

"I would have detected a persistent residue, either in the air or the ground." I shook my head. "But I didn't."

"Because it was . . ."

"Decomposed and distributed. At the molecular level. In real time. Tech that violates everything I know about physics."

She sat back hard, brushed the gray, pebbly matrix with bright red poly-alloy fingers. "Then *this* is what the Crabs were afraid of—or whoever put it here. It's the cause of G-mat's sterility."

It answered so many questions while begging so many more. Just what have we stumbled upon, here? Bile rose in my throat.

"Hilde, I need to—"

Every nerve in my body seemed to fire at once.

THE AGONY WAS BEYOND ANYTHING I'VE EVER KNOWN, LANCING DOWN THROUGH my skull and obliterating all perception under wave after wave of pain and stink, flashes of light and color that tasted of memory and impossible sensations all blended together. Filling my body and mind until all I knew was pain and chaos and undifferentiated perception.

I thought I'd inured myself to the threat of overstimulus years ago after I instructed Hilde to dual-route my frame's sensors—including the left hand's high-detail array—through both tactile *and* olfactory nerves. I'd come to peace that even the simplest acts would subject me to intense flavors that would take me years to differentiate and interpret. That the sour-acrid sharpness of organic putrescence might easily prove the most benign new flavor I would savor, deconstruct, and accurately catalog in alien environments.

I've tasted protomatter directly from within a nebular burst and savored the impossible heat of a red giant's corona. I've taken in the flavors of nonhydrocarbon plant life (fuchsia, oily-aromatic, piquant, frictionless) that grew more than a kilometer tall and shimmered with shifting UV patterns.

I thought I was immune to any kind of sensory overload. But I was wrong. This was too much to process. Far too much.

Anything. Please. Just make the agony stop.

THEN IT WAS GONE AND I LAY FLAT ON MY BACK TRYING TO UNDERSTAND WHAT just happened.

"Are you okay?" Rachel asked.

I blinked against the stark contrast of her red helmet against an inky black sky, the bright yellow-white disk of the sun hovering just above her head. Nausea flooded me and I rolled over, tried to recover myself as I stared down at gray cottage cheese that tasted of chalk and ozone. Small curd.

Rachel's trueface appeared on my heads-up, piercing hazel eyes under shocking red hair. Not as it really was now, soaked in hyperoxygenated equalization fluid and webbed by a neural net encased in an armored compartment within her frame's torso. But as it was before, years ago, when we were all younger and healthier and walked on our own legs. Before we sold our lives to the Planetary Assessment Corporation.

It was comforting. We didn't use our trueface icons very often. It was easier to commit to the illusion if you ignored your organics.

"Did you feel . . . that?" I asked in a shaky voice.

"Like being stabbed in the head with an icepick? Yeah."

I rolled over and tried to stand, then thought better of it and sat on the ground.

Rachel gasped. "But you smelled and tasted it, too. No wonder it knocked you down."

"I would rather have skipped that part." I glanced up-right. "Hilde? What just happened?"

"There's been an unexpected discontinuity in my backup system and it bled over. Evaluating."

I let Rachel help me stand on wobbly legs, tried to remember the insight that had dominated my thoughts only moments ago. Absorbent cat litter and Crabs and . . . something else.

Medeiros called out. "Ten minutes are up. Time to go!"

I turned and saw his matte black frame bounding across the flat, featureless plain from the east. The sky above his head was dominated with the unmistakable outlines of a massive silver and blue stellar ship, easily more than a kilometer long. Not ours; had to be Crab. It was angled steeply toward the ground and fell in what seemed like slow motion.

My entire body went weak and I reflexively switched to video broadcast on all channels, suddenly unable to speak. Medeiros turned and his needle rifle fell to the ground.

And I remembered. Fear. There was someone the Crabs feared more even than Humans, who could kill them by the hundreds without real weapons or a single loss. Someone or something even more threatening.

"Hilde!" Klein shouted over the comm. "What am I seeing?"

There was a long silence as the ship continued inexorably down, then Hilde finally spoke.

"We misunderstood how serious they were. I'm sorry."

The ship struck directly over our landing zone, then continued its slow motion descent, the thunder of its impact rumbling through the ground.

"Please die quickly, and without pain," Hilde said quietly.

There *was* pain. Crushing, gasping agony. But only for a moment, then nothingness.

IT TOOK A LONG TIME TO REORIENT. MUTED, PANICKED VOICES. NUMBED FINGERS seeking in the dark. Desperate fatigue and a desire to sleep.

Not yet. People were lost; my people. I can help.

Vision returned, then sensation. I looked back toward the lander site, saw the squared tail of a huge silver and blue stellar ship bending slowly toward the ground as it broke free from its own crushed and ruined fuselage. Eighty klicks away; a ten-minute run at full speed.

My left foot tangled as I stepped forward and I looked down to see Rachel's bright red arms flung forward, her knees hunched under her and her face planted into the pebbly ground.

"Rachel! Are you okay?" I said on team-comm as I knelt down and pulled her flat, rolled her over. No response. "Klein. Takashi. Anyone?"

Nothing.

I unlatched the manual data panel on her right chest, hit the status button. Frame systems green. Bio-functions green. Hilde interface red.

I sat back. The Hilde system had failed, which meant Rachel was cut off inside her armored cocoon. Isolated from the frame's sensory inputs and floating in pressurized equalization fluid that doubled as sensory deprivation chamber.

Alone and disoriented. But alive.

"I'll come back as soon as I can," I said out loud and latched the panel. "I'm sorry."

I checked Medeiros. Same as Rachel. I took off for base, running as fast as I could. As long as the frame systems were active, they could live for up to a year. But without sensory input, they would slowly lose their connections and their sanity.

I had to either repair the Hilde system (Zbilski's specialty) or find a safe place to crack their suits and let them out (Takashi's expertise). Either option started with whatever was left of the lander.

"Hilde," I called as I ran, but of course the AI didn't respond. I checked the status on my heads-up, and it flashed red and yellow. The system was unresponsive, but clearly working well enough to allow me to function normally.

Repairs were still possible.

I checked my systems. Sensory input was muted but operable, and control systems were normal despite the flashing indicator. I checked Takashi, Zbilski, and Klein—the same as Rachel and Medeiros. I was the only one online.

I flipped among the comm channels, found one filled with wheezing and chittering sounds. Clearly organized, but totally incomprehensible. Crabs?

"Hello?" I said. The chittering stopped. "My name is Jacob Stern. Can you understand me? I need help."

There was a brief pause, then a high voice screeched, "Die! Vanish! Die!" over and over again. I tried to interrupt, but it was relentless. I flipped to a different channel and found the same. After ten channels commanding me to die, I muted the comm.

I was two minutes from the lander when an icon flashed on my heads-up. Red hair and piercing eyes. "Rachel!" I shouted. "You're back!"

". . . primary destroyed . . . failover damaged . . ." Hilde's distinctive alto voice said on private channel. ". . . protect data . . . activate failsafe . . . please, Jacob—"

The signal cut off, then: "Die! Vanish! Die!" I muted it again.

Protect data? Activate failsafe? What did that mean?

The landing site was not how I remembered. Not merely because it was crushed under the mountainous debris of the Crab mothership, but because it was a hardened bunker cut deep into the ground instead of the armored lander and lab that I had helped dig into the surface myself just five days ago. Remnants of military-grade tactical armor still stood amongst the wreckage. That armor could take hits from field disruption weapons—only the overwhelming mass of this kind of physical impact could have shattered it.

It was impossible to build this kind of bunker in only five days.

The picture came clear in an instant. Sensory feeds. Hilde had fed us bogus data to hide the fact that we were not the first arrival team. Now that Hilde was down I was truly seeing it for the first time.

But why hide it at all? We were all security-cleared and fully committed. I needed more data.

I picked my way through the rubble, past hundreds of unarmored Crab corpses and the twisted debris of strange tech. Cloying, coppery seawater stink rose from each corpse, then faded as I passed. I brushed everything with my left hand and tasted minerals, ceramics, interesting alloys that used radioactive metals to enable near-superconductivity—spicy and sweet and aromatic like menthol or wasabi. I found a gap leading down.

There's a detached, surreal quality to the massively unfamiliar that makes it easier to deal with. Though untold questions swirled, two basic ideas anchored my mind.

First, given a choice, it would always be Humanity first, no matter what lies I'd been told or by whom.

Second, no one is left behind. I may not save everyone, but I would give everything I had in the attempt. We're a team.

It *had* occurred to me that I might still be living some kind of sim, that once I committed to sensory induction through Hilde so many years ago, everything I'd known since might be an elaborate ruse serving unknown uses for manipulating bastards back at the PAC.

Doesn't matter. I choose who I am inside my own head—and how I act as a result. The rest takes care of itself, in time.

I worked down through a half-dozen crushed sublevels. No sealed areas or protected places where I could crack the frames and let my friends out; no operable comms that would let me call down a rescue pod from our unmanned mothership; no functioning access to facility datasystems. As the darkness deepened, I used picowave reflection imaging to retain adequate vision.

Hilde appeared again on my heads-up, still wearing Rachel's trueface. "... discontinue . . . activate failsafe . . . core data taken . . ." Her distinctive alto voice distorted, broke up, then changed into Rachel's thin soprano. ". . . dying . . . only you . . . give them peace . . ."

Sudden rage rose up, and I cut off the transmission, then instantly regretted it. Though Hilde had obviously lied to me, she was also my only guide and partner at this point.

I found the crushed ruin of Hilde's hardware on level eight. Row after row of toppled and crushed server racks fiber-linked together. A half-dozen Crab corpses were scattered among the debris, all wearing hard suits. A panel at my feet read, "Harbaugh Induction™ Life-Comm Duplication Environment."

Beyond salvage, even for Zbilski. Not without working fabrication tech, stable lab space, and more time than I think my people have left. I wondered where the backup was.

I found our own bodies on the next level down.

Though the room was mostly intact, the forward structure of the Crab mothership and hardened ceramic debris from our own ceiling had fallen across the far side, precariously propped against the smashed tops of the last two of six massive black boxes. Curled, yellowed strips of old masking tape were stuck to the end of each box, our names hand-written in blue marker.

The box with my name was fully crushed, only the forward-left corner still intact and bearing the weight of the Crab bulkhead, the pale stains of evaporated fluids all around its base. Medeiros' box was mostly smashed, but its angled lid and three stable corners held the ruin of the ceiling and kept it from destroying the remaining four boxes. Five unlabeled indicator lights below the names on the first four boxes showed green, flashing yellow, red, red, red. Mine and Medeiros' lights all glared solid red.

How was that even possible?

Hilde appeared again. Instead of just an icon on my heads-up, this time she projected a full image in the center of my display. She still wore Rachel's head, but it sat atop a bare-breasted figure clad to the waist in billowy white linen and carrying a huge broadsword held up to block my path. Angel wings flowed from smooth shoulders. I recognized it from a game sim and laughed.

"What are you supposed to be? Some kind of electric valkyrie? Come to reap among the dead?"

The image shifted and the body was now tall and lithe, fully clad in chrome armor. She pointed the sword at me.

". . . no time . . . dying . . . afraid. Only you . . . give peace." She used Rachel's voice.

"Don't you dare speak to me with that face and that voice!" I shouted. "Those things don't belong to you."

"Limited resource . . . library destroyed . . . rebuilding . . . too slow . . ."

I saw how closely her face mirrored my own frustration and my rage subsided. She had critical intel but suddenly lacked the tools to share it. A perfect inversion to own my frantic search for knowledge.

"How?" I whispered. "Anything. Just explain this to me."

Fierce satisfaction transformed her eyes as she lunged forward and stabbed at my head with the sword. In the instant before it struck I saw the fine traces of circuits dancing on its surface and opened myself to the blow.

"Understand," she said in her own rich alto voice.

THE DATA TRANSFER WAS INSTANTANEOUS AND NEARLY OVERWHELMED ME. BUT I had learned long ago to interpret through multiple streams, and unlike the random noise that knocked me flat before, this signal was organized. So I simply took it in on all channels, through all senses until I felt that I could see and hear, smell and taste, savor and feel through every cell in my body.

The picture came clear.

The sensory-induction boxes were a precaution. Frames were too expensive to repair remotely, so it was critical to instill caution in the pilots to protect their frames by believing their lives depended on it. That pragmatism enabled both safety and operational convenience, so the lie was maintained.

That we'd been fed sims to fill the mundane gaps between missions *was* disappointing. It seems only in-frame experiences were true, original sensory induction. A lie, to be sure. But not quite betrayal. And actually permitted by contract.

But we had never been told of the wormhole that extended our reach by a hundred light years or the remote bunker gouged out of the surface of the planet on its far side by robot drones. Or the arrival to that planet of the Crabs a year later, who declared a prior claim and ordered us to leave.

Humanity's first contact with intelligent alien life.

A planet that was outside our contracts, which clearly specified a fifty light-year exploration radius—well beyond the reasonable lifespan of a human, even if protected by permanent encasement. The mission itself was permitted, but the location was out of bounds. And there was no time to mount a new expedition before the Crabs secured the first surface-accessible, geologically stable planet we had found—and our best chance to establish a forward operating base.

They could have told us; we all would have accepted the amended terms. We had long ago committed our lives, knowing that the nature of sensory induction would destroy our bodies. We came for precisely this kind of experience that was impossible by any other means.

How could they so misunderstand who we are?

Hilde negotiated with the Crabs by remote; they had no idea she was an AI. But they spoke nonsense, religion, hokum. The "Seed Bearers" would return if they detected our lives. They would rebuke first the Crab homeworld, then Earth. We've been once chastened and must never test them again. The proof lies below. Stop. Leave. Now.

Clearly an excuse. They needed time to cool down, so we cut contact. The tactic was Earth-approved. We got here first and refused to acknowledge some fanciful prior claim. Exploration began; Hilde filtered out Crab communications to prevent confusion.

Earth thought the Crabs would negotiate. Instead they sent clerks, laborers, teachers, and farmers from their great colonization ship, rerouted to warn us away. Poorly equipped and untrained, but willing to die to make us leave. Our tech could stay; just not our organic selves.

We believed it was just a tactic. Until the great dive made the error of our thinking clear.

It would have succeeded, except that Hilde had used her own initiative to create a vast extension of her core systems, an orbiting array of simple lasers and scaffolding; brute-force replication of her core systems using gross materials. At first to expand her mind; later to replace it. The Crab colony ship pierced it in its long suicide; gave her orbiting brain a stroke that accidentally destroyed Hilde's failover interface as the ship intentionally crushed her primary system.

That's what we felt as stabbing pain. That's when Rachel and Klein, Takashi and Zbilski were doomed to abandonment, locked inside the sudden void of total sensory deprivation but full cognitive awareness when Hilde was suddenly cut off.

I cannot save their lives, but I can give shape and comfort to their deaths. Real experience through sensory induction that they can now know only through the technology of their frames.

I will leave no one behind. Not one.

I mourn for Medeiros, whose ebon tomb blocked debris and protected his squad—guardian to the last. And my own organic body, lost in the same instant.

The seat of consciousness is not in the brain alone. *Also* there, but not exclusively. It can also reside in the senses, in the spaces between cells. But only if it has discovered how, as mine did when it learned to smell and feel and taste as a single act, a new perception among and between synapses. As it proved when it re-invigorated a frame it had long recognized as self, rather than accept an end.

As it does now in Hilde's vast machinery.

I have acquired her knowledge and control of her systems. I feel the solar breeze and taste its subtle salt. I hear the last surviving Crab move and smell the empty place where deep data stores once purred. Secrets of our lives and our technology.

We must stop that theft. Not out of revenge, but simple security. Humanity first.

I re-enable the Hilde interface, hear the collective gasps of my friends through their own ears and see through their own eyes as light pierces the imprisoning darkness and they are themselves again. I seed their displays with data and feel their recognition, smell their need to respond.

We converge on the crash site and feel the rumble of rocket ignition from an escape pod in the tail section of the ruined Crab ship. I grip as Zbilski, with powerful servos optimized for heavy loads, crushing the side of the emerging pod and slowing its rise. I slash as Klein, gripping Zbilski's thick leg and slapping at stabilizer fins that force the craft into slow rotation as it continues to rise, searing heat from rocket exhaust consuming my legs in exquisite agony that proves my reality. I leap as Rachel and Takashi into impossibly bright flames that taste of pure breath and the stuff of life, climbing deeper into the maelstrom and pinching feeds, tearing nozzles, rupturing lines, and finally breaking through the upward wall—content to know as brighter light fades to black that we have stopped the theft of that which we hold precious.

Not lost, alone in darkness, but liberated by a difficult choice gladly made. A worthy end.

I feel the rocket explode, taste its brief sweetness only barely salted with coppery seawater in the burst of liquid fuel that dissipates quickly in the vacuum, then is gone. I see lights atop four secret monuments flash briefly red, then go dark as batteries fail and power is lost, forever.

With a word, I activate Hilde's systems again and detonate the field disruption charges placed many years ago to close the gate that leads back to Earth. That is what Earth asked of Hilde, and Hilde asked of me. I accept their wisdom.

Now we wait.

We, the beloved of the electric valkyrie who protected us to the best of her ability. Who came to me in a moment of panic and showed me how to give honor to my friends and lead them to peace in the realm of the blessed dead.

I let their valor fuel me. Klein, Zbilski, Rachel, Takashi, and Medeiros. And the Crabs, willing to sacrifice thousands to protect their billions from a power that they feared more than death itself: unknown aliens capable of obliterating planetary ecologies under a blanket of grainy matrix as punishment for an unnamed sin.

Beings they call Seed Bearers, but I know only as Enemy.

So I remain. Here in the debris of abandoned technology and the spaces between earth and sky. Waiting for them to return to this place and consider the results of their cruelty. Until that day when we will finally meet and I can show them the error of their ways.

The Oysters of Pinctada

Larry Hodges

Tell me where they come from!" Captain Orata of *The Akoya* had grown weary of torturing the Pinctadans. The high-pitched screams irritated him.

He glanced at the viewscreen, which showed a pursuing ship against a background of stars. The rapidly closing ship would catch them in fifteen minutes.

Orata picked up the head-sized Pinctadan pearl he had stolen from the palace. He held it in front of the trembling man he was currently torturing. Between cries of pain, the man stared back. With a flick of his wrist, Orata increased the electric current to near lethal levels, trying to ignore the foul smell of this degenerate human who writhed on his office floor carpet.

He stared at the pearl as it fluctuated in the light between a lustrous pink and milky white. The pink and cream swirled into the background, pulling him into its depths. With difficulty, he averted his eyes.

The pearl was worth more than anything he could ever earn in an honest year's work. Why should he struggle while the Pinctadans grew rich and fat? He glared in disgust at the king's fat belly as he took a sip of his now cold Capella tea.

His own sculpted physique bulged under his tight-fitting blue uniform. His black ponytail was clasped in the back, warrior fashion, by a leather cord he'd cut from a living army lizard from Sirius. Off to the side, strapped to a chair, King Fucata silently watched the torturing of his man. A guard stood by the door.

Orata found this resistance unbelievable. The Pinctadans didn't seem the type. Fucata and his forty royal guardsmen were the most pathetic creatures Orata had ever seen—all short, pot-bellied, bald men, with mud-colored heads and tiny, beady eyes. He could barely tell them apart except for their colorful, loose-fitting outfits. He couldn't believe he shared human ancestry with them.

He turned off the current and shook his head in irritation as he put the pearl back on the shelf behind his desk. "Put him with the rest, and not too gently," he ordered his guard. The guard dragged the unconscious man away under the amused eyes of the many framed pictures of Orata on his office walls: sword fighting, throwing a spear, aiming a laser, hitting the *fire* button on *The Akoya*'s bridge.

Orata scowled at Fucata. "Someone will talk. They always do."

"None will talk," Fucata said, his voice weak from hours of his own torture. "You simply do not understand honics."

Honics. Orata snorted in disgust. He had read up on Pinctadans before launching his scheme, but had breezed over that part. Wasn't it some sort of religion, adopted by some of the early settlers from Earth? It didn't matter. Men were men, and no matter what their philosophy, they will break when tortured. Eventually.

"Yes, I know about your honics," Orata said, pronouncing "honics" with his high-pitched imitation of a girl. "Honor and ethics. Somewhat redundant, don't you think?" Just what he needed, he thought, a bunch of fat "holier than thou" prisoners.

Fucata locked his tired eyes with Orata's. "Honor is honesty, fairness, integrity, and altruism in a person's beliefs and actions. Ethics are the standards that govern a person's conduct. All Pinctadans are drilled in honics from childhood, and their conduct is governed by the highest level of honics. None will betray our secret."

"What is this big secret?" Orata demanded. "They're just big pearls, and you're just a bunch of gem dealers. You must have giant oysters somewhere on Pinctada. Or do you make them, mine them, grow them, or what? Whatever it is, I will find out."

"Not in any honorable way," Fucata said.

"So says the fat king," Orata said. "Some honor." He patted his own firm stomach. "I drink pretty well myself, but nothing like what your people must do every night."

"We do what we do," Fucata said.

Orata jabbed his finger into Fucata's bony chest. "You're parasites. With your monopoly, you keep the supply of these stupid pearls down, run the price up, and make a killing. And leave the rest of us out of the money loop. Well, no more. I'm starting my own business."

"And what will you do when *The Feathered Oyster* catches up?" Fucata asked. *The Feathered Oyster* was Fucata's royal cruiser, which had pursued them since they had fled Pinctada after the kidnapping. "It is faster and better armed than you."

Orata smiled inwardly but kept a straight face. "What do you think's going to happen?"

"It'll laser your engines to disable your ship, and then board you. They have far more soldiers than you."

"We didn't just kidnap you and your honor guard," Orata said, grinning. "We also planted a bomb in your ship's laser. The minute it fires, *boom!*" He raised his arms, simulating an explosion. "They are as good as dead." There had been no point in blowing the ship up while it was at Pinctada; the Pinctadans would just send another ship. As the ship approached, Orata had tried to set the bomb off by remote control, but as he had expected, the pursuing ship's shielding blocked that.

Fucata's muddy face drained of color, turning it a dirty white. "You can't do that! Viren, Chem, they'd be on that ship!"

"Princess Viren, Prince Chem? A pity, but it's up to you. You want to save them?" Orata knew that the heirs would die either way. He stood up and put his face close to the king's. "*Then tell me what I want to know!*"

The king closed his eyes. "I cannot."

"Then your heirs will die. Your men will be sold into slavery. And you will be held for ransom. Whether you tell me the secret of the pearls or not, I come out ahead."

"WHAT IF CANT SAVE," Princess Viren tapped with her index finger on her armrest in Morse code. She sat in the middle of the bridge of *The Feathered Oyster*, in hot pursuit of the kidnappers on *The Akoya*. Under full magnification, their prey was barely visible on the viewscreen. She wore the red and blue striped robe she had worn at court when she had been alerted to her father's kidnapping. The ship had waited for her and her brother before taking off in pursuit, since it was their responsibility, under honics, to join in the chase. As the heir, she was in command.

"DO WHAT NEEDED," tapped back Prince Chemnitz, her eighteen-year-old brother, two years her junior. Chem, as he preferred to go by, sat in an adjacent chair, wearing a green and black striped robe, nibbling a benthic bar made from red seaweed. Their mother had died years before of a mysterious DNA-related illness.

They were both short, bald, and pot bellied like the other Pinctadans. The two had been tapping back and forth in the ancient code their father had taught them when they were very young, allowing them to talk secretly when others were present. While useful for discussing important issues without others hearing, in the hands of Viren, it was a way to crack her father up in the middle of important meetings.

"*The Akoya* is now in sensor range, Highness," Helmsman Tobiah said, interrupting the tapping. "I'm reading fifty-two life forms." Several other crew sat quietly at their stations, surrounded by buttons and blinking lights. Except in a battle situation, none were needed; Tobiah could run the ship alone.

Viren bounded over to Tobiah's station and looked over his shoulder, examining the readings on his console. "That would be my father, the forty men in his honor guard, Captain Orata, and ten others that must be his crew." Her hands trembled; hoping nobody had noticed, she clasped them together to still them. What if they harmed her father? Or even . . . killed him? She decided it was best not to think about it.

"Can you read their condition?" she asked. Normally her father would be asking such questions, but now she was in command. She did not feel ready.

Tobiah stared into his instruments, crinkling his eyes. "No. We can barely read anything through their shielding. Just whether they are alive or not. We can't even place their locations on the ship."

She stared at the fifty-two flickering yellow lights on Tobiah's console that indicated life. One of them was her father's. Which one? They all looked the same. If Orata harmed a hair on her father's back . . . she took a deep breath.

"How soon before we'll be in laser range?" Chem asked, still nibbling on the benthic bar.

"Ten minutes," Tobiah said.

"The minute we're in range, take out their engines," Chem said.

"But not without my order," Viren added.

Chem glanced at his sister. "Why wait? There's nothing to talk about. We take out their engines, we board them, we capture or kill Orata and his pirates, and we rescue our father and his men. They better be okay, or I'm gonna introduce Orata to a laser, one small piece at a time." His benthic bar lay forgotten on his armrest.

"I hope that simple," Viren tapped. "But why do this. He know cant outrun outfight us. He must have plan." Whatever Viren wanted to do to Orata, she would one-up him. But her dad had taught her to be careful when in command, and to be even more careful when nervous. Right now, her heart raced well beyond the nervous range.

"He probably hoped to be out of range before we realized what happened," Chem said, not bothering to tap it out. "Or perhaps he's just stupid. After all, what does he expect to get out of kidnapping our father? Does he have the faintest idea about honics?"

ORATA SIPPED HIS CAPELLA TEA AS HE STARED SILENTLY AT FUCATA. THE KING occasionally yanked at the ropes holding him to his chair, but to no avail. The color had returned to his face, which was now a bright red. He stank from sweat and blood that poured down his face, drenching his robe.

Orata restrained himself from speaking. There was no need. The king was broken, and would soon be ready to deal. Let him make the first move. Patience was a virtue he'd learned to use to his advantage.

It had taken years to get in the good graces of the king. Once that was done, a simple invitation to tour his ship—with lies about all the wonders they would find—was all it took to trick the king and his men onto his ship and ambush. Planting the bomb on *The Feathered Oyster* had also been easy—the ship's guards trusted Orata right up to the moment he lasered them.

"You can't sell my men to slavery," Fucata finally said in a croaking voice. Orata knew he had won, but kept a straight face. He could gloat later.

"Nothing could be more dishonorable," Fucata continued. "You wouldn't understand this type of honor."

That was too much for Orata. "Honor? What type of honor do you speak of? You think you're better than others because you were born a king?"

"I'm king because someone has to lead."

"Ever hear of democracy?" *Not that I'm for it*, Orata thought.

Fucata's eyes glinted. "Democracy? What's the point? If a group of intelligent, honorable and ethical people run for office, shouldn't they all come to the same conclusion on each issue? They would under honics, and I'm king as long as I act under its guidelines. If I do not, my men will remove me, if I did not resign first."

"Yeah, whatever you say. Now be a good king and save your men the dishonor of enslavement. You know what I want."

The glint left Fucata's eyes. The king lowered his eyes for a moment. When he spoke, it was barely a whisper.

"I'll tell you the secret of the pearls. In return, you must not sell my men to slavery. And before I tell you the secret, you must warn *The Feathered Oyster* about the bomb."

"No deal," Orata said firmly. "The minute I warn your ship about the bomb, I'm at their mercy. No, the deal is I tell them about the bomb *after* you tell me the secret of the pearls."

Fucata shook his head. "Once I tell you the secret, you won't have any reason to uphold your end of the deal, except honor, and you have none."

Orata started to retort but rethought his strategy. "If you won't trust me, then your children are already dead. There's no way I'm going to warn them until I have the secret of the pearls." *Nor will I warn them after*, he thought. "We'll be in their laser range in minutes, so decide quickly or you'll have murdered your children."

The king looked up and stared into Orata's eyes for a moment, then looked away. "You have no plans of telling them even if I tell you the secret. In your eyes, it's your only leverage. Admit it."

There was no use denying it. "You're right."

Orata watched as the king looked upon him with pleading eyes. "Contact them, let them know about the bomb, and release the prisoners, and I give you my word as king, with honics, to give you the secret and let you go, with no pursuit. You may keep me as a hostage."

Orata had already considered this possibility. "Sorry, I don't trust you or your honics far enough to risk my freedom and life. Letting them know about the bomb isn't an option. It's the only thing that keeps my freedom assured."

The king was silent for a moment. "Any deal we make, I'll have no way of enforcing. If I tell you the secret of our pearls, what'll keep you from selling my men into slavery anyway, for the extra profit?"

Which was exactly what Orata planned to do. "Why would I bother?" he asked. "Their worth is small compared to the value of the pearls." *But money was money.*

Fucata's eyes flashed. "I can't take that chance. It'd be better that they die."

"That can be arranged."

"No," Fucata said. "The men must choose their own fate, and must do so before we deal."

"And you think they'll choose to die?"

"All of them will, to avoid slavery."

"Then why bother having them kill themselves, if they will all choose to die?" Orata asked. "I could have my men kill them and get it over with."

"They must make that honorable choice themselves. That is honics."

"And how do we arrange that? You want me to just hand over forty lasers?"

"The holding cell is laser-proof from the inside, correct?" Orata nodded. "And you have surveillance equipment, so you can watch us?" Orata again nodded. "Then give us a single hand laser, and let those who wish to die do so."

Orata's eyebrows rose. Give the prisoners a weapon? It didn't seem a smart thing to do. And yet, if that was what it would take to get the secret of the pearls, what did he have to lose? They had no way out of the holding cell. If anything went wrong, he could flood the cell with knock-out gas in seconds. It was a strange deal, but he was dealing with strange people.

"Here's what we'll do," Orata finally said. "After you and your men are secure in the holding cell, I'll have a hand laser put inside through the food opening. We'll find out just how—*honical*—your men really are. And when your men are done, you will tell me the secret of the pearls." The nice thing about the deal, Orata thought, was that due to honics, he should be able trust Fucata to fulfill his word and tell him the secret. Honor was a wonderful thing to use against your adversaries, as long as you weren't risking your own life or freedom on it. At worse, he'd have a bunch of dead Pinctadans.

They put the plan into action. Orata watched on the murky surveillance screen as Fucata, holding the laser, spoke to his men.

Fucata lined them up against the wall. Then the king raised the laser and quickly shot the first two men, from head to heart. This caught Orata off guard. Hadn't Fucata said the men had to do it themselves? Fascinated, he watched as Fucata shot another unresisting man, then another, and a few seconds later, another.

The king leaned over one of the dead men. When he stood up, he held up a large, round object. Orata stared—could it be? *It was!* A Pinctadan pearl! But where had he gotten it?

Fucata looked directly at the surveillance camera. Then, with a half smile, half grimace, he reared back and threw the pearl at it. It smacked into the camera as Orata flinched. The image blacked out.

Orata donned his laser-proof body armor, including helmet, and motioned four guards to follow as he made his way to the holding cell.

Helmsman Tobiah sat up suddenly. "Highness, two of the life forms just died!"

Viren and Chem hurried over to Tobiah's station.

"There goes another!" Tobiah said, staring at his sensor readings. Looking over his shoulder, Viren had seen the light flicker out. She gasped. *Father?*

"How long before we are in firing range?" she asked. She could now see *The Akoya* on the viewscreen, a double-engine Hawk-class freighter.

Tobiah pushed a few buttons. "About one minute. Highnesses, another just died!" He paused. "And another! That's five. They're killing them!"

"Can't you just start firing?" Chem asked as Viren stared at the remaining lights. She'd watched them blink out, each one a hammer blow to her pounding heart.

"Targeting system won't lock in yet, not at this range," said Tobiah. "Two more just died, that's seven!" A moment later, "And two more!" He paused. "And there goes two more—they're killing them two at a time now!"

Viren slammed his fist into a console. "I don't care what it takes, we have to stop this! The instant we're in range, take out their engines." He began pacing.

"They just killed two more," Tobiah said. "And there go two more." Viren watched as the lights blinked out. She took a deep breath, and stepped back, pulling her eyes away from the unwatchable sight. She was in command; she didn't have her father to fall back on. *I need to focus!* she silently screamed to herself. Which didn't help. She took several slow, deep breaths, and focused on the situation.

Something was not right.

"Why would they kill off the prisoners?" she wondered. "They could use them as hostages. They must know we'll attack in response."

"And that's exactly what we'll do, sister," Chem said.

"Two more dead," Tobiah said. Chem watched over his shoulder as Tobiah continued to count off the deaths. Three more died, one at a time.

Viren couldn't watch; she needed to think. What was happening in that ship? Why were they killing the prisoners one or two at a time? Her head seemed to clear as she thought furiously.

"Highness, we're in range now, and ready to fire on your orders," said Tobiah. "I've got their engines targeted."

"Then fire!" Chem said.

"Belay that!" Viren cried, her voice cracking. "*Do not fire!*"

Chem spun about and shook his sister. "What are you saying! Our men are dying! And our father!" He turned to Tobiah. "Take out their engines!"

"*No!*" Viren exclaimed, shoving her brother out of the way and standing over Tobiah and his station. "Don't you see what they're doing?" She spun to face her brother. "Two died right at the start. Then three died one at a time. That's dah, dit, dit, dit. Then two died at the same time, and this happened three times in a row. Dah, dah, dah. Then two died at the same time, twice in a row. Dah, dah. Then two died at the same time again, followed by three dying one at a time. Dah, dit, dit, dit. They're dying in Morse code—they just spelled out B-O-M-B!"

Brother and sister stared at each other. "What are they trying to tell us?" Viren finally asked. "We don't have any bombs, just the laser."

"Doesn't matter," Chem said. "We need to stop this killing. We can disable their engines as a warning. Tobiah, fire the laser!"

"Tobiah, if you fire, your career is over," Viren said. Disabling Orata's ship wouldn't stop the killing. They had to figure out what the message meant. "Need I remind you that *I* am the Princess, and the Prince my little brother?"

"Then these deaths are on your hands!" Chem cried. "Including our father's!"

"Highness, two more just died," Tobiah said. "One at a time."

"That's dit, dit," Viren said. "An 'I'. I bet . . . next will come a dah, then a dit. Two deaths together, then one by itself. An 'N'."

Tobiah stared up at Viren. "I don't know about this dah and dit stuff, but two more just died. And there goes another. You were right." He was gripping his chair's armrest with a white-knuckled grip.

"B-O-M-B-I-N," Viren exclaimed. "Bomb in what?" She looked over Tobiah's shoulder, not bothering to hide her trembling hands.

"Maybe it's B-O-M-B-I-N-G?" Chem asked.

"There's another dit, so it's not a 'G'," Viren said as another light disappeared. As they silently watched, two lights went out together. Then another. Then another. "That's dit, dah, dit, dit. An 'L'. That's BOMBINL." She suddenly straightened, and her face flushed. "Oh no!"

"What?" Chem asked.

"If it's what I think—*do not fire the laser, no matter what!* Chem, I think there's a bomb in our laser! Take some men and check it out."

As she watched helplessly, the lights continued to blink out as she had expected, until there were only fifteen left. If eleven were Orata and his men, then. . . .

ORATA ENTERED THE PRISON CELL IN HIS BODY ARMOR, ACCOMPANIED BY TWO armed guards. He held a hand laser, one far more powerful than the one he'd given Fucata. He didn't need it.

Orata had seen some pretty nasty sights in his years, as you'd expect for someone who didn't always operate on the right side of the law. Yet his stomach did a back flip at what he saw.

Nearly all of Fucata's men lay dead in pools of blood on the metal floor of the cramped holding cell, lasered by their own king. Only the king and three of his men still stood. Fucata turned to face him."

"You want to know how we create our pearls?" Fucata cried out, his voice hoarse as tears ran down his face. "You want our secret? *Here is our secret!*" He lasered one of the remaining men, who fell to the ground on his back. Standing over him, Fucata lasered the man's pot-like belly, cutting a hole. Guts poured out, and then a large, round object covered in blood. Fucata grabbed the object and wiped most of the blood away on his robe. It was a Pinctadan pearl, about ten inches wide, mostly white with a slight bluish tinge.

"Now you know our secret!" Fucata yelled, tossing the pearl at Orata, who stumbled as he caught the heavy object, blood spattering about. "We grow them in ourselves, through DNA manipulation, one in each of us, a fortune to be extracted and sold upon our deaths! *We* are your oysters!" As he said this, he lasered the last two of his living men in quick succession. "If others learn of this, then it will be hunting season on Pinctadans *everywhere!*"

Orata stared about wild-eyed. Realization dawned on him. There were forty-one pot-bellied Pinctadans, each hiding a fortune in their bellies!

He spied an extra hefty man on the ground, and lasered the man's belly. A huge Pinctadan pearl covered in blood came out.

"That's a fourteen-incher!" he exclaimed, barely noticing as Fucata turned the laser on himself.

SHORTLY AFTER CHEM LEFT THE ROOM WITH HIS MEN, THE MESSAGE WAS NEARLY complete: "BOMB IN LASE." Another died; then two more. "I get the message, you don't need to kill anyone else," Viren cried. She knew who the last person was, the final dit in 'R'; who else over there could know Morse code? "*Please!*" she pleaded.

One more light flickered slightly; as she watched, it blinked out, the final "dit" of the dit, dah, dit of the final 'R' in the message.

She returned to her chair and slumped backward. Tears flowed down the face of the new queen of Pinctada.

Soon the tears stopped flowing. She stared nearly unblinking out the viewscreen at *The Akoya*. Her eyes narrowed. A coldness entered her body, but she did not feel cold, only determined and yet lifeless.

It took Chem and his men only a few minutes to disable the bomb hidden in the ship's laser and return to the bridge.

IT BARELY REGISTERED ON ORATA WHEN THE SHIP SHOOK AS IF STRUCK BY LASER fire. He looked up, and—realizing that Fucata and his men were all dead—ordered his guards out of the room. He tore his helmet off.

He lasered the other Pinctadan bellies, watching in awe as the pearls rolled free. He tore a blue robe off a dead man and used it to wipe the blood off the pearls. He piled them carefully in a corner, admiring their colorful luster. Some were cream white; most were tinged in red, blue or green. He rubbed a large, red one against his face. It was still warm; he closed his eyes, enjoying the hard, wet embrace.

He barely noticed the armed boarding crew that entered and surrounded him—but that ended when the Princess slapped him. He looked up, rubbing his cheek. He caught a quick look at eyes that blazed like a thousand Pinctadan pearls, and then she turned away and knelt by her father's body. After a moment she lowered her face and whispered in her father's ear. Fear rose in him as she continued to whisper. *What was she saying?*

She kissed her father's bloody forehead. Then she looked back at him, and her eyes were now dark and lifeless. He dropped the pearl.

"Everyone out," she said, her voice equally lifeless. A moment later they were alone.

"Look—" he began.

"Shut up," Viren said, her lips bright red with her father's blood. She held up her laser, her dead eyes looking him over as she debated where to begin.

Spirit of the Vangaurd

Jenny Perry Carr

Jeffers ripped blood-soaked mech gear off Landon, wounds squelching as he removed the metal. "Hold on, man." Sweat fogged the edges of Jeffers' visor.

Landon pinched his lips tight and grunted an affirmative.

The grizzled sergeant major scrambled to assess the damage to Landon's midsection. The broken edge of a N'Goi bayonet blade protruded from his best friend.

He sucked in a breath. It was all his fault.

Smoke and burned flesh tainted the thick air of the desolate moon orbiting the ringed yellow planet. White flashes from laser weapons whizzed overhead.

If it weren't for Jeffers, Landon would have never gotten hurt. He would have never even been there. Jeffers convinced him to join the Astromarines. Then got him to volunteer for the Mech Vanguard, guaranteed adventure.

He ripped open Landon's shirt, revealing the extent of the damage, and swallowed hard. The blade had to come out. It was the only way he could attempt to stop the bleeding.

Jeffers promised this would be their last tour—clear out a few nuisance aliens, earn enough credits to open their shop. Easy-in, easy-out mission. Hardly.

He yanked the medpak from his suit and dumped it out, frantically searching through the contents, hands shaking. Jeffers pressed gauze against Landon's chest, which instantly turned red. He grabbed an injector and pushed it against Landon's skin. Grabbing the device with both hands to steady it, he pumped a numbing agent repeatedly around the object sticking out of his friend.

How many times had Landon saved his bacon? Even as kids, he took Jeffers in when his parents fought and never left his side all these years later. He needed Landon.

Jeffers gripped the jagged chunk of metal. "I'm sorry, man. So sorry." He inhaled and slid the sharp steel out of Landon's abdomen. He tossed the blade into the medpak.

Landon cried out, then gritted his teeth. Blood bubbled out of the wound, saturating his ripped shirt.

He squirted irrigation fluid to clear away blood, then squeezed a packet of mending glue into the gaping wound. "We got this." His voice cracked. A field patch should hold until he could get him out of there. It had to.

Jeffers dared a look from behind the rocky outcropping where they sheltered, hydraulics within his suit whining with each movement. His gaze darted across the active battlefield, tech and bodies strewn across the barrens, red and blue rivulets of blood crisscrossing the surface.

Were the rare minerals worth all this?

Landon's face paled.

"Think of our circuitry shop back on Hera 10." He had to keep him conscious. His stomach flip-flopped. He couldn't lose Landon. "I don't know jack about conductors. I'm the deal man." Landon was the real talent. All Jeffers was good at was talking, and it was bull. He wasn't smart like Landon.

But Landon believed in him. Always told him, "You've got something special there." What was so special about him? What did he see?

Landon coughed and gave a weak thumbs up.

A crackle of static came through his radio. *Kshhh, kshh, kshh.* ". . . contact. Break contact. All units, return to LZ. Exfil in thirty mikes." *Kshh.*

"That's our cue." Jeffers gathered up the medpak supplies and snapped the kit back onto his suit. He wrapped his arm under Landon and hefted the man to his feet.

Landon pushed him away and stumbled on his own. "I got this." He tore off his helmet and sucked in a deep breath, then exhaled a soupy, ragged sound.

"That's the spirit." He clung to Landon's positive words, clung to the belief that Landon would be okay.

THEY HURRIED PAST LIFELESS SOLDIERS, FRIEND AND FOE.

A woman from another unit lay prone on the ground. She lifted her head.

Jeffers lumbered to her side. Two stripes were emblazoned on the arm of her suit. "You okay, corporal?"

She repositioned her off-kilter helmet. "Don't know." Unsteady, she rose, each step of her heavy mech suit reverberating against the rock.

She bobbled, and he braced her. He glanced at the nameplate on her chest. "You with me, Rodriguez?"

"Roger." Despite the reassurance, she held fast to Jeffers' arm.

Her heavy suit weighed him down, his own hydraulics straining. She would slow them down, and he needed to get Landon to the landing zone ASAP.

Landon took Rodriguez' other arm to ease the burden. "Let's get out of here."

Jeffers peered across the battlefield, scanning for a clear path forward. "There." He pointed, and the three zig-zagged through the fray, dodging bursts of blaster fire. They raced toward the extraction point two klicks away, where they were dropped in last night for the surprise attack. Surprise was enemies were waiting for them. They had walked right into a trap.

Their intel said the N'Goi were primitive, and it would be easy to remove them from the small moon. Their overconfidence was their downfall. The aliens were far more superior than anticipated, with a mix of simple and technologically advanced weapons that seemed to target every one of the Astromarines' weaknesses.

Alien and friendly fire lit up the wasteland. He yanked Rodriguez down as a shot grazed his helmet, the scent of molten metal seeping into his suit. His stomach twisted in knots. The N'Goi wouldn't let the foreign soldiers retreat without a fight. Jeffers chest heaved as he weighed their options. "I don't know if we can do this." He tipped his head toward the wounded woman.

Landon swooned, then took a knee.

Acid crept up his throat. "I don't know if *you* can do this."

Landon waved a dismissive hand. "Don't worry about me. You're the toughest man I know. You can do this. Lead us out of here."

He didn't know about being tough, but Jeffers had led more successful missions than he could count. If anyone could get them out of there, it was him.

He nodded with resolve. "I got this."

Jeffers rested Rodriguez against a rough boulder, then assessed another wounded Mech Vanguard soldier crumpled on the ground. His helmet had come free and laid crushed beside him. The left half of the lieutenant's suit was shredded from one of the N'Goi's powerful acoustic weapons. Bits of shrapnel were embedded into his skin along the length of his exposed body. He tore off his gauntlet and gripped his cool hand.

Maybe they got what they deserved. They had no right to take resources from an alien world by force.

"Help me." The lieutenant's voice was weak and raspy.

But no one deserved to suffer like that. The blame was on their leaders. Jeffers just needed to get as many evacuated as possible.

But there was nothing he could do for this soldier. He would never make it off this rock alive. He let his hand go and stepped away. He crunched through the gravel and bent to pick up Rodriguez.

Landon hovered over him. "What are you doing, man?"

"Getting us out of here."

"You can't leave him." Landon's voice echoed inside his helmet. Landon's field bandage was spotted red. The patch wasn't holding. They had to move, now.

Jeffers stood upright and whispered, "He's almost dead."

Landon stiffened. "So? We don't leave men behind."

He shrugged, gears within his suit whirring. "How am I supposed to carry him?"

Landon leaned against the boulder beside Rodriguez. "You're the brains behind this operation. Figure it out."

Jeffers sighed. They lived by a code. Landon was right. He couldn't leave the living behind. It was every soldier's fear to be left for dead in enemy territory. He searched the field for something useful, trying to avoid detection by staying low and at the edge of fighting.

Jeffers shifted the wounded man onto a flat piece of steel vehicle shielding he had found. He salvaged cables from a fallen mech soldier and used the cording to drag the makeshift sled behind them. Sweat soaked his fabric neck sheath, and a musky tang saturated the inside of his suit. He pushed beyond the limits of his gear to haul the sled and hold Rodriguez steady.

Landon grinned. "You've got something special there."

He sneered. Hopefully the extraction ship would still be there when they finally got to the landing zone. His nostrils flared. "Can we go now?"

Landon smiled.

THE HEAVY SLED SCRAPED ACROSS THE UNEVEN, ROCKY GROUND OF THE foothills, away from the battlefield. Rodriguez leaned against his arm. Jeffers took this route to stay out of sight, but it added significant time to their trip. They crested a small hill and found another survivor.

A wounded infantry soldier straddled a uniformed officer, pumping his chest with rhythmic thrusts. Blood pulsed from a gash across the kid's shoulder with each of his chest compressions. The commander's eyes were open and fixed, staring off-planet, clearly dead. The fallen officer's face was already blue.

He unhooked the sled and stood beside the determined private. He touched the twenty-something's back, and the kid flinched. "Stand down, private. It's time to go home."

The soldier fell away from the dead man onto the ground. He collapsed in on himself and sobbed. His voice stuttered. "He can't be gone. I can't be the last one left. Can't."

Jeffers began to reattach the sled to his suit. "I know it's hard. Come with us to the extraction point. Let's get you out of here." The kid was so busted up about being the last of his unit, it wasn't clear if he understood or would follow.

Tears saturated the young man's eyes. "Couldn't save him."

"But we can save you. Let's go." He extended a hand and helped the private to his feet. Landon patted the kid on the back.

A three-fingered hand stirred beside Jeffers' foot. He drew his blaster and pointed it at the smooth gray head of the injured N'Goi soldier sprawled on the rocky landscape.

"Don't." Landon touched the barrel of his pistol.

He clenched his jaw. "Why not? It's war." They had lost so many of their comrades.

"We don't shoot 'em when they're down. It's not a fair fight. Not honorable."

Jeffers aimed his weapon at the back of its head, finger tense on the trigger. How many had this N'Goi killed?

Landon shook his head. "We're not executioners."

"Fine." Their orders *were* to break contact. He exhaled and holstered his weapon.

Jeffers led them down the hill along the edge of the barrens and into a clearing. The young private staggered behind in a daze, but he was able to ambulate himself. Fighting had lessened as the Astromarines retreated, but the open debris field felt exposed, nonetheless.

Rocks shifted and pebbles clattered onto the path behind them. He spun around toward the noise.

Up on the hill, the alien he had spared steadied its rifle and aimed a blue laser targeting beam at Rodriguez's head. Jeffers dove in front of her, blocking the blast that pinged off his titanium chest plate, armor shuddering from the force.

He reached for his sidearm, but the alien was too fast. A flash of white heat slammed against his suit, shattering his weapon and severing his hydraulics. He buckled to his knees, the weight of the suit dragging him down.

The blue laser searched for a new target.

His heart thrummed against his chest. He had to stop the alien, but no one else carried a sidearm, all discarded tending wounds or lost in battle. They were away from the battlefield, so no other weapons were in range. Why had he listened to Landon and let the alien live? He should have listened to his gut and ended him.

The blue laser zeroed in on the young private.

Now they were stuck, out in plain sight, about to be executed.

Stuck.

Jeffers eyed the blood-soaked bandage covering Landon's midsection.

The bayonet.

He stripped off his medpak and searched through the bloodied supplies. He pulled out the broken N'Goi blade. With a flick of his wrist, it sliced through the air and thunked into the forehead of the alien.

It flumped over, dark blue blood trickling onto its face.

He sucked in a breath and strained to lift his leg to stand. He eyed the wounded soldiers around him. How would he get them all to the landing zone now?

Dust swirled as they entered the basin of the exfiltration site. Rescue ships streamed in from the orbiter, engines screaming as they slowed for a landing.

Jeffers struggled to drag the wounded toward the nearest craft. He handed off the soldiers one by one to the medical staff that raced out of the ship with gurneys and medical supplies.

The medics took over, immediately triaging the injured. One medic shouted over the whir of the engines, "How did you manage this? And her in a full suit, no less. They're going to give you a medal for carrying three soldiers to safety."

"Couldn't have done it without Landon." He thumbed over his shoulder.

"Who?" the medic hollered.

Jeffers turned and froze. His stomach dropped. Landon wasn't there.

Jeffers stomach vibrated along with the hull of the rescue ship as it approached escape velocity. He gripped the shoulder harness that held him in place. He could have sworn Landon was right there with him.

But Landon hadn't survived the bayonet through the chest. All their mech gear couldn't protect him. He couldn't save him. All his fault Landon was dead. So stupid to think this would be an easy mission.

He could have never made it out with the others by himself. No way.

The shaking of the ship smoothed as they entered orbit.

How would he do this alone? He needed Landon. A heaviness filled his stomach despite the weightlessness.

"Don't know what I'm going to do now." The young private stared forward, his face pale. He mumbled, "Whole unit's gone. Got nothing."

The kid snapped Jeffers out of his own thoughts. "What's that?"

"I got nothing to go back to."

He understood. He was in the same situation. What did he have to go back to? He couldn't run the shop alone. He didn't have Landon's skills. Landon helped him with everything. "What about your parents?"

"No. They were lost in the Haggian insurgency."

"Sorry for your loss."

Landon wasn't lost. Jeffers had it all wrong. No. He hadn't been alone that day. Landon might have died, but he'd spoken to him every step of the way. He wasn't gone. He was in his heart. And he'd be with him forever.

The kid pointed to Jeffers' wrecked suit. "See you took damage to your hydraulic valve control unit."

He touched the frayed metal. "Yeah."

The young soldier nodded. "I can fix that for you."

He raised an eyebrow. "Oh?"

"I'm good with my hands."

"Is that so? What's your name, kid?"

"Chen."

Jeffers studied the young private's face. Maybe he could help the kid the way Landon had helped him. He nodded. "I'm Jeffers. Know anything about circuits, Chen?"

"Circuits, conductors, capacitors, you name it. Second nature to me."

A warmth spread across his chest. He smiled. "You've got something special there."

The Flight of Captain Kowalski

K. Z. Richards

W e've got a Code Alpha, Bay 12. Code Alpha, Bay 12."

The announcement echoed through the break room of the Galactic Veteran's Retreat vessel where I and three other crew members sat at a small table, MREs in hand. We eyed each other, each of us waiting for another to volunteer, but nobody moved.

"Not it," Tyrone said, taking a bite of his lunch.

"Not it," I said, beating Diego's "not it" by a fraction of a second.

Amara, my supervisor sat up straighter in her seat, puffing out her chest with the privilege of authority. "Sorry, Henry, it doesn't work like that. Report to Bay 12, pronto."

I scoffed. "But I said it first."

"Now, Henry. Unless you want me to withhold my recommendation?"

The only thing standing between me and a position on the Intergalactic Space Corp's med squad was her stamp of approval. Either I earned that letter of recommendation, or I'd face a lifetime of Code Alphas.

Reluctantly, I dropped my food pouch on the table. "Yes, ma'am."

As I stood to leave, Amara turned her attention back to her lunch, fanning the steam as it curled in the starship's filtered air. "Better hurry. If you're fast enough, you can get there before he yanks his catheter out."

Tyrone and Diego sniggered as I trudged out of the break room and into the starship's corridor.

Ten more weeks, I told myself. *Only ten more, brain-numbing weeks.*

When I reached the door to Bay 12, I found it ajar, a loop of plastic tubing draped over the threshold. As I slid the door open, I found the usual suspect sitting in the pod seat, staring out the convex window, his hands busy at the keyboard on the dash. Thankfully, none of his tubes had disconnected from their designated spots on his pale, half-naked body. A small mercy.

"Going somewhere, John?" I asked, unzipping my crewman jacket. I draped it over his bare shoulders.

"It's the Voltons again," he said, keeping his yellow eyes fixed to the window. "They're attacking the ship. ISC's going to need reinforcements." He pushed a series of random buttons, none of which did anything. We had learned from John's first escapade to keep the escape pods locked and triple password protected. Corporate might have forgiven one incident, but they would not forgive two.

Careful not to step on the IV bag on the floor, I squatted beside him. "We've gone over this, John. The Voltons are friendly. We signed a peace treaty with them years ago. Now, why don't we get you back to your room? I hear they're serving carrot pudding."

He smacked his hands on the dash. "Carrot pudding? *Carrot . . . pudding?* We are at war, young man. War!" He shook his bald head quickly, making his jowls jiggle. "Carrot pudding, my a—"

Suddenly, the starship lunged forward, throwing me into the controls. I peered out the window, gripping the back of John's seat to stand up. "What on Pleiades cluster was that?"

"Voltons," John grumbled, grabbing a joystick. "Probably hit us with a dark falcon. But don't worry, I'll show them. Once I figure out how to work this darn thing."

Outside, the familiar orb of Venus' hazy atmosphere and a spattering of stars filled the sky, but there was no sign of anything that might have collided with the ship.

"It was probably just the gravity simulator glitching again," I told John, though I did not believe it myself. When the simulator glitched, it created brief sensations of sudden weightlessness, not violent jerks. Dementia or not, John was right—something had hit our ship.

"I'll tell you what, John. Why don't we let the ISC handle this one, and I'll let you know if they call for reinforcements. Sound like a plan?"

John grit his teeth. "Nope, I don't like it. Tell the ISC I'm in position and ready to engage. I'll just need a few more minutes to get through the last security clearance."

"Wait. What do you mean the *last . . .* ?" I checked the screen on the dash, and sure enough, John had already figured out two of the three passwords. "How in the Seventh Sister did you do that?"

John shifted in his seat, his gaze flickering to something between his knees. There, poking between the folds of his thinning skin, was my personal communicator, the screen unlocked.

Panic surged through me. If John managed to launch the escape pod using my credentials, I'd be in serious trouble. Forget joining the ISC's med squad; I'd probably get banned from ever setting foot in space again.

"Give that to me," I said, reaching for the communicator.

He swatted my hands away. "No."

"John."

"Young man, you must understand the urgency. The Voltons—"

"No, John, you can't—"

John jerked to move the device out of reach, and the strap holding his catheter bag caught the side of the chair, yanking the bag, and the rest of the tubing, free. The bag seemed to fall in slow motion, hitting the floor just out of reach where it ruptured, drenching my shoes and filling the room with its acrid scent.

"Oh. Whoops," John said, staring at the mess.

I counted to ten before reaching for my communicator again, frustration coursing through me. This time, John let me take it without a fight.

"I need backup in Bay 12, please," I spoke into the device, using all my strength to keep calm. "Backup in Bay 12."

"Sorry, Henry, no can do," Diego replied. "We've got a situation here."

My heart skipped a beat. Had they identified what hit us? Was it dangerous? "What kind of situation?"

"Lunch," he said. In the background, I heard Tyrone chuckling.

"What about the crash? Did you look into it?"

"Amara says it's nothing to worry about. Probably just debris. You worry about getting John back to his room. And make sure this time he stays there, okay?"

With a sigh, I grabbed John under the arms and hoisted him to his feet. "Time to go, John," I said, deciding I'd take care of him and his mess first, and then figure out what the blazes hit us. Because it sure as hell wasn't debris.

"Was that the ISC?" John asked.

"It sure was," I lied, bending down to pick up the IV line and empty catheter bag. "They want you in your room. General's orders."

John sighed. "Very well. But make sure the general knows I'm willing to fight."

"Don't worry, I'll tell her," I said as we made our way into the hall, plastic tubes trailing behind us.

Once we made it to John's room, I placed the IV bag back on its hook, dressed him in a new gown, and began taking his vitals. John sat on the bed, staring at the wall across the room, his expression vacant. The reflection of the stars outside his bedroom window speckled his cheeks.

"You never imagine yourself here when you're there," he said. "You don't imagine that the glory and honor will fade."

I followed his gaze to the framed space naval uniform on the wall, its sleeve crested with the insignia of the Intergalactic Space Corps. Three platinum rings on his cuff marked his rank as captain, and a collection of service medals decorated the front, overlapping so much I could hardly tell them apart.

"You miss it?" I asked.

He nodded. "Every day. Don't get me wrong, the retreat is a thoughtful gesture on the ISC's part—'Retirement in the Stars' and all—but it's not the same."

He blinked, and a tear fell to his lap. For a moment, I glimpsed the man behind the years, the man who'd done so much to earn our planet's respect in the cosmos. He didn't look it now, but John had once led hundreds of missions as Captain Kowalski, earning us intergalactic admiration and solidifying so many of the alliances we valued today. Now, here he was, struggling to maintain basic human dignity, his only company a handful of corpsmen who couldn't wait to put their medical certifications to better use.

The guilt washed over me like a cold shower. No one liked chasing down residents or cleaning up after their inevitable messes, but John deserved better than what I'd given him so far.

John blinked again, and as quickly as it had come, the moment passed. He flinched, jerking his head toward some imaginary sound. "The Voltons. They're at it again." He swung his legs off the bed, but before he could stand, I grabbed him.

"Easy, John. You have to stay here, remember? General's orders."

"Forget the orders. We need to get to an escape pod."

I sighed, hating what I would have to do next. Reminding myself it was for John's own good, I moved quickly, flattening John against the mattress. Grabbing a strap from under the bed, I fastened it to the other side, cinching it tight across his waist.

"What are you doing?" John protested. "The ISC needs help. They need me."

Ignoring his pleas, I fastened a second strap across his chest and a third across his legs.

"No!" he cried. "You have to let me go. This is a matter of life and death."

"I'm sorry." I grabbed my jacket and pulled it back over my shoulders. It smelled of urine and sweat, but for the moment, I didn't mind. "I'm truly sorry, John."

Making sure I had my communicator with me this time, I slid the door closed, silencing John's wails.

THE MESS IN THE ESCAPE POD DIDN'T TAKE NEARLY AS LONG AS I THOUGHT IT would to clean up. After a quick mop and a heavy application of sanitizer, the space was good as new.

I had just finished wiping down the keyboard when the ship lurched again, banging my head against the dash.

Grasping the lump forming there, I pulled my communicator out and paged the entire crew.

"You guys want to tell me *that* was debris, too?"

After a brief silence, my supervisor responded. "All crew members please report to the bridge. All crew members to the bridge, please."

Without bothering to return the cleaning supplies to the closet, I ran toward the bridge, my heart racing. My limited military training had taught me what kinds of threats lurked in space and how to handle them, but discussing them in a classroom in California and facing them in outer space were two very different things.

Praying the gravity simulator wouldn't choose that moment to glitch, I sprinted as fast as my legs would carry me, charging onto the bridge just as another object made impact.

I stumbled into Amara, Tyrone, and Diego who were huddled around the ship's large front windows, smashing the three of them into the glass.

"Geez, Henry," Tyrone said, pushing me off him. "Watch out."

I scrambled to my feet and peered out the windows. Blocking the light from Venus with my hand, I searched the dark sky. "Can you see it? Where did it come from?"

"No idea," Amara said, taking a seat at the controls. "Nothing shows up on radar."

"What about infrared?"

"Nothing."

"So, they're invisible?" I asked. "But the only beings we know of that have dark weapons are—"

"The Voltons, I know." Amara pursed her lips.

I placed a hand on the glass, steadying myself. "But we have an agreement with them. They're not even supposed to be in this part of the galaxy. What are they doing firing upon a civilian spacecraft?"

She shook her head. "No idea."

I took a deep breath, trying to calm my shaking legs. "We've got fifty-six veterans on board and limited defense capabilities. How are we supposed to protect them against a Volton warcraft?"

"I've already contacted the ISC requesting support," my supervisor said. "The only thing we can do is cross our fingers and pray the ship holds until they arrive."

"Shouldn't we at least fire back?"

"We could try, but we'd be firing blind. Even the most experienced fighters have trouble hitting dark weapons. I know I couldn't hit one."

Tyrone and Diego stared blankly at me, their chins dripping with chili mac. Despite their years aboard this ship, I doubted either one of them had the military expertise to help. Fortunately, I knew someone who did.

"I'm going to check on the residents," I said, marching toward the hallway. "Keep me updated on anything you find."

When I reached the door to John's room, I was relieved to find his wailing had ceased. In an effort not to startle him, I knocked before sliding the door open.

The room inside was unrecognizable. Bed sheets thrown to the floor, bedside lamp toppled, John's old uniform lying in its shattered frame on the ground. John, himself, was MIA. The straps securing him to the bed were still fastened, but John had somehow managed to wriggle out of them, and his new hospital gown, ransacking the room in the process.

My first thought was to call in another Code Alpha, but I paused as I lifted my communicator to make the call.

Even if someone did show up to help, they wouldn't approve of what I planned to do next. Best case scenario, they'd sedate John and lock him back up in his room—the last thing I wanted. They wouldn't understand that dementia or not, John was the most experienced, most capable person on this ship.

Pocketing my phone, I grabbed a pair of clean slacks then retrieved John's uniform from the shards on the floor, shaking the glass from its silver fabric. I folded the uniform into a neat square, tucked it under my arm, and ran for Bay 12.

I had only taken a few steps when the impacts started to come in rapid succession.

Bang.

Bang.

Bang.

My chest hit the floor, my arms sprawling out in front of me. John's clothes were knocked from my grasp, landing on the floor just out of reach. I army-crawled toward them, but before I could grab them, another impact knocked me flat.

As I started to get up, my stomach did a funny flip, like I'd been turned upside down. The weight left my body, and I started to drift further and further away from the starship's floor.

The last hit had taken out the gravity simulator.

I reached for the wall for support, but another crash set me flying into the top of the ship, knocking the wind out of me.

I gasped, cradling my throbbing side as the reality set in.

We were not going to make it. We were a civilian ship, little more than an orbital nursing home. We didn't stand a chance against whatever wanted to destroy us. I closed my eyes, praying the attacks would stop long enough for me to find equilibrium, when a hand grabbed me by the wrist.

"Haven't earned your space legs yet, young man?" John said, pulling me toward him.

"John! What are you doing here?"

"Just checking to make sure all passengers are secure. This is no time to be wandering the halls, young man. We are under attack. You need to get yourself to a holding room and prepare for oxygen breach."

"I can't. We need to get to an escape pod and fight back."

"Already tried. Couldn't figure out the passwords. Someone's changed them again."

The ship jolted, but John curled himself around me, cushioning the impact with his bare torso. I grasped his arms, careful to avoid the IV protruding from his forearm.

"I've got the passwords," I said. "I just need someone who can operate the pod. You got any experience with dark weapons?"

A grin spread across his face. "Hell yeah, I do."

"Great. Then, you'll need just one more thing." Still holding onto John for support, I reached for the jacket and pants, floating midair. "You can't fight dark weapons in nothing but your undies." I grabbed the clothes and handed them to John.

"What's this?" He turned the jacket over to see the front, and his yellow eyes widened. "Oh. It's been so long . . ." He patted his bare chest, his cheeks flushing.

"We should move quickly. Who knows how much longer the ship will hold."

I let go of him to free both his arms.

"Yes, no time to waste." Effortlessly, he slipped into the jacket and pants, maneuvering himself and his tubes midair like someone who had never known arthritis, muscular dystrophy, or half the other conditions that now plagued him. Fully dressed, he straightened himself to his full height and looked at me with an expression so commanding I hardly recognized the old man behind it.

"To the escape pod?" he asked.

For a moment, I considered the gravity of what I was about to do. If we survived, it would cost me more than a letter of recommendation. The ISC would probably never let me set foot in one of their vessels again, let alone grant me a position on their med squad. But I knew it was the right thing to do—for John, and for all of us.

"Aye-aye, Captain," I said, raising my arm in salute.

The barrage continued as John and I made our way to Bay 12, knocking us into the walls with every hit. I held onto John the entire way, not letting go until we reached the escape pod. While John fastened himself into the seat, I quickly typed the passwords into the computer.

"All systems go?" he asked, weaving a seatbelt between his dangling cords.

An impact sent me flying forward, but I caught myself on the dash. "Almost." I copied the third password from my communicator and was about to hit enter when an announcement echoed through the room.

"We've got a Code Alpha, Bay 12. Code Alpha, Bay 12."

"I guess they know we're here," I said.

My communicator lit up. "Henry, can you take care of that Code Alpha?" Amara's voice said. "The rest of us are busy securing the ship."

Despite myself, I smirked. "On it."

"Good. And hurry. The ship's outer shell is down to seventeen percent strength, putting us at extreme risk of breach. Anyone not in a secured room is in very serious danger."

I looked back at John.

"You heard the lady," he said. "Better get yourself to safety." Despite the wrinkles lining his face, he looked younger than I'd ever seen him.

"It's not too late to back out."

In response, he reached past me and hit enter on the keypad, submitting the last password. The dash lit up, and he seized the controls. "Thanks, Henry. I'll take it from here."

I pushed myself toward the exit but lingered just outside. "Be careful, Captain. I want you back in one piece."

"Son, I've been doing this my whole life. You worry about getting yourself to a secure location, and I'll worry about whatever's trying to blow us to smithereens."

The doors closed between us and locked with a definitive thud. As the escape pod's engines roared behind the door, I gave John a silent salute then pushed myself toward the bridge.

Without John, I moved more clumsily down the corridor, bumping into walls as I overshot my handholds. My head and shoulders throbbed when I finally reached the bridge, but I ignored them, taking the empty seat beside Amara.

"Henry, you're here. Good. Securing the bridge now." She pressed a button, and a door closed behind us. Diego and Tyrone didn't look up but continued with their task of securing the rooms. Their voices carried through over the hum of the ship's engine.

"Room 42, secure."

"Room 43, secure.

"Room 44 . . ."

"How long until ISC arrives?" I asked.

"Too long, I'm afraid," Amara said. "They are three to four days out."

"*Days?* What's the strength of the outer shell at?"

"Three percent. It could breach at any moment." She gripped her armrests, staring into the windows ahead.

"Tell me we have at least figured out what's hitting us."

"Negative."

"Nothing at all on radar?"

"Nope. It's like they're coming out of nowhere." She pointed to her screen. "See for yourself. No matter which—wait. I think I see something. Tyrone, bring up sector nine on the screen."

The feed from sector nine's exterior camera played, showing the familiar backdrop of Venus with a small spacecraft flying across it.

"That . . . doesn't look like an enemy ship," Tyrone said.

"No, it doesn't." Amara enlarged the image until we could clearly see the writing on its side.

I kept my gaze fixed on the screen, avoiding eye contact.

"You've got to be kidding me," Diego said. "It's—"

"John," Amara finished for him. On the screen, "Galactic Veteran's Retreat" emblazoned on the side of the ship in bold, undeniable print.

"Henry, I thought you said you were going to take care of that," she said.

"I did," I said. "Don't worry, John knows what he's doing."

"You mean you let him go? On purpose?"

The escape pod turned, firing a stream of red lasers into the emptiness of space. At the same time, another invisible something hit our ship, making the room go momentarily dark.

"Outer shell at two percent," Diego said.

Amara turned to me, glowering. "I hope you have a good reason for sending that poor old man to his death. If we live, I'll make sure you pay for this."

"If we live, it will be because of John," I said. On the screen, John's ship continued to spin around, firing into nothing.

"You can't hit dark weapons from an escape pod," Diego said. "No one can. It's like shooting blind."

"John can." I turned to the screen where his ship continued to swerve back and forth, its beams shooting off into space.

As another object made impact, our ship jolted, triggering an alarm.

"System breach imminent," a voice said. "Prepare for catastrophic failure. Outer shell at one percent strength."

Come on John, I thought. *Come on, you can do this.*

Just then, one of the red beams made contact with an invisible something, exploding into a sphere of white light.

"He hit one!" Tyrone said. "He really hit one!"

Moments later, a second sphere of white light appeared, followed by a third, then a fourth.

"He must have found a way to detect them!" Amara said, leaning over her monitor. "But how?"

"I'm gonna guess it has something to do with his fifty years of experience," I said, smiling.

For several minutes we watched as John lit up the sky with a hundred explosions. Again and again, his shots met their target, with improving accuracy, until the ship finally came to rest.

"Do you think he got them all?" Tyrone asked.

I watched the ship hover, motionless.

"Do you think he's just waiting to see if there are more?" Diego asked after another couple of minutes passed.

I shook my head. "No, I think something might be wrong." I turned to Amara. "Can we bring him back in from here?"

"I already tried," she said. "He's disabled remote override."

Suddenly, John's spaceship swerved, turning toward the ship. Somewhat erratically, it bobbed toward Bay 12, docking with a crash that rocked the whole ship.

I unstrapped myself from my seat. "Quick, open the doors." I hurled myself toward the exit just as the doors opened.

Not caring how it would cost me later, I launched myself down the corridor, colliding with walls, floor, and ceiling along the way. When I reached Bay 12, I found the doors already open, John slumped in the pod seat, his forehead slick with sweat.

"I think I . . . got 'em all," he said through shallow breaths. "Took me a minute, though."

I squatted beside him, medical training kicking into gear. "Your pulse is through the roof. How do you feel? Dizzy? Nauseous? Any pain?"

John slowly turned his head, a big grin on his face. "I feel better than I've felt in years. And even if I didn't, I'd do it all again." He closed his eyes, resting his head on the back of the seat. "I was right, by the way."

"Oh?"

"Yeah. They were dark falcons. Volton-made. Only they were free-floaters. Leftovers from a past battle, adrift in space. You'll have to let the general know you've found some out here. She'll want to sweep the whole area, check for others."

I patted John's hand. "I'll let her know. I promise."

At the end of the corridor, my supervisor appeared. When she saw me, she launched herself down the hall, catching herself on the edge of the door. "Is he hurt? Is he okay?"

"He's doing just fine," John answered. "Thanks for asking."

My supervisor looked at me, her expression severe. "Henry, you are—"

"Fired, I know."

"Well, no. I was going to say, 'a genius'. Asking John to help, that was brilliant."

"Oh, I didn't have to ask John anything. It was all his idea. I just handed him the keys, so to speak."

John frowned. "Why on Earth do you think that'd get you fired, young man?"

"Well, for one, I put you in danger. For two, I disobeyed a direct order. Then, there's the damages." I pointed to the escape pod, whose side was dented from the rough docking.

"You were merely helping me follow my own wishes," John said. "Which, if I'm not mistaken, saved the life of everyone on this ship."

Amara smiled. "Yes, that is true. But I think we should note that the ends don't necessarily justify the means. And while I don't plan on firing you, Henry, I'm afraid I cannot in good conscience provide a letter of recommendation."

John scoffed. "And by 'means' you mean giving veterans, like me, the power to make their own decisions."

"Mr. Kowalski—" Amara began.

"*Captain* Kowalski," I said.

"Yes, of course. *Captain* Kowalski, it is my job to determine whether or not Henry has earned my letter of recommendation, and frankly, I don't think he has."

John stared blankly at her. "Okay, fine. He can have mine, then."

"Your what?" she asked.

"Letter of recommendation. I'm sure the recommendation of a captain carries more weight than that of a . . ." He studied her slate gray uniform, unable to guess her rank.

"Supervisor," I said, stifling a laugh.

"I see. Yes, I'm sure the general values a captain's recommendation more than a supervisor's."

Amara's face turned scarlet, but before she could respond, I said, "I appreciate the offer, Captain Kowalski. And someday I do hope to join ISC's med squad, but I think I still have a few things to learn. If Amara will still have me, I'd like to work here a while longer."

Amara's expression softened. "Well, certainly, if that's what you want."

"It is," I said, turning to John. "Where else would I get the opportunity to learn from the very best?"

John smiled, his eyes glistening. "I already know what the first lesson will be: How to navigate zero gravity without looking like an idiot."

I laughed, rubbing a particularly sore spot on my head. "I'm looking forward to it."

"I'm glad you'll be staying with us," Amara said. "But just so you know, being the captain's favorite won't get you out of handling Code Alphas."

I looked back at John, strapped into the pod, his tubes sticking out from under his uniform.

"Oh, don't worry. I'm counting on that."

Jaguar's Ghost

Devin Miller

The bound girl reminded Jaguar of his niece. He saw her by the amber glow of a geothermal-powered lamppost, which stood in a courtyard of ruined townhouses. Ashy volcanic clouds roiled low overhead, choking the light to a dim halo through which three men dragged the girl by her arms.

Hard to believe there's a bright yellow planet out there, Jaguar thought.

The planet was Carpathia, a beautiful gas giant with several habitable moons, including this one, Hurrono. Although, since the planetary governor had dropped buster bombs into the deep volcanic shafts and infested the surface with Mithra decades ago, *habitable* was a generous description.

Jaguar watched the girl from outside the range of the lamplight. He was at home in the dark, and had been for a year. Another shadow in the ruins. His black combat suit covered everything but his eyes.

He spotted a green glow in the distant sky, rising over the husks of bombed out buildings. A gravity egg, heading to space.

Nearing mission objective, said a voice in his head—Meteor, his sniper companion. *Former* sniper companion, since his squadron had all been sent back to the void in an ambush more than a year ago, their bodies consumed and incorporated by Mithra.

I'm getting off this awful moon, Jaguar thought, *and I'm not letting anyone or anything stop me.*

The vehicle ascended toward the cloud cover, trailing a stream of green-white light. He could see details on it—the capsule door, the viewing window, the humming engine compartment—so close to salvation now that he burned with a fever to move.

So why was he hesitating?

We live for a reason, Bulldozer's voice said. *To make a difference.*

His niece came to mind again. He could almost see her, hear her laugh. His brother's daughter. He hadn't thought of her since before the ambush. Nothing on Hurrono had reminded him of her, or anything cheery or optimistic. Those things were dead here.

Except that girl.

Jaguar shook his head. He'd never respected a squad leader more than Bulldozer, but he no longer believed the big man's optimism. Jaguar wasn't the man he had been. He wasn't alive for any *reason*. He was alive because he'd been scouting when the squad was ambushed, and he'd found a place to hide when the shooting attracted the Mithra.

He knew who the girl was. He had overheard the locals talking about her since he snuck into the city of Tomoyo two days ago. Clean skin, bright dress, curly dark hair. The planetary governor's daughter. Jaguar watched the gravity egg disappear into the ashy canopy high above, leaving a trail like a teasing path to deliverance.

Might it be useful to have her around when he got up there? The gravity egg was like an elevator that would take him off the moon to a Cultural space station in geosynchronous orbit. He would be debriefed extensively, his loyalty questioned. He didn't want to trade one prison world for another. What if she could vouch for him to her father?

The three men wore the handmade uniforms of an amateur paramilitary group, little more than a gang. Dark pants and shirt, hair cut short. Two had steel bars across the left shoulder—rank, Jaguar assumed. They had scarred faces and dirty hands. The third was cleaner, and had five steel bars.

Not bars, Jaguar realized. *Mithra claws.*

They were arguing with each other, debating which abandoned townhouse to usurp. They wouldn't choose Jaguar's hiding place—it was a leaning ruin, though he had found a blessing inside: working pipes and lukewarm water. While they spoke, the girl stared at something on the ground. A skeleton. None of the others noticed. Jaguar also paid it no mind, more interested in the vehicle the group had come in.

It was a small ground transport, but it would have a fuel cell, and Jaguar had a few explosives. He wasn't an expert in them—that had been Kerosene. He also had a sidearm with some projectile ammunition, and he had Claw, his dagger.

Jaguar was never one to collect dust. He slunk into the shadows, which were deep enough that Jaguar could circumvent the courtyard without the three men noticing, absorbed as they were with each other. He kept clear of the lamplight's halo. This was his expertise. Few people ever saw Jaguar once he decided he didn't want to be seen, and if they did, they rarely had a chance to tell anyone about him.

He reached the vehicle's rear bumper and briefly considered hotwiring; it would help him reach the gravity egg sooner, get off this world, be closer to home.

A wet smack made him turn. The three men loomed over the young woman. Someone had slapped her to the ground. It didn't stop her from unleashing a string of curses at them. One of them bent and tore a strip from the hem of her dress, which was already ragged. Jaguar realized that a length of it had been tied around her wrists. The man shoved the cloth into her mouth.

From her place on the ground, she spotted Jaguar manipulating the vehicle undercarriage. Her eyes went wide, body stiffening, a sharp inhale of breath. Instinct told Jaguar to disappear.

Instead, he drew Claw.

As soon as the dagger's point cleared the sheath, the battery in the hilt sent power through the blade, making it glow red-hot along the edge.

The girl's reaction and the glowing blade drew the men's attention. Three armed and hostile men, fully aware of him—a phenomenon that hadn't happened for months. They formed a line between him and the girl. Jaguar's heart pounded. But his grip on Claw was firm and steady.

"He's the one Derry saw cutting through the fence, Hurst," one of the men said. Jaguar cursed silently. Slicing through Tomoyo's perimeter barrier had been an exposed act, but he thought he'd gotten through unnoticed. He would have to be even more cautious. Tomoyo had eyes everywhere.

"Quiet." Hurst had a rifle, and stared at Jaguar with a hunter's gaze. "Keep your gun on Miss Naïve."

"By the Yellow God, that's the Culture soldier," the first man insisted. He looked to his other friend for help. "Tell him, Derry."

The friend nodded. "He's the one. Has to be." He pointed his pistol in Jaguar's direction. "I'd like a knife like that."

"He doesn't look like much, now that he's out of the dark," said the first man. "Skinny little mangy mongrel."

"Now you've hit on what makes him so dangerous," Hurst said. "Not looking like much, letting you underestimate him. He probably has some trick ready for us, some—"

He stopped short, glancing at the vehicle. He gasped and leapt for cover. Jaguar did the same. Then the explosives he'd hidden detonated, and shrapnel from the vehicle's shell flew in a hot cloud at blazing speed. The two men with the pistols grunted and collapsed.

The blast lifted Jaguar and flung him, farther and harder than he'd predicted. Shrapnel bit into his combat suit, and a few pieces tore ragged tracks across his back. He landed and rolled, finding his feet and his target.

Snarling, Hurst spun to a knee and raised the rifle.

Jaguar fired Claw.

A red beam appeared from the dagger's tip and pierced Hurst's shoulder. The man yelped and fell back. His arm spasmed, the rifle went flying, and the beam sheared the barrel clean in half.

Jaguar released the trigger. Claw cooled, red glow receding. He watched it fade, and realized belatedly that all his vision was fading, too. A dizzy wave tipped him over. He caught himself, blinking furiously, and glimpsed Hurst fleeing past the townhouses and away.

Footsteps sounded from behind him. He spun but lost his balance. Someone caught him before his head hit the stone formation under the lamppost. The girl. Her hands were half free; she wriggled them the rest of the way out and tossed the cloth from her mouth.

"Sorry that took a second," she said. "Had to do some unladylike stretching to get my hands in front of me. Let me see your back."

Jaguar's vision spun. He grabbed the ground but still felt as though he were falling.

"Lots of blood," the girl muttered.

"The suit . . . will heal it," Jaguar said. His tongue felt heavy and dry, his words slurred.

"You're Jaguar, right?" the girl said. "*The* Jaguar? Dad told me about you. I'm Elena. Come on, let's get you inside."

A wave of nausea made Jaguar gag. He pulled his mask under his chin.

"Don't throw up on me," Elena said. "I've gone through enough today without that, thank you very much."

She put Jaguar's arm over her shoulder and heaved him up. "Blood? Fine," she said. "Vomit? No way."

"That one," Jaguar said, pointing to the half-collapsed townhouse he'd hidden inside earlier.

"That one? That's a ruin. These look much better."

"That one," Jaguar insisted. Now that he was upright and moving, pain flared to life in his back as if he'd been whipped. *Stupid explosives,* Jaguar thought. *Where was Kerosene when you needed him?*

Back to the void, that's where.

Elena stepped over a crumbled wall and into the teetering structure. The pipes Jaguar had found earlier emptied into a low tub. Elena helped Jaguar sit and turned on the water by the glow of Jaguar's headlamp. "You have to clean that wound. No arguing. And anyway—don't take this the wrong way—when was the last time you had a bath?"

Jaguar didn't answer. He couldn't. His head was swimming.

"Thought so."

Elena pulled off his boots. He didn't have the energy to protest. The top of the combat suit unbuckled on his left side, and Elena peeled it away from the wound. It stuck in places, making Jaguar hiss and clench his teeth. A smell came with it, part metallic, part body odor. Elena grimaced, but she said, "I'll set it over the tub to air out."

As she did, he saw the hole the explosion had burned away—large and jagged, with cracks in the protective material. Its quality had degraded. The suit simply wasn't meant to be worn for a year.

"In you go."

He slid in, the warm water climbing over the combat suit's pants and his flat, pale stomach. He could count his ribs. His lean muscle had withered. He had changed so much in a year. Once, he had been a gung-ho soldier, never happier than on a mission with his squad, knowing the work he did kept his home planet safer. But fighting those three men earlier, he had been something else. Something more savage than a soldier. A darkness had descended on him as if the clouds overhead had swirled into his soul.

Beside him, Elena smelled of conda flowers. It shocked him. A smell he had completely forgotten could exist, though they grew rampant on his home planet. A pleasant, slightly spicy aroma. It brought the power of memory with it. Memories of home, of family. He wondered if other things might come back to life inside him, too. Maybe that was just shock talking.

Then he got his shoulder submerged, and the water ran red. His spinning head became worse than ever.

"Listen, now that we have a moment," Elena said. "Thanks for what you did back there."

"Don't let me drown," he said. It was first time he'd depended on anyone else since the ambush.

The dim light faded to black.

JAGUAR AWOKE TO SOMETHING STICKY ALONG HIS SHOULDER—THE SUIT HAD secreted some wound gel, and the healing skin itched.

He sat up in the tub. Elena had propped his headgear on a pile of concrete to give him light from the lamp. In the tub with him were a few big bricks covered in an old tarp—a makeshift footstool to keep him from sliding under. *She's resourceful.*

He tested his shoulder. Stiff, but manageable, the pain well-controlled at a constant low throb.

Jaguar crawled from the tub without a splash and dripped dry. He turned off the light and let his eyes adjust. Then he cupped his hands under the faucet and drank his fill.

"Don't drain it," Elena whispered.

He spotted her lying flat on a fallen slab of concrete, staring out a hole in the townhouse wall. She held a finger over her lips.

Jaguar slowly pulled the combat shirt back on, slid his feet into his boots, and moved to her position.

A single Mithra prowled the courtyard. Medium-sized, maybe fifty kilograms, depending on how much metal it had consumed. Its shoulders were low, hips high above skinny, taut legs built for chasing and pouncing. As Jaguar watched, the Mithra found a piece of the vehicle's torn casing and began to gnaw on it.

"So they consume metal," Elena whispered, "*and* people?"

"Most of them do okay with concrete, too—they go after the rebar."

"Fascinating."

"Organotech," Jaguar said. The Mithra snorted and moved toward Jaguar's two victims. "It'll clean up my mess, and tomorrow it will be bigger."

The Mithra's steel claws gleamed in the lamplight. Jaguar wrapped his hand around the hilt of his own weapon. He could hit it from here, but he didn't fully understand the Mithra hive mind. Killing one almost always attracted more.

"Best to slip away," Jaguar said.

"Right."

Jaguar led her to the back of the townhouse, careful not to dislodge any rubble. The Mithra would investigate. They were designed to be endlessly curious, for maximum destruction. Jaguar hadn't saved this girl to get her eaten by Mithra.

Why *had* he helped her?

The gravity eggs were his only chance off this moon. No ship would be unguarded enough, not in this environment, with desperate people and powerful, armed factions. Only the eggs, which serviced the farming palaces—massive, fenced-off districts where the moon's ruling class grew food in enormous greenhouses. The eggs were a direct line home to the Culture.

Jaguar's best chance of sneaking into such a place was alone.

Except he hadn't always been alone. He'd had a squad once, and together they were a formidable force. He had lost them to the void. Now he had Elena, smelling of conda flowers and bringing back memories of home and family, of his life before being alone. He wasn't sure how he felt about it. It felt risky, exposed.

He wanted the familiar loneliness back.

Squatting at the rear of the townhouse, Jaguar looked down a ravine carved into the cityscape. The trail dug out by a crash landing, no doubt—he had followed it into Tomoyo's outer districts. Elena crouched next to him. Up close, he saw sweat and ash had matted her dark hair in places. He pointed into the heart of Tomoyo, along the ravine.

"I'm going that way," he said. "To the farming palace at the city center, and their gravity eggs, and I'm taking one of them off this moon."

"Perfect," Elena said. "I'll go with you."

"You can't," Jaguar said. "I am a trained stealth agent. You're a politician's daughter in a bright dress who Hurst will have everyone looking for once he gets back to whatever gang."

"You don't know me," Elena said. "I know how to hide."

"It's not about hiding." Jaguar sighed. "Look, I can't protect you out there. I'm out of explosives, only have a few bullets left, and Claw. That's it. That's not enough to fight our way through gangs of humans and a growing Mithra infestation. I don't pick fights. I sneak around them."

"You picked a fight with the three men who kidnapped me."

"That was different."

"Why?"

"I don't—" Jaguar stopped, reminding himself that a Mithra lurked nearby. Quieter, he said, "I was in a ten-man squad. All elite soldiers. They could help you. Bulldozer especially. He was the leader. He could get you there. Or Meteor, our sniper. But not me."

"Well, forgive me, but they're all back to the void now. So that makes you much more qualified to help me than them."

Jaguar thought about his men, the emptiness he felt when the void took them. Some thought of space as the void, something above the cloud blanket where the "Yellow God" waited. But the void was death, and it had infiltrated his chest, freezing his heart and his breath. He had been reduced to something animal by that loss.

Was this a chance to be something else again?

An outside chance, Jaguar thought. *An impossible mission.*

But what would be the point of escaping this moon if he brought no humanity with him? Maybe he should take Elena, not because he needed a ticket past the Cultural station, but because it was the right thing to do.

He knew his squad, what they'd say. None of them liked unnecessary risk, but one thing none of them would ever do is give up on themselves or each other.

"Listen carefully," Jaguar said, kneeling and looking directly into Elena's blue eyes, out of place and far too bright and hopeful beneath these clouds. "If you stay with me, you have to move like me. When I move, people never know I was there. You have to stay so close and tight to me that they will never know you were there, either."

"I understand," Elena said. "I'll be your shadow."

"No, no," Jaguar said. "You aren't getting it. People can see shadows. You have to be a ghost."

She nodded. "I'm Jaguar's ghost," she said.

The girl was a quick study. Unusual for someone of privilege. She was made of interesting stuff. Not a soldier, but neither would she give in to fear.

So what right do you have, Bulldozer said, *to let your emotions control you? Get moving, soldier. You aren't one to collect dust.*

From the courtyard, the Mithra emitted a call—a haunting, echoing shriek. Jaguar listened. Answering calls came seconds later. Many more individuals. The horde, coming closer to the city.

"We've got to move," he said.

They slunk into the ravine.

JAGUAR DISLIKED BEING BELOW TWO RIDGELINES, WHERE ANYONE COULD LOOK down on him. But the walls were steep enough that no light could reach them at the bottom, unless the clouds revealed the bright planet above. He led them through the thick shadows, largely feeling his way over concrete obstacles and muddy patches where the output from leaky pipes had collected. A stench hovered in the low spots, like rust and sewage.

They didn't see any people in the ravine, though some clearly came there. Scorch marks revealed the sites of old camps. Under two unusual rock piles, Jaguar found caches of blankets. He cut a hole in the middle of one and draped it over Elena's head. He rubbed mud and dirt on the parts of the dress it didn't cover, as well as her forearms and legs. Beneath the cache, they found fruit inside steel containers, locked with a code. Claw's heated edge sliced through the lock, and they shared a sweet and energy-rich snack.

"I feel bad stealing someone's food," Elena said, though Jaguar noted she ate ravenously.

"It's war," Jaguar said. "Things get lost, taken. Destroyed."

"Too many things," Elena said.

"Wish we could have taken that vehicle," Jaguar said. Overhead, another green-and-white gravity egg rose toward the dark clouds. Ashy particulate floated through the tail of light streaming behind it. So close now, he could taste the clean, filtered air inside, feel the cool breeze of climate control and the gentle press of the seat below him until that old weightlessness returned.

Space.

Home.

"You wouldn't have wanted that vehicle," Elena said. "It smelled like a Mithra had died inside."

Jaguar considered her, examining the smudges on her cheeks, a yellowish bruise rising where she'd been slapped. "You're pretty out of your depth here, huh?"

Elena looked up from the fruit can and wiped her face. The juices cleaned her chin, making her look like she was wearing a mask—dirty above her mouth, clean below. She shrugged.

"What exactly did you come down here for?" Jaguar asked. "Couldn't wait on a committee for something?"

"Were you familiar with Hurrono politics?"

"No. And I don't really care."

"All you need to know is Hurrono wanted out of the Culture," Elena said. "The Culture doesn't tolerate secession. My father was tasked with ensuring the moon's compliance. The war started. He dropped the buster bombs, the volcanoes erupted . . . ."

She gestured to the ashy sky.

"Not all the populace was for secession," she said. "Those people were given sanctuary in the farming palaces. They've lived in relative luxury, hiding behind fences and in underground bunkers, while the rest of the population begs for food, forms gangs, and goes mad for two generations until they actually start to think that Carpathia is a god. The Mithra were sent for them."

"A cruel decision," Jaguar said. "Set that can down gently. People will hear if you drop it. Let's keep moving."

The next few hours were tedious. They trekked over uneven ground until they came to the wreckage of three military aircraft, fuselages half buried, barely recognizable but for their wings and tails protruding like tombstones. The wind through the shattered hulls made a deep noise that Jaguar felt in his gut. He crouched on the ridge above the planes and considered them.

"Could there be people inside?" Elena whispered.

"Don't think so," Jaguar said. "Too vulnerable from above. They'll have been picked clean for supplies and weapons. The Mithra will devour the rest when they come."

"The more I learn about the fate of this moon, the more horrible I feel about it," Elena said. "It deserves better than what my family did to it."

The note of sadness in her voice struck Jaguar. It was as unusual and unfamiliar as her perfume.

"You're not responsible for what your father did," he said.

"Someone has to make it right. But the only way the Culture will get involved—meaning, sending a fleet to mop up the Mithra and terraform the moon—is with a formal petition from the populace, and an agreement to a century of military occupation. I came to convince them to accept that."

She stared at Jaguar, frank and open, as if daring him to call her *Miss Naïve* the way Hurst had.

"Could be caches down there," Jaguar said. "Too risky to investigate, though. Better to hurry past in case someone comes."

The gloom above the ridge gave way to a dim glow after another hour: the farming palace, getting closer. Voices came with it, sporadic but unmistakable. Jaguar spotted figures moving on rooftops. He made them crouch for two hours in a muddy pit until a patrol—led by Hurst, arm in a sling—had moved on.

"Wish I could convince that man what a fool he is," Elena said. "He thinks he's a king. Doesn't realize he's part of a bigger culture, *the* Culture, humanity throughout the galaxy."

"Quiet," Jaguar said.

"Brought a whole ship's worth of aid and none of it mattered." She flung a rock into the dark. Jaguar started to admonish her, but something reminded him of his niece again. He couldn't recall what, or why. It had been too long since he'd thought of her, of family, and far too long since he'd seen them. A heavy longing settled in his gut.

"The only thing that kept him from shooting me is he thought he could ransom me," Elena said. "Now I'm stuck here."

"Just until we reach the gravity egg."

"Doesn't seem like your preferred mode of transport."

"Reliable enough, and easy to hotwire."

"No need for that. I know how to program them."

"You do?" He peered through the darkness at her. Her eyes caught the distant farming palace's greenhouse lights and shone.

She grabbed his hand briefly, just a reassuring squeeze, then said, "You can trust me."

Jaguar didn't respond for a long moment. Then he said, "First, we have to get there. And no more throwing rocks. Ghosts don't throw rocks."

Though he was eager, he slowed their pace. People appeared all around now, darting through nooks and crannies in the rubble, at home in the dead city. Shadows flashed in and out of the ravine, strange shapes in the distant blue glow.

They spent the night in a tight space underneath a fallen wall. Jaguar awoke with foggy dreams of distant shrieking, howling, growling . . . and gunshots. Had that been a dream? Or had the Mithra horde reached the city limits? Jaguar snuck out of their hiding place, Claw in hand, alert for an ambush.

All was quiet save the hot wind.

No sun rose to mark the morning, but it seemed the cloud layer had thinned some. Jaguar saw individual wisps dashing and swirling in the murk above, rather than one continuous thick totality.

Was there a splash of yellow in there? Or just his imagination? *No wonder people here worshipped the orb above.* In the thick gloom, even a flicker of light seemed divine.

The cityscape changed as they followed the ravine inward: the greenhouse lights grew brighter, the structures taller. Towering husks made up most of downtown. Many buildings had fallen, a crisscrossed network of once-proud megaliths, steel and concrete skeletons laid to rest atop their smaller neighbors. Nothing could withstand a Cultural barrage from orbit. The husks were like the dead city's bones, the people who thrived here long gone, and those who replaced them were more like bacteria decomposing a corpse—hardened, hungry gangs, armed with weapons leftover from the war.

"You should see the documentaries of what this once was," Elena said.

"Little to do now but wait for it to die," Jaguar said.

"It's heartbreaking."

Jaguar put a finger to his lips. A vehicle approached, wheels crunching on gravel. They lay on their bellies. Jaguar felt the vibrations against his rib cage and watched the headlights shine off rubble, bouncing erratically over potholes. Elena started to get up once it had passed, but Jaguar held her down. Moments later, he heard footsteps coming down a metal staircase somewhere to their right. Light steps. A child. A glimmer of shadow that vanished into a broken building. Jaguar motioned with his head to their left, and they hurried away at a crouch.

He pointed to what had once been a meeting place, perhaps a convention center, and indicated a collapsed storefront that leaned against it and provided a way to the roof.

Elena followed as best she could, not quite his ghost but doing well. A fast learner.

From the roof they could see a mile south, the way lit by sporadic lampposts. The main landmark was a toppled skyscraper that cut through the previous grandeur like a horrid scar. It appeared to run just alongside the city's farming palace. It would be easy to find. Easy to follow. Alone, Jaguar could do it in a day. His scouting instincts told him he had found his path.

Then he thought about supplies. They had few, even after plundering the caches. But the building they stood upon was large, and perhaps harbored a few working pipes.

"Follow me," Jaguar said. "As a ghost, remember."

They descended through the windows.

They found more locked steel containers and cut into them. Beans this time. They devoured them while Elena described more video footage of the vibrant moon decades before the bombings had made it a black abyss.

Jaguar realized that, for the first time since he had lost his squad, he was relaxed. His instincts still reigned—he had a good view of the door and the street through the window. But his fight-or-flight response wasn't running at full speed the way it had been for the previous year. Maybe it wasn't so bad to have a little companionship again, even civilian companionship.

Voices came through the window. Jaguar saw three boys run into the street, sneering playfully at each other and passing something between them that Jaguar realized with a shock was a Mithra skull. One of the boys put it down, and another took a sack from his shoulder and dumped its contents: a dozen small, silver balls that reflected the amber lamplight.

The boys were scrawny, young adult frames grown but nothing fleshed out on them. Jaguar had been the same once, back home. A lifetime ago. They took turns trying to bowl the balls into the open Mithra jaws. Jaguar noticed the jaws and teeth were half bone and half steel—a well-fed specimen. Each time a ball rolled inside the skull, the boys would shout, *"Ka-Boom!"* and fall over laughing.

"Hurst would give you a gun for that throw!" one of them said.

Jaguar stiffened.

Elena appeared beside him, watching, fascinated. The game went on for a while, long enough for Jaguar to wonder if they should sneak out some other way and continue on. But then one of the boys, who had yet to bowl a ball into the target, rushed to the skull and snatched it. The other two shouted and gave chase. A scuffle followed. They tugged at the skull. The one who tried to steal it yelped and flapped his hand. The teeth had cut him.

"Well you shouldn't have tried to take it!" one of his friends said, and gave him a hard shove that sent him tumbling into the decrepit door of the convention center. It banged open from the force, and the boy sprawled inside.

For a few seconds, the only sound was the squeaking hinges as the door rebounded. Light from the street poured over Jaguar and Elena, and the boy's head snapped around. Jaguar drew Claw and let its red-hot glow illuminate him. A look of stark terror appeared on the fallen boy's face, ghastly in the eerie light. He screamed and burst back into the street.

"*Soldier!*" the boy shouted. "*It's the soldier!*"

The boys fled, puffs of dirt thrown up in their haste. Jaguar stepped outside. He sheathed Claw and listened. He heard only the wind, making a strange whistling sound as it carved its way through the Mithra's eye holes and nose cavities. Jaguar spotted a red tooth, but the blood looked dry already, as if even dead it was still absorbing the organic material that would help it grow.

Jaguar crouched by one of the balls. He picked it up and brought it to his eyes. "Do you know what this is?"

Elena squinted. "No."

"It's a dud from a cluster bomb. The Culture would drop these long bombs from space—no thrusters necessary, they were really just suitcases—and inside would be hundreds of these little explosives. They'd open over the city. That's probably what destroyed most of these buildings. There could be thousands of these duds."

Elena looked pale, and Jaguar knew she must be thinking about what might happen to those boys if a dud decided to explode after all. "The duds all have the same defect," Jaguar said. He undid a clasp mechanism on the shell and unscrewed the cover. Kerosene had shown him how, ages ago. He heard the explosives expert's voice talking him through exposing the simple guts of the bomb, the pressure trigger, the defect, how to detach it without affecting the charge. His fingers worked quickly but carefully, threading the detonator out of the shell and turning the pressure trigger into a manual one.

"Now it's a grenade," he said.

"I don't like it," Elena said. "I don't trust it."

"Do you trust me?" Jaguar said.

"Yes."

Jaguar blinked. A strange feeling came over him, a fluttering in his chest and a warmth in his face. How odd, to be trusted again, after everything he had suffered and done in the last year.

"We might need them," Jaguar said. His words came out softer, gentler. "Those boys are going to tell their minders about me, and word will get back to Hurst. They'll come for you. And me, too."

Elena hesitated, her eyes on the dud. Then her gaze flashed to something along the road in the other direction. A look of horror overcame her. Her hands flew to her open mouth.

Three Mithra charged them.

They were hideous, misshapen creatures. Bulbous knee and shoulder joints, eyes rolling with hunger, tongues lolling, jaws glinting metal. Organotech monstrosities with single-minded programming—consume and grow and reproduce. The one in the middle had two extra limbs, small and useless, that would eventually be the forelimbs of another individual.

If it lived that long.

Jaguar fired Claw and traced the red beam through the chests of the first two. They slumped in pieces with a thud on the dusty street. The last one leapt for Elena. She didn't scream, but she did flinch when Jaguar's pistol barked out two shots.

The creature spun in midair and landed at her feet, still.

Elena showed him again that she was made of the same stuff as a soldier. "Let's take the grenades."

By noon, Jaguar knew something was wrong. The atmosphere of Tomoyo had changed—a prickly sensation in his skin, a sense of being watched, an unsettling hum beneath his feet that meant activity. People—maybe Mithra?—moving about, being loud and angry and alert. Sounds of distant motors reached them from around ruined buildings, difficult to localize. Lights glowed in windows. Flickers of red and orange hit the bottoms of the roiling black clouds.

"You were right," Elena said. "Those boys raised the alarm."

"Hurst will be after us soon. He's stirring up the crowds, and crowds attract Mithra."

"I thought they'd only just gotten to the city," Elena said.

"They swarm," Jaguar said. "You kill a few, a few more come. A few get fed, hundreds will come."

Elena shivered.

"If Hurst finds you again, he won't care about ransoming you," Jaguar said.

She clutched her blanket tighter around her chest. "We've got to get to the gravity egg."

"The farming palace is on the far side of that skyscraper," Jaguar said.

It had become a carcass of shattered glass and twisted steel, crushing upper stories of other buildings like thin aluminum under a boot. Navigating below it could be dangerous, and loud with all the broken glass, but going around would take time, and Jaguar was no longer willing to wait. He sensed his window of opportunity closing.

"Let's go."

They hurried down an alley beneath the behemoth structure. The echoing distant crowd became muffled. Jaguar chanced a light. He paused. Elena gasped. Along the curb, next to a shattered wall, was some kind of office lobby, obviously fallen straight through from the building above. Chairs and tables had landed weirdly intact, as if a conference had just ended. Cushions were rotted away, picture frames cracked. Several potted plants stood, leaves gone and trunks desiccated and grey.

A pile of bones lay beyond the potted plants.

Jaguar and Elena gave it all a wide berth. Trekking slowly, stepping carefully, they spotted other debris of what had once been a bustling enterprise. Computers, tangled wires, communications stations mangled. A set of cutlery. Scattered dress shoes and a ragged suit jacket.

The alley ended. Across a final street, the greenhouse lights shone. Electrified fencing surrounded the complex and cast crisscrossed shadows on a dead lawn. The roaring crowd grew in volume at the edge of the skyscraper ruin. Nearby, a refrigerator lay on its side, gleaming white in the glow. It was missing a large chunk out of its metal door.

"Fresh," Jaguar said.

Elena touched the jagged edge. "The mouth that bit this must be . . . ."

"We'll double back north a bit, put some space between us and Hurst, then cut through the fence. Let's hurry."

She didn't need telling twice. They stepped out from beneath the fallen skyscraper and took off running.

THEY STOPPED, PANTING, AT A MOUNTAIN OF DEBRIS AND A GRAVEYARD OF wrecked vehicles that stretched across the dead lawn to the fence. Jaguar felt the ground vibrating. *The Mithra horde. Already close.* At the same time, the human voices had only grown louder, more urgent, sensing they were close to their targets. Jaguar knew it was time. Elena waited for his signal, her chest heaving. They ran toward the fence.

Jaguar dodged the broken glass in the street by intuition, which Elena had never learned in her conference calls and study halls and meetings. Her boots crushed the shards to grit with pops like gunshots—*pop! pop! pop!*—a pattern that couldn't be mistaken for anything other than footsteps.

She stopped, eyes wide and imploring to Jaguar, hoping it wasn't bad.

Jaguar's instincts screamed at him to move, to leave her, to get across the dead lawn and through the fence, to the egg and up before it was too late. Men were coming. Mithra were coming. Elena's predicament was her own fault.

No matter what you call yourself, Meteor's voice said, *you're not an animal.*

Running away from who you are? Kerosene asked. *Man, that's the same as the void.*

From the shadow of the fallen skyscraper, a figure stepped into the light. Jaguar heard him exclaim something, saw a finger point toward them. Then another figure appeared beside the first, arm in a sling.

Hurst.

He awkwardly lifted a rifle. Jaguar sprang forward and grabbed Elena. They ran over the broken glass at a crouch, her blankets fluttering. The whiz of a bullet passing overhead echoed louder than the shards underfoot. Then their boots were on grass, their bodies flashing through the fence's shadows.

A chorus of bullets sang all around. Hurst shouted to his men. Jaguar drew Claw. Elena wheezed beside him. They slid into the shadow of an overturned transport truck next to the fence. It smelled of oil. Its tires had been stolen long ago. The fence hummed menacingly.

"You're going to run ahead of me," Jaguar said. "No matter what you hear, don't look back. Don't stop. Run as fast as you can for the gravity egg."

Elena looked as though she wanted to protest, but instead she clenched her jaw and nodded.

Jaguar fired Claw's beam through the electrified fencing. It popped and sparked, then shorted, and the ubiquitous hum disappeared. In seconds, Jaguar had cut an arch large enough to step through. He kicked it in.

Elena sprinted away.

A bullet pinged off the overturned truck. Jaguar leaned out and fired Claw's beam, slicing horizontally and ducking out of sight again as more bullets hit his cover. He heard men crying out, wounded. He rolled through the gap in the fence.

A rectangular building with five-meter-high windows along the top loomed ahead. The greenhouse. Elena followed a paved path around its corner, out of sight. As Jaguar ran after her, he felt he had been transported to another world, one preserved from war, where arc lights still shone and ash never lay over the ground like a suffocating blanket. The black clouds overhead even seemed thinner here, the sky less dark.

He stared upward as he ran, and realized with growing awe that the clouds really were thinner. They were parting. Yellow light poured through the gaps. The planet appeared—yellow gaseous surface and glowing orange and brown rings shining like polished gems. Jaguar slowed, staring, eyes burning from the light—brighter than anything he'd seen in a year—but he refused to close them. It was too beautiful.

Behind him, cries of praise and wonder replaced the bloodthirsty shouting. Jaguar looked over his shoulder. The men in front of Hurst dropped their weapons and fell to their knees. They raised their hands in supplication.

"*The Yellow God!*" they sang. "*Hail the Yellow God!*"

"Don't stop!" Hurst yelled. "Up! Up!" But he might as well have commanded a wall. Jaguar felt his heart lift. A little luck, at just the right moment. They might make it.

A massive black wave appeared from under the fallen skyscraper. The charging Mithra looked like a single hungry, stalking organism.

The Mithra fell on the crowd of men—claws shining, gleaming yellow in the sunlight reflecting off the god above. The prayers took on a horrible timbre. The fence collapsed, disappearing inside snapping jaws. Hurst got off a single shot.

Jaguar didn't stay to watch.

"They're through the fence!" Jaguar shouted, rounding the corner. "Elena! Start the launch!"

She reached the closest gravity egg, one of five on their landing pads, and wrenched the capsule door open. She began working the controls. Between Jaguar and Elena stood a line of parked vehicles on a concrete slab—big trucks with beds for distributing food throughout the city. They looked as if they hadn't moved in ages, sagging on their tires, windshields grimy, almost opaque. Jaguar hoped their fuel cells hadn't leaked. He dropped a remade grenade under each as he sprinted by.

The ground shook. Glass shattered somewhere. People inside the greenhouse began to scream, their sanctuary lost. The shrieking grew in intensity, coupled with the scraping of metal claws on concrete. Jaguar leaned against the last truck and caught his breath, quieted it, listening for the horde to circle the greenhouse.

He could get to the egg. Secure himself inside. Maybe even reach full power. But the swarm would wash over them, and a gravity egg was a civilian vehicle. No armor. The Mithra would send them both back to the void.

What are you a soldier for, the voice of Bulldozer said, *if not to protect people?*

Jaguar stood up straight, in plain view, Claw in his right hand. From the greenhouse on his left, the shrieking grew louder until a window broke in a shower of shards, like yellow rain in the planet's light. A lone Mithra appeared in the frame. It scanned the ground below, gripping the ledge with metal claws that punctured the outer wall. It opened its mouth and let out a hissing shriek from between jagged teeth, stained red.

The horde turned the corner at last and spotted him. Their calls escalated. He noticed several with hands of flesh instead of metal, shoulders and rumps of organic material. Their victims, recycled and reused. Several were huge, bulbous, swollen with grotesque extra limbs.

All of them charged.

Their footsteps pounded across the concrete. Jaguar listened hard. Elena shouted from behind him, pleading with him, but that pitch was high. He listened for the low pitch he hoped for—perhaps his only chance—and heard it when the horde was halfway across.

He fired Claw's laser, sweeping side to side, and kept his finger on the trigger. Mithra fell, tumbling in their charge, shrieking, tripping those behind. The red beam severed flesh and cut through the living metal. Mithra poured from the greenhouse window, and Jaguar caught several on their way down.

More came. Dozens, maybe hundreds more, of all sizes. The swarm wouldn't be stopped. Jaguar looked over his shoulder at Elena, who leaned from the gravity egg door, tears on her cheeks.

He waved her on.

Then the red beam dwindled as Claw's battery faltered. He pointed it toward the wheel well of the closest vehicle, and the waiting grenade, which started to glow. The Mithra closed in. Claw's beam faded, faded, then vanished. Overhead, the clouds swirled in a colossal eddy, and the wind pulled the shroud over the planet once again. The yellow light vanished, and darkness fell.

The only light now came from the gravity egg ascending behind him. He felt the engine's pulsations in his belly, heard the hungry Mithra only meters away. He barely noticed. His thoughts were of his squad, of his niece, and of Elena, rising to safety.

The heated grenade detonated.

The chain reaction lifted him off his feet. When he came back down the ground had disappeared. A stronger blast than he had expected, but he had never been great at explosives. A storm of concrete, twisted metal, and rebar leapt first up, then down through a hole blown in the roof of a subterranean structure. The rubble flowed like an avalanche, and Jaguar rode down with it.

ALL WAS DARK AND DUST AND ASH AND QUIET FOR AGES, BUT JAGUAR DIDN'T mind. He had survived a year like this—what was a little more time?

The rubble consisted of concrete boulders, mangled vehicle frames, shattered building material, and dead Mithra. It hadn't taken long for the surviving horde to lose interest in him—with the farming palace open, there would be easy prey to seek. But Jaguar lay still in the dark and dust for a day before moving.

He followed the sound of running water to a busted pipe and drank. It tasted of rust and silt, but it energized him for the climb.

Jaguar hauled himself from the ragged hole over the course of the next day, moving and waiting. Listening. Peering through the tumbled debris for any Mithra left alive, keen to avoid any fight, as Claw was only a simple dagger now —a millennia-old weapon against the cruelest of modern war.

But it was a human voice he heard that made him freeze at the top of the hole, beneath a precarious concrete slab.

"This is where he was."

"You saw the footage?" a male voice answered. They were whispering.

"He was alive when he went in," the first voice said. It cracked with excitement. "He should be the new leader. Wouldn't that be great? If we could just find him . . . ."

The companion chuckled. "Kid, no one finds a soldier like that unless he wants to be found."

Jaguar listened as their footsteps went away. He waited ten minutes, then climbed up.

The gravity eggs were gone.

He thought about what he'd overheard, and decided no one would see Jaguar anymore, because he was done with the Jaguar persona. He had the skills, the stealth, and would need them to get to Plotoyo, another city ten miles away. But he would keep his humanity. Now that Elena had helped him find it again, he would never let it go.

Lieutenant Commander Javier Ortega was never one to collect dust. He sank into the darkness and disappeared.

The Battle of Donasi

Elaine Midcoh

Captain Linae Tower walked through the entrance of Earth Space Command HQ, grateful the security team manning the detectors pretended to not recognize her. She tried to ignore the people in the crowded lobby. Some stared, others glanced away, a few nodded at her, but one young Marine private stopped and came to full attention, blocking those around him. She resisted the urge to slug him. "Move on, Private."

She went to the elevators. The people waiting there parted, allowing her to board first. No one else got on. Linae thought about promising not to infect them, but the elevator doors closed before she could say anything. She was startled by the image reflected on the metal doors. Though only thirty-two, her eyes, red-rimmed and worn, belonged to someone ninety-five. And she spotted new gray hairs mixed in with her auburn strands. As the elevator rose, she patted her inside pocket and felt a sharp prick from the corner of the envelope holding her resignation letter.

Linae emerged on the top floor at the end of a long hallway. Directly across from the elevator doors, shimmering bright on the maroon walls, were large gold letters: "Earth Space Command—Chief of Staff." And right beneath them, sitting on a gold-colored textile padded bench, was Ash, complete with his trademark smirk.

Lieutenant Commander Asher Betowan, Medical Corp, rose to his feet, managed a legitimate, yet sloppy, salute and said, "Commander Destructo, I presume." Then he pointed at the red stripe across her shoulder. "Oops. I mean Captain Destructo."

Linae smiled, an expression so long unused that it felt foreign. Ash appeared rested; his dark brown skin had a glow to it. The three months home with his family in Nairobi certainly had helped his recovery. The scar on the left side of his face had faded to a barely visible crescent moon. She hugged him. "Looking good, Ash."

"This isn't proper military protocol."

She stepped back. "As if you would know. What are you doing here?"

"Like you, I have been summoned."

"Why? To make sure I don't commit suicide when they fire me?"

Ash's eyebrows shot up.

"I was joking," she said.

"Uh huh." He gestured toward the padded bench. "Let's sit."

"But we have been summoned."

Ash checked his watch. "We have five minutes, thirty-six seconds." He sat down. Sighing, she sat next to him.

"You did what had to be done," he said.

"Which part? Genocide or bringing biological warfare to space?"

Ash frowned. "That article got it wrong."

She didn't answer, but Ash knew her too well. "Earth's Gift to the Universe: Biological Weapons!" the headline had read and beneath it a photo of her at the World Parliament building receiving the Medal of Valor from President Sagun. That damned editorial went viral. On vid they discussed it endlessly and always, always, the morality question. Then one of the talking heads labeled her "Captain Destructo." That's when her stomach began launching acid up her throat, that's when sleep wouldn't come without a pill or two, and that's when she couldn't stand people anymore, like the Marine private in the lobby.

"You can talk to me," Ash said. Of course she could—Academy classmate, friend for a dozen years and shipmate for the past three. She'd been "best man" at his wedding and was "official auntie" to his toddler son. She could talk to him. She knew it . . . but.

Ash waited, then shrugged. He peered at his watch. "We have four minutes and twenty-seven seconds. Quiz. How many Earth ships were lost in the battle at Cerium 3?"

Linae laughed. Ash was back in Academy cadet mode, when they'd relentlessly drilled each other before exams.

"378," she said.

"And how many people did we lose?"

"174,452."

"And if we hadn't beaten the Hiturans at Cerium 3, what would have happened?"

"They'd have continued into our system. Europa, Mars, the Moon, Earth."

"And what would they have done?"

She stared at him. "They would have killed us, Ash."

He nodded. "And who started the war?"

She hesitated. "They did—we think."

"Incorrect. They did—definitely. The idiots who say we somehow provoked them, that we must have unknowingly violated a 'sacred Hituran cultural norm', ignore that they attacked first. We tried to contact them. We asked other planets to intercede. Do you remember when President Sagun broadcasted that, 'Don't know what we did, but we're sorry, please forgive us' speech? She sounded like a confused lover. But the Hiturans didn't care. They ignored every attempt at dialogue."

Ash rubbed the scar on his face, the place where a piece of their ship's buckling hull had sliced into him. "And we were losing, our pulse weapons slightly more than useless. What would our military history instructor have said? 'Throwing rocks against tanks.' That was us." He pointed his finger at her.

"Then you, Commander Tower—oops, I mean Captain, saved us."

She remembered her excitement when she'd come up with the idea. With their ship damaged, weapons offline, and Captain Arayas dead, Linae had taken command. Through grit and luck they managed to bring the *David Roy* to the fallback rendezvous point, only to find they were the only battle cruiser to get there. It was supposed to be a place for a regrouping of forces, a place to organize a second stand, but the devastation at Cerium 3 had eliminated that possibility. Then Linae had seen the eight robotic supply ships standing by and got an idea.

The Hiturans would never board an occupied human ship without carefully eliminating biohazards, but automated supply ships were designed to be bioclean. That was how the worlds conducted trade with each other. The Hiturans would be happy to steal the supply ships and their cargo. All she had to do was plant a surprise for them. And then she saw the medical ships and got another idea.

Ash checked his watch again. "Final question: Was it your goal to commit genocide?"

Linae stiffened. "No. But who cares? I'm 'Captain Destructo'."

"No, you're Captain Tower. The Hiturans going extinct didn't happen because of you. You know our protocol in such circumstances?"

She had reviewed it several times since Cerium 3, always wondering about the Hiturans. "If a space crew gets infected with an unknown disease, we send in a medical ship. Hopefully, they can help. If not, then both ships and crews get quarantined in their own private mini space station until such time as a cure is found—or forever, if no cure is found."

Ash nodded. "That's the only smart course of action. There was no reason to think the sick Hiturans would go back to their planet. We still don't know why they did. Maybe it was a 'sacred cultural norm,' maybe dying Hiturans have to go home. But they made that choice. All you did was come up with a defense strategy designed to defeat enemy forces in the middle of a battle." He tapped her on the knee. "You know that, right?"

"Sure, absolutely." Linae tried to smile, but her face just couldn't get there.

He stood up. "Thanks for saving us, by the way. I like being alive. We have forty-five seconds."

When they entered the conference room Linae saw two officers already sitting at one end of the long antique oak table. Her heart skipped when she realized that the gray-haired man at the head of the table was the Chief of Staff himself, Admiral Ideema.

She and Ash both came to attention and saluted. This time Ash's salute wasn't sloppy at all. "Captain Tower, reporting," she said.

"Lieutenant Commander Betowan, reporting," Ash said.

Admiral Ideema stood up, as did the other officer, which was strange because they both outranked Linae and Ash. Then she realized it was her Medal of Valor pin. Tradition required that all officers present, regardless of rank, stand when a Medal of Valor recipient walked into a room. Damn.

"Captain, Commander," Admiral Ideema said. "Sit down."

Linae wondered if the fancy chair was designed to be deliberately uncomfortable or if the erupting muscle spasm in her back was her body's response to this meeting.

Admiral Ideema introduced the other officer as Vice-Admiral Coyman, a sharp-looking woman in her fifties. She was Earth Space Command's Chief Medical Officer.

Admiral Ideema said, "Before we begin, I want to thank you personally, Captain Tower. Without your innovative strategy employed at Cerium 3, I doubt any of us would be sitting here today. Or anywhere."

Innovative strategy, Linae thought. *Nice phrase for genocide.* She nodded in acknowledgment.

He said. "What do you know of the planet Donasi?"

Donasi? Linae had to think for a moment. "Of the thirty-two worlds known to have intelligent life, Donasi—"

"Thirty-one," Admiral Coyman interrupted. "There are now just thirty-one planets known to have intelligent life."

Linae saw Ash's hands clench into fists. Admiral Ideema regarded her without expression. *Screw them,* she thought. *If they want to fire me, fine, but I'm not going to punch out a superior officer and give them the satisfaction of a court-martial.*

"Thank you, Admiral Coyman. Of the thirty-one planets known to have intelligent life, only thirteen have developed interstellar travel."—*Thought I'd say fourteen, didn't you?*—"The remaining eighteen, including Donasi, have not developed space flight and are each at different stages of cultural and technological development. Donasi is considered a 'D' planet, at a technological stage roughly the equivalent of Earth in the early twentieth century, about where we were two hundred years ago. They've just begun to develop electricity as a power source. They have multiple nation-states across the planet, ranging from dictatorships to democracies. They are located in an isolated part of space, away from the interstellar trade routes and shipping lanes. Their planet is not known to hold any unusual natural resources that would make it a target for exploitation."

Admiral Ideema grinned. "So you still remember your Academy textbooks. But do you know when that textbook entry was written?"

"Sir?"

"Your information is nineteen years out of date. That's the last time an Earth Space Command ship surveyed Donasi. We want you to go back. Do a new survey."

"Why?" It made no sense. Donasi was a nothing planet. No special location, no special resources.

"Why not?" asked Admiral Coyman. "We don't have another war for you."

Ah, so that was it. She wasn't being fired. She was being sent away. Give the war hero a medal, then hide her in isolated space.

Admiral Ideema gave Coyman a hard look. "There's more to it," he said. "It's important for us to show the other worlds that we're not interested in war. Going back to routine missions is a start. Having you lead such a mission emphasizes that point." He smiled. "Also, I'm sure you won't mind: We're giving you the *David Roy*."

Linae and Ash glanced at each other and Linae felt a surge of joy. As for Ash, he could barely contain himself. "The *DR*'s been fixed?" she asked.

Admiral Ideema said, "We're repairing all the ships we can, even those we might normally scrap. It's not as if we have a lot left. We prioritized the *David Roy*. It's the first one off the line and is ready for a shakedown. That's another reason for this mission."

"What about our crew, Admiral?" Linae said. "We lost about a third at Cerium 3, but I'm sure the rest will be pleased to return to the *David Roy*."

"We've already assigned you a crew, Captain. Admiral Coyman, if you please?"

Coyman nodded to Ideema, then turned to Linae. "About half the crew will be your own, but the other half, and all the officers except for you and Dr. Betowan here, will be from other ships, ships that fought at Cerium 3."

"Ah, survivors," Ash said.

For the first time, Coyman smiled. "I see you haven't forgotten your psychology studies, Doctor."

"No, ma'am," Ash responded.

Ash clearly understood what was going on, but Linae did not. She said, "I haven't had psychology studies."

Coyman folded her arms and gazed at Ash.

Ash turned to Linae. "We lost a lot of ships at Cerium 3, and people too, but there are always survivors."

Linae flinched. *Not for the Hiturans.* If Ash saw it, he pretended not to notice.

"Many of the survivors of Cerium 3 are traumatized. There've been multiple medical conferences over the past months. We've been trying to figure out effective treatments. It's clear that some crewmen and officers will end up leaving the service, perhaps never returning to space. Others will need to gently ease back in. But some should return to space duty now, immediately. For them, the sooner, the better."

Admiral Ideema said. "They've fallen off a horse, Captain, and if they don't get back on right away, they might never ride again."

Is that why they picked her for this, as part of some psychological treatment? Then it hit her. "I'm commanding a therapy ship?" That's all she needed, a weak, whiny crew. She felt her face reddening.

Admiral Coyman glared at her and leaned forward, but whatever she was going to say was cut off with a quick hand gesture from Admiral Ideema.

"Captain Tower, no Earth Space Command crew needs coddling. If this mission is . . . somewhat therapeutic, then your crew's therapy is that they're not in therapy. They are all Space Command personnel, and you should hold them to the same high standards as any crew." He smiled again. "They'll expect nothing less from the hero of Cerium 3."

THE JOURNEY TO DONASI WAS UNEVENTFUL, EVEN BORING, THE PRIME DEFINITION of a milk run. Linae ran a series of drills to test the *David Roy* and her crew, including battle scenarios. She half expected Ash to protest. Maybe battle drills were too stressful "therapy" for this damaged crew. But Ash laughed when she set up the exercises. "Y'know the war's over, right?" he asked.

The renovated bridge was just as crowded as the old one, with the captain's chair smack in the middle of its long rectangular shape, surrounded by the various stations. Ash spent a lot of time on the bridge, sitting in the observer's chair that was to the right and slightly behind her own. He complained that the crew was too healthy to keep him busy and that the refurbished sick bay smelled funny. Linae didn't mind his presence. Though she made a point to meet and chat with all of the officers, Ash was the only one she knew well. Of course, there was an advantage to being on a ship with Cerium 3 survivors, even if they were strangers. Not one gave her a funny look or called her "Captain Destructo."

Only when they reached the outer edge of the Donasi system did they get a surprise.

Ensign Irena Terry, working the forward helm, made the discovery. "Captain, we're scanning an unmanned craft up ahead, either a probe or a satellite."

Terry was one of the Cerium 3 survivors on board. Unlike other survivors, she did not consider herself lucky. Her husband and sister had both died in the battle with the Hiturans. She rarely talked about her loss and she performed her duties with an intensity that Linae admired. "Main screen on, Ensign."

Terry had to magnify the screen five times before the object's features became clear: a simple metallic box with solar panels on all sides.

"Not very stylish," Lieutenant Batak said. Batak was the ship's navigator and another survivor, but—to Linae—he didn't seem troubled at all. He was jovial and happy, a cheeriness that went well with his short roly-poly body.

Terry looked up from her instruments. "Captain, even though the object has solar paneling, its primary power source is nuclear. It's leaking radiation, though there's no danger to us. I've heard of stuff like this, but only in museums."

"Captain Tower, we're receiving a signal from the object," Ensign Flare's booming voice echoed across the bridge.

"Audio on."

Flare stood close to seven feet, tall for a human, but which Flare swore was small for a Texan. He loved hand-to-hand combat and continually challenged other crewmen to meet him in the ship's gym. Linae felt tempted to match him, but wondered if that was appropriate for a ship's captain. Still, she appreciated Flare's aggressiveness. He would have been a great crewmate at Cerium 3, but had been on leave when the Hiturans attacked. He missed the entire battle. His old ship, the *Venture*, was lost with the entire crew. Flare didn't talk about them— ever—but he often said that he would never take leave again. Flare hunched over the station at tactical. "Ma'am, it's not an audio signal, it's visual."

"Then visual on," Linae said, drumming her fingers.

The main screen filled with an image of a male. He had the distinguishing characteristics of the Donasi: blue, hairless, short, barrel chested, powerful arms and long elegant fingers that seemed incongruous with the rest of the body.

Within seconds the Donasi began to wave his arms in front of his body.

"It looks like he's waving us off," Terry said.

"We don't know that, Ensign," Ash replied. He had entered the bridge just as the signal came through. "We don't know their customs or body language. Maybe this is the Donasi way of saying hello." He took his observer's seat.

Linae nodded a greeting. "We do know it's crazy for the Donasi to have this technology. Less than twenty years ago they barely had electric power. How likely is it that they developed space flight in so short a time?"

"Maybe they're intelligent," Batak said.

Linae frowned. "Maybe. Or perhaps they had help."

"Another world? Why?" Ash asked.

"Captain, look." Terry said.

On the screen appeared an animated image of the planet. The Donasi stood in front of it and began to swing his arms, first to the right and then to the left.

"Go around, maybe," Ash said.

Then the Donasi crossed his arms across his huge chest, with his long fingers resting lightly on his powerful arms. His face took on an angry look as he planted his feet firmly in place. His body shielded the animation of Donasi, completely blocking it as it disappeared behind his defiant stance.

"You're right, Ensign Terry. He's not saying hello," Ash said.

Linae stared at the Donasi's image. *So they don't want visitors. Okay, but that didn't answer the question of how they got to space so fast.* She said, "Ensign Flare, of the known inhabited worlds, how many planets developed space flight within twenty years of developing electricity?"

Flare responded immediately without having to check with the computer. "None."

"How about thirty years?"

"None."

"That doesn't mean they didn't do it on their own," Ash warned.

"No," Linae said, "but it's unlikely. One of the other worlds is here or came here. I want to know why." *Was it the Hiturans? Could some have survived? Had they come to Donasi to make a new home? A lonely planet off the grid would be a good place to regroup.*

Ash leaned forward. He whispered, "I know what you're thinking. Forget it. They're all dead."

"Someone's here, Ash. We're going to find out who."

Linae folded her arms and her face took on an expression eerily similar to that of the Donasi on the screen. "Ensign Terry, take us to Donasi."

Exactly three minutes and forty-two seconds after the *David Roy* entered orbit around the planet, the first Donasi ship approached.

"They knew we were coming," Ash said.

"That welcome wagon probe sent a signal," Batak replied.

Linae turned to Flare. "Will we be able to communicate with them?"

"Yes, ma'am. We've been monitoring their broadcasts since we entered the system. The computer's translation matrix has us at ninety-seven percent clarity."

"Excellent. Establish commlink. Put it on the main screen."

"Commlink open."

Linae faced the screen. "My name is Linae Tower. I'm the captain of the Earth Space Command vessel *David R———*"

"I am Ben Ami," a gravelly voice cut Linae off as the image of the Donasi filled the screen. He was clearly old, yet strength emanated from him. There were wrinkles around his green-blue eyes, but the eyes themselves were bright and alert. Ben Ami reminded Linae of an old half-dingo/half-husky dog she had watched over one summer, all folded up and contained within itself, ready to uncoil and strike at the first sign of danger or prey. "I am the commander of the Donasi Defense Force. You have invaded our space. Surrender your ship immediately."

Linae felt her eyebrows shoot up and forced them down. "Commander Ami—"

"Ben Ami," he said, again cutting Linae off.

Linae reminded herself that so far there was no cause for hostility. "Commander Ben Ami, we mean you no harm. Our mission is peaceful—"

The channel shut off. Linae turned to Ensign Flare.

"It wasn't me," Flare said.

"Then get him—"

"Ma'am, there's a power surge in the Donasi ship," Terry said.

This was the fourth time that Linae had been stopped mid-sentence, but at that moment she didn't care. "Engage shielding, Battle Alert."

A microsecond later the *David Roy* was bathed in a sparkling bluish-green light. Linae squinted her eyes until Terry filtered out the brightness.

"Analysis," Linae said.

"It's an energy pulse," Batak responded. "They meant to disrupt the ship's structural integrity. Their weaponry seems similar to the first experimental pulse weapons we developed years ago. It's too weak to hurt us. Our shielding dispersed the energy before it could do any damage."

"A warning shot?" Ash asked.

"I don't know," Linae said. "Ben Ami doesn't strike me as a warning-shot kind of guy. Mr. Flare, damage report?"

"Reports coming in. No damage, no casualties. A few inquiries asking about the pretty light. Some of the crew don't even know we've been attacked. Shall I return fire?"

Linae saw Ash watching her, not with his usual smirk, but with a seriousness that made her stomach contract. Another battle. Damn.

"No. Resume commlink," she said.

"Captain, two more Donasi ships approaching," Terry said.

"Mr. Flare?"

"I'm trying to reestablish comm, but they're refusing to respond."

The two Donasi vessels immediately flanked the first ship. Linae noted that they positioned themselves in such a way as to provide for maximum defense, while still enabling them to initiate an attack.

"Mr. Flare," she repeated.

Flare's hands flew rapidly across his board. "Captain, they won't answer, but their comm system is pretty simple. Got it. They may not respond, but they'll hear you."

Linae nodded. She leaned toward the main screen. "Commander Ben Ami, I know you hear me. We are not here to fight. I only want to talk with—"

Ben Ami's image filled the viewscreen. "There is no reason to talk. You trespassed in our space. Surrender or be destroyed."

And then Ben Ami waited. He did not break off communication, he did not make more demands, and he did not order his ships to fire. He simply gazed at Linae. Though Ben Ami's gaze was calm, there was something else there . . . something Linae could see, almost recognize. *What is it? What am I missing?*

Ben Ami was waiting for Linae's response . . . but what response? *I'm not a damned diplomat, just a dumb captain.* She glanced at Ash, hoping he might have an idea, but he just stared back at her. Great.

"Ben Ami," she began, "It was not our intention to trespass. We came in response to your probe. We were surprised to find a space-faring people in this region—"

"No doubt," Ben Ami said. His image disappeared from the screen. Seconds later it was replaced by the luminous bluish-green light of the Donasi energy pulse weapon.

"All three Donasi ships fired simultaneously," Batak reported. "No damage to us. If this is the best they've got, they can shoot at us for months. It won't even dim the lights."

"That went well," she said to Ash.

"At least this time we're the tank and they're throwing the rocks," he replied. "I wonder why."

"That's the question, isn't it?"

"Captain, shall I return fire?" Ensign Flare asked.

Linae rubbed her forehead. "Fire a warning shot across the bow of Ben Ami's ship."

"Aye."

The pulse blast flew across space.

Linae sighed.

Ash whispered, "This isn't your fault. They started it." She wondered if he knew he had said the same thing about the Hiturans.

"Ash, it's pretty clear Ben Ami won't talk with me. Monitor their communications. See if you can learn something."

"Aye, Captain." Ash turned to his seat's screen.

Twenty minutes later Linae shook her head. Now there were five Donasi ships and four more on the way, expected within the next fifteen minutes. Once again the five ships fired, this time aiming at the propulsion systems. Once again the *David Roy*'s shielding easily absorbed the energy pulses. By now the Donasi had to know that their weapons were useless. Earlier they had fired simultaneously. When that failed, their ships fired one after the other, creating a continual flow of energy that still couldn't penetrate the *David Roy*. One time they concentrated their energy pulse on just one section—oddly enough the area where the kitchen mess was located—and later they dispersed their fire so that the whole *David Roy* was bathed in the bluish glow from their weapon. It didn't matter; the Donasi energy pulse was too primitive a weapon to break through.

The *David Roy* vibrated slightly as the Donasi attacked yet again. Ensign Flare checked his board, then looked up at Linae. "Still no damage. Shall I fire another warning shot? Again?" His lips formed a thin line.

Linae understood. She wouldn't mind giving the Donasi a thorough lesson in modern weapon technology. Still, she knew she hadn't a clue as to why this was happening. Just like with the Hiturans, a fight and not knowing why.

"No, don't fire another warning shot. Ash, have you found out anything?"

Ash looked up. "Not in terms of helpful information, but there is something of interest. Our 'battle' is being broadcast across the entire planet. They have an extensive mass-communication network and right now it's focused on us. I know you want to keep your eyes on them"—he gestured toward the Donasi ships on the main screen—"but listen to this."

Within seconds an excited voice filled the bridge, "and so Commander Ben Ami and the five Defender ships have stopped the invader. This is the first time the enemy has not returned fire—"

Linae turned in her captain's chair. "Ensign Flare, prepare to fire on all five ships."

"Aye, Captain."

"Hey, wait a sec," Ash said.

"I can't have them think we're weak. Don't worry, I won't rip them apart, but they need to know they can't win. They need to understand that their only option is to talk to us. Mr. Flare, set weapons to minimum strength. Do not damage their ships. I repeat, do not damage them, but make sure they feel it. Fire when ready."

"Aye, Captain. Firing now."

The five Donasi ships lit up with the impact of the pulse beams.

Terry said, "Good God, they have no shielding."

"I know that," Flare said. He bit his lip as he examined the info coming across his board. "I made adjustments. They shouldn't suffer damage, at least not much."

"Captain, you'll want to hear this," Ash said.

Again the Donasi announcer's voice played across the bridge. His words came out in huffing breaths. "By the Divine, all five defender ships have been hit. For so long we have prepared and now the invaders are here and, by the Divine, we don't know if we can defend—"

Ash shut it off. "They don't think we're weak now, do they, Captain?"

Linae ignored his icy tone. "He said they had 'prepared for so long,' as if they knew we were coming—or someone was. At some point someone must have come to their planet. Ash, keep monitoring their communications. We need more info."

She turned to Flare. "Did we damage them?"

Flare reviewed his board. "One ship lost about half their engine output. The other ships haven't suffered much damage."

"Open the commlink." At Flare's signal, Linae began, "Commander Ben Ami, there is no need for continued hostility. We mean you no harm—"

Once more the *David Roy* screens glowed as the Donasi fired their energy pulse weapons. Linae didn't bother to ask for a damage report. She knew there wasn't any.

"Captain, the other four Donasi ships have arrived," Batak reported.

Linae watched the four new Donasi ships as they positioned themselves. Ben Ami was no fool. Now with nine ships at his disposal, Ben Ami arranged his ships so that they completely surrounded the *David Roy*. Apparently, it didn't matter to Ben Ami that there was no chance of winning. He had to know that. Still the Donasi ships kept firing and Linae sat in the captain's chair, wondering how this mission was going to end.

"Oh no," Ash said.

Linae turned to him. Ash was focused on his screen. "What?" she asked.

Ash looked up, eyes wide. "I was monitoring one of their broadcasts. They were doing a review, a history of events. I found out who their alien visitors were." He rubbed his scar. "It was us."

The entire bridge crew stared at Ash. Linae said, "We just got here."

"Not us, the *David Roy;* us, Earth Space Command. Nineteen years ago when Captain Zared and the *Pueblo* came here, they were seen."

"But that's not possible," Batak said. "The Donasi didn't have scanners back then. They barely have scanners now."

"No," Ash said, "but they did have telescopes, and some good ones. Apparently, the Donasi have a strong interest in astronomy."

He turned to Linae. "I checked the *Pueblo* logs. Captain Zared had a hobby. He liked planetary geography."

Now Linae's eyes widened. "Are you telling me he did low sweeps?" That was in direct violation of Space Command rules when surveying an inhabited world.

Ash said, "Not exactly. The sweeps weren't low enough to be spotted with the naked eye, so he thought he was okay. But while the *Pueblo* was here, the largest Donasi moon was full in the night sky. Initially, the *Pueblo* was spotted by a young astronomer. At first he thought the *Pueblo* was a comet, streaking between Donasi and the moon, but then the *Pueblo* changed course."

"And comets don't change course," Linae said.

"Right. The Donasi knew that it was a ship. For the next three nights, they had dozens of telescopes searching the sky and four different course changes were noted. Captain Zared was mapping the planet. It was us, Earth Space Command. We were the ones who showed the Donasi that they weren't alone."

"So they were surprised," Linae said. "But that still doesn't explain their hostility. The *Pueblo* didn't attack them."

"No, but they didn't introduce themselves, either. The Donasi are afraid. They couldn't understand why the *Pueblo* would visit their world and not stop to say hi. Eventually they decided that the *Pueblo* must be a scout ship for an invasion. Everything in their society is based on that. All of the Donasi resources were turned to planetary defense. They developed flight, then space flight. They went from electricity to nuclear power in just a few years." Ash shook his head.

"They're remarkable. They set aside their differences, created a world government—mostly based on democratic principles, though with a strong military—and they made astounding technological advances in a very short time. All of it done in anticipation of this moment. They spent years and years waiting and planning, until today, Invasion Day. That's what they call it. And we're it, we're the invaders."

There was silence on the bridge. Terry's face went pale. Linae studied her bridge crew, hoping someone would have an idea. Instead, she saw that they all looked to her. *How wonderful to be captain.* She turned to Ash.

"I don't know," he said. "I don't know how we make this right."

Linae didn't know either. She had ignored the Donasi "stay away" message determined to find out what alien species had come here and why, only to learn that Earth Space Command was at fault. And now the situation had become hostile. Captain Destructo at work.

So she gave the only order she could think of. "Let's go home."

The nine Donasi ships completely encircled the *David Roy*, blocking all avenues of exit. Linae would have to get one of the ships to move. Of course, the *David Roy* could attack the Donasi vessels to clear a path. Linae refused to consider that option. No, Linae would have to get through to Ben Ami. Linae told Flare to open the commlink. "Commander Ben Ami, we acknowledge that we trespassed into your space. We respectfully request permission to leave."

Immediately the nine Donasi ships responded with a unified blast of their energy pulse weapons. It barely shook the bridge.

"Why are they so stupid?" Flare's fist banged against the console.

"What do you mean, Ensign?" Ash asked.

"They know they aren't hurting us. They know we can hurt them, yet still they keep at it. They can't win. It's stupid."

"No, it isn't," Terry said. "It's courage. It's Cerium 3 all over again. An invader, impossible odds, yet a refusal to give in. It's my husband and my sister and all the other Earth officers who died." She flushed and her voice shook. "The only difference is that this time we are the Hiturans."

No one answered her. Now Linae knew what she had recognized in Ben Ami: the face of all warriors who willingly enter into hopeless battle. She had seen it on her own captain and crewmates just a few months ago. *Terry is right, this is Cerium 3. But she's wrong, too.*

Linae stood up. She glared at each member of the bridge crew. "We are not the Hiturans."

Flare actually seemed to grow taller under Linae's gaze. Terry nodded her head and so did Batak. Ash gazed at Linae and gave her a small smile.

Linae addressed the bridge. "I want each of you to think. We want to create a path through the Donasi ships, but we don't want to damage them or cause casualties. Suggestions?"

"What if we grazed them with our pulse weapons, kind of pushed them instead of doing direct hits?" Ash asked. "Could we clear a path?"

"No way, Doctor," Flare said. "You saw what happened when we hit them with a blast at minimum power, and we weren't trying to push them then. Also, we'd probably have to hit them multiple times to push them in a controlled way. I doubt their ships could take that.

"Couldn't we modify the pulse beams to make them weaker—much weaker, enough so we could push the Donasi ships, but not damage them?" Terry asked.

"Maybe," answered Flare. "I've never tried to weaken one of our weapons. We'd have to hit their propulsion systems first, knock them offline and then push. We could try." He looked at Linae.

"How long?" she asked.

"I'm not sure, ma'am. At least twelve hours I think."

"Captain," Batak said. "Six more Donasi ships are on their way. They should be here in about seven minutes."

"I don't think we have twelve hours," Ash said.

Flare said, "Sure we do. Those six ships won't matter. They can fire on us for twelve years and our shielding would hold."

Ash said, "According to their broadcasts, this is the last of their fleet. They have no more ships. I'm not worried about their weapons. I'm worried what they'll do once they realize that six more ships don't matter. I think they may already realize that."

Linae nodded. "I think you're right. I'm surprised Ben Ami waited this long."

"Waited for what?" Batak asked.

"They're going to ram us," said Terry. "That's what we were going to do at Cerium 3. Captain Milton gave the order. But then the Hiturans withdrew. It was this ship that did it, that saved us." She laughed. "That's why I was so happy to get this assignment, to be on the *David Roy*, the ship that stopped the Hiturans. Now look at us, the evil invaders."

"Ensign Terry," Ash said.

"It's okay, Doc. I'm fine," she answered.

Linae sighed. "Mr. Flare, if they ram us, will our shielding hold?"

"We would have damage. Of course, the Donasi would not survive."

Batak said, "Captain, their ships are nuclear-powered. If any of their ships rammed us, depending on what debris falls into the atmosphere, parts of the planet may be contaminated. Thousands of the Donasi could become sick or die."

Linae felt her heart thudding. *No. I can't infect another world.*

Flare said, "Maybe we should blast one or two of their ships now and clear a path. Yes, it would destroy those two ships, but we could hit the debris before it enters the planet's atmosphere. If they ram us and we're damaged, we might not be able to contain the debris. Taking out two of their ships now is better than letting their atmosphere get poisoned."

Ash leaned over. "Linae, once these last ships arrive, eventually Ben Ami will reach the same conclusion we have, if he hasn't already. They will ram us. There's no other choice for them."

Linae stood in silence. The rest of the bridge crew waited quietly for her decision.

She asked, "How long until the other six ships arrive?"

"Approximately two minutes," Batak answered.

Flare said, "I've targeted two of their ships. Respectfully, Captain, if we wait for the other ships, then we may have to target three or four of them."

"It's all right, Linae," Ash whispered. "It's not like you have a choice."

Ash always seemed to be saying that. We have no choice. We do what we have to.

Linae looked at each member of her bridge crew. Flare's hands were poised above his board, waiting for the order. Batak checked his screen.

"Captain, the ships will be here in one minute."

Linae gazed toward the main screen. She knew she should give the order, but a thought floated in her brain and wouldn't leave. *Why isn't there a choice?* She wondered if, when the Hiturans started the war with Earth, they also thought there was no choice. *Maybe we did do something to them. Maybe we just didn't understand.*

Now no one would ever know.

"Thirty seconds," Batak said.

Linae knew what to do. It was, she realized, the only act that would have made the Earth Space Command ships pause in their suicidal efforts against the Hiturans. Linae sat down in the captain's chair. "Open the commlink, Mr. Flare."

Flare's hands still hovered over the weapons board. "Ma'am?"

"Commlink, Mr. Flare. Now."

"Yes, ma'am." Flare hit the switch and nodded to Linae.

"Commander Ben Ami, this is Captain Tower of the Earth Space Command vessel *David Roy*." Linae took a deep breath. "We surrender."

Linae ignored the surprised reaction from her crew and waited for Ben Ami. For several seconds, the Donasi did not respond.

Ben Ami's image filled the main screen. "Repeat yourself, *David Roy*."

Linae stood. "We trespassed in your space. It was wrong. We wish to surrender. What are your terms?"

Around Ben Ami chaos erupted. Several Donasi, some in uniform, some not, were hurrying behind him, while others manned what appeared to be a communications network. One small Donasi kept trying to hand Ben Ami something, an earpiece perhaps, then shoved a tablet at him, but Ben Ami ignored them all. He stared at Linae. She stared back.

Batak said, "The six other Donasi ships have arrived."

Linae did not acknowledge Batak. She kept her eyes locked with Ben Ami. Slowly the chaos behind Ben Ami quieted. The *David Roy's* bridge crew barely moved. It was just Linae and Ben Ami.

Finally, Ben Ami began to sway his head side to side. His blue-green eyes closed slightly and the wrinkles deepened in his face. And then he barked what could only be a Donasi laugh.

"Captain Tower, our terms are simple. We want you to leave and not come back."

Linae nodded. "Ben Ami, you lead a brave people and a generous one. We accept your terms."

Ben Ami gestured to two of his aides.

Batak said, "Three of their ships have moved away. We're clear to leave."

Ben Ami raised both his hands even with his head. "Good bye, *David Roy*. You are not the invaders we expected. We may need to rethink this 'victory' of ours. Perhaps one day, we'll meet again."

"I welcome that day," Linae said. She nodded to Flare and the commlink was broken.

"Ensign Terry, get us out of here," she said.

"Yes, ma'am!"

Linae sank back in her chair.

"That was magnificent," Ash said. "What would you have done if his surrender terms had been unreasonable?"

She shrugged. "I don't know. Negotiate, I guess."

Ash laughed. "Well, so long Captain Destructo. What will it be now? Captain Peace? Captain Surrender?"

Linae smiled. For the first time in months, her stomach felt fine. She was even hungry. "Captain Tower will do."

Tower Farm

Vonnie Winslow Crist

The buzz of the tower farm's perimeter alarm woke Crowe. He fumbled for his pistol, then sat up, flung his legs over the side of the bed, rubbed his eyes, and studied the status console. Jax already stood in front of the flashing screens and monitors. She glanced over her shoulder at him and gave a slight wag of her tail.

"What have we got, girl?"

Crowe laid his handgun on the desktop in front of the console, leaned forward, and scanned the displays. Something had disrupted the current which electrified the security fence surrounding Demon's Spine Tower Farm. Since no sentient, human or otherwise, had tried to enter the facility since Jax and he had been stationed there, Crowe figured it was a nocturnal animal.

It hardly seemed worth starting the rover up to check it out. All they would find was a fried critter of one sort or another, cooked and ready for the morning scavengers.

What am I thinking? he mused. He knew the carcass would likely be consumed before the first moon set. Still, he and Jax were duty-bound to identify what had tried to breach the facility's perimeter.

"Duty-bound," he grumbled. His fingers drummed the desktop in frustration. Guarding a Sarkar Prime tower farm, no matter how vital to planet-wide operations, was a far cry from the battlefields, heli-drops, and rescue missions of the past. Jax and he had been one of the elite teams called into action when a situation looked dire. They had been the best of the best, but that was before The Explosion.

He pulled on his pants, laced up his boots, slipped on a combat vest, and filled its various sheaths and holsters with weapons, including the pistol. Granted, the gun was old tech and only good for up close encounters. But he had slept with that pistol ever since a band of deserters murdered his parents and younger sister not two days' rover ride from the base of the tower farm.

Luckily, Crowe was visiting with his uncle when the attack occurred. Otherwise, he would have been killed, too. Afterward, he never went anywhere without a gun. Even to bed.

Jax sat by the door to the rover's bay patiently waiting for him to dress her for the nighttime outing.

"Probably nothing," Crowe told her as he Velcro-ed on her burn vest.

The Explosion had burned both of them severely. People rarely noticed Crowe's repaired face and back, but cosmetic surgery was not approved for military dogs. Instead, Jax had been issued a specially designed vest that shielded her scarred and nearly hairless right shoulder and side from sunburn and chilly temperatures.

"And we had better put this on as well. Just in case," he said as he lashed a heavier combat jacket over her burn vest.

Jax barked three times. One of her signals for "yes".

"Let's go, partner." Crowe could not keep the eagerness out of his voice as he unbolted the steel door between the rover's bay and the living compound, pushed open the heavy barrier, and stepped into the bay. He also couldn't help but hope they saw some real action, as they had done little more than busywork since The Explosion. Maybe there really were enemy combatants trying to knock out communications, or scrappers after the copper used to ground the towers. Or something, anything, that would require the skills of an experienced K-9 and her handler to neutralize the threat.

"Not likely," he muttered. "Everyone thinks we are has-beens assigned to a babysitting post on Sarkar Prime's frontier."

Jax looked at him, tilted her head, and seemed to understand his longing to engage in battle one more time.

The bay was much colder than the living compound, but they would not be staying there long. He punched the unlock code into a panel embedded in the wall, unplugged the power charger, then manually lowered the door in the belly of the rover. It formed a ramp, which Jax and he walked up. The inside of the cabin rumbled as Crowe turned on the rover and closed the belly ramp.

Once everything locked secure, the cab swiveled one hundred eighty degrees until they faced the outer hatch. Crowe flicked the switch and waited impatiently as the door slowly lifted. Finally, the rover quietly rolled from its subterranean lair onto the gravel road that led to the main tower farm area.

With all three moons out, a blanket of stars overhead, and the flickering of the towers' aircraft warning lights, Crowe doubted they would need to turn on the spotlight attached to the rover's roof to determine what had triggered the alarm. Thanks to the rover's electric engine, they traveled in near silence down the road that circled the tower farm just inside the fence searching for the culprit. He rolled the window down, just a crack, until they could hear the wind whoosh across the mountain top and whistle through the towers.

Tonight, the direction and speed of the gusts were just right. The wind seemed to sing as it rushed between monopoles, lattice towers, guyed towers and their anchor wires, and all the various antennas that sprung from the metal structures like spindly appendages.

A quick scan and we will be done and back at the living compound in no time, he thought as Jax and he surveyed the chain-link fencing.

A low growl stopped Crowe's musing. Jax's ears pricked as her lips drew back exposing her teeth. He followed her gaze and saw a breach in the fence about seventy-five feet ahead. Razor wire lay useless on the ground. And where it had been cut, the damaged chain-link fencing curled back like torn paper.

"Geezus. That was no critter." Crowe stopped the rover but decided against using the spotlight. If someone had gone to the trouble of winding their way through the vast network of canyons surrounding Devil's Spine, climbing to the high desert plateau below, then scaling six thousand feet of sheer cliffs to reach the tower farm, he assumed they would still be somewhere on the premises. The quiet approach of the rover might give Jax and him an advantage against whoever had entered the remote tower farm.

He touched his lips with a forefinger. Jax saw his signal and stopped growling. With the calmness of a seasoned warrior, Crowe picked up his semiautomatic. Antiquated in most battle situations, a semiautomatic fitted with a night-vision scope in the hands of an expert marksman was the weapon of choice on a tower farm where destruction of the towers and their equipment was to be avoided at all costs. A pulse rifle, blaster, or explosive of any sort could not only damage the towers and their antennas but also blow to bits the satellite dishes scattered among the towers.

It had been made clear to Crowe that government accountants frowned upon the cost of replacing such valuable equipment because a soldier would not obey orders. And even on this lonely mountain top, Jax and he were still part of Sarkar Prime's military.

Before exiting his vehicle, Crowe studied the displays in front of him. According to the rover's instrument panel, the temperature on Demon's Spine was thirty-nine degrees. Taking into account the strong gusts, Crowe figured the wind chill was below freezing. He pulled a pair of zee-foil gloves from one of his pockets and slipped them on. Snug as a second skin and thinner than parachute silk, they wouldn't interfere with his ability to fire the rifle but would prevent his fingers from going numb if he was outside for a prolonged period of time. After making sure no one was nearby, Crowe lowered the rover's access ramp. Then, he and Jax slipped outside.

Directing Jax with barely discernible nods and gestures, they moved to the nearest tower complex. Built of thick, steel-reinforced concrete, the shelters at the foot of the towers housed a base transmitter station for each tenant. He checked the door. It was still locked.

His jaw clenched in grim realization. Whoever broke in was not after copper. Scrappers would have stripped the shelters closest to their entry point, then made a quick getaway.

Crowe took several deep breaths of the frigid air. He hoped this *was* a second chance to show that Jax and he were still real soldiers.

With a tilt of his head, he sent Jax to the next complex. Making little sound, his dog raced through the scrubby grasses, checked around the far side, then turned her head and nodded the *all clear* signal. Crowe followed Jax's path until he stood by her side. He reached out and tested the shelter's door. Again, everything was secure.

They repeated the process two more times with the same results. He knew the importance of the towers' tenants grew as they moved toward the center of the facility. The towers on the outer edges of the farm were used by mining companies, cell phone firms, and other commercial tenants. The highest towers, located in the center of the farm, were utilized by the government, military, public safety command, defense contractors, and classified entities.

He considered who would be interested in sabotaging or destroying the base transmitter stations of those tenants. Maybe humans with plans to hold a shelter's worth of transmitters for ransom. Perhaps a radical group with a political agenda to unseat the monarchy wanted publicity. Of course, there was the possibility of nonhuman sentients. But it seemed unlikely as he was not aware of any recent alien attacks in this quadrant. Then again, the caretakers of Demon's Spine Tower Farm had limited contact with the nearby military and civilian centers where such information might be known.

He was about to send Jax to the next shelter when she froze in place with her nose pointed in the direction of a tower about a hundred fifty yards to the west of their location.

Crowe followed her line of sight and spotted a group of bipeds attempting to pry open the tower shelter's metal entrance door. He frowned. Even from this distance, the fluidity of their movements did not seem human. The oversized shelter the trespassers had chosen contained the base transmitter stations for two five-hundred-foot military guyed-towers and a public safety self-support tower. It was one of the most vital shelters on the farm. Once inside, they could not only disrupt the legal tenants' signals but alter the programming and use the towers to send their own messages.

Likely as not, those messages would be antigovernment—maybe even antihuman. Though stationed on the outskirts of a remote Sarkar town, Crowe knew that Jax and he were still essential to planet-wide security.

His pulse raced as he realized this was no group of amateurs. These potential insurrectionists knew what they were doing. With his left hand, Crowe slowly reached up and felt for the emergency button built into his vest which activated a distress signal on the rover. Once he located the device, he pulled off the protective cover and pressed the button. As he lowered his hand, he felt himself slip into a calm, clear-headed battle mode. He knew by now the distress signal had reached Fort Destiny. Though they would not arrive for twenty minutes, Special Forces were at this moment being deployed to Demon's Spine. But until they got there, it was up to Jax and him to protect the tower farm.

Using satellite dishes, towers, and shelters for cover, they crept closer. As they got within Crowe's optimal firing range, he raised his hand slightly. Jax and he stood still as stone and studied the individuals who had illegally entered the restricted area. Three bipeds who appeared human were working on the door and nine biped guards carrying some sort of long-barreled weapon formed a semicircle around them. Three of the guards also looked human. The other six appeared to be four-armed beings with long, oddly shaped fingers.

Crowe pressed his lips together and raised his weapon. Pressing his eye to the scope, he tried to get a better look at the bipeds by using the device. He was rewarded for his effort as—through the scope—the bipeds' faces appeared slightly furred and their eyes huge. The four hands clutching each weapon seemed to have suckers on the ends of their fingers. Whatever they were, he did not recognize these particular aliens from his training manual. Unless their existence was above his clearance level, they were a new threat to Sarkar Prime and her inhabitants. A threat Jax and he had to deter.

Studying the bipeds again, he could imagine how handy those finger suckers had been in scaling the cliff up to the top of Demon's Spine. Who knew what else they were capable of?

Though the temperature was near freezing, sweat broke out on Crowe's brow and trickled down the side of his face. He tore his eyes away from the aliens for a second and glanced at Jax. Her eyes shone and the corner of her mouth twitched. He smiled as he realized she, too, felt the thrill of adrenaline again coursing through her veins at the prospect of entering combat once more.

With back-up forces still ten or more minutes away and the bipeds determined to break into a shelter housing high-priority base transmitter stations, there was no choice. Crowe reinforced Jax's stay command, then charged his weapon.

As he took aim, one of the human-appearing guards transformed into a four-armed alien.

Hell's bells, biomorphs! Crowe's gut clenched as he realized how easily they could blend in with the human citizens. For all he knew, the planet was crawling with them. Were they an alien threat intent on invasion? Or worse, were they an indigenous species bent on eliminating the human presence on their planet? There was little doubt in his mind the entire population of Sarkar was threatened.

Whatever their intent, right now Crowe and Jax were the only obstacle between them and success.

Jax stood next to him, ready to follow his commands. Battle trained, she didn't flinch when he shot the first biomorph. Before the aliens could react, Crowe hit four more. Dead or wounded? It didn't matter so long as they were not able to return fire.

Screeching in rage, the remaining biomorphs assumed their natural form. All of them turned toward Crowe and Jax, eyes intense with what Crowe could only assume was hatred. He ducked behind cover and fired again as the four guards shot burning projectiles from their weapons at Crowe and Jax. Where the fireballs landed around them, the wind-dried vegetation burst into flames.

Crowe's ears pounded and bile climbed his throat as the radiant heat threw him into a flashback. For a moment, he was back on Perseus Three:

Jax and he left the cave where his unit had hunkered down to walk the quarter mile or so back to base camp and get some grub. They had remained on guard duty while others took their turns, so they were the last pair to head for chow. Everyone else, dog and soldier alike, had a full belly and were settling in for the night. He could hear his comrades' muffled voices and laughter as they waited to drift off to sleep. Then, a high-pitched whine cut the night air. Instinctively, he and Jax turned around in horror, but there was nothing they could do as the incoming missile targeted the cave. Their whole squad disappeared in the fireball.

Crowe had spun away and attempted to escape the blast zone, but the fire roared all around him. Jax, who had been clear of the fireball, had rushed headlong into the flames trying to get to his side. Crowe remembered seeing the reflection of the blazing hillside in his dog's eyes before he blacked out. When he had come to hours later, the medics told him Jax had dragged him nearly back to camp before collapsing from the burns she had sustained in his rescue. She had lost the tips of her ears and been severely burned because she came back for him. He owed her his life.

Returning to the present, he clenched his teeth and suppressed the urge to retreat as the flames licked closer and the aliens continued to fire. Sensing his elevated level of anxiety, Jax turned her muzzle up and gazed at him. Just like that day on Perseus Three, he saw blazing brush reflected in her eyes. Hating the necessity, he gave her the signal to send her through the flames toward the biomorphs and their fireball guns.

He pointed at the aliens, nodded, then lifted his weapon and began to shoot at the advancing biomorphs. Without hesitation, Jax rushed forward, her jaws slightly open. With a grim expression on his face and a rapidly pounding heart, Crowe followed his partner. Despite the fire-retardant fabric of his pants, his legs screamed with pain, and higher on his body, it felt like a swarm of yellow jackets were stinging his jaw. Crowe ignored the pain and the terror licking at his insides. He held his weapon steady and shot again at the advancing biomorphs. Three of them fell beneath his fire as Jax tackled the fourth.

His dog ripped out the biomorph guard's throat, then looked up for orders. Crowe gave her another nod toward the remaining targets. Jax leapt over the body of the guard and raced toward the remaining bipeds.

The biomorphs gained access to the shelter just as Jax and he neared the reinforced concrete building. A pair of the four-armed aliens remained outside the damaged door while their comrade slipped inside the shelter. The two biomorphs on guard raised their fireball guns and shot at Jax. Unable to dodge away, the war dog collapsed as the fireball engulfed her.

Crowe screamed. Charging forward, he fired a stream of bullets, and kept firing until he was out of ammo and the biomorphs outside the shelter were dead. After bursting through the shelter's door, he attacked the remaining alien with a serrated blade he kept in a sheath on his belt. He stabbed and slashed the last biomorph until its lifeless body slumped to the floor, then glanced around. Alien blood and tissue matter splattered every surface, but other than the door, it appeared the biomorphs had not had time to damage the base transmission station's equipment.

Ignoring the sensation of thousands of fire-ants biting his legs, he kicked aside the biomorph's body, shoved open the door, and ran to Jax. Moaning, he knelt by his dog. Even with the protection offered to her by the combat jacket and burn-vest, she was badly injured. A quick glance told him she would lose the lower part of her front legs. *If* she survived the burns. His brain latched onto that thought. The legs could be replaced, thanks to modern bio-mechanics, but Jax could not.

She raised her charred head, looked Crowe in the eyes, and tried to wag what was left of her tail.

"Easy, girl," he whispered as he ripped the zee-foil glove from his hand. He wanted to touch her, but had to restrain himself from caressing the side of her face.

As his adrenaline drained away, he felt light-headed from the agony of his leg burns. Between the pain and the smells of burnt flesh and dead aliens, his stomach turned. He clenched his jaw and resisted the urge to retch. Looking down at Jax, he told himself that it was the smoke from the scorched grass making his eyes tear.

Stay conscious, Jax needs you, he reminded himself as the wind sang through the towers soaring above him like a chorus of angels.

Suddenly, shouts and gunfire brought his focus back to his surroundings. Through the smoky haze he saw soldiers running toward them while other uniformed men and women finished off the still-breathing biomorphs. A third group of soldiers bagged alien bodies and collected the fireball guns.

Crowe was vaguely aware of soldiers stopping beside him, then kneeling as they laid a stretcher down. Their mouths moved, but he was too numb to make out the words. He recognized the cross emblem on one soldier's uniform, and realized she was a medic. And as she readied an IV, Crowe surrendered to the pain and slumped down beside Jax.

He fought to remain conscious as the medic grasped his wrist and cleaned a spot on his arm for the IV needle.

"No!" he screamed. "Jax first. Treat my dog first."

"Sir, you are injured. We need to stabilize you and get you back to the base." The medic then looked over at Jax, "To be honest, I don't think the dog is going to make it."

"I am not leaving without her." Crowe struggled against the soldiers who were trying to restrain him so the medic could stabilize his vital signs before he was loaded onto the waiting 'copter for transport.

The lieutenant commanding the unit walked over to see what the commotion was about.

"Please, my dog," Crowe begged. "Please, try to save her."

The officer shook his head. "She doesn't look good, son."

"She saved my life. Helped save this facility from alien attack. She has served with honor for years."

The world seemed to stop as he waited for the lieutenant to speak.

The officer knelt down and studied the critically injured Jax. "Do as he asks," he said, a hint of warmth in his gaze.

The medic started to protest, but the officer cut him off, "That is an order. You will treat and transport both soldiers. This war dog deserves a chance."

We got to make a difference again, thought Crowe as he drifted in and out of consciousness. *Maybe now, they won't consider Jax and me has-beens.*

But the future remained hidden as the military helicopter flew through the darkness and murmured words about an alien invasion hung in the air like smoke. The last thing Crowe remembered before he passed out from pain and meds, was looking over at the stretcher next to him and seeing Jax gazing back.

He knew they'd make it. He knew, though a little worse for wear, they'd both be ready for action again if called upon to serve.

Hardship Posting

Ben Beckstrom

The two Al-Khidr Marines stood at a bored attention in front of the Terran Embassy on Dri'eva. Their post, guarding the basement entry of the embassy, was usually uneventful. Today's shift, however, held some promise.

"Hey Bugs," said Broomsucker—known to his mama as Malik Levsky—"how long has that wagon been sitting there?"

Bugs—born Jarom Russell Vaipulu—shrugged. "It's been idling since before we got here. You think it's worth a look-see?"

"I can checky-check it. Make sure they know where they is headed and all'at, ya know?"

"Roger, roger, Broomsucker." Bugs shifted his gyro-gun. "Be back right quick or I'll have to hit up Her Excellency."

"You don't need another wife, chief."

"Do you want me or flattie over there to blow you back to Brooklyn?"

"I'm going, I'm going."

Broomsucker sauntered over to the stalled vehicle. Through one of the windows, he saw a frightened looking native Dri'evan. Her flat head and bulbous eyes twitched from side to side nervously as he approached. Before he could knock on it, the window deflated.

"Please help," said the female. "Our eggman, he . . . he eats the larvae."

"Your husband is eating your children?" Broomsucker, behind his back, tapped two fingers on his levjet. He heard Bugs mumble into the internal network. "Ma'am, we can't help you. Is there anyone we can call for you? Your vehicle hasn't moved in some time."

"No, no, no, understand us please." The female leaned in. "Eggman is from the Sliver. His friends from the Trades and the Deviancy Commissions, they hunt us. They say we are larva-eaters. That we are traitors. He calls me 'Terran bug'." Her antennae were waving frantically. "Asylum is the word we must use, yes? Please let us be asylum in Terran castle."

Broomsucker toggled off his external comms. "Hey Bugs, you getting any of this?"

The low rumble of Bugs' voice came through on the internal network. "Yeah. I forwarded it to the Ambassador and Colonel Shabazz. We don't want to annoy the Sliver too much, but political asylum . . . it's the Labor Coalition's policy." Bugs stopped talking for a moment. "Alright, Shabazz says to let the lady in. Even if Her Excellency doesn't care for it, it's regs. And apparently we have an ID on her eggman. We've had eyes on him for a minute."

"Oh?" Broomsucker was still staring impassively at the trembling female.

"You remember the flattie who shot up a Greenie hangout on Lorcan? The one you said you'd kill if you saw him again? It's him."

Broomsucker tightened his grip on his gyro-gun. "I'll wave her through." He toggled his channels back to external comms. "I hope you enjoy Terran hospitality, ma'am."

Her Excellency Anahita Cupul, Ambassador of the Terran Federated Union, granddaughter of Fleet Admiral Cyrus Yazdi, ex-Duumvir of the Federated Union Mint, former Assistant Chief Metallurgist of the Labor Coalition, was out of her league and she knew it. Facing her was a delegation from Dri'eva's most dangerous political alliance. In front of her was the one who called herself Jackie, President of the Deviancy Commission. Flanking Jackie was one calling himself Fred, a planner for the Sliver who moonlighted as a Trades Commission attorney. Fred's wife was hiding in the basement of the embassy. On Jackie's other side was Lana, an enforcer for the Sliver who also held the official title of Fixer for the Council of Matriarchs, presumably a more violent type of chief of staff than was normal for Terran politics. The only human physically near Anahita was Colonel Darwin Shabazz, who only had his cultural sidearm, a six chambered revolver, and his muscles in case it went ugly.

Of course, this was still the Terran Embassy, and therefore *her* house.

"How can I help you?" A verbal salute before the duel.

Jackie waggled her antennae invitingly. "May I sit, Your Excellency?" Without waiting, she sat. "It seems that we have an Undesirable hiding in your basement. We would be more than happy to help with any pest control needs, particularly in this nasty weather."

Anahita inhaled. "I have to say, thank you for getting to the point. My government has made it clear that anyone who seeks political asylum, particularly if they say those words in Standard Terran, must be accepted."

"Anyone? Even a terrorist?"

"I'd be happy to submit a complaint to the Terran Senate, if you'd like."

"No matter." Jackie, presumably for human benefit, waved her top hand at Fred. "Go ahead."

Fred stared beyond Anahita, into Colonel Shabazz's eyes. "I'd like to request political asylum."

Anahita's eye twitched. "On what grounds?"

Fred's antennae were waving almost uncontrollably. "I fear for my life. The extremist group the Sliver has designs on my life. If you don't accept me—"

"If you don't accept him," said Jackie smoothly, "we have compelling evidence to suggest that Sliver militants will brutally murder him in the near future. If that happens, we are inclined to submit his body and our account to the Terran Senate. I'm sure the Triumvirs would be *ecstatic* about that. They might even summon you home!"

Colonel Shabazz fidgeted with his revolver. "You wouldn't dare."

Jackie's mandibles arranged themselves into an approximation of a smile. "The Sliver is very influential, here on Dri'eva. All it seeks is a pure society and a withdrawal of Al-Khidr Marines from disputed territory." She paused. "Or so they say."

Anahita flexed her hands under her desk. "That won't be necessary. Of course we'll accept Fred." She fixed her eyes on him. "Welcome to Terran jurisdiction. Colonel, if you wouldn't mind?"

Shabazz had caught her undertone. "Dri'evan identifying as Fred, I arrest you under suspicion of terrorism, murder, anti-Senatorial behavior, and discharging a weapon with intent to kill TFU armed forces according to Terran Penal System Regulation 126.42.4.5b3 due to your actions on Lorcan one half-standard Terran revolution ago. Further, you are charged with fraud against a diplomatic officer for acting as a threatening agent of a foreign power under Terran jurisdiction as governed by the Convention on Reprisals, Asylum, and Refuge section A subhead 7 clause 14. As you are under Embassy Law, your legal counsel will need to coordinate with either Al-Khidr Marines or Embassy personnel as per the same Convention, section C, subhead 13. You will exit with my Marines or be considered as resisting arrest."

Fred sputtered. Lana looked languidly at Jackie, then shrugged. Jackie waved at Fred as two Greenies (that was the slang, right?) marched in and shackled him to their waists. As Fred was escorted out, Jackie began to clap.

"Oh, that was brilliant! I would never have guessed this was your first posting. And what a useful head of security!" Her mandible grinningly gaped toward Shabazz, who shuddered. "We won't miss him too terribly. Some of the Sliver's agents are too clumsy for their own good. I hope you shoot him, that would be excellent."

"He'll have a trial, don't worry."

"How boring. This was fun, though. We'll need to do this again sometime. You have some gumption! I'll need to think of a better test."

"Test?"

"You don't think I would actually come down to help Fred with his marital problems, do you? I told Linda to leave him years ago. But what this has taught me is that you're more flexible than other Terrans. I hope I can work with you again. Good day." Jackie stood, bowed, then towed Lana to the door.

Anahita and Shabazz were left alone, dumbfounded. "Well, Colonel. That was not quite what I anticipated."

"Agreed, Ambassador. We'll have to keep a closer eye on further developments."

BUGS AND BROOMSUCKER SAT IN THE GREENIE LOUNGE. BROOMSUCKER STARED into his maté. Bugs sank into the leather couch. "You good, man? We got the baddie. You were instrumental. And the flattie chick'll be safe."

"Yeah, I'm chill, doc." Broomsucker sipped his drink. "Bugs? Can I ask you a question?"

"Shoot, bro, if you can't, then shove me out an airlock."

"Something about this felt too easy. We'll have to deal with a big Sliver thing soon. Mark my words."

"Well, Broomsucker," Bugs somehow sank deeper into the couch, "as long as we got Shabazz and Her Excellency we'll be jayyid."

"You gonna ask her out?"

"The Dri'evan or the ambassador? Cuz I'm thinking about going native."

Broomsucker threw a magazine at Bugs and the two Al-Khidr Marines burst into laughter. The next shift was hours away. The Sliver could be forgotten, for now.

Lagrange Contact

Joe Monson

May 1, 2116
WNN News Report

This is Yolen Jakkin with breaking news. A shuttle has reportedly launched from the Deep Desert Spaceport in central Sudan early this morning.

"According to an anonymous source who watched the launch, it appears to have been one of the *Sirocco*-class shuttles operated by the Group 16 Consortium. These shuttles are just under fifty meters in length and weigh about ninety thousand kilograms before fueling and cargo. They usually have a crew complement of two to four.

"The G16 is a reclusive group of countries that refuses to work with anyone outside their borders, despite numerous outreach efforts. In recent years, there has been an increase in cooperation among their leadership. There have been reports regarding their own space program, but they have been very secretive about their goals and the level of their technology.

"As the G16 did not announce this launch, we have no specific details regarding its mission. As more information becomes available, we will share them with you, our viewers. This is Yolen Jakkin, reporting for WNN."

May 12, 2116
Earth-Sun Lagrange Point One

CHIEMI STRETCHED IN THE HARSH GLARE OF THE SUN. IT WAS COLD ON HER TINY asteroid, but her glittering black skin absorbed enough light to keep her warm. As she settled back, her rippling scales sparkled in the stellar light and the reflected light from the Earth. She loved how shiny her scales became in the vacuum of space.

She had taken up residence on the lazily-spinning rock because it allowed her a good—and mostly unchanging—view of Earth, her former home. The rock stayed in roughly the same place, slowly tumbling in the mild gravity currents from the Earth and the Sun. Chiemi was younger than most starkind who left home, but she was confident in her ability to survive the cold of space. Starkind had done so for thousands of years.

One hundred sixty-nine years after Chiemi had first journeyed above the Nesting Grounds near an active volcano on Earth, the humans had ventured into her domain. Now they had a small and growing collection of metal objects floating near her home. There was even one that had four humans inside it.

What was it they called them? Chiemi thought hard for a minute, it had been a while since she'd left the Nesting Grounds. Then it came to her. *Satellites. I think that's what they call them. I wonder how many more they'll send here. If it gets too crowded, they might notice me.*

She watched as the four satellites glinted in the sunlight. The newest one— the one with the humans in it—had arrived only a few years earlier. Chiemi found the humans fascinating, and she loved watching their little metal boxes as they came and went.

"How are you enjoying your new home?"

The question came suddenly into her mind. She smiled as she recognized the quiet thought patterns of her mother.

"I'd forgotten how peaceful it is here, Mother. Thank you for suggesting it as a good home," she thought back, sending a burst of bright yellow joy and pastel happiness along with the words.

A rainbow ripple of amusement arrived several seconds later. *"I thought you might enjoy that place. It has machines created by the humans and a good view of both the Brightstar and the Nesting Grounds."*

"Why don't you just call them 'Sun' and 'Earth', Mother? That's what the humans call them. It's much shorter than using our names for them." Chiemi sent a burst of greens and blues along with her thought to indicate she was only half serious.

Though her mother tried to hide it, Chiemi caught a brief flash of red against the otherwise calm blues of her mother's thoughts. It was gone just as quickly as it showed.

"You know that I am not as enamored of the humans as you are, my daughter. When you have lived as long as I have, and seen what horrors they can produce, you may change your mind."

Chiemi sighed to herself, careful to not broadcast the bright pink of annoyance. *"I've seen them, not long after I was born. I've seen far more good from them, however. They're even traveling out where we live."*

"I apologize, my daughter. I should not let old grievances bother me so. It has been hundreds of years since we starkind were directly attacked by humans. Most humans no longer believe we exist, thankfully."

" 'You are too young to truly understand'," Chiemi mimicked. She sent a splash of dull green grumpiness laced with a rainbow halo of mirth.

An echoing rainbow splash came back but was suddenly cut off with the sharp red and orange of alarm and bright white flashes of pain before going black.

"Mother?" Chiemi's head rose from her reclining position, her mind swirling with the same orange and red her mother had sent. *"What's wrong? Mother?"*

There was no reply.

Lucky Dragon central station module
Earth-Sun Lagrange Point Two

Alarms wailed and flashed all across the *Lucky Dragon's* Command and Control.

"What was that bump, Ai?" Lieutenant Commander Vasiti Taake asked as she checked her own monitors.

"Radar and cameras are not showing anything, Lieutenant Commander," Second Lieutenant Aiono Maimoana said. "There's nothing—large or small—anywhere near the module. We were moving orbit around the Lagrange point when it felt like we hit something."

"Anyone injured?" Lieutenant Commander James Tezuka commed from the medical bay.

"No injuries we're aware of, Doc. We'll keep you updated." Vasiti keyed off the comm, focusing her attention back on her screens. "I need more details, Ai. We hit something, that's for sure."

"I don't know." Ai quickly switched from one screen to the next as she searched for answers. "I'm working on that, ma'am. We seem to have hit . . . something in Quadrant A by Hydroponics. It didn't sound like an asteroid—it was softer than that—and we couldn't see anything there."

"So what's causin' all this racket, Taake?" Commander Leah Brackett floated through the door and muted the alarms. "It sounded like we hit somethin', like gently bumpin' a cow or a horse. Ain't no cows in space, though. Any injuries?" She grinned.

"None reported." Vasiti grinned slightly. "We're still trying to figure out what we hit, Commander. Whatever it was, it's not hard enough to be an asteroid, which is all that should be out here. Maybe an old satellite? The system reports no significant structural damage to the hull, and there are no pressure drops in either of the labs there." She scanned the video monitors, then pointed at one of the feeds. "Ai, what's that on LA-A2? It looks like something's blocking it."

Ai glanced over and frowned. "I'm unsure, Lieutenant Commander. It appears something is obscuring the camera, as you said. Let me try LA-A1."

They watched as the LA-A1 slowly panned, the star field changing on the screen until it was pointing toward LA-A2. Almost half of the view was obscured by the object.

"Ai, turn on the floods in Quadrant A," Leah said. "That should help things a bit."

"Yes, ma'am."

Glare from the floodlights showed in several of the feeds, but the obstruction remained mostly dark. Some of the feeds showed more twinkling in spots, but the dark object showed little change.

"Hmmm," Vasiti continued, "Cameras both show nothing but empty space with the occasional star twinkling, which shouldn't be happening here in a vacuum. See?"

Leah pushed off from her console, quickly floating over to grab a handhold above Vasiti's station. The large high-definition screen above the station showed blackness, with a few glittering yellow-white points of light.

"Show me." Leah's rural Idaho drawl always sounded relaxed to Vasiti. She half-expected Leah to be holding a cold drink.

Vasiti pointed in turn at each of several points. "These 'twinkles' shouldn't be twinkling, ma'am. There's no atmospheric distortion here. They also move too much and change shape. Watch."

She zoomed in with one of the cameras. They watched the screen as one of the dots moved slowly down, then shrank to a thin line before expanding so that it appeared be pointing in a different direction.

"That doesn't look natural." Leah's brow furrowed as she watched for a few more seconds. "Any idea what's causin' it?"

"Whatever it is, we're having trouble focusing on it, ma'am. It appears to be moving, and it appears to be very close to us."

Leah looked thoughtful as she watched the feed from the cameras. Vasiti continued adjusting the cameras as she tried to get something—anything—to stay focused.

"Since stars don't twinkle in space," Vasiti continued, "there must be something else there. Whatever we hit is pretty much invisible to our cameras. Even radar shows nothing. There aren't any windows on that side of the module because of the labs, so the cameras are all we have. We may have to do an EVA to determine the extent of the damage."

"Who's on EVA duty, Taake?"

"Now that you're here, ma'am, I am, along with Lieutenant Maimoana. We can be suited up in ten minutes."

"Go through Airlock B since A might be damaged."

"Yes, ma'am. On our way," Vasiti said. They launched toward the door.

"Lieutenant Dvoretskiy, please report to C&C," Leah commed while studying the camera feeds. Ten minutes later, Vasiti and Ai cycled through Airlock B, attaching the tethers from the anchor points just outside the airlock to their belt clips.

"Okay, Ai," Vasiti said over the suitcomm, "We've got 200 meters to work with on the tethers. Let's see what we can find. Keep the suitcomm open."

"Acknowledged, Lieutenant Commander."

The magnetic soles on their boots helped steady them as they trekked across the outer edge of the *Lucky Dragon,* passing Dock 1 of Cargo Bay B1 just a few meters from the airlock. It was like walking down the middle of a wide, metal suburban street that curved out of sight very quickly.

Vasiti paused for a moment to look around at the darkness. The sun was occluded by the Earth and the *Lucky Dragon,* so it was very dark. Without the interference of the atmosphere, the night sky was more focused, the stars intense points of light against the inky blackness of space, brighter than she had ever seen them. The arch of the Milky Way crossed through most of her view, and she had to remind herself to breathe as she turned her head to follow its path.

"Isn't it gorgeous?" Ai's voice spoke softly, reverently over the suitcomm. "There are so many stars out there. Wouldn't it be wonderful to visit them?"

"Yeah." Vasiti replied in a half-whisper, slight sadness in her voice, before she started walking again. "Not in our lifetimes, though."

"It's even better than night out on the Pacific." Ai continued talking quietly as they approached Dock 2 of Cargo Bay B1. "I love going out on a canoe at night when the winds are calm. The sky stretches on forever. That's what got me into astronomy."

"Yeah." Vasiti was quiet as she nodded, taking in the countless stars and the dense arch of the Milky Way. "Much as I would love to stare at the stars, Ai, we have to see what we hit. I'm glad we have the floods because these suit lamps aren't bright enough for this job."

A brief sigh came from Ai before she gave Vasiti a thumbs up. Vasiti smiled, keying her comm.

"C&C, please turn on the floods in Quadrant B, too. We're going to need a lot of light to assess any damage."

"Will do, Lieutenant Commander," First Lieutenant David Dvoretskiy replied as he settled into his seat in C&C. "Switching them on now."

Moments later, everything was bathed in the brightness of daylight LEDs. Vasiti's visor darkened slightly at the sudden illumination, but everything on the hull was very visible now.

Just past Dock 2 of Cargo Bay B2, Vasiti could see the spoke collar jutting three meters out from the hull. This was one of four spots where the spokes for the outer ring would be connected.

"What's that?"

Ai's voice broke into Vasiti's thoughts. She saw Ai pointing past the spoke collar and noticed an indistinct area of darkness against the stars. Her eyes wouldn't focus on it. The area absorbed light despite the flood of illumination while also sparkling here and there, which caused Vasiti's mind to rebel.

"I'm not sure," Vasiti replied. She keyed her main comm. "Commander, there is definitely something here, but it's hard to tell what it is. I suggest recording our suitcam feeds so we can review it later."

"I agree, Taake," Leah said. "Please switch to open station comms instead of your suitcomms."

"Acknowledged, Commander. We are switching to open comms." Vasiti responded, with Ai repeating a moment later.

May 12, 2116
Earth-Sun Lagrange Point One

Chiemi's mind swirled with the oranges and reds of alarm and concern mixed with the swampy greens and grays of fear. She chomped down on a smaller rock as it drifted past, crushing and swallowing it quickly.

Mother's thoughts have never cut off like that before. Is she hurt? In danger? Something must be wrong. She sent another message. *"Mother?!"*

Still hearing no response, she sent a general distress call in all directions. She was probably the only starkind nearby, but there were always others passing through the inner system or the rocky boundary with the outer system. Maybe someone was nearby who could help.

Chiemi glanced at the four satellites near her home. They were all oblivious to her existence. She ate a few more quick mouthfuls of her rock before turning her back on the Brightstar. She had been resting for a full rotation of the Earth, absorbing the energy from the Brightstar, and she felt the energy coursing through her.

She spread her inky black wings, catching the winds from the Brightstar to lift her slowly and gently from her asteroid home.

The winds are moving quickly today. It shouldn't take too long to reach Mother. Hopefully, I'll make it in time to . . .

Chiemi wasn't sure what to expect.

Several minutes later, she silently passed high above the icy southern cap, the blues and whites of her birth world moving beneath her. She had enjoyed playing in the snow there when she was a child. All too quickly, the winds—augmented by the energy she was expelling—pushed Chiemi beyond the Nesting Grounds and toward the outer system.

Flashes of ever-deepening purples cascaded in waves across her scales as her speed increased. When the dark purple glow completely enveloped her, she disappeared.

Lucky Dragon central station module
Earth-Sun Lagrange Point Two

THE LARGE, DARK SHAPE RESTING NEAR THE AIRLOCKS FOR THE HYDROPONICS AND biochemistry labs had, surprisingly, not drifted away from the *Lucky Dragon*.

"We're approaching the object, Commander," Vasiti reported. They were within four meters now, and she looked back and forth, guessing at its size. "It appears about thirty or forty meters long and about ten meters high. There's not a lot of space around it, so I can't get around it easily without turning off the boots."

"It also seems to be breathing, Lieutenant Commander. Look." Ai pointed, and Vasiti could see the shape slowly compressing and growing.

"Ai is correct, Commander. The movement of the object does suggest very slow breathing, though I'm not sure what it would be breathing out here. Atmospheric molecules are pretty sparse this far from Earth." Vasiti continued watching the object as she waited for a reply. "How would you like us to proceed, ma'am?"

"Mother!"

Vasiti thought she saw a flash of orange. "What was that, Commander?"

"I didn't say anythin', Taake," Leah replied.

"I could have sworn . . ." Vasiti began.

"Mother!"

This time, she was sure she saw the flash of orange, perhaps with little red patches in it, but it wasn't her eyes seeing it. Vasiti looked around at the vast darkness of space, seeing source or cause of the light flashes.

"You didn't hear that?" she asked.

"Hear what? Other than you talkin', I haven't heard anythin', Taake," Leah replied.

"I didn't hear anything, either," Ai said quietly. "What are you hearing?"

"Mother!"

"I've heard someone shouting 'Mother' three times now."

After a few moments of silence, Leah's voice came over the comm. "Dvoret-skiy, please verify any anomalies on the comms channels."

"Yes, ma'am, checking for alien influences!"

Vasiti heard him grinning as he said it.

"No time for your aliens right now. Just check for anomalies, Corporal." Leah's voice was not amused and lost its drawl.

"Understood, ma'am!" Dvoretskiy responded cheerfully. After a few seconds, he continued. "No anomalies detected, ma'am. The comms were silent at the times Vasiti heard the voices."

"Thank you, Dvoretskiy. Taake, have you heard the voice again?" Leah asked.

"Mother! Where are you? Mother!"

"Yes, Commander. Just now. This time, it sounded like it was in my head rather than coming over the comms. It's calling out to 'Mother'. It sounds worried."

"Hearin' voices is not considered a good sign, Taake. You ain't goin' crazy on us, are you?" Leah's voice slipped back into her country drawl, so Vasiti knew she wasn't being completely serious.

"At least it's not telling you to kill anyone," Dvoretskiy chimed in, his big grin coming through.

"Thanks, David. I'll be sure to submit myself for evaluation when we get back home." Vasiti smiled as she said it. "This last one, I don't know, felt like it was closer than the others. It came in much more clearly. Louder, somehow."

"Interestin'," Leah said. She was silent for a few moments before continuing. "I know this may sound weird, but have y'tried answerin' the voice?"

Vasiti considered that for a moment. "Um, no? How would I do that? I don't even know where it's coming from."

"Well, since you're hearin' it in your mind, try thinkin' back at it. Kinda like telepathy."

"I'm almost there, Mother!"

The voice returned, this time more insistent, and accompanied by cascades of vivid oranges and reds, splashed with patches of pinks. A halo of murky greens and grays surrounded the other colors. The colors bursting behind her eyes were almost overwhelming, causing Vasiti to gasp.

"I . . . I've never felt anything like this, Commander. I'm seeing intense colors, too, now."

"Do you need to come back inside?" James cut in. "What's your oxygen level?"

Vasiti wanted to cradle her head in her hands, but the intensity was subsiding. "I'm fine, Doctor. I'm still at ninety percent in my reservoir, and the rebreather is at ninety-eight percent. The mix looks okay, too, so I'm not hallucinating."

Ai walked up behind Vasiti and accessed her suit information from the panel on the back of the suit. "I confirm those numbers, Doctor. There are no anomalies showing up on any of my scans, either. Other than this large object, there's nothing out here. I can help her if she needs it. We should be fine."

"I still suggest you should try replyin' to the voice, Vasiti." Leah's voice came in on her private channel. "You can obviously hear whatever it is, so maybe it can hear you, too. Go ahead an' try it. Switching back to the main channel."

"Thank you, Ai," Leah continued. "If you think she's okay and you can handle it, continue as you are. Taake, if anything changes, let us know. Just focus on the voice."

Vasiti gathered her thoughts and concentrated on the voice she had heard.

"Who are you? Where are you?"

Silence. She wasn't sure if it had worked right, so she concentrated on the voice and tried it again.

"Who are you? Where are you?"

The silence continued. Outside of the quiet hiss of the air scrubbers and the slight humming of her suit's onboard systems, the only thing she heard was her heart pounding in her ears. It was loud, too, though it faded into the background when she focused on anything else.

"I'm not getting anything, ma'am. Just . . . nothing."

"Try it again." Leah's voice was soft on the comms. "Go ahead."

Vasiti closed her eyes. Concentrating on the voice she had heard, she focused on how it had felt, remembering how the colors had swirled in her mind the last time she heard it.

"Who are you? Where are you?"

Vasiti felt the words leaving her this time. There wasn't any other way to describe it. The words moved away from her as she thought them.

A sudden rainbow burst with splashes of greens and blues entered her mind and then was cut off, replaced by words.

"Who is this? I don't know you. Where are you? Show yourself!"

The words came in more clearly this time, accompanied by a splash of muted yellow speckled with reds and oranges and a feeling of caution.

Vasiti opened her eyes in surprise. "I got a reply!"

"What did they say?" Leah said. "Keep talkin' to them, and find out who they are. Looks like we may not be the first people here, after all."

"They asked who I was and where I was." Vasiti closed her eyes and thought of the voice. It was easier this time.

"My name is Vasiti. What is your name?"

The reply came more quickly than before. It felt even closer than before.

"I am Chiemi. Where are you? I can not see you. Where is my mother?"

"I don't know where your mother is. I didn't know anyone else was here. We're supposed to be the first people here." Vasiti paused to gather her thoughts. *"I'm in the L2ISO module Aorab'a Rákon."* She thought of what the module looked like from when they had flown by it at Perseid Station on the way to their current location, and then sent the image the same way she sent the words.

Vasiti received a confusing splash of mixed colors in reply. Chiemi did not respond in words for another several minutes.

"Where are you from? I do not recognize your voice. Are you from Outside?"

The last word came with a feeling of location, and therefore capitalized itself in Vasiti's mind.

"I'm from Kiribati. I don't know where 'Outside' is. Where is that?"

Another few minutes of silence followed before Chiemi replied. A bright splash of orange and red that faded into hot pink with yellow slashes. A feeling of concern and suspicion accompanied the colors.

"'Outside' is beyond the influence of the Brightstar. Through the ripples. Are you human?"

"Brightstar?" Vasiti murmured to herself. "Sorry, Commander. The voice—she calls herself 'Chiemi'—was asking if I was from 'Outside'. I asked her what she meant, and she said 'Outside' was beyond the influence of the 'Brightstar'. And then she asked me if I was human."

"Well, that's an interestin' question. What did you tell her? And how do you know the voice is a 'she'?"

"I just get that sense in what she's sending to me. I knew when she was getting closer. I think she's almost here. I haven't replied yet."

Leah was silent for a few moments.

"May as well tell her we're human. Either she is, too, or she isn't. Makes it interestin' either way, I think. Could be first contact! Wouldn't that be excitin'?" Vasiti heard her smiling.

"Yes, we are human," Vasiti replied. *"Aren't you?"*

The reply came very quickly.

"Of course not. This is the first time I have encountered a human who talks normally. I can see your module." The last comment was accompanied by a vivid picture of the *Lucky Dragon* seen from a high approach angle.

Vasiti opened her eyes. "She's coming toward us from Earth, or at least from that general direction. High, maybe two o'clock, and about one or two kilometers out."

"Dvoretskiy!" Leah barked. "Are there any other ships in this area? Modules? Maybe somethin' the G16 sent up without tellin' anyone?"

"Negative, ma'am," he answered quickly. "Nothing on radar. The cameras on that side are not showing anything, and none of the Earth L2 satellites are in that direction right now."

"Mother! Are you hurt? What did they do to you? Mother!"

Had it not been for her magnetic boots, Vasiti would have jumped. She heard Chiemi's voice as if standing right next to her.

A dark shape—smaller than the shape next to the *Lucky Dragon*, but still much bigger than Vasiti—suddenly flashed into view, shimmering deep purple waves cascading off it. There was a brighter flash of purple and she felt the *Lucky Dragon* lurch as if pushed. Her boots held her fast to the side of the module. A chorus of surprised exclamations came over the comms as the *Lucky Dragon* began drifting away from the two dark shapes.

"Status! All stations report. Dvoretskiy!" Leah's voice broke through the exclamations.

"Internal pressure appears steady, Commander." After a short pause, Dvoretskiy continued. "Confirmed. No hull breaches. We are slowly drifting away from our previous position and are now at fifty meters and continuing to drift, ma'am."

"Understood. Can we get back on course and return to our previous location?"

"Absolutely, ma'am," Dvoretskiy replied. "Maneuvering thrusters are green."

"Please stop the drifting for now, Lieutenant."

"Yes, ma'am!"

Vasiti felt the rumble of the maneuvering thrusters through her boots, and the drifting slowed. It was hard for Vasiti to distinguish between the shapes. She saw the smaller one moving around, but only because of the quickly fading glittering violet ripples moving across her form.

"Any ideas what happened?" Leah asked over the comm. "Taake, has Chiemi said anything new? Maybe she knows what happened."

Vasiti concentrated on Chiemi again and felt an instant connection, as if a door was opened in her mind.

"What happened, Chiemi? Did you see what moved us?"

Splotches of bright red came through just before Chiemi's reply. *"I moved you. You attacked my mother. Why did you attack her?"*

"Commander, she says we attacked her mother. Maybe that's the object we hit?" Vasiti mentally turned back to Chiemi.

"Chiemi, when we arrived, we hit something, but we didn't know what it was."

The red spots—interspersed with some purples turning to blues—were less intense when Chiemi's wordless reply came through.

"I apologize, Chiemi. It wasn't our intention to hurt her. We don't have any weapons. We didn't even know she was there. We had begun slowing down as we approached the Lagrange point—that's what we call this location—so we were moving quite slowly at the time. I hope she is okay."

The larger shape started moving, though still more slowly than Chiemi. Much less agitation came from Chiemi, though no reply came as the pause stretched into several minutes.

"What's happenin', Taake?" Leah's voice broke the silence.

"I don't know ma'am. It seems Chiemi is examining her mother, the way she's moving around over there. I guess we just need to wait."

After fifteen minutes with no reply, Vasiti tried again.

"Chiemi? Is she okay?"

The reply came quickly this time. *"She is waking up. She does not appear to be seriously injured. She was unconscious because of being hit."*

"I'm glad she's okay."

After a few moments, a different voice came into Vasiti's mind, much older and more powerful than Chiemi's. It was quiet, but vast and strong, reminding Vasiti of the ocean that surrounded her home.

"Human, my daughter tells me you are able to hear our speech."

Vasiti swallowed, her mouth suddenly dry. "Commander, Chiemi's mother is awake. She just spoke to me."

"This day is gettin' more and more interestin'! I doubt they thought we'd encounter aliens when they sent us up here, especially this close to Earth. Go ahead and talk to her. Let's see what we can do. Also, try to verbally repeat the conversation as it happens so we have a record of it."

Vasiti refocused on the mother. "*I first heard your daughter calling out for you, and thought I was hearing things. My name is Vasiti. What is your name?*"

"*You may call me Ekoha. It is not common for humans to hear our speech, but it is not unknown. I have met others with this ability, though your thoughts are much clearer than most. Human, why are you out here, so far beyond the Nesting Grounds?*"

"*The 'Nesting Grounds'? I don't understand. Where are the Nesting Grounds?*"

"*My daughter reminds me that you call the Nesting Grounds 'Earth'. Why do you come out here, beyond Earth, where you cannot live? There is no air here.*"

"*We are here because we are exploring, trying to move beyond our world. We want to understand space and learn everything we can about the Solar system. We are curious.*"

Vasiti's mind filled with bursts of tans and browns and a sense of understanding.

"*Humans have always been curious, sometimes too curious for their own good.*" Bursts of greens and blues laced with patches of rainbow colors swirled briefly. "*Why did you come to this place, to my home? Is there not enough room elsewhere? I have lived here for a very long time, and you have never come here before.*"

"*We have only recently learned how to create places for us to live in space. This location, this place, is special because very little energy is required to keep us here. We call it a Lagrange point. This one is called Earth-Sun Lagrange Point Two. The gravity—that's the force that pulls us toward the Sun and the Earth—is equal here. Do you understand?*"

"*I am familiar with the concepts. That is also why I live here. It is peaceful. I am surprised humans have progressed so far since I last visited the Nesting Grounds.*"

"*A hundred years ago, we couldn't have done this easily. In the last fifty or sixty years, we have started moving farther into the space around Earth, even traveled to other planets, like Mars.*"

Vasiti sent pictures of the research station on Mars, emphasizing what Mars looked like. Tans and browns came back, laced with rainbow splotches of amusement.

"*The orange planet is a dry wasteland for the most part,*" Ekoha replied. "*It moved too far from the Brightstar to be useful as a nesting ground many lifetimes ago.*"

"*It used to be closer?*" Vasiti asked, surprised.

"*Many, many lifetimes ago. There are legends among my people about a great battle with an ancient enemy that caused it to be moved from its place. It has been lifeless since that time.*"

"*My people, the people on Earth, have wondered if there used to be life on Mars. We never thought it was because of a change in orbit, though. We concluded that there may have been some lower life forms, like plants and bacteria, but we didn't think there had ever been any higher life forms.*"

"Yes," Ekoha said. *"There are a great many things humans must still learn. Your first steps into the Great Cold are only a beginning for you. Let us begin with some questions . . ."*

FORTY MINUTES LATER, VASITI AND EKOHA WERE STILL DEEP IN THEIR discussion.

"You gonna to be finished soon, Taake?"

Leah's voice broke into Vasiti's thoughts, and she pulled herself out of her trance. She quickly sent a message to Ekoha.

"Ekoha, Commander Brackett is asking me a question. I'll be right back."

"You've been silent for the past forty minutes," Leah continued. "You'll need to write up a report when you come back inside."

"Sorry, Commander. I lost track of time. Ekoha is very interesting."

"What'd y'learn?"

"Several things. Mars used to be in a different orbit and used to be inhabited. I don't know exactly how long ago. Ekoha only said it was many, many lifetimes."

"Really? That's definitely interestin'. I bet the scientists back home have a field day with that one. Anythin' else?"

"The dragons—I'm not sure what else to call them, since they really look quite a bit like dragons from all those legends. The dragons have been using Earth as a nesting ground for longer than humans have been around. In fact, many of the legends about dragons are about *these* dragons. They've been embellished, though. Dragons don't breathe fire or anything like that."

"That's nice to know. Makes me feel a bit safer." Leah chuckled. "I don't suppose they are magical, either."

"No, though we discussed how Chiemi was able to get here. Apparently, she lives in the 'quiet spot' on the other side of the Earth. I think she means Earth-Sun Lagrange Point One based on how she described it. I think they can intuitively feel gravity currents, too, ma'am. She was describing this spot and the one where Chiemi lives as if they were calm spots in a river, so it makes sense."

Vasiti paused for a moment. "Anyway, they somehow collect the light from the Sun—all of it, the full spectrum, from what Ekoha said—and use that to reach what they call a 'flashpoint'. They can travel really fast that way. Ekoha couldn't explain the physics of it, but Chiemi flew from L1 to this location in less than thirty minutes!"

Leah gave a low whistle. "That's somethin' worth exploring. Imagine how that'd change things in the Solar system! Travel times would be almost equivalent to travelin' on Earth in some cases."

"I was thinking the same thing, ma'am."

"Did you ask for permission to stay here? If we aren't gonna be able to stay, we need to know now so we can see what ISEF wants to do. I don't think they had a contingency plan for if this location was occupied." Leah chuckled.

"Very true, ma'am. I'll ask Ekoha. Be back in a few minutes."

Vasiti turned her attention back to Ekoha. Making the mindlink was easier than before.

"Ekoha, thank you for your patience. Commander Brackett asks if we have your permission to stay. We want to study the Solar system, and some of the things can only be studied here. We didn't realize this location was already occupied. None of our satellites gave any indication you were here."

A halo of rainbows sparkled through Vasiti's mind. *"We are very good at not being seen."*

"May we share this place with you? We hope to have many of us living here eventually, inside modules that attach to the one I am on. We would orbit this spot, about ten kilometers out." She sent an image of the spot where Ekoha was, with the completed *Lucky Dragon* moving in a circle around it.

"Let me consider what you have said, Human Vasiti. I am impressed with the knowledge and history you have shared, and you are a very honest person. The same cannot be said of other humans I have encountered in the past, so perhaps your people have changed. I will discuss it with my daughter."

"Thank you, Ekoha. I will wait here."

"The damage is minimal, Lieutenant Commander," Ai reported. "While you were talking with the dragons, I went over every centimeter of Quadrant A. Outside of a few minor dents, there is no damage. David did some testing from the inside, too, and everything looks good. We were lucky."

"Thanks, Ai. Lucky in more ways than only that, too." Vasiti said. "It's unlike anything else. I can't even begin to describe it. Feelings come along with the words, which makes it so much easier to understand them."

"I wish I could hear them," Ai said wistfully. "It sounds so exotic."

"The closest thing to it is listening to an audiobook, except you aren't hearing the voices in your ears. I can actually hear their voices in my head. They have different voices, too, just like our spoken voices. It's really easy to distinguish between them, at least for these two."

"Human Vasiti," Ekoha's voice rumbled into her mind. *"You may stay here provided you maintain your module where you described. There is enough space for both of us here."*

"Thank you, Ekoha," Vasiti replied, relief flooding through her. *"I'll tell Commander Brackett. She'll be very pleased. I need to go write my reports and sleep. It's been a*

long day, though I really enjoyed talking with you. I've learned more today than I ever expected to learn coming out here. See you again tomorrow."

"I have learned much as well, Human Vasiti. I look forward to further discussions."

May 22, 2116
Earth-Sun Lagrange Point Two and Jarvis Island Spaceport, Jarvis Island, Kiribati

"THINGS ARE GOING WELL, KALANA."

Vasiti sat in front of the comms panel in her quarters, speaking to a small picture of her sister. There was a five second delay, which wasn't bad as far as communications went. The people on Mars had a much bigger delay.

"A lot of experiments to do," she continued, "and a lot of getting everything ready for the spokes and the outer rings. The four spokes should be here in early June, so we don't have much time. Each one comes with two more crew members, so it will be getting more crowded."

"I'm sure that explains some of the activity I'm seeing here, Siti," Kalana replied, "but there's something else going on. I've never seen so many commercial launches pushed back before. What's happening out there? ISEF security is everywhere now, monitoring everything that comes or goes out of this place."

"You know I can't tell you any more than I have, Sis. My hands are tied. They'll announce things at some point, but it's not up to me. I'm lucky they let me talk to you at all. It's probably because you're Director of Jarvis Island Spaceport. Congratulations on that, by the way. You deserve it."

"They still don't tell me anything. If they keep this up, we'll start losing our commercial contracts, and that's what pays the bills here. It's not like ISEF normally has enough traffic to keep JIS busy more than a couple weeks out of the year. In the last three weeks, they've had multiple launches a day. A day! I don't know how they can keep it up!"

Kalana sounded exasperated and looked exhausted. Vasiti saw the dark spots under her sister's eyes.

"You ought to let your second take care of things more so you can get some real sleep," Vasiti said.

"I know, I know, but ISEF has a really demanding schedule. None of us are getting all the sleep we want. Hopefully, things will slow down a bit soon. Unless they give us money to increase our staff, we can't keep up with all of this. Not that we'll tell them that. All this traffic is helping Kiribati, and the government rep keeps telling me to just do whatever they need done, so someone's getting paid a lot somewhere. I'm not seeing any of it showing up in my budget, though."

"Maybe it's time to ask them for an *increase* in your budget, Sis, so you can hire more people. There are a lot of talented people who would jump at the chance to work at JIS."

"Maybe." Kalana didn't look convinced. "Hey, there is one thing. In the comms traffic this morning, there was something confirming an orbital launch from somewhere in Africa about three weeks ago. I'd seen a news report about it, but it was really vague. The message indicated it might be Group 16. Maybe have Commander Brackett ask Perseid Station. It may be nothing, but you never know."

"I'll do that. Thanks, Kalana."

They were silent for a few moments before her alarm beeped and Vasiti spoke again.

"I've got to go, Sis. Give Mom and Dad a hug for me. It was good talking to you. See you in about eleven months."

"Sure thing. They do miss you. We all do. Too bad you can't just call them and chat. Maybe in a month or two, if things change. Talk to you later, Siti. I love you."

"I love you, too." Vasiti waved at her sister, waited a few more seconds, then disconnected. She leaned back in her chair and stared at the ceiling, her foot hooked through the footbar under the desk so she didn't float away. Her quarters were certainly not luxurious, but at about eight square meters, they were larger than she thought they would be.

"Human Vasiti." The rumbling mindvoice of Ekoha interrupted her thoughts.

"Hello again, Ekoha. How are you doing? Is Chiemi still visiting, or has she returned home?"

"My daughter is still here. She finds you humans fascinating. She enjoys watching your preparations."

Vasiti smiled. *"I'm glad she finds us so interesting. I always enjoy talking to both of you. I've learned so much through our conversations."*

"As have I." A rainbow splash filled Vasiti's mind as Ekoha spoke. *"I am contacting you because more"*—and the word didn't make sense to Vasiti—*"have arrived here to watch your progress."*

"What is that word?" Vasiti tried to mimic what Ekoha had sent.

"That is the name we call ourselves. In your language it would mean 'starkind' or 'dwellers among the stars'. Chiemi tells me the human word you use is 'dragons'. You may call us any of those names."

"That's an interesting name. I like it." Vasiti sent mixed pastel colors to indicate she was happy to learn more about the dragons. *"So more than just you and Chiemi live here?"*

"Yes. There are many others who live under the influence of this Brightstar. They wish to observe you and the other humans because you are now journeying into our home, far beyond the Nesting Grounds."

Vasiti sent a mental nod and keyed a private channel on her desk comm. "Commander Brackett."

"Go ahead, Taake."

"Ekoha informs me that several other dragons, or 'starkind' as they call themselves, have arrived and will be watching our progress. We should advise those piloting the incoming spokes and other sections of the *Lucky Dragon* to be cautious so we don't accidentally hit one. Again."

"I agree, Taake. They don't show up on radar, so we'll have t'figure out some other way to watch out for them. Maybe ask Ekoha to advise the other dragons to watch out for us, too, since they *can* see us."

"Yes, ma'am. She contacted me this time to let me know of the arrival of the other starkind. I'll pass along your suggestion."

"Sounds like you're makin' some good progress talkin' to them, then, if they're contactin' us now. Keep me informed, Lieutenant Commander."

"Will do, ma'am. One other thing. I was just talking to my sister—she's Director of Jarvis Island Spaceport—and she said there was a report of an orbital launch from Africa about three weeks ago. She said it might be the Group 16 Consortium. Maybe we should contact Perseid Station to have them watch for anything headed our direction."

"Yes, I remember seein' that in the command reports back then. Interestin'. Thank you for remindin' me. I'll see what I can find out. Thank you, Taake."

Vasiti leaned back in her chair to stare at the ceiling, her gaze wandering randomly as she thought about all the breakthroughs made over the last three weeks.

Alien life confirmed, right here in the Solar system. Not only that, but friendly, intelligent alien life! At least so far. Her mind raced with excitement. *And I'm right in the middle of it all! I came out here to study physics, and now I'm the front line ambassador and negotiator for ISEF. I wish I could tell someone back home. Speaking of physics . . .*

"*Ekoha, I have a question about something Chiemi said when we first met. She said something about 'ripples' and 'outside'. What do those mean?*"

"*We call other places like this one 'Outside' because they are not here. They are outside. The ripples are how we travel to places outside.*"

Vasiti thought for a few moments before replying. "*Places like this? You mean the Sun—the Brightstar—and the Nesting Grounds? The Solar system? You can travel to other stars like this one?*"

"*That is correct. If we have need, we can travel to other places. This method of travel is very fast. I do not think you have the correct tools to make the journey. Many of the starkind do not think you are ready for such things.*"

"*Why not?*" Vasiti asked.

"*Starkind have very long memories, and some that live here still feel animosity toward humans because of how humans treated us in the past. Many starkind were attacked, and some were killed. Some of us fear you may now do that again.*"

"*That makes sense. Humans have certainly done some stupid things in the past.*" Vasiti nodded even though Ekoha couldn't see it. "*And probably still do, too. Perhaps we could form a treaty or something.*"

"*What is this 'treaty'? I am unfamiliar with that word.*"

"It's an agreement where each group lists concerns and how they should be handled in the future. So humans and starkind would each list any concerns they had, and then come to an agreement on how to resolve those concerns. This helps avoid any problems in the future. Does that make sense?"

A splash of tans preceded Ekoha's reply.

"Yes, we have had such agreements with humans in the past. Starkind very rarely broke such agreements, but humans often did. This is why we rarely show ourselves to you anymore. Our councils decided you were too dangerous."

Vasiti was silent.

"Our interaction with you here has given some starkind hope that things might be different this time," Ekoha continued. *"While our first encounter was bumpy, you and your crew have been very forthcoming and open with me and with my daughter."*

Vasiti laughed. *"Did you just make a joke, Ekoha?"*

A rainbow halo came in reply, and Vasiti heard Ekoha chuckling. It was an odd sensation.

"Yes. My daughter has explained some human things to me, and she said that humans like humor. She says it puts you at ease." Ekoha sent mixed pastels with splashes of rainbow colors. *"It would seem it has worked."*

Vasiti grinned, sending her own halo of rainbows back to Ekoha. Ekoha's voice was more serious when she replied.

"Everything you have agreed upon here has happened as agreed. You have made a very positive first impression this time. So, perhaps those voices of dissent may change. Much depends upon you and your crew."

"We've been trying to make up for accidentally running the module into you," Vasiti replied, nodding. *"You're the first non-humans we have encountered. We want to learn from you."*

"She's correct that many treaties have been broken in the past," Vasiti thought to herself. *"Even now, there are countries that refuse to trust each other."*

Ekoha's voice came again, suddenly.

"We must call a council among the starkind and others to discuss these issues. We will contact you again when that is finished." Ekoha's presence withdrew from Vasiti's mind before she could respond.

May 31, 2116
Earth-Sun Lagrange Point Two

Vasiti sat in a corner of the mess hall, her feet hooked under the footbar so she felt like she was sitting rather than weightless. The room was mostly deserted, with only Jonas and Cristina working in the kitchen. A half-empty squeeze packet of orange Jell-O floated near her head.

"Lieutenant Commander?"

She felt alone, even though Commander Brackett had given her plenty to do to prepare for the four station spokes arriving in ten days.

I got used to having Ekoha and Chiemi around to talk to, she thought. *It feels weird to not sense them nearby. It's like part of me is missing, and I didn't even know it was a part of me until Chiemi screamed into my mind.*

"Lieutenant Commander?"

I've tried multiple times to contact them. Both of them, but they just don't reply. Maybe they've gone Outside. Maybe these other starkind and the 'others' she mentioned aren't here in the Solar system. Perhaps this mindspeak has a distance limit?

"Excuse me, Lieutenant Commander?" Ai gently shook Vasiti, startling her out of her thoughts.

"What? Oh, sorry. What can I do for you, Ai?"

"Commander Brackett wants you in C&C. She's been paging you for the last ten minutes." Ai smiled, her face a mixture of excitement and friendly mirth.

"Thank you, Ai. I'm on my way."

Vasiti untangled her feet and pushed off toward the door, nearly crashing into David on the way.

"Sorry, David!"

"No problem, Lieutenant Commander." David gracefully slipped out of her way and into the mess hall.

Vasiti sped down the hall to the zero-G tube access, moved through the tube with practiced ease, and exited on the main level and going around the corner to C&C. Leah looked up as Vasiti floated through the open door.

"I'm glad you could join us, Lieutenant Commander," Leah said sternly, though Vasiti saw a slight twinkle in her eyes. Leah gestured at the largest screen. "I thought you might be interested in our new visitors."

Vasiti looked at the monitor, currently showing a camera feed from the outside edge of Quadrant B. At first, the object it showed appeared to be a small round asteroid—unusual, given the irregular appearance they usually took. Then she looked closer.

This sphere was quite smooth, and it wasn't pocked with small craters. She saw straight lines on its surface, but it had no visible windows or ports. It looked artificial.

"What is it, Commander?"

"That ship—yes, it's a ship—is carryin' a number of representatives from the halfen. They've stated that Ekoha invited 'em here to watch us."

"Another first contact?"

"Yes and no. They want to meet with us to discuss what they've been discussin' for the last several days."

"That's a good thing, I would think." Vasiti looked at her superior, whose face suddenly sported the beginnings of a devilish grin.

"Specifically, they want t'meet with you. No one else."

Vasiti's looked surprised. "Why me?"

"It appears your reputation precedes you. They said that Ekoha and Chiemi spoke highly of you, and so they would deal only with you. Get suited up and out Airlock B. Don't tether down. I'll let them know you're coming."

"Yes, ma'am!" Vasiti launched herself toward the door, using the handholds to swing around the corner toward the airlock. She tried reaching out to Ekoha and Chiemi on her way.

"Ekoha? Chiemi? Are you back?"

"Human Vasiti, we are here," came Ekoha's familiar mindvoice. *"We will talk after you speak with the halfen."*

A wave of relief swept through Vasiti. Her mind burst with a rainbow of pastels shot through with bursts of bright yellow. Her happiness at hearing Ekoha's voice immediately lifted a weight she hadn't noticed until that moment.

"We missed you, too, Vasiti," Chiemi chimed in with a splash of amused colors.

Vasiti had to slow herself down to make sure she didn't skip any steps while donning the EVA suit. When she was satisfied she hadn't forgotten something that would kill her, she stepped into the airlock and started the cycle. One minute later, she opened the outer airlock door and swung out onto the side of the *Lucky Dragon* using one of the many grab bars.

"I'm in position, Commander," she reported.

"You're just in time, then, as they've dispatched a shuttle to retrieve you."

Vasiti turned toward the halfen sphere. It was larger than it had appeared on the camera feed. Much larger. The shuttle coming toward her was significantly smaller and more egg shaped.

"Their ship is huge, Commander! It looks like it's at least three or four times wider in diameter than the *Lucky Dragon*."

"That sounds 'bout right, give or take, based on its radar signature," Commander Brackett replied.

The shuttle grew closer, finally coming to a stop and hovering three meters from Vasiti. A small hatch opened in the side, so Vasiti released her magnetic boots and pushed off toward it.

The ovoid shuttle was about seven or eight meters long and about four meters tall and wide. As soon as she was inside the hatch, it closed and the airlock cycled. When the inner airlock door opened, she found herself in a small room with several large seats in rows. She also noticed the pull of gravity toward the floor.

"Artificial gravity?" she murmured to herself.

A voice spoke over her private comm channel.

"This shuttle is equipped with artificial gravity, though I can turn it off if you find it uncomfortable. Please have a seat, Lieutenant Commander Vasiti Taake. We will be arriving at the *Cauqua Odmarluu* shortly. Please enjoy the flight."

"You speak English?" Vasiti asked.

"Yes, and many other languages. It is how I was programmed."

"Programmed? You're a computer?"

"Yes, though I am much more advanced than anything you have. I am an artificial intelligence."

"Cool." Vasiti didn't know what else to say.

"I can turn up the temperature if you are uncomfortable, Lieutenant Commander. I did not increase the temperature because you are in your environment suit. Does it not control the temperature?"

"What? Oh, no," Vasiti laughed. "No, that was an expression. It means I was impressed that you were an AI. Like you said, we don't have anything close to as advanced as you. My suit temperature is fine, thanks."

"I will note that for future reference. We do not always have the most current slang terms programmed into us. We have arrived, Lieutenant Commander."

"Already? That was quick! I didn't even feel the ship moving." Vasiti stood up. "Please, just call me 'Vasiti'. You don't have to be so formal."

"As you wish, Vasiti. My designation is *Chosu Nomh*. You may call me 'Nomh'."

The airlock doors opened simultaneously, and light from the docking bay flooded into the dim interior of the shuttle.

"Thanks for the ride, *Nomh*."

"The environment in *Cauqua Odmarluu* is suitable for humans, so you are welcome to preserve your suit resources and leave it here, if you wish. You will not need it during your meetings. The meeting rooms are not designed to allow easy maneuvering while wearing such a suit. You may place it in this storage unit."

A previously-hidden door opened to reveal a storage unit near the airlock.

"I guess that makes sense. Thanks, *Nomh*." Vasiti removed the suit and placed it in the storage unit. "How do I close the storage unit?"

"I will close it after you exit. You may retrieve your environment suit when your meetings today are complete. I will then return you to your module. That is what the starkind said your ship was called."

"The module is only part of a space station that will be built soon. The rest of the pieces will arrive over the next few months. Its name is *Lucky Dragon*. Seems especially appropriate, given who we've met over the last month or so."

"That is indeed an auspicious designation. I will wait here for you. Good luck!"

"Thank you, *Nomh*," Vasiti said as she walked through the airlock and onto the walkway next to *Nomh*. The shuttle was berthed in a docking bay large enough to fit thirty such shuttles.

The bay was utilitarian, with very little in the way of decoration. Greenish metal was used everywhere. Spaced evenly around three sides of the bay were banks of windows, though Vasiti couldn't see through them. Boxes and other containers were stacked in designated areas near many of the berths. Everything looked very organized and clean.

A group of four humanoids waited at the end of of the walkway, dressed in forest green military-style uniforms accented with golds and reds. A small angled oval insignia adorned the right side of their chests. Three stars clustered near the bottom left, and a single star sat at the top right of the oval.

Each of the halfen wore a rounded helmet with a dark visor, preventing Vasiti from seeing any of their faces. Despite the helmets, they were not threatening. Dark brown belts, gloves, and boots completed the uniforms. As she approached, one of the them removed her helmet and stepped forward.

The halfen's hair was very dark bluish-black, tightly braided intricately down the center of her back. Stray curly wisps of hair poked out here and there along her braid, making her seem less severe, despite an imposing two meter height.

Her hair and uniform contrasted sharply with her light brown sandy skin, and served to highlight the slight point near the tops of her ears. Deep green eyes considered Vasiti intelligently.

Space elves! Vasiti thought, a slight grin forming on her face. The halfen grinned in response.

"I am Sheran Mehse. Welcome to *Cauqua Odmarluu*, Lieutenant Commander Vasiti Taake. I am here to escort you to the meeting room. If you will come this way."

"Does everyone speak English?" Vasiti asked as she moved in the direction Sheran Mehse gestured. The other three escorts followed about three meters behind them.

"Many of us do, as well as other languages from your planet. We have studied humans for many years," Sheran Mehse replied as she led Vasiti through a doorway and down a wide hallway. "We have anticipated this meeting for centuries, though perhaps not quite this soon."

The hallway was wide—about three meters wide—and adorned in some sort of darkly stained wood. The overhead light appeared dappled on the floor, shadows and light moving slightly as if affected by a slight breeze. And she could feel a slight breeze, too.

After several turns and about eighty meters, Sheran Mehse led Vasiti through an open a door on the left side of the hall. The room appeared very much like an executive board room on Earth. A round table filled the center of the square room, and twenty chairs were arranged at intervals around it.

Vasiti looked around the table as she stopped just inside the door. All but one of the chairs contained a willowy yet sturdy halfen. The occupants stood as one as she entered, looking as interested in her as she was in them. Many of them were smiling. They varied in height and weight, but all were slightly taller than most humans.

I've never seen a human with blue or green skin, she thought as her eyes continued looking around the table. *Pink hair is a little unusual, too, and it looks natural, not dyed. All of them have pointed ears, too! They look like the elves from all those fantasy movies Kalana likes to watch. If they covered their ears, most of them could pass for humans.*

One of them stepped away from the table and walked toward her. He had close-cropped auburn hair, with graying around the temples. His skin was golden brown, his dark eyes piercing, and his voice deep and friendly when he spoke.

"Lieutenant Commander Vasiti Taake of the International Space Exploration Force of Earth, welcome. Ekoha has spoken much of you, and we are honored to finally meet you. I am Sendiherra Vastaar. We welcome you to the *Cauqua Odmarluu* on behalf of the Halfen Kongsveld."

"Thank you, Sendiherra Vastaar. It is an honor to be invited here and meet all of you."

Sendiherra Vastaar's smile grew. "I am the royal ambassador to the humans, and those seated around the table are representatives from various organizations: business, education, ministerial, and so on. In addition," he gestured at three large monitors, each featuring a dragon in a large bay, "we are joined by three starkind, representing their Council of Elders. They each have a translator we provided to them so they can communicate freely with you and us, though I understand you have the gift allowing you to communicate directly with them." He raised an eyebrow in question.

"Yes, though I have only spoken with Chiemi and Ekoha so far."

"Wonderful! Wonderful!" He clasped his hands together twice in front of his face. "Let me show you to your seat and we can begin our discussions."

SEVEN HOURS LATER, SHERAN MEHSE LED AN EXHAUSTED AND OVERWHELMED Vasiti back to the docking bay and the waiting shuttle.

"I hope your meeting was productive." Sheran Mehse asked.

"I think so, but it's a lot to take in. They asked a lot of questions about recent history, various scientific things, and pretty much anything and everything about Earth. They were especially interested that I wasn't from a large country. I'm surprised they had even heard of Kiribati." Vasiti yawned. "I didn't know answers for some of the questions, though. I hope they don't hold that against me. I got the impression they already knew the answers to a lot of their questions."

"I'm sure you did well, Lieutenant Commander. It is unlikely they would have asked you here if they didn't already know most of what you discussed with them." Sheran Mehse smiled as they walked into the docking bay and stopped at her shuttle's berth.

"Thank you for the escort, Sheran Mehse. I don't know that I could have found my way back very easily."

"It was my pleasure. Have a good evening, Lieutenant Commander. I will meet you here tomorrow morning," she said before leading the other guards out of the bay, leaving Vasiti alone in the large bay.

"The meetings are over for today, Nomh."

"Welcome back, Vasiti. I am ready to depart as soon as you are settled."

"Yes, *Nomh*, thank you," Vasiti said as she flopped across multiple seats in one of the rows. "I'm ready to go to sleep!"

"Acknowledged. We should arrive at your module in about five minutes. I uploaded recordings of today's meetings to the recorder on your suit. Please enjoy the ride."

Vasiti's head spun with all the new information she had learned. The halfen had studied Earth for over ten thousand years, and they had tested her knowledge of recent Earth history.

"Ten thousand years, Nomh! Ten thousand years!" Vasiti laughed. "No wonder they know so much about us. They know more than I remember learning in all my history classes, and I took a lot more of them than most people."

"It is true that the halfen have studied your planet for many millennia. I have only been witness to their study for the last three hundred fifty-seven of your years. They take great pride in learning as much as they can about every life form they encounter."

"I'm just overwhelmed, Nomh. So much information!" Vasiti stared at the ceiling.

"That is completely understandable," Nomh said. The next few minutes passed in silence before he continued. "We have arrived, Vasiti. I will return at 07:00 tomorrow morning, your shipboard time."

"Thanks for the ride, *Nomh*. See you tomorrow."

Vasiti suited up, cycled through the airlock, and leapt across the meter of space between *Nomh* and the airlock on the *Lucky Dragon*. She felt Chiemi's mind touch hers as she opened the airlock on the module.

"How do you feel, Vasiti?" Chiemi's voice was quieter than usual. *"How did your meetings go?"*

"I'm tired. The halfen really enjoyed the meetings, though." Vasiti sent a rainbow splash of amusement as she closed the airlock and started the cycle. *"Most of it was answering questions, even though they already knew the answers to all of them."*

Chiemi replied with an answering rainbow halo.

"It's overwhelming, Chiemi. I signed up for this mission thinking it would be a standard one-year deployment to study astrophysical phenomena from space. I never thought I'd meet two different alien races, let alone learn about wormhole travel to other star systems! This is an astrophysicist's dream come true!"

The airlock finished its cycle, and Vasiti sent multiple bright yellow bursts while removing her EVA suit, then walking toward her quarters.

"The halfen offered to take me and two others through a wormhole to visit another star system. It may be normal for you and the halfen to travel like that, but it's only been wishful thinking for us. Wormholes were only a theory until now."

"I'm pleased that you're so happy, Vasiti. There are some beautiful star systems Outside."

"Will you be coming, too, Chiemi?" Vasiti asked as she entered her quarters and flopped down on her bed.

"Mother and I will be coming. Did Sendiherra Vastaar say when you would be leaving?"

"The day after tomorrow." Vasiti stretched and yawned. *"Tomorrow will be more discussions with the halfen. Some of them seem unsure about supporting the trip. There aren't many of them, so I'm hoping it won't be a problem."*

Chiemi was quiet before responding, sending muted yellows with a few bright pink bursts to indicate cautious annoyance.

"When Mother and I originally met with them, there were several of them who wanted to get started as soon as possible, but some of the halfen and starkind elders are not convinced humans are ready to be taken Outside. You have impressed many of them, however. They won't block those of us who think you're ready."

"I think my government is eager, too." Vasiti nodded while sending bursts of tan and brown. *"I wonder when they'll announce this to the public? Commander Brackett doesn't want me saying anything to anyone."*

"Mother said this is a common discussion when a young race is introduced to the 'galactic community'. Some people are always concerned about the impact of learning about other life out here."

"So there are other races, too, not just you and the halfen?"

"Oh yes, many others. Most of them are very far from here, many days' travel even using the ripples. You will probably meet a few others soon, should everything go well."

"I'll try not to worry about it then—"

An alarm cut off Vasiti's thought. It was followed quickly by Leah's voice.

"This is Commander Brackett. All hands to stations. This is not a drill. Repeat: all hands to stations. This is not a drill."

"There's an alarm, Chiemi." Vasiti sent bright orange and red bursts laced with muted yellow. *"I'll talk to you later."*

May 31, 2116
Earth-Sun Lagrange Point Two

Vasiti pulled on her uniform jacket and was out the door before she finished zipping it closed. A few moments later, she entered the bridge.

"What's happening, Commander?"

"Perseid Station was hit by four missiles about an hour ago. Only two exploded, but the other two were going fast enough to do damage. They're still sorting out what happened. The attack killed four workers, including my uncle, and damaged their comms and one of the spokes. Uncle Low was getting workers out of the damaged areas when something exploded . . ." Leah trailed off, her face grim.

"I'm so sorry, Commander," Vasiti said. "Do we know who it was?"

Leah's face became even more grim.

"We're not one hundred percent sure, but a couple of freighters in the area said it looked like a Group 16 shuttle design. They also said the shuttle didn't stop and was headed this way on full burn."

Vasiti felt her stomach sink and closed her eyes briefly before looking up at Leah. "Do we have anything we can use to defend ourselves?"

"Based on the information passed along by the freighters and Perseid Control," Leah said, "they will likely be out of fuel by the time they get here, so they won't be able to maneuver much. This is a one way mission. Their missiles aren't all that reliable, either."

Leah was silent for a moment as she looked around at her crew. All of them were gathered now, holding on to various grab bars to keep steady. Their faces showed a range of emotions, from anger to shock to determination.

"Perseid Control says the attacking shuttle is moving much faster than we were on our trip out here. They hit Perseid as they flew by on full burn, so it might be here within a couple hours. We need to figure out some way of protecting this module, and we don't have a lot of time. Ideas?"

There was silence for a minute before Ai quietly spoke.

"Should we let the halfen and the dragons know what's happening? If that ship really is from the G16, and it really is coming here, they could get hurt by whatever the people on that shuttle decide to do."

"Good point." Leah nodded as she spoke. "Taake, contact Chiemi and Ekoha, then contact the halfen. Anyone else?"

"We have radar," Dvoretskiy said, "no weapons, but we can make sure we see them as far away as possible. I think we should keep active radar pointed in the direction of Perseid Station."

"Agreed. Do it, Dvoretskiy. Anyone else?"

Emilia spoke up next. "If the dragons can help, we might be able to grab some big asteroids and use them as shields? Or maybe see if one of them could help us fling them at the shuttle?"

"Maybe Chiemi and Ekoha can help with that," Vasiti suggested. "I don't know if they have anything that's capable of moving asteroids, but the halfen might. I'll ask."

"Good. Anyone else have ideas?" Leah looked around the crew.

"We do have something that might be used as a weapon, maybe," Vasiti said. "The booster we used to get here. It still has about one-third of its fuel. We already disconnected it, and it's just floating about one hundred meters away."

Leah nodded. "After you're done talking to Chiemi, work with Dvoretskiy to see how we can do it. It's already rigged for remote operation, so we should be able come up with something useful using it."

"David," Leah continued, "go secure the mess and living quarters. Doc, make sure the medical bay is ready in case there are injuries. Ai, secure the labs and cargo bays. Everyone, make sure your quarters are secured after that. In sixty minutes, we'll seal the bulkheads until this is over, so be at your assigned stations by then, and make sure you're in your EVA suits. I'll give warnings at ten and five minutes before they close. I'll also keep an eye on the radar, in case that shuttle shows up earlier than we think it will. Let's get to it!"

Fifty-five minutes later, Vasiti and Ai were the last to return to C&C. Leah looked up as they entered.

"You're the last ones, Taake," Leah said. "Please seal all the bulkheads."

"Yes, ma'am. Chiemi and her mother know of a few asteroids in the area, but none of the big ones are close enough to move here in time, Commander," Vasiti reported as she and Anahera launched toward their stations. "We have the booster ready to fire. We'll have to use its attitude jets to point it first. It will basically be a battering ram, and we won't be able to make many adjustments once it's moving. The compressed air supply for the attitude jets is mostly gone, and we didn't have time to replenish it."

"Understood," Leah replied. "We'll make do with what we have. Reminds me of being back on the ranch. It usually didn't involve incoming missiles, however."

"All bulkheads reporting sealed, Commander," Vasiti smiled grimly as she strapped in.

"Acknowledged." Leah looked up from Dvoretskiy's station. "We have a shuttle headed this way. It doesn't have a transponder, so it's not an ISEF shuttle. It's about thirty minutes out at its current speed. It could fire missiles at any moment, if it has any more, and they would be here in less than ten minutes."

A grim silence settled over the command center. Everyone focused on their own stations, trying to think of something that would help.

"Did the halfen say anything, Taake?" asked Leah. "Do they have any ideas?"

"They have not responded, Commander. I've sent two messages. Shall I send another and update them?"

"Do it."

Vasiti opened a channel to the halfen.

"*Cauqua Odmarluu*, this is the *Lucky Dragon*. We have detected an unknown shuttle inbound about eighty-four thousand kilometers out. We anticipate it will be here in under thirty minutes and may fire missiles at any time. We estimate the missiles will arrive in less than ten minutes once fired. We plan to launch our booster toward the shuttle, but we will have little control over its trajectory and attitude once launched. We have no other weapons with which to defend ourselves. Are you able to assist?"

Vasiti waited two minutes before turning to Leah.

"Still no response, ma'am. Let me contact Chiemi and see if she has any ideas."

"Good idea. Do it."

Vasiti concentrated, finding the open mind door to Chiemi.

"Chiemi, can you hear me?"

"I am here, Vasiti."

"The halfen are not responding to messages. We have detected a probable hostile shuttle inbound. It's likely going to try to kill all of us, and may try to hurt you and the halfen. Do you know why the halfen aren't responding?"

A rainbow halo laced with bursts of bright red and pink came through. *"The halfen do not like to interfere in internal issues. They are probably trying to see what you will do to resolve it. My mother agrees and doesn't want me to do anything at this time."*

Vasiti sent bright red and orange bursts laced with the murky green of fear.

"These guys have already killed people! The Commander's uncle was killed at Perseid Station trying to save some of his workers, but four people still died. We're sitting ducks out here!"

"I understand, Vasiti. I want to help, but they have forbidden me from doing anything. They say that you have to figure out how to resolve this." Bright pink burst with dull green halos indicated Chiemi's unhappiness with the decision.

"Commander!" Dvoretskiy's voice broke in. "Two missiles inbound."

"Acknowledged," Leah replied. "Taake, try to put the booster between the missiles and the *Lucky Dragon.*"

"Acknowledged, ma'am. The halfen and the starkind are still choosing to not engage. Chiemi has no additional ideas."

Vasiti sent a brief *Gotta go!* to Chiemi, then called out to Dvoretskiy. "David, send the tracking data for the incoming missiles to my station."

"Already on it," Dvoretskiy replied. "It should be coming up for you now."

Vasiti studied the radar information. The missiles were in a tight pattern. She linked the tracking information to the subroutine for the attitude jets, made a few small adjustments, and initiated the program.

The booster moved slightly in one direction before coming to a relative stop. The infrared sensors lit up as the ion rockets ignited, moving the booster toward the incoming missile blips.

After an eternal three-and-a-half minutes, the infrared sensors flashed intense white before fading back to black. Everyone was silent until Dvoretskiy reported.

"No incoming missiles! We got 'em!"

C&C erupted in cheers. Vasiti looked around at her crew members, her eyes finally stopping on Leah's bowed head. As if sensing Vasiti's gaze, she looked up, a relieved smile on her face.

"Looks like we made it through this one, y'all." Leah's voice sounded tired, and Vasiti understood. She relaxed in her harness, the adrenaline high fading. Dvoretskiy's voice cut through the joy, however.

"Commander, I'm tracking a single incoming object. Based on the size, I've identified it as the shuttle that fired the missiles. It's headed directly for us. At its current speed, it will be here in less than five minutes, ma'am."

Vasiti tensed. They had only attitude jets at their disposal.

"Turn Cargo Bays A and B toward the shuttle. That may help lessen the impact. Then brace for impact." Leah's voice was quiet and determined.

"Executing," Ai replied. "Fifteen seconds clockwise should do it, followed by fifteen seconds the other way to cancel the spin. Hold on."

The jets fired.

"Brace for impact." Leah said quietly, yet her words felt like a knife. Vasiti gripped the grab bar near her station, closed her eyes, and offered a silent prayer.

Thirty seconds passed, then a minute. Vasiti looked up tentatively, her eyes cracking open as she looked around. Dvoretskiy was staring at his screen.

"Commander, radar is showing the shuttle stopped one hundred meters from our hull. It's just stopped there."

"*Lucky Dragon*, this is *Cauqua Odmarluu*. We have stopped the incoming craft."

Vasiti looked up at Leah, then tapped the comm button.

"*Cauqua Odmarluu*, this is *Lucky Dragon*. Thank you. How did you stop it? It was moving pretty quickly."

"We negated its kinetic force. We are moving to intercept it. We had to wait to see how you would handle the situation with an obviously hostile force. You handled it well."

Vasiti watched through the cargo bay cameras as the shuttle hung motionless when it suddenly blossomed into an enormous fireball. Moments later, the shockwave rocked the *Lucky Dragon*. Shrapnel from the disintegrating shuttle hammered the hull, tearing holes into its smooth, metallic skin. Vasiti felt her suit seal as a small piece of shrapnel burst through the bulkhead in C&C, causing the pressure to drop.

"*Lucky Dragon*, this is *Cauqua Odmarluu*. We are sending assistance. You are venting atmosphere. Is anyone injured?"

"*Cauqua Odmarluu*," Vasiti replied. "We appreciate the assistance. We're assessing damage. Please enter at Cargo Bay C. That airlock appears undamaged."

"Commander, the *Cauqua Odmarluu* is sending assistance," Vasiti said as she turned her attention to the crew.

"Lieutenant Commander, you need to come over here." Ai's voice was softer than usual.

Vasiti looked up, finding Ai next to Leah's chair. Leah's helmeted head was tipped to one side, and the Commander was not moving. The side facing her looked undamaged.

"Doc, the Commander is hurt," Ai said into the comm.

Vasiti unstrapped her harness, grabbed the medkit from the side of her chair, and propelled herself toward Leah's station, dreading what she would find.

As the rest of the helmet came into view, she looked into the remnants of what had been Leah's visor. The small object had smashed through the visor, passed through the middle of Leah's head, and tried to exit the back of the helmet. The helmet stretched out at least two centimeters where the object had stopped. There was a tiny crack in the middle of the protrusion.

She heard someone giving orders as she examined her friend, only slowly realizing she was the one giving the orders, her training taking over automatically.

"I need damage reports now, Ai. David, get to Cargo Bay C to help the halfen crew that's probably docking right now. Doc, I need you in here now!"

"Don't worry," Doc said as he came through the door. His EVA suit was scuffed in several places. "The passageway is open to vacuum, too. Let's see what we have here."

He took a couple moments to look over Leah's injuries. "The object killed her instantly, Lieutenant Commander. I wish there was something I could do."

Several hours later, Vasiti was going through Leah's quarters, gathering personal effects to send back to Idaho on Earth. She was exhausted. As she sorted the items, she recorded a log entry.

"The halfen arrived shortly after the explosion and helped repair the *Lucky Dragon*, so we are no longer venting atmosphere. Hydroponics was undamaged, luckily, so replenishing the oxygen won't be a problem. Sheran Mehse, the guard captain on the *Cauqua Odmarluu*, led the repair and rescue party. It was good to see her again, though I wish it had been under better circumstances.

"Using some technology I don't yet understand, the halfen stopped the shuttle just short of it hitting the *Lucky Dragon*. Someone onboard the shuttle rigged it to explode, and a piece of the shrapnel killed Commander Brackett. She never had a chance. It killed her instantly."

Vasiti picked up a picture frame showing Leah and her uncle. She had taken it for the Commander during their brief stopover at Perseid Station on their way to their current location. They both looked so happy in the picture, making silly faces for the camera. Now their families had to deal with two sudden and senseless deaths.

"No one else was killed here. Doc Tezuka was banged up a bit due to the sudden decompression, but it was just some bruising. Cargo Bays A and B took the brunt of the explosion, and we're still sorting out which supplies are too damaged to use. I should have that report by the end of the day."

Vasiti stopped and looked around Leah's quarters before placing the frame into the last box. All of Leah's personal effects were boxed up now, and the room felt oppressively empty.

This has to be the worst duty for any commanding officer, acting or otherwise, Vasiti thought. *I'm not looking forward to writing that letter to Donald and their kids.*

Vasiti took one last look around Leah's quarters. While she had only been her CO for a short time, Leah had become a mentor, a confidant, and a good friend. This room had become so familiar. Whenever she needed to discuss something or work through a problem, it had often been in here. She took a deep breath, then waved her hand over the light control and walked out the door.

You'll be missed, Leah. Safe journeys, wherever you are.

June 14, 2116
Lucky Dragon, Earth-Sun Lagrange Point Two

Doc looked concerned.

"You'll do fine, Doc." Vasiti patted him on the shoulder and smiled. "It should only be for two or three days. We'll be safe. Chiemi and Ekoha are coming, too. If you can handle med school, you can handle this. The halfen said they'll stay here to help, should you need any."

Vasiti looked behind her. The halfen had insisted that only three of the humans could come through the wormhole this time, so she had picked David and Ai to go with her. They looked simultaneously excited and concerned.

Just a week earlier, ISEF had held a press conference to announce contact with the halfen and the starkind, as well as the suspected Group 16 Consortium attack on Perseid Station and the *Lucky Dragon*. The talking heads on WNN and all the other news channels had discussed nothing else since, even clamoring for permission to send reporters out to both places.

The newsies were not happy when they learned about their pending first trip through the wormhole. They demanded it be delayed until they could get people out to cover it, but the halfen declined to change their plans. This made Vasiti like the halfen even more.

"I should be back before the first three spokes arrive next week. Command of the *Lucky Dragon* is yours until I return, Lieutenant Commander Tezuka. Treat her well."

"Yes ma'am. I'll keep the lights on for you." James snapped a salute. "Have a safe trip, Commander."

Commander Vasiti Taake—newly promoted only two days earlier—saluted in return, turned to Ai and David, and led the way into the airlock toward the waiting halfen transport.

A Request

If you liked this anthology, please take the time to leave a review on the site where you purchased it and/or on one of the social media reading sites like Goodreads. Tell your friends that you enjoyed it. Suggest it as reading for your local book club. Request it at your local library (or more than one local library).

Please use these tags when posting about this book:

#forgloryandhonoranthology
#hemeleinpubs

Thank you for your time, and thank you for reading this book!

Find more exciting books to read at hemelein.com.

HEMELEIN PUBLICATIONS

About the Contributors

Ben Beckstrom is an aspiring author, a student of political science and the Middle East, and a fan of blueberries. He can be found either hiding in the library, wrestling large dogs, or reading books the size of Monaco. Initially from Oregon, he served his mission in Southern California and then fell in love with Brigham Young University. Keep an eye on this space!

Jenny Perry Carr is group vice president of scientific services for a medical communications company by day, budding sci-fi/horror/fantasy writer at night, which sounds much like the beginnings of a superhero's bio. But alas, her only superpower is remembering random facts, like the human body contains trillions of microorganisms that outnumber our own cells by 10 to 1! She has a PhD in molecular neurobiology from Yale University and unleashes her scientific insights into her spine-chilling tales.

You can find her captivating stories in the anthologies *Dog Save the King*, *Troubadours and Space Princesses*, *Rhapsody of the Spheres*, *Mythical Monsters* (The Horror Lite Anthologies), and *Murderbirds: An Avian Anthology* (Unhelpful Encyclopedia). She's a Minnesota native living in North Texas with her husband and currently working on a sci-fi trilogy. She can be found on her website, jennyperrycarr.com, or on Facebook @JennyPerryCarr.

JALETA CLEGG was born some time ago and has filled the years since with plenty of make-believe. She writes science fiction adventure, fantasy of all flavors, and silly horror. When not writing, she enjoys playing with yarn, cooking weird vegetables, designing costumes and quilts, and generally messing around.

She has published eleven volumes in her Altairan Empire series, has written many short works and has multiple collections collecting them, most recently *Waiting for Elephants*. Jaleta is co-editor of the LTUE Benefit Anthologies series. Learn more at jaletac.com.

VONNIE WINSLOW CRIST, SFWA, HWA, is author of *Beneath Raven's Wing, Dragon Rain, The Enchanted Dagger, Murder on Marawa Prime, Owl Light, The Greener Forest, Shivers, Scares, and Goosebumps,* and other award-winning books.

Her speculative short fiction appears in *Amazing Stories, Lost Signals of the Terran Republic, Black Infinity, Cirsova Magazine,* in the *Neptune* and *Uranus* volumes in the Planetary Anthology Series, *Deep Space, Sci-Fi: Space Opera Mashup, Sci-Fi: More Future Earth, Troopers Quarterly, Storming Area 51, Defending the Future: Dogs of War, Re-Launch,* and elsewhere. Believing the world is still filled with mystery, miracles, and magic, she strives to celebrate the power of myth in her writing.

Learn more at vonniewinslowcrist.com.

KATE DANE writes offbeat stories with heart. She has published a collection of her speculative fiction, *Plus or Minus Forever,* and a werewolf romance. Her stories have appeared in a number of anthologies. She's always asking "What if?" and writing an answer. Learn more at katedane.com.

MICHELLE J. DIAZ lives in the Pacific Northwest and has been writing since she first picked up a pencil to try her hand at it. Thankfully, that particular manuscript will not see the light of day anytime in the near future. Her stories have grown since, covering a wide scope from sci-fi to fantasy and occasionally the places between. To advance her skills, she has taken courses from David Farland and Wulf Moon. To see more of her work, visit michellejdiaz.com.

David Hankins is the award-winning author of *Death and the Taxman, Death and the Dragon,* the forthcoming *Death and the Immortal,* and the companion *Grimsworld Tales* collection. He writes from the thriving cornfields of Iowa where he lives with his wife, daughter, and two dragons disguised as cats. His short stories have graced the pages of *Writers of the Future Volume 39, Amazing Stories, DreamForge Magazine, Escape Pod, Unidentified Funny Objects 9,* and others.

David devotes his time to his passions of writing, traveling, and finding new ways to pay his mortgage. You can find him at davidhankins.com.

LARRY HODGES, of Germantown, Maryland, is an active member of the Science Fiction & Fantasy Writers Association, with over two hundred short story sales and four SF novels. He's a graduate of the Odyssey and Taos Toolbox Writers Workshops, a member of Codexwriters, and a ping-pong aficionado.

As a professional writer, he has twenty-one books and over twenty-two hundred published articles in 180+ different publications. He's also a member of the USA Table Tennis Hall of Fame, and claims to be the best table tennis player in SFWA, and the best science fiction writer in USA Table Tennis! Visit him at larryhodges.com.

LIAM HOGAN is an award-winning short story writer, with stories in *Best of British Science Fiction* and in *Best of British Fantasy* (NewCon Press). He helps host live literary event Liars' League and volunteers at the creative writing charity Ministry of Stories. More details at happyendingnotguaranteed.blogspot.co.uk.

CANDICE R. LISLE is an fantasy and science fiction writer currently living in Iowa. She is a member of Codex, SFWA, DreamForge Writer's Group, and Wulf Moon's the Wulf Pack Writers Group.

She had a story published in the *Murderbugs* anthology, as well as on Amazon Kindle, *Daily Science Fiction, Galaxy's Edge Magazine, Martian Magazine, Sci Fi Lampoon,* and the LTUE anthology, *Parliament of Wizards.*

Her story, "Follow the Pretrons", won the Critters Award 2022 Best Positive Future Short Story.

Elaine Midcoh (a pen name) loves reading and writing science fiction short stories. She's a past winner of the Jim Baen Memorial Short Story Award and the Writers of the Future contest. Her stories have appeared in the anthologies *Writers of the Future* (volumes 37 and 39, Galaxy Press) and *Compelling Science Fiction Short Stories* (Flame Tree Press) and in the magazines *MetaStellar, Escape Pod, Galaxy's Edge, Daily Science Fiction, The Jewish Fiction Journal, Flash Fiction Magazine,* and *The Sunlight Press.*

Before jumping into writing, she worked as a college professor, where she spent many happy years teaching criminal justice and law courses. She lives in South Florida. For her publications list, see elainemidcoh.wordpress.com. You can also connect with her on Facebook @Elaine Midcoh.

Devin Miller writes science fiction and fantasy when he's not putting patients to sleep for surgeries . . . hopefully with approved medications, and not with his fiction. Learn more at devinmillerwriting.blogspotcom.

Joe Monson loves reading, books, and butter mochi. He has worked at a couple dozen different jobs during his life. In his current job, he valiantly battles worms, trojans, viruses, corruption, hardware, and updates to keep computer systems running.

He has co-edited multiple anthologies with Jaleta Clegg in the LTUE Benefit Anthologies series, and he's the series editor of the Legacy of the Corridor publication series from Hemelein Publications. His most recent anthology, *The Horror at Pooh Corner,* was a successful Kickstarter and was released in bookstores worldwide in 2024.

Joe writes short stories and is outlining a space opera adventure series. He collects science fiction and fantasy art, but not as much as Paul[a] (as if that was even possible). He lives in the tops of the mountains with his thoroughly amazing wife, three miracle children, and their pet library. Learn more at joemonson.com.

John M. Olsen edits and writes across multiple genres and loves stories about ordinary people stepping up to do extraordinary things. His short stories have appeared in dozens of anthologies. He's also written the Polecat Protocol science fiction series and several other novels across multiple genres, including books in the JTF13 and Four Horsemen shared universes. He loves to create and fix things through editing and writing, just like when he's working in his secret lair equipped with dangerous power tools. In all cases, he applies engineering principles and processes to the task at hand, often in unpredictable ways.

He lives in Utah with his lovely wife, a variable number of mostly grown children, and a constantly changing subset of extended family and pets. Check out

---

[a] See http://www.paulgenesse.com/.

his ramblings on his blog at johnmolsen.blogspot.com. Safety goggles are optional but recommended.

Scott R. Parkin is is an award-winning author with more than sixty short story sales across a wide variety of genres, from romance to military sf and slice of life to absurdist fantasy. A winner in the international Writers of the Future Contest, Scott is currently at work on a fantasy novel set in ancient China, and a companion novel to his short story, "Beloved of the Electric Valkyrie".

Jacob Pérez was born in Ponce, Puerto Rico, but spent most of his young adult life in Boston, Massachusetts, earning a nursing degree. He now lives in Portland, Connecticut, with his wife and three beautiful kids. He spends his days off writing about monsters, spaceships, superheroes, and the most bizarre creatures.

He loves crossing genre boundaries and exploring the complexity of human nature. Currently, he's working on expanding his writing portfolio. You can find him on X/Twitter @jacobperez86, Facebook @jacob.perez.98096, and jacobperezauthor.com.

K. Z. Richards writes speculative fiction from her home in Ohio, where she cares for her five children and two budgies. Her stories have appeared in *Neo-opsis Science Fiction Magazine, Triangulation, Flash Fiction Magazine,* and other publications. In her free time, she enjoys running circles around her neighborhood and binge-watching completed tv shows with her husband. You can find her on Facebook @kzrichards and BlueSky @kzrichards.bsky.social.

Brandon Sanderson is the internationally best-selling and award-winning author of dozens of novels. His most recent works include *Wind and Truth* and *Isles of the Emberdark* in his Cosmere universe, as well as the *Tailored Realities* collection of his short fiction. His works have been translated into many different languages. You can find out more at brandonsanderson.com.

Liz Silverthorne is an aspiring author from New Zealand. She loves her dog, drawing, and occasionally closeting herself away from the world to hammer out new ideas. No stranger to the madness of writing, she enjoys creating stories about ordinary people in extraordinary situations, strange places, and futuristic times.

Ethan Skarstedt is a member of the National Guard who served in Kuwait, Senegal, Iraq, and Afghanistan. He's authored several short stories, including "H.A.R.R.E.: Heuristic Algorithm and Reasoning Response Engine" with Brandon Sanderson (originally published by Baen in the *Armored* anthology), "The Light Goes Out", "Among the Apple Trees", and others. He's currently working on at least two different novels. You can find out more at ethanskar.com.

Kevin Wasden is an artist, storyteller, poet, and educator. His artistic journey began in childhood, sketching comic book heroes and doodling for friends. Mr. Sylvester's 6th grade art class at Fillmore Middle School flipped a switch. There he discovered the magic of light and shadow, forever altering how he saw the world.

He went on to study at Utah State University, where mentors such as Glen Edwards and Gregory Schulte helped hone his drawing and painting skills. His quest for artistic excellence led him to study figure painting under Andy Reiss in Brooklyn, New York. As a professional illustrator and designer, Kevin created art for numerous book, periodical, and game publishers, including Avon Camelot, Baen, Fantasy Flight Games, and Alderac Entertainment Group.

Kevin played a pivotal role as the creative director at Alinco Costumes, where he helped guide the creation of many famous mascot characters and costume designs for the Chicago Bulls, the Arizona Diamondbacks, the Oklahoma City Thunder, and others.

Throughout his career, Kevin has felt a deep desire to share his knowledge and skills with others. For many years, he served as a private art instructor and high school art teacher. In 2023, Kevin turned most of his creative energy toward making more personalized artwork for shows and galleries. He is currently an exhibiting artist at Urban Arts Gallery in Salt Lake City. He also participates in numerous local and state art shows. Learn more at kevinwasden.com.

Additional Copyright Information

Also from Hemelein Publications

An LTUE Benefit Anthology
TRACE the STARS
Edited by
Joe Monson
& Jaleta Clegg
Featuring 17 space opera and
hard SF stories by:
Kevin J. Anderson
David Farland
Nancy Fulda
Eric James Stone
Brad R. Torgersen
Julia H. West
and more!

An LTUE Benefit Anthology
A DRAGON & HER GIRL
Featuring twenty fantasy adventure stories by:
Mercedes Lackey & Elisabeth Waters
Bryan Thomas Schmidt • Michaelene Pendleton
Alex Shvartsman • David VonAllmen • M. K. Hutchins
Gerri Leen • Sam Knight • and more!
Edited by Joe Monson & Jaleta Clegg

An LTUE Benefit Anthology
TWILIGHT TALES
Featuring 31 light horror stories by:
Dan Wells • D.J. Butler
Kary English • Joe Vasicek
Edward Ahern • Wendy Nikel
Vonnie Winslow Crist • Jude Reid
Gustavo Bondoni • Kelly A. Harmon
...and more!
Edited by
JALETA CLEGG & JOE MONSON

Featuring 24 science fiction and fantasy wizard stories by:
Michael R. Collings • D.J. Butler • Sarah E. Seeley
Gerri Leen • Eric James Stone • Jodi L. Milner
Scott R. Parkin • Berin Lee Stephens
...and more!
Parliament of Wizards
An LTUE Benefit Anthology
Edited by
Jaleta Clegg and Joe Monson

A
HERO
OF A
DIFFERENT
STRIPE
An LTUE Benefit Anthology
Featuring 21
science fiction and
fantasy hero stories by:
D. J. Butler
Wendy Nikel
Eric G. Swedin
Jessica Guernsey
Scott R. Parkin
Emily Martha Sorensen
...and more!
EDITED BY
Jaleta Clegg and Joe Monson

TROUBADOURS
and
SPACE PRINCESSES

EDITED BY
JALETA CLEGG AND JOE MONSON

DOG SAVE THE KING